THE *Illicit* PLAY

KATY ARCHER

THE ILLICIT PLAY

Nolan U Football #4

www.katyarcher.com

ISBN: 978-1-991403-00-1 (Kindle e-book)
ISBN: 978-1-991403-01-8 (paperback)

Archer Street Romance
www.katyarcher.com

CHAPTER 1
BLAKE

The sun is warm on my face as I lean my head back and soak in the rays. The worst of the winter is over, and spring is teasing us with the odd day like this. I can't get enough of it. I'm a summer girl and cannot wait to hit the lake in July. I'm gonna jet-ski and sunbathe on the pontoon like I do every year. It's going to be epic.

Is it?

My stomach twists and I snap my eyes open, irritation sizzling through me.

It *is* going to be epic.

But not like old times.

Not after what went down in Chicago.

You can't hide the truth forever.

Gritting my teeth, I glare at the sidewalk, leaning back against Wily's truck and not wanting to think about it. No one needs to know for now, and they might not even have to know this summer. I don't have to face shit until the new school year, and that's months away.

Crossing my arms, I dig my fingers into my leather

jacket and force myself to think of something else. Anything but school.

Thoughts of Grady Newman immediately flicker through my mind. My lips twitch. I can't help it. They do that every time the hot running back jumps into my brain. And it's been doing that a *lot* since the bathroom incident.

I knew moving into Football Frat to help my brother after his knee surgery might mean I'd bump into half-naked football players. I was so okay with that.

But I never counted on the hottest human body to ever exist walking in on me shaving my legs. He was shirtless, a fine sheen of sweat glistening on his dark skin, and holy sex bomb, he was fiiiiiinnnneee!

His ripped torso was droolworthy, and it took everything in me not to stand there gaping at him, drinking in every valley and curve of his naked torso. When my eyes trailed down to that defined V disappearing into the towel wrapped around his waist, my lady-parts started dancing.

I was desperate to know if he was naked under there, because if his goodies looked as divine as the rest of him, I was in for a treat.

It took maximum effort to hide my attraction to the delicious hottie.

But I had no willpower when it came to him checking me out.

I was totally naked, my foot perched on the edge of the bathtub while I shaved my legs. I really should have scrambled for a towel to cover myself, but he'd stunned me stupid with his beautiful body, and then he was the one gaping at me.

I'm pretty sure, in most normal circumstances, he would have spun back out the door, mumbling apologies, but he just stood there, wide-eyed and drinking me in.

I could tell he thought I was something pretty, because his eyes trailed down my body, and his desire was so potent my skin started to tingle... in all the right ways.

So I let him look.

I even turned to give him better access so he could check me out.

A smirk tugs on my lips as I recall asking him if he was enjoying the view.

The look on his face. I couldn't resist teasing him just a little more.

"I've shown you mine. Maybe you can show me yours."

That got him moving. He bolted out of the bathroom mere seconds later, and I was left standing there with a weeping pussy as I tried and failed not to imagine what it would have been like if he'd dropped that towel and taken me against the bathroom wall.

Sweet mercy, that would have been the hottest moment of my life.

I can't stop thinking about it.

About him.

Wondering. Wishing.

But the guy is flat-out stonewalling me now. It's so frustrating. He won't even look at me, even when I put myself right in his path.

I bet he hates that I'm living in the same house as him, but I'm not gonna move out just because he's trying to avoid me.

I'm here for Wily.

It's only been a week since my brother's surgery, and he needs the support. Sienna has Zoey to look after, and Satch has classes. We can't expect them to drop everything. My time is more flexible, and I want to be here for him.

He's my favorite person in the world—my best friend—and moving to Nolan to help him out was a no-brainer. My mom's kinda pissed about it, but she can go suck an egg for all I care.

As far as she's aware, I'm keeping up with my classes online. And I will keep selling her that lie for as long as I can.

Because I am staying here for Wily. My big brother would do the same for me, so I will drive him to every freaking PT and doctor's appointment, I will make him food, serve him drinks, and even sit there playing boring-ass *Madden* with him—whatever he needs to get through this heart-crushing nightmare.

I refuse to let him give up on his football dreams.

It's the only thing the guy has ever wanted, and I won't shut up about this injury simply delaying his plans. I won't let him fall into some kind of depressed stupor. He's getting back. He's fighting for his dreams.

I won't have it any other way.

Although...

I glance up to check the various pathways leading into the Nolan U campus, my lips stretching into a smile when I spot her.

Maybe football isn't the only thing Wily wants anymore.

His girlfriend is walking toward me, holding her bag straps while she chats with a woman who looks about her age. I bet they've just finished a class together. They look like poster children for hardworking, well behaved college students, with Satch in her cute skirt and cardigan and the other girl sporting a pair of jeans with a loose plaid flannel shirt tucked into them.

Satch is giving her a shy smile and nodding while the woman goes on about something, laughing and talking a mile a minute.

They dribble to a stop at an intersection in the pathways, and I tip my head to watch them, wondering what they're talking about. Probably studying, or an upcoming assignment.

I snort and shake my head.

Boring!

Shut up, you used to be just like that.

I frown, crossing my arms again and glaring across the campus, watching students come and go after their classes, all studious and disciplined.

Fuck.

With a sigh, I pull my shoulders back and stare at Satch, willing her to see me so she can wrap up this conversation and we can get the hell out of here.

She's waving goodbye to Little Miss Chatterbox, so I pull Wily's keys from my pocket and am about to raise my hand and get her attention when she spots something to her left.

The skin on her round, normally rosy cheeks goes instantly pale and she stiffens, crossing her arms over her body and kind of shrinking in on herself.

I ping straight, stepping away from Wily's truck and making a beeline toward her.

He warned me about this. Told me all about those

bitchy girls and what they did to Satch at her birthday party.

That's why I'm here to pick her up. He hates that she's still walking around campus, alone... vulnerable. He hates that he can't be here to protect her. He's put us all on guard duty, and I'm about ready to unleash a little hellfire if those girls so much as look at her.

But then my pace slows and I stutter to a stop when I notice Satch pulling herself upright, like she's just made a decision.

Lifting her chin, she glares up at the girls walking past, looking... well, shit, Satch is looking fierce right about now. A freaking warrior princess.

I grin, wishing I could pull my phone out and snap this shit, but the girls are already gliding past her, and she's sinking back down like she's just withstood a tsunami.

I run forward, my boots clipping on the concrete, alerting her to the fact that I'm approaching.

She glances at me, her posture relaxing when she sees who it is.

I smile a little wider, stopping beside her and asking, "Team Evil?"

"2.0." She breathes the words more than says them, so I throw my arm around her shoulders, supporting her against me while I shout to their backs, "Have a nice day, ladies!"

Raising my middle finger, I flip them off, delighted when they turn around and take me in.

I make sure my smile is bright and unmissable, and I can't get enough of the way their pretty little faces scrunch in annoyance.

"Whatever," one of them mumbles before they all spin and strut away like they're practicing for the catwalk in Milan.

Oh man, I'd do anything for one of them to stumble and knock the others down.

Now *that* would be epic.

If only.

Lowering my hand with a sigh, I glance down at my brother's girlfriend and let out a soft laugh. "What?"

She's gazing up at me like I just invented orgasms or something.

"I think I just fell in love with you," she whispers.

I tip my head back and laugh before kissing her cheek. "Well, I'm already in love with you, so that works out great. Now..." I loop my arm through hers and start dragging her toward Wily's truck. "Let's get you back to Football Frat so I don't have to hear my brother whining about missing you. He's been going on all freaking day, and it's doing my head in." I bulge my eyes at Satch.

She lets out a soft giggle, her cheeks tinging pink as she climbs into the passenger seat. I walk around the truck, gripping the handle to help me jump up into this beast. Honestly, this truck is ridiculous. I should have driven my Mini down from Chicago, but as soon as I heard what happened to Wily, I jumped on a plane. I had to get here as fast as I could, and now the thought of going back up to the Windy City is...

Well, it can wait.

Not forever.

Shit.

I grit my teeth, starting the engine and gunning it toward Football Frat. I don't want to think about my stuff, my car, and how I'm supposed to get it back. I don't want to think about any of that shit.

I just want to focus on my brother.

"You know, if it's too much, you don't have to stay." Satch worries her lip. "I don't want this to encroach on your life. I can try to rearrange my schedule or—"

"No way." I shake my head. "You're already busting your ass making sure you get to all your classes and get Wily's work for him. You're doing your own studying and assignments, plus tutoring him. You can't take on any more than that."

Satch fidgets with her fingers in her lap. I glance at them before looking back at the road, pausing at the crosswalk to let a bunch of students pass.

"At least he'll be back in class next week, although it's gonna be so hard for him, hobbling around on his crutches."

"Yeah." I sigh. "He's gonna hate it, but he'll be able to handle it, and I can sit in on classes with him. I don't mind."

"What about your work, though? You're sacrificing so much to be here."

I glance across at her again, giving her the brightest smile I can muster. "It's fine. Honestly. This year has been kind of chill for me. Keeping up with my classes is not a big deal."

"So watching videos of the classes at night isn't bumming you out? How will you keep up with the workload if you're going to Wily's classes as well?"

"I'll manage," I assure her... just like I'm assuring everybody.

Because it's not like I can tell them the truth.

CHAPTER 2
GRADY

I can't tell.

I can *never* tell a fucking soul that I walked in on Blake Wilson bare-ass naked.

Oh shit, her bare ass.

I only saw the side of it, but that curve...

I can picture my hand molding over it, cupping those perfect white cheeks and giving them a squeeze.

Her skin's so pale. It's porcelain, delicately painted with a dusting of freckles.

Damn, the shape of her is fucking beautiful.

Delicate lines that douse me with guilt every time I think of them.

I wish I could block her out of my head.

I've been doing everything I can to forget about what I saw, avoiding her at every turn. But it's like she's making a game out of it.

Every time she sees me, she gets this playful twinkle in her eye, like I'm her target and she's gonna enjoy bringing me down.

But I can never let that happen.

She's Wily sister. He's my teammate, one of my best friends, and I respect the guy too much to let myself go and do what I want with that hot sister of his.

Fuck.

Even now as I'm on the field, doing light fitness drills to keep us active in the offseason, she's haunting me.

It's like my brain took multiple photographs of her smoking hot body and has been torturing me with them ever since.

Every morning, I wake up with a granite woody, and I'm not proud to admit it, but I gave in to temptation this morning and pictured exactly what I wanted to do with that woman as I stroked myself, then pumped until I had nothing left in me.

But the image of holding her up against the bathroom wall and burying myself inside her while she cried out in my ear was too fucking much.

I couldn't resist it.

And I've been racked with guilt ever since.

Are you fucking kidding? You've been racked with guilt for days! And that's not the only time you've pictured her while you polished the banister, my friend.

Squeezing my eyes shut, I take a beat before sprinting back down the field.

It doesn't seem to matter how fast I run. I can't shake her.

And it's making me feel like shit.

I'm still processing my breakup with Teah. She tore my heart out, and now I'm lusting after my best friend's little sister? What the fuck is wrong with me!

"Flash, let's go, man. Pick up the pace!" Carson barks at me. "Don't let those fuck nuggets beat us!"

I glance to my right and put on an extra burst of speed, reaching Carson just before Lincoln reaches Peters.

Fuck, this race makes me feel like I'm five years old, but during the offseason, the coaches like to mix it up and give us drills that are lighter and more fun. It definitely brings out our competitive sides, and I force myself to join in, clapping and encouraging Carson as he sprints back toward us, slapping Zander's hand when he crosses the line.

We watch our quarterback compete against Fleischer, Carson yelling extra loudly.

"Don't you fucking let him beat you, Zan Man!"

I snicker and shake my head, watching my captain dominate. He deserves to play pro ball. He belongs on that field, and I'm so fucking proud of him. He had the best time at the Scouting Combine, and things are looking good for him. He's not sure who he'll get drafted to, but he'll definitely be picked up by someone.

Just the way Wily should have been.

Shit, it's such a tragedy what happened to him.

Can't believe it.

The guy's still set on making it, but it's gonna be a long, hard road to recover from the injury and get himself back into playing condition. Coach Jones says it's never too late, but I can't tell if he's just using words like that to comfort Wily or whether he actually means it.

Our head coach seems pretty determined to help Wily get there.

And I believe it.

If anyone's gonna go the extra mile for his players, it's Coach Jones. Wily's in good hands. He's counting on Wily getting drafted with an injury. He's pretty sure it will happen. Sometimes teams take injured players with big potential, so it's not out of the question. That's what Coach keeps saying, anyway. Wily won't be a top pick anymore, but he'll still be in the running.

"We just gotta have faith." Coach's mantra rings in my head.

We'll all do everything we can to support the guy.

Shit, I hope it comes together.

I know from experience that life doesn't always turn out the way you want, even if you map it out in painstaking detail. I don't mean to do it. My brain's just wired that way. I like to plot, plan, picture my future.

After my parents' divorce, I became obsessed with scheduling my life. I thought if I had a plan, set my goals and fought hard to achieve them, then I could control everything.

And it worked.

It fucking worked great.

I got into the school I wanted with a full scholarship. I've been playing running back for the team I wanted. I scored myself a gorgeous girlfriend who was everything I wanted.

My life was set.

Until she dumped me. I didn't even see it coming, although I probably should have. We'd been bickering a little more than usual before she slapped me with the breakup talk. I thought we'd just hit a rough patch but would work our way through it.

But nope.

She was done.

And I was shattered.

My plans were unraveling around me, and that thread got pulled a little harder last week when I saw her making out with Finn Macalister. Everybody calls the badass basketball player Mac for short, but I don't give a flying fuck what his name is.

His hands were all over my girl.

His tongue was in her mouth.

And I wanted to tear his fingers off... smash his face into the concrete.

How dare he touch her!

How dare he? my brain scoffs, mocking me for my stupidity.

He dared because she wasn't mine anymore. She hadn't been mine for two months, and I was still pining like a fucking sap while she was moving on.

So, no, you can't control life with long-term plans and goals.

Life is still gonna kick you in the balls and point at you, laughing its head off while you writhe on the ground in pain.

And it's fucking doing it again.

Mocking me with thoughts of a blonde hottie who likes to shave her legs butt naked in my bathroom.

Fuck!

CHAPTER 3
BLAKE

Music is pumping through the kitchen as I stand over the chopping board, grating carrots for the salad Satch wants to make. She's beside me, preparing chicken tenders and singing along. I don't know the song. It's some old tune that my grandparents probably listened to growing up... or maybe even my great-grandparents.

Seriously? That's taking old-school to the extreme.

As much as I want to tease her about it, I keep my mouth shut because she sounds ah-mazing! The girl's got a set of pipes on her, and I think it's totally shit that she's majoring in English when she should be doing performing arts, or at least studying music. She's thinking about becoming a teacher. Well, duh! Teach music, girl!

But Wily's super protective of her, and I can't go challenging her on that shit.

Besides, I can't risk anyone turning around to challenge me on what I'm studying.

Or not studying.

Glancing over my shoulder, I check on my brother,

grateful he can't read my mind. Thankfully, he's too busy staring at his girl, a small smile on his face. He loves watching her.

Kinda creepy if you ask me, but his dopey, loved-up grin is too cute.

The guy is gone.

I mean, I knew the romantic sap would end up falling hard one day, but I thought it'd be later on, once his football career was underway.

Satch took him by surprise, that's for sure.

And the timing couldn't be better, because the poor guy needs something to help him through his shitty situation.

My gaze creeps down to his bandaged leg propped up on a chair, and I can't help that burn of disappointment on his behalf. He'd had it all mapped out. For years. And now he's sitting there with crutches leaning on the wall behind him.

It's so fucking unfair.

He doesn't deserve this shit.

Not like you.

My insides writhe and I shake off the thought, focusing back on my carrot situation.

Cooking for a house full of athletes and their partners is a mission. Every meal has to be just so, with the correct amount of protein and carbohydrates and nutrients.

Why they don't just eat at the athletes dining hall, where all that shit is provided, is beyond me. Wily used to eat there all the time last year, but then Zander's baby mama appeared back in his life, bringing with her an adorable two-year-old who just loves seeing her Daddy's *bess fens*. So now they do dinner on the regular like some happy, clappy family.

It's the most un-college-y thing in the world, if you ask me.

And cooking? Why?

Has no one ever heard of takeout before? Uber Eats? DoorDash?

These aren't new concepts, people. And it would save me having to grate carrots.

Satch doesn't seem to mind slaving over a hot stove, but I'm not used to...

One: being in the kitchen.

And two: dealing with quantities like this.

I grew up in a family of four, and when I moved to college, I spent the first few weeks eating in the dining hall and then the last few months...

Dipping my head, I hide my grimace, not wanting to give anything away.

Thinking about how I spent my last few months is the last thing I should be doing right now.

If Wily knew who I'd been hanging out with, and what I'd been doing with them, he'd hit the roof.

But it's not like I meant to get caught up with my roommate. She just made a different way of living look so exciting. And she was right! It was fucking epic.

We had so much fun together.

Until the trouble started, and then fun turned to shit, and shit turned to life-changing decisions that I couldn't take back.

Decisions that forced me to—

Snapping my eyes shut, I grate this carrot like my life depends on it. Stupid idea when you're trying to dodge things you can't fix and your eyes aren't open... because the chances of grating the top of your knuckle off are a guarantee.

"Ow! Shit!" I drop the carrot stub in the sink and quickly suck my stinging knuckle.

"Are you okay?" Satch whips around to look at me while Wily starts struggling out of his chair.

"What have you done now, butt face?" His teasing grumble would usually appease me, but I'm too pissed off that my big brother, who I've literally been looking up to my entire life, is now wrestling to get his crutches so he can limp across the room to help me.

"No, I'm fine," I quickly tell him. "Sit your ass back down, shithead." After throwing him a pointed look, I examine my finger.

Gross. I've managed to grate a decent flap of skin off my knuckle, and it's bleeding everywhere.

"Quick." Satch pulls my hand over the sink so I don't drip blood all over the floor. "Wash it off, and I'll find the first-aid kit."

Wily directs her and I wash off my finger, irritated by the burn and that it's even happened in the first place. It freaking hurts! And it's so not helping my mood.

"I can't reach it." Satch pops her head back into the kitchen with an apologetic frown.

"Let me help you." Wily struggles to stand once more.

"No, I'll get it." I head for the pantry.

"Not sure you can reach it either."

"Let me fucking help!" Wily shouts at our backs, his crutch clattering to the floor. "Shit!"

I spin around, blood dripping from my finger when I

point at him. "Don't bend down to get that. You'll topple over."

"Stop telling me what to fucking do and let me help you!"

"You helping me is gonna get you hurt, and then we'll have two injuries on our hands, so just sit your ass on that chair and—"

"Shut up, butt face!"

"You guys, I can just grab a chair." Satch tries to squeeze past me out into the kitchen, her cheeks flooding red, as she obviously hates the rising voices in the room.

"I'll get the chair," I bark at her.

"Stop shouting at my girlfriend. You're such a little shit," Wily snaps.

"Oh, *I'm* the shit?" I point at myself, managing to wipe blood on my shirt. I growl. "You stubborn asshole. Don't you get that trying to help us is just making everything worse?"

He glares at me, plonking back down in his chair, then wincing in instant regret.

Satch hisses. "Baby, be careful."

His dark expression folds when he hears her voice, and shit, is he about to start crying?

He's been way more emotional since the injury and—

Satch shoves me aside so she can get to him, and I pop my finger back into my mouth before I bleed on anything else.

The front door pops open, and a bustling sound indicates that the guys are home from practice.

I can hear Tyrell's low voice and then Zander's reply. He laughs at something, and Carson replies about everybody being assholes. This causes all of them to start laughing, and I wonder what they were teasing him about.

Then Grady's voice chimes in, and I feel that familiar tingle race through my body.

Shit, even his voice gets me going.

I glance at my brother, grateful he's not looking at me.

Satch has her hands on his cheeks, and she's murmuring something to soothe him. He reaches forward, lightly grabbing her hips as she leans down to kiss him.

Rolling my eyes, I look away from their lovefest, fighting a sizzling irritation that I don't even understand.

I should be apologizing for yelling at Wily when all he was trying to do was help. That's his thing. I *know* that's his thing, and not being able to do it is probably killing him.

I need to be more fucking understanding.

My heart crumples into a ball of trash when the guys lumber into the kitchen with their gear and I watch a sad, devastated expression flitter across my brother's face before he manages to put on a bright smile.

Shit.

I'm the worst!

Catching his eye, I wince an apology at him. He shakes his head, giving me the finger and winking at me, before asking the guys how practice went.

Damn, I have the best brother in the world.

No wonder I love him so much.

No wonder I'm so guilt-ridden every time I look at him.

His dreams are shattered because of nothing he did.

Mine are torn to shreds because I acted like an idiot.

Fuck, I don't even know what my dreams are!

I've never felt so lost, and as I hover in the pantry doorway, listening to the guys talk football and trying to make Wily feel part of it, all I can do is quietly slip out of the room.

I don't want to hear this. See this.

Sucking my aching finger, I head up to the bathroom and rustle around in the cabinet for some form of bandage but come up empty-handed.

"Seriously?" I mutter, rising with a string of soft curses.

Walking out the bathroom door, I examine my knuckle, wondering how long it'll take to stop bleeding, when I jolt to a stop just before crashing into a sweaty shirt and a wall of rock-hard muscle.

Stepping back, I glance up with a soft gasp and then forget how to breathe.

Grady is standing there, gazing down at me, his handsome face puckered into a small frown.

"What happened?" Taking my hand, he studies the torn flap of skin.

"I was grating carrots." It's hard to talk normally when he's standing this close. My words tumble out in a husky whisper.

Sweaty men should not smell this good. I should be repulsed, but this manly scent of his is doing weird things to my brain.

"I've got a first-aid kit in my room," he mumbles, spinning away from me and silently expecting me to follow.

At least I think that's what he's expecting, so I trail after him, my socked feet padding across the wooden floor. Pausing outside his bedroom door, I steal a quick glance into the room and notice how tidy it is.

Wow. A man who can clean.

My eyebrows rise and I creep a little closer, standing in the frame while he pulls out a plastic storage box from under his bed and flips the lid.

It's so freaking organized in here.

Everything has a place. His desk is set up for optimal study conditions. His bed is made, the navy blue duvet pulled tight, the surface of his nightstand uncluttered with just a few charging portals for his different devices.

On the far side of the room is a chest of drawers with a mirror on the wall and a corkboard with neatly placed images, evenly spaced and tacked on with tiny pins. I see one of him smiling with an older man who looks just like him; they're standing in a forest looking sweaty and proud. Then there's a picture of him decked out in football gear surrounded by his buddies... and what's that one? An image of him and some pretty girl with strawberry blonde hair and perfectly applied makeup. She's laughing at the camera while he kisses her cheek.

Is that his girlfriend?

My insides twist and I force my gaze away, checking out the posters on the adjacent wall. They're framed, large images of mountains and lakes, one of a waterfall, another of the sun rising over a massive boulder.

Wow. They're really stunning, and I stare at them, wishing I could somehow step right into those places. If only magic were real.

Grady walks back toward me, filling my view with that delectable body of his.

"Let me see." He flicks his fingers at me, and I hold up my hand again.

His touch is delicate, his expression serious as he examines the cut, then nods and rips open a little alcohol wipe.

"Ouch," I hiss, the burn making me wince.

"Sorry," he murmurs, but doesn't stop torturing me.

Once it's clean, he gently rearranges the flap of skin back over my knuckle, then carefully wraps a Band-Aid around my finger.

Hmmm.

Who knew first aid could be so damn sexy?

I smirk, eyeing him as he throws the scraps away. When he bends down to collect the one thing he missed, I take advantage and check out his ass.

Damn.

Those cheeks look like they're made of pure steel.

What I wouldn't do to give them a squeeze.

A hot yearning pools between my legs, and when he stands up to look at me, I'm obviously not hiding anything because he blinks, then bites his lips together and takes a step back.

No wonder. He has a girlfriend, you little homewrecker. Stop staring at him and behave yourself!

"You good?" He swallows, not even looking at me when he says it.

Ugh. I must be making him so uncomfortable.

Putting on a bright voice, I force a smile. "Yes. Thanks for your help."

He nods, his head bobbing erratically.

"I like your room." I try to keep this going, because part of me is evil, another portion deranged, and I obviously like watching this unavailable man squirm. It's too much fun to resist.

"Yep." He looks around. "Thanks."

With a bemused grin, I go to take a step inside, but he quickly shakes his head.

"Nope." He holds up his hands.

"What?" I stop in the doorway.

"You can't be coming into my room."

"Why not?"

"I can't have you in my room." His voice is strained as he chokes out the words.

"Because..." I inch a little farther into his space.

"Uh-uh." He's shaking his head, obviously battling something as he walks toward me.

I stop, crossing my arms and narrowing my eyes at him. "What is your problem? It's not like I'm about to jump your bones. I just wanted to... look around."

Shaking his head again, he avoids eye contact and gives me the lamest excuse ever. "I need to get started on homework."

"Oh really?" I scoff. "I call bullshit."

He glances up at me then, his dark gaze burning holes right through my forehead. "Call it whatever the fuck you want. But you need to get out of my room. Right now."

"This is ridiculous."

"It's what it's got to be," he mutters under his breath, striding toward me and clamping his hands around my arms.

With one swift move, he lifts me off my feet and places me in the hallway, then gives me a polite smile before closing the door in my face.

"Are you kidding me?" I yell at the wood.

"Uh... everything okay?" A deep voice catches my attention.

I spin, looking up at Tyrell, who towers above me the same way my brother does.

Giving him a tight smile, I nod, desperately trying to play it cool as I stalk away from Grady's closed door.

Tyrell gives me a quizzical frown, but I ignore it, brushing past him and murmuring, "Just going to get some studying done."

He doesn't need to know that.

And the truth is, I should be down in the kitchen helping Satch with dinner, but the thought of playing pretend right this second is too much.

I just need to hide away for a minute and pull myself together. Because I can't walk back into Wily's space with everything so close to the surface.

Making a beeline for the guest room, I close the door behind me and rest my back against the wood, sucking in a few short breaths.

"Check yourself," I whisper, pulling my mask back on as best I can.

Testing out my bright smile, I feel the movement on my face and will myself to keep it there.

Grady's rejection is a slap in the face. And a well-deserved one. He's taken, and I have no right putting a single one of my flirty toes into his bedroom.

It doesn't matter that he's obviously attracted to me. He's a loyal boyfriend.

Shit, that only makes me like him more.

Snapping my eyes shut, I groan.

What is wrong with me?

There's no way I can handle going downstairs. I can't deal with the idea of letting something slip when my guard is down. Because my family can't know what a fuckup I've become. It'll break their hearts, and I'll never get over it.

Which is why Grady not letting me in is a really good thing.

That controlled girl I used to be... she doesn't seem to exist anymore, and I can only imagine Wily's horror if he saw me getting it on with his teammate the way I want to.

His *unavailable* teammate.

Grady was right to push me out his door.

I should seriously stay away from that man. He makes me feel that addictive thrill that got me in trouble in the first place. And I can't be that person in Nolan.

Not with Wily so close.

Not when I could get busted and have all my shit laid bare for everyone to see.

CHAPTER 4
GRADY

Damn, man. Trying to avoid Blake Wilson is impossible.

Seeing her standing in the bathroom bleeding put a vise around my chest.

Watching her cute little ass hover in the doorway of my bedroom nearly did me in.

I'm losing my fucking mind.

Running a hand over my head, I pace my room, from the poster of Half Dome in Yosemite to the edge of my bed and back. I try to regulate my thundering heartbeat, which is insane because she should not be affecting me this way.

I'm still in love with Teah.

Glancing at the photo of me and my girlfriend—ex-girlfriend—makes me feel like shit, and I move to my corkboard, slowly unpinning it and laying it face down on my chest of drawers. I should have put the damn photo away weeks ago. She's not mine anymore, but my heart can't seem to let her go, and now Wily's sister—*his little sister!*—is wreaking havoc on my body.

I don't need this shit.

What I need is a run, but my PT has made it clear I've been pushing it too hard, and I can't risk an injury. The sound of Wily's knee popping still echoes in my brain, and I shudder at the memory.

"If you can't fucking run, you can at least walk," I mutter, quickly changing out of my sweaty clothes and snatching a hoodie off the end of my bed.

Throwing it on, I wrestle with the zipper and walk out of my room, checking the hallway is clear before darting down the stairs. My heart spasms when I reach the bottom and find Wily waiting for me, leaning on his crutches with a frown.

"Hey, man." I try to play it cool, wondering if he's about to bawl me out for talking to his sister... or thinking about her naked body and what I wanted to do to said body if I'd lost all willpower and invited her into my room.

Fuck!

"Hey." Wily gives me a distracted nod, looking up the stairs in obvious frustration. "You seen my lil' sis up there?"

"Oh, uh..." I glance over my shoulder, swallowing and trying to keep a level head on this thing.

Yes, you saw his sister. That's it. You just saw her and talked to her. No crime in that.

"She took off, and I want to make sure she's okay. She hurt her finger."

"Yeah, I saw that." I nod, forcing a smile to try and ease his tension. "I patched her up, and I think she's gone to her room to study."

"So she's okay? The cut wasn't bad?"

"Nah, just a decent nick. Those things always bleed a lot, but fingers heal up quickly."

Wily's shoulders slump in obvious relief. "Thanks, man. I got..." He huffs. "Distracted. And then when I looked up to find her, she was gone."

"No problem. I found her in the bathroom, probably looking for a Band-Aid or something. Anyway, I gave her one from my stash. Made sure the wound was clean. You know." I shrug, trying to play it casual and not let slip that feeling her breath skim across my cheek when I leaned over to wrap the Band-Aid around her finger was the fucking sexiest thing ever.

Which is insane, because scientifically, breaths are nothing more than nitrogen, oxygen, and carbon dioxide. Throw in a little water vapor and I should be repulsed by the idea of gasses hitting my skin like that, but fuuuuuuuck.

Yep, losing my mind. That's what is happening right now.

But I've got to keep that shit on lockdown, because I can't go complaining to Wily that his sister is too damn sexy and I need her to move out because being around her is awakening some kind of primal instinct inside me that I didn't even know existed.

"Thanks so much for looking after her." Wily gives me a half-hearted grin. "I hate that I'm injured right now." His lame smile turns into a wince. "And I got shitty with her when she couldn't reach the first-aid box in the kitchen and she wouldn't let me get up and help her." He lets out a heavy sigh. "I fucking hate this, man."

"Hey." I rest a hand on his shoulder. "This is temporary. Those crutches will be gone soon, and you'll be running up and down these stairs just like before."

Wily flashes me a closed-mouth smile before nodding, then shouting up the stairs, "Hey, butt face! You okay?"

I can't help a soft snicker as we wait for Blake's reply.

It takes a moment longer than I thought it would... unless she didn't hear—

"All good, shithead! Now leave me alone. I'm trying to study up here."

"Got it. I'll help Satch with the rest of the dinner prep, then," Wily calls back up to her.

Her laughter is muffled as she shouts back, "Probably safest. Unless you want your salad with a side of Blake."

Yes, please.

I swallow, darting my eyes at Wily and hoping he can't read minds.

But he's too busy laughing. "Gross. No thanks." He shares a bemused look with me before calling up the stairs again. "Love you, loser!"

"Yeah, yeah, love you, too, jackass."

He snickers and grins at me, obviously relieved that his little fight with Blake has been resolved so easily.

"You sticking around for dinner?" He points at me.

"Nah, I'm gonna go for a walk."

He gives me a quizzical frown, but I just shake my head and walk past him, not wanting to explain.

How can I?

He'll never be cool with me lusting after his sister. Not when my heart is still hurting over Teah. It's messed up, and I won't go there.

Which means I have to get out of this fucking house.

Closing the door behind me, I trot down the stairs, embracing the cool night air. I need that shit to wake me up, slap some sense into me.

Thank fuck spring break is only two and a half weeks away. Coach is giving us a long weekend, meaning spring training doesn't start until Tuesday afternoon. That'll give me three entire days in the forest… and I can't wait.

It'll be good for me to get out of Nolan and hike my favorite trails. It's a much-needed getaway with my buddies. Unfortunately, not all of them can make it anymore. Which sucks. Big-time. It was Wily's idea, and now the poor guy is injured. I offered to cancel, but he told me no way. He's gonna spend the weekend with Satch, and I think he's looking forward to having the house to themselves.

Zander wanted to come, but Sienna's parents are taking them away in the camper van, and I told him that family time was more important. So he's doing that, which just leaves me, Carson, Tyrell… and I invited my dad too. Because the guy is awesome and taught me everything I know about the outdoors.

Since my breakup, I've only seen him once. I went down and spent a weekend with him and his girlfriend. It was good to get away, and he let me mope around his house, not asking anything of me. But I couldn't hide away there forever, so I forced my butt back to Nolan.

It'll be good to see my old man again.

He asked me if I wanted to invite my big brother, Owen, and was probably bummed out when I said no. But I'm going away to feel better about myself, and bringing that dick along will only ruin shit.

He wouldn't want to come anyway.

Ever since the divorce, Dad's been trying to get back into Owen's good graces, but I say it's an impossible task.

My brother made the choice not to forgive. He sided with Mom, whereas I supported Dad. It caused a rift we all have to live with now.

That idiot is missing out on a relationship with the best father in the world. That's his loss.

Still, it breaks Dad's heart, which then pisses me off.

Yes, my old man made a mistake. He fell into a one-night stand that he instantly regretted. It destroyed his marriage. But only because Mom couldn't get past it.

He was instantly remorseful and would have done anything to make up for his mistake. Mom wouldn't have it. Not one tiny bit, and I can't help wondering if she used it as an excuse to bail, because within one year of the divorce, Mom was married to Emilio and pregnant with my half-brother, Jamar. I was fucking salty over that one, and as soon as I was old enough to choose for myself, I moved in with Dad.

I didn't sign up to live with an overactive toddler and a crying baby.

My two half-brothers aren't all bad. Now that they're ten and eight, I'm starting to like them a little more, although Luis can still be a pain in the ass. But Mom's happy, and so I do my duty and spend a few weekends there each year, like the good boy I am.

But Dad's the guy I spend the majority of my time with, because unlike Owen, I refuse to hate on him.

He made a mistake.

It was a shitty one, but he tried to fix it, do what he could to make it right, and Mom wouldn't let him.

Even at the age of ten I understood that. I don't see why my brother can't.

Picking up my pace, I speed-walk away from Football Frat, hating this restless, antsy feeling inside me. I want to break into a sprint and burn this shit off, but it never works, and now my PT is on my ass telling me I'm doing too much.

I have to rest or my body is gonna hate me for it.

So I'll fucking walk like I'm supposed to.

But damn... this energy inside me is burning hot lava.

I just want things to go back to the way they were.

I miss Teah.

I miss how uncomplicated it all was.

She wasn't related to any of my friends; she was simply a sweet sorority girl who caught my eye. We knew each other from school, and I'd hang with her at sorority parties or college events. And then last spring break, things shifted between us.

I didn't fall in love with her instantly. Sure, I was attracted to her. Who wouldn't be? The girl's a hottie, and she knows how to dress that body of hers in all the right ways.

She's got an amazing laugh. She's kind and smart and...

Damn, I miss her.

I miss having a girlfriend who I can share my life with.

I miss texting her when something funny happens or I get a good grade on a test or assignment. She was always so awesome at celebrating with me.

I miss picking her up and taking her out on dates.

I miss holding her hand as I walked her to class.

I miss her in my bed.

Shit.

I sigh, shaking my head and trying not to relive the last time she was in my bed, that uncertain look on her face just after we'd made love. I didn't know what it meant... and when I asked her if she was okay, she said yes.

She fucking said yes!

Only to break my heart two days later.

I know what that look meant now.

She knew.

I lay on top of her, fucking clueless, but she knew it was the last time we'd ever be doing it. Because she was just trying to find the right time to dump me.

"Fuck!" I spit out the word, burying my fists in my pockets as I head down the dark street and make my way to Offside.

I don't even know why I'm going there.

To get drunk?

Not really my scene. I'll have the odd beer, but I'm not a big drinker. It's not that I'm opposed to it, I just don't love the idea of not being in control of my senses. I've seen Carson lose it way too many times. Stupid shit happens to drunk people, and if I'm wasted, who the hell is gonna step up and help the other guy, you know?

Checking the street, I wait for two passing cars before crossing to the other side.

Bring on spring break.

I need fresh air, forest, some quality time with people who aren't gonna break my heart or do my head in.

Thank fuck for Carson, Tyrell, and my dad. They are gonna be the perfect balm. They'll keep me distracted, and I can have a break from all the shit that's eating me up.

Pulling the big wooden door open, I step into Offside, glancing around the sports bar and taking in the action.

It's the usual energy for a Wednesday night—not too busy, but still pumping with the regular crowd and an indie artist who is getting his turn onstage. I watch him for a second, shuffling farther into the room before looking at the bar. His sound is pretty cool, like a mix between Jason Mraz and Adam Levine.

Yeah, I can dig this.

Walking around the first pool table, I make my way to the bar, figuring this is the perfect distraction... until I angle my body to avoid a pool cue in my eye and find myself looking at the last girl I need to see right now.

CHAPTER 5
BLAKE

The dining room table is surrounded as everyone from Football Frat joins in on the meal. Everyone except Grady Newman.

Well, shit. There goes my eye candy for the evening.

Not that every other man at this table isn't something to look at. Except my brother. Gross.

But there's something about Grady that gets me going in a way no one else has. Maybe ever.

I dated a few guys in high school, nothing too serious, and I got pretty hot and heavy with a couple of guys in Chicago, but none of them hold a candle to the Nolan U Cougars running back.

My lips twitch just thinking about him standing in the bathroom staring at me, the top half of his hot bod on full display. Ooooo, mama.

"Ty, no phone." Zoey points across the table at the towering center. He's been texting ever since we sat down to eat, frowning down at his screen and quickly replying, then trying to catch up on the conversation before his phone buzzes again.

"Zoey." Sienna laughs, lighting touching her daughter's hand. "It's okay."

"No phone, Mommy." Her sticky little finger points to Zander. "You say no phone table."

"That's true." Sienna picks up a fish stick and holds it out for her daughter. "But different families have different rules, and you're not the boss of this table, so..."

"Me boss." She points at her chest, making Zander laugh. She pouts at her father, then looks back at Tyrell with a stern frown. "No phone table."

I can't help a snicker as I share a glance with Wily, who is grinning at Zoey with the cutest, most adoring smile.

"Better do what she says, man." Wily raises his eyebrows. "Don't want to piss off the boss lady."

Tyrell slips the phone into his pocket. "Sorry, lil' one."

"She is not the boss," Sienna clarifies, then grins at her daughter. "Eat up, kidlet."

Zoey takes an aggressive bite of her food, chewing it between huffs while Nylah distracts us all with a story about fish that she learned in class today.

This leads into a discussion about conservation that I find pretty interesting. Bottom trawling should seriously be banned around the world. It's destroying our ocean floors.

"Have you guys seen that David Attenborough documentary on the ocean?" Nylah asks the table. "It's so good. Grady recommended it to me."

"And you made me watch it." Carson's upper lip curls.

Nylah laughs at his expression, quickly kissing his

cheek. "You loved it, caveman. Don't tell me you didn't find it interesting."

He gives a noncommittal shrug.

"And thank God we did watch it, because Professor Moore put me on the spot in class today."

"Ugh, I hate it when they do that." Satch shudders. "That *all eyes on me* feeling is the worst."

Wily glances at his girl, brushing his hand down the back of her hair and winking at her.

She blushes, smiling back while Nylah agrees with her, then starts looking all triumphant when she gave an answer that had the professor "Nodding her approval. It was like getting a gold medal, because that woman is hard to please."

"Moore?" Zander asks. "Yeah, she's a hard-ass."

"You're so lucky you're doing your classes online until spring break." Satch smiles across the table at me, like she's trying to draw me into this conversation.

She really doesn't need to do that, but I force a smile when she does.

"You don't have to be put on the spot like that." Her cute little nose wrinkles.

"Yeah, it's pretty easy this way. I like that I can watch the lectures in my own time."

"You managing to keep up with everything okay?" Sienna glances at me before darting out her hand to catch a flying sippy cup.

"Ooops." Zoey giggles, taking the drink off her mother and loudly guzzling down her water.

I grin, sharing a quick look with Sienna, who gives me a comically pained frown.

"Drink nicely, lil' bug." She tucks one of Zoey's wayward curls behind her ear.

Tyrell's back to texting, and I start playing with the food on my plate—my appetite disappearing as knots crowd out my stomach. "Yeah, it's fine. The work hasn't been that challenging, and..."

"You're a smart-ass." Wily winks at me, then starts laughing when Satch tells him off for being rude. "But it's true, baby." He rests his hand on the back of her neck. "My sister here has always been the smartest girl in the room. Although... that title might be yours now." He nuzzles her cheek, and I roll my eyes.

"So, you're one of those annoying brainiacs, huh?" Carson smirks at me.

I can't help a soft laugh. "Yep. That's me."

"She was valedictorian," Wily murmurs between kisses.

"Stop." Satch giggles, but she doesn't really mean it.

Seriously, people! We're trying to eat here!

Reaching under the table, I try to kick my brother, but I only give him a light tap, just in case I get the wrong leg.

He shoots a look at me, and I bulge my eyes, then mouth, "We're in public."

His eyebrows buckle into a frown, and he obviously can't understand what I'm saying, so I just roll my eyes and go back to poking at my salad.

"Valedictorian is impressive. Well done." Sienna grins at me.

I can't help a soft scoff. "Didn't really have much choice. You've got to be the best when you're a Wilson. Wily dominated on the field, I dominated in the classroom, and..." My words trail off as I shake my head.

Wily won't get it if I start ranting about Mom and Dad and the ridiculous pressure they always put on us. He never seemed to feel the same way because he loved football so much.

"Aw, come on. You love it." Wily proves my point with his throwaway comment, and I grit my teeth, forcing a smile when he continues. "She's the best because she works so damn hard and hates coming in second. Do you remember that time you got beaten by 1 percent and threw a massive hissy fit?"

I cringe, hating this story.

But I was fourteen and hormonal, and Haruki Sato was not allowed to beat me, dammit. That guy was an arrogant ass.

And I made sure he never beat me again.

I had no life while I was doing it, but I did manage to stand on that podium and give the graduation address, right?

Oh so fucking triumphant.

As I gazed down at my classmates, I didn't feel the pride I should have. All I felt was loss.

Loss of my teenage years as I strove for something I didn't even want.

Being the best was seriously not all it was cracked up to be.

But no one in my family seems to get that.

Clearing my throat, I squirm in my seat, needing this conversation to wrap up like five minutes ago.

"So..." I jab my fork into my last bite of chicken. "Where's Grady?"

What the fuck? Why did you just ask that?

I don't know!

And shit, now I'm blushing. I can feel the heat in my cheeks, and when I glance up and find Wily staring at me with a quizzical frown, I have to quickly improvise.

Waving my forkful of chicken in the air, I glance around the table. "I'm just wondering if we have to save him dinner or if I can finish up the last of the... broccoli."

"Go for it." Satch nudges the bowl toward me, and now I have to finish the freaking broccoli. Dammit!

"Saw him leave earlier," Wily murmurs. "He was heading out."

"Not for another run, was he?" Zander darts his eyes at my brother, obviously concerned.

"Nah." Wily shakes his head, then shrugs. "Actually, maybe."

"But you guys already had training today. I know you're on lighter sessions, but..." Nylah trails off, obviously concerned too.

"PT's on him not to push it." Carson shrugs. "But the guy's getting over a breakup he never saw coming."

"It's been two months." Sienna winces. "It's hit him so hard."

My insides twist.

What?

Breakup?

So that girl in the picture *isn't* his girlfriend anymore.

I should seriously not be so happy about that.

Don't ask about it. Don't you fucking open your mouth right now!

"They were in love." Nylah's lips dip into a sad frown. "At least he was. Losing someone you care about that much is brutal." Her eyes dart to Carson, and she reaches for his hand. "Do you think he can win her back?"

Great, now my stomach is starting to writhe. There's no fucking way I can finish this damn broccoli. Grady's in love with another woman. She might be his ex, but Nylah just said it loud and clear—*they were in love.*

I should be grateful. It'll help with the whole "trying to resist him" thing.

Oh, you mean like earlier today when you thought he had *a current girlfriend and still wanted to check him out, walk into his room?*

Seriously. You're despicable.

Although, now that I know he's single... maybe he needs a good screw to get that girl out of his system. Maybe that's why there's so much sexual tension between us. Because it's *supposed* to happen. Like my little gift to him.

My lips twitch, a zing firing through me as I think about just how helpful I could be. It's an effort to hide my smirk.

"I'm not sure if they'll be able to work it out," Tyrell murmurs, sliding the phone back into his pocket. "From what I've heard, Teah's moved on with another guy."

"No way." Sienna's eyes pop wide. "Who?"

"Not sure. Just heard she was dating someone new. A guy on the basketball team, I think."

"I wonder which one." Zander leans back in his seat, resting his arm on the back of Sienna's chair and lightly playing with the ends of her hair while looking at Nylah. "You heard anything? Your roommate's dating one of them, isn't she?"

"Yeah." Nylah nods, finishing her mouthful. "Jolie didn't mention anything to me, but I can ask."

"Nah, I'm just being nosy." Zander flicks his hand

through the air. "Damn, that's gonna kill Grady." Turning to Sienna with a worried frown, he murmurs, "Think I should go find him?"

Without hesitation, she gives him a nod, and I have to resist the urge to offer my help as well.

I'll come. I'll find your friend and make sure that girl is the last woman on the planet he's thinking about.

"We'll come too." Nylah rises from her chair, pulling Carson up beside her. He wraps his arm around her waist, and I clamp my lips together.

Keep your mouth shut, Blake!

"I'll clean up," Satch offers.

"No way. You cooked dinner." Wily frowns. "I'll clean up."

"I can do that." I jump all over the task, needing the distraction, while Zoey starts to cry that Daddy won't be reading her a story tonight.

Unca Wywee jumps in and saves the day, offering to read Zoey's favorite book while I start gathering dishes off the table and heading for the kitchen.

Yes, cleaning up is just what I need.

Boring!

I know, but at least it's not trouble.

Just be the good girl you're supposed to be, dammit.

You can do this.

CHAPTER 6
GRADY

"Hi." I breathe the word more than say it, my heart jackknifing at the sight of my ex.

She's still so fucking beautiful it hurts.

"Grady." She gives me an awkward smile, and it's taking everything in me not to rest my hand on her hip the way I've done a thousand times before. "How are you?"

Her smile is tighter than usual. It's her polite "I don't really want to talk to you, but I shouldn't be rude" smile, and it breaks my fucking heart all over again.

Why am I missing her when she doesn't even want me around?

I take a small step back and nod. "Yeah, I'm..." I shrug, wondering how to play this. Do I go for fake happy, like she hasn't affected me? Or do I let her know that this shit is real and I'm still an open wound, bleeding out right in front of her?

She swallows, twitching in her heels and dancing from toe to toe.

Fuck. I should really let her get on with her evening, but I can't seem to stop staring at her, drinking her in.

Why does she have to be so beautiful?

It's fucking unfair.

"Well, I..." She tucks a lock of hair behind her ear. "It's, um... it's nice to see you again."

I frown at her, hating how fake she's being. I want to call her on her bullshit, but I don't get the chance because Finn Macalister appears. Like an apparition from the deathly fucking hallows, the white boy is suddenly there, staring at me with his intense blue eyes. They're gleaming as if there's some hilarious joke I'm unaware of. Flicking his tongue over the piercing in his bottom lip, he smirks at me, and I want to punch him right in his straight little nose.

His pale fingers curve around Teah's waist. He's staking his claim loud and clear, and Teah, although she's trying to hide it, loves every fucking second of his hands on her body.

Seriously?

What does she see in this guy? He's everything I'm not.

That's what she sees. That's what she wants.

NOT you.

The thought is a punch to the balls, and rather than lashing out the way I want to, I take another step back, sending the guy a silent warning: *You fucking look after her.*

He glares right back at me, and I can sense Teah's discomfort, so I play the bigger man.

Flicking my gaze to hers, I softly mumble, "Have a good night," before spinning away and stalking to the bar.

Fuck!

Fuck, fuck, FUCK!

I plunk onto one of the free stools and glare at the dance floor. Macalister is pulling Teah onto the floor and she's smiling at him, obviously loved-up and into it. Wrapping his arms around her, he suctions their bodies together, and I can't stop staring at them.

Yeah, call me a masochist, but I can't seem to fucking help myself.

"Can I get you something?" A pretty woman with springy black curls and a bright smile grabs my attention.

"Oh, uh..." I tap the bar with my finger. "Yeah, just grab me a beer."

"ID?"

I pull out my wallet, showing her my driver's license, and she nods. "What's your flavor?"

"Whatever." I shrug. "Corona?"

"With lime?"

"Yes, please."

"Got it." She heads off to get my drink, and I pull out my phone, ready to pay. I'm only gonna get one tonight. Don't want to get off-my-ass drunk, although for the first time in my life, I am *seriously* tempted.

I don't even know why I'm still fucking here!

I should have bolted out that door the second I saw Teah, but no, I decided to torture myself.

When she first broke it off with me, I had these hopes of winning her back.

She said the relationship had gotten boring. That we were acting like an old married couple already and we were still in college. It seemed so wrong to her, and apparently that was a sign to end it.

I told her I could be more exciting.

But she argued that the things that excite her are not the things that excite me.

I wanted to tell her that was bullshit, but the more I've thought about it, the more I know she's right. I'm just not ready to fully admit that.

But I can change, be the guy she needs.

Glancing back over my shoulder, I watch her head tip back in laughter, Macalister murmuring something against her neck as they sway on the dance floor.

Guess she doesn't need me to change anymore. She's moved on.

Fuck, maybe she had before she broke up with me. Or maybe she'd met Macalister, and he was the catalyst she needed to get out of her humdrum relationship.

It makes me feel like complete shit.

"Here you go." The woman sets down my beer, then holds out the machine for me to pay.

I do, then grab the bottle, slugging back half the beer before slamming it down on the bar.

"Hey, Grady," a soft voice says, and I turn to spot Teah's best friend, Bella.

"Hi, Bells. How are ya?"

"Yeah." Her shoulder hitches as she rests her hand on the bar, looking past me to the dance floor.

It's instinctual to turn and see what she's looking at, and I instantly regret it. Mac and Teah are playing a serious game of tongue twister, his hand palming her ass while she fists the back of his hair.

I grit my teeth, spinning back before I can shout at the top of my lungs, *"We're in public! Get a room!"*

But I don't *want* them to get a room. The thought of them doing—

Nope, don't you fucking go there.

Gripping my beer bottle, I train my eyes on the bar while Bella lets out another sigh. "They got together a few weeks after you broke up."

I work my jaw to the side, tempted to ask if she was cheating on me and only revealed the relationship after we were done. Shit.

"It's been so... stressful," Bella ends in a whisper.

My eyes dart to hers. "What do you mean?"

"I don't know." Her face puckers with distress. "He's just so... wild. And we're worried about her. She was so steady and stable when she was with you. Mac is... pulling her away. I don't like it. I wish she'd never dumped you. It's like she lost her mind or something. You are... a million times better than him." Her lips form a deep pout. "I'm really sorry, Grady."

I shake my head, my throat swelling as I wrestle my way through this conversation. "Do you... think she's safe?"

Bella brushes her teeth over her bottom lip, obviously considering her answer carefully. My insides coil into tight, painful knots while I wait her out.

If he's hurting her, I'm going to end him. I don't give a shit if she's over me and I'm not her man anymore. I won't let someone cause her any kind of pain.

But then Bella nods. "Yeah. As far as I'm aware, he's not hurting her or anything. He's just... bringing out another side of her, I guess. She seems to love being with him—is constantly running out of the house with this big smile on her face. She's giddy and excitable and..." Her nose wrinkles. "I just prefer you. All of us do."

I nod, not sure how to respond to that. She's not the

only one who's been against this breakup. Teah's parents still check in with me—a little text or phone call every week or so to see how I'm doing. They're heartbroken that their daughter ended things. I wonder if they know about Mac.

Unable to stop myself, I glance over my shoulder again. They're not kissing anymore, but they're dancing close, lost in their own little bubble. His vampire hands are running up her back, those long pale fingers squeezing her close. Yeah, I can't imagine her parents being cool with a guy like him. Their country club friends would be horrified if he walked in with his messy black hair and multiple piercings. His bad boy rocker look and "fuck off" vibes aren't exactly high-class.

"Anyway." Bella sighs, her smile sad when I swivel back to face her. "You take care of yourself." Patting my arm, she says a silent goodbye and walks back to the table of sorority girls.

I watch them for a second, knowing half of them, then having to wave when a couple of them smile at me. One of them blushes, her eyes dipping with a coy smile.

Oh, fuck no. Please do not go falling for me. The last thing I need is another sorority girl from the same house as Teah. Forget it.

Turning my body to face the bar, I focus on my beer, running my thumb up and down the condensation before taking another swig, then slapping it back on the counter.

"Someone's having a bad night," a gruff voice murmurs behind me, and I spin to find Carson and Nylah giving me sad smiles.

Shit, I'm not sure how many more of them I can take. Their sympathy is killing me.

Zander saunters up just behind them, his hard gaze on the dance floor. "Is that Finn Macalister?"

"Yeah," I mumble, hunching over my beer with a dark frown.

His hand lands on my shoulder. "I'm sorry, man."

I shake my head, not even knowing how to respond.

"Did she leave you for him?" Nylah takes a seat on the other side of me while Carson flags down the bartender.

I sigh, tracing the blue letters on the bottle with my thumb. "I don't know. I want to think she didn't cheat on me. But who the fuck knows." I growl.

"It sucks." Zander nods, resting his elbow on the bar, then holding up a finger to indicate that he wants a beer too.

I sit there in silence while my friends order their drinks, then let them drag me to a table where my back is to the dance floor.

As soon as I take a seat, I start to feel better. At least I think I do.

Two beers down now, and my shoulders aren't so tense. In fact, everything is a touch looser, and my tongue starts to flap before I can stop it.

"This wasn't the plan," I mumble.

"What?" Carson leans closer to hear what I'm saying.

"I had it all fucking mapped out, and she—" I flick my hand in the air. "She dumped me. And it wasn't the fucking plan!"

"You can't control life, man." Carson tips his beer bottle at me. "It throws shit at you, and you can either turn it into fertilizer or stand there smelling like ass."

I frown at my roommate while Zander snickers. "Where the hell did you get that?"

Carson tips his head at Nylah. "My girlfriend said it."

"I did *not* say that."

"I'm paraphrasing." He winks at her.

She rolls her eyes but then gives me a kind smile, resting her hand on my arm. "It's sort of true. From one closet control freak to another... it's a mantra I have to remind myself of all the time." Running her hand down to my hand, she curls her fingers around mine. "I know life is shit right now, but you can handle it. You just have to let go of trying to fix it and trust your gut. For once, why don't you let life just happen to you and see where it goes? There's a certain freedom to that, you know?"

I scoff and shake my head. "What if my gut's not saying a fucking thing? What if life is leading me straight into a shithole?"

Nylah laughs and shakes her head. "Your gut is talking to you all the time. You just have to shut up and listen. Stop getting in your own way and just... be still. You know?"

Be still.

My brain mumbles and mocks those two words until they start to really sink in.

Be still.

The only place I can ever truly do that is in nature.

Damn, I need that spring break trip now more than ever.

Gimme tall trees and cold lakes. Gimme campfires and trail mix. Just gimme anything that isn't a strawberry blonde woman making out with a pale-skinned basketball player on the dance floor.

CHAPTER 7
BLAKE

I've been on nursing duty for nearly two weeks, and it's safe to say that...

I'm done!

I love my brother. He's one of the best people I know. Possibly *the* best person I know. But watching him process his disappointment—more like devastation—over his football plans going up in smoke has been painful.

That makes me sound like a selfish bitch. The poor guy has had his dreams shattered. I've tried to tell him they're only dented and he'll get them back—a plan is already in place. But every time we leave one of his PT sessions and he's clenching his jaw, fighting the agony of recovery, he slumps back into that mode of "my life is over," and "I'll never get drafted," and "what's the point of fighting so hard?"

Of course, the second Satch walks through the door, he manages to find his happy self again. It's only me who is truly getting all of his mournful angst.

And I'll take it.

Seriously, I will.

I'd do anything for Wily.

Except tell him the truth.

Scowling at the rows of nail polish in front of me, I try to focus on which color I'm in the mood for, but my mind is still cluttered with complaints.

I had to get out of Football Frat. I told Wily I was popping into town to grab some necessities, making it sound like I had my period or something. He didn't bat an eye, just kept staring at the TV screen with this glum look on his face.

With a huff, I grabbed my phone and jacket, then bolted out the door. Despite the rain, I decided to walk into town. It only takes about twenty minutes to get to Main Street, and now I'm standing in the drugstore, wasting time prowling the aisles and not really needing anything. I've tried out the tester hand cream and checked different shades of lipstick on my hand, but it's doing nothing to still the restless wasps buzzing in my brain.

What I need is some kind of release.

A decent hookup or getting wasted at a party.

Or maybe… I gaze at the nail polish bottles, twisting the closest one around and staring at the color. The blue shimmer mesmerizes me for a moment as my mind jumps back to Football Frat, running through the week I've just had… and the fact that I can't see an end to this thing.

Putting on a smile, pretending like I'm the studious girl I used to be. It takes a lot of effort, and I'm so over it.

Part of me just wants to bail and head back to Chicago, but I can't.

I shouldn't.

Reconnecting with Cleo is a terrible idea. My roommate is nothing but trouble.

Yet I can feel that itch. That tickle that's telling me to play those games again. To seek that thrill. To go against the grain and break all the rules.

I spent my entire life being the good girl. The child who did exactly as she was told. The one who aced all her tests and got the gold stars. I was constantly accepting awards and accolades, and my parents were so fucking proud.

Yet I'd never felt more alive than when I was in Chicago, ditching classes, getting drunk at parties, having sex in the back seat of Simon's car. Damn, that boy was a hot ride. I'd never date him in a million years, because he can be a first-class asshole, but I'll always love his dick... or at least the thrill of having it inside me. Of doing it in dangerous places. The thrill of nearly getting caught. Now that was a rush.

My eyes dart back to the nail polish.

My fingers start to tingle.

Don't do it, Blake. Just turn and walk away.

But damn, it's tempting.

I need this.

I'm losing my mind at Football Frat. It's so fucking boring, and I just need...

Glancing over my shoulder, the good girl in me starts to wail, but it's drowned out by a flood of temptation that I can't resist.

Snatching the metallic blue bottle, I slip it into my pocket, my heart rate picking up a notch as I play it cool, pretending to check out other colors, before glancing around me again.

My insides are dancing, my pulse a thick beat that reminds me of that nightclub we snuck into a few months ago. I can't remember the whole night, but flashes of color and laughter and pleasure make my lips twitch with a grin. A thrill sparks inside me, lighting me up like a fuse running to a stick of dynamite that's going to explode the second I walk out the door with the stolen item safely in my pocket.

Shit, I love this rush.

I want that explosion.

I need that thrill.

Clamping my teeth together, I force myself to walk calmly, playing the innocent girl I'm not.

It's impossible to fight my smile, so I let it grow across my face, nearly giggling when I spot the door and make a beeline for the exit.

I'm less than ten steps away when a man appears from the end of the aisle, blocking my path and glaring at me.

I give him a confused frown, the pulse in my neck shifting from a steady thump to an erratic trembling.

Shit.

Spotting his name tag, I try to hide my reaction when I notice that he's the store manager.

Shit, shit, shit!

You're busted.

This has never happened to me before. The thrill of

nearly getting caught is what I've been craving. Not *actually* getting caught.

Forcing a smile that better be fucking innocent, I veer to move around him, but he darts into my path, barking in a voice that will alert the whole fucking store, "I don't think so, lady! Give me back that nail polish!"

CHAPTER 8
GRADY

"The nail polish!" someone shouts again. "I saw you take it!"

I glance over my shoulder but can't see whoever the store manager is yelling at.

I was just in here restocking my first-aid supplies for my upcoming hiking trip when I noticed the guy storm past me, muttering under his breath.

Then he started shouting, and it's oh so clear.

Shoplifting little punks.

I shake my head, irritated by stupid people who think they have a right to just take stuff they don't deserve.

Nail polish?

That's not a necessity.

I can get over someone shoplifting food or feminine products or something like that. It's not right, but I get it.

Nail polish, though?

Give me a fucking break.

"You did take it! I saw you on camera!"

The woman's voice rises a little to match his. "I don't

know what you're talking about. Yes, I was looking at the polishes, but that's it."

Wait.

I go still, my hand poised in the air above the box of Band-Aids.

I know that voice.

Swiveling left, I head down the aisle, my lips parting when I spot the back of Blake's head.

And I should know what it looks like, because every time she's passed me in the house and I've desperately tried to ignore her... yeah, I've turned back to drink her in, to let my gaze travel down those stunning blonde curls and across the curve of her perfect ass.

Shit, I'm a creeper.

But I can't seem to stop myself.

I should be getting a fucking trophy for the fact that I've been avoiding contact all week. I'll graduate to not checking her out next week... after I've stopped this asshole manager from yelling at her.

"Everything okay over here?" I step forward, keeping my voice low and calm. The manager looks at me, and I smile. "Hey, Kevin."

He frowns. "Uh... hey?"

It's clear he has no idea how I know his name, but I'm not about to admit that I just read it off his name tag. The truth is, I recognize the guy. He's been working here for a couple of years now, and I see his face around all the time. I probably knew his name was Kevin in the back recesses of my brain. His name tag was just reminding me.

Looking at Blake, I try to catch her eye, but she's

staring at the floor, obviously embarrassed by what this guy's accusing her of. But it can't be true, right?

The way Wily always talks about her, the girl's allergic to getting into trouble, which means she'd never do anything as reckless as shoplifting.

Stepping a little closer to her, I try to form a barrier between her and Kevin, angling my body so that she's tucked just behind me.

His confused frown turns into a scowl. "You in on this too?"

"In on what?" I glance over my shoulder.

Blake's eyes dart up to meet mine, and she gives me a look of flustered confusion.

I can read her SOS signal loud and clear.

Being falsely accused of anything sucks, and this guy's got it wrong. Blake wouldn't shoplift.

"Listen, man, I think there's been some misunderstanding here. I can vouch for this woman. She's my roommate's little sister, and I'm telling you, she wouldn't shoplift anything from your store."

"You can check my pockets if you really want to," Blake drawls behind me, obviously just as unimpressed by these accusations as I am.

"Okay." Kevin squares his shoulders, grabbing her arm and pulling her out from behind me.

I step forward with a soft growl and quietly warn him, "Get your hands off her."

Rolling his eyes, Kevin releases Blake's arm and gives her a pointed look. "Come on, then. Empty your pockets."

She frowns, clearly irritated that he's taking her up on her offer.

For just a second, a wave of doubt rushes through me.

She didn't actually take something, did she?

But my doubts quickly fade as she pulls out her phone, then pats her jean pockets. "I've got nothing else in here."

"Turn around," the man barks.

I glare at him as Blake does a slow spin and he eyes up the back pockets of her jeans. "She doesn't have anything."

"And your jacket pockets." The man ignores me and points to Blake's leather jacket.

She glances up at me again, her blue eyes so bright—they look just like Wily's.

I gaze back at her, my lips curling into a closed-mouth smile as I try to reassure her.

With a soft sigh, she pulls out the insides of her jacket pockets, proving that they're empty.

"What?" Kevin balks. "But I saw you."

"You didn't," Blake gently argues. "I was looking at nail polish. I picked up a bottle, thought I might get it, then changed my mind. I wasn't walking out of this place with it in my pocket."

"But..." He huffs and looks at me like he's wanting my help.

I frown back at him. "I told you she wouldn't."

"I saw her!" His face starts turning red as he storms down the aisle, heading for the makeup section. "She took it from here and put it in her pocket! I watched her do it!"

"I don't have anything in my pockets, sir," Blake calls back to him.

"We're leaving now." I back her up, tucking my arm

around the curve of her elbow and urging her toward the exit.

"Don't you need to get some stuff?" She points at the supplies in my hand.

Dumping it on the shelf by the door, I shake my head and walk out into the light drizzle. It's been raining on and off all day, which isn't too bad after the heavy downpour we had all night. Hunching my shoulders, I lift the collar of my jacket and watch Blake do the same.

I'll come back and get my stuff later. Right now, I just need to get this woman away from false accusations.

Steering her toward the overhang of the building down the street, I make sure she's under shelter before glancing back over my shoulder at the pharmacy.

I don't relax or let her go until we're five stores down.

Slipping my hands into my pockets, I softly check on her. "You okay?"

She glances up, her smile warm and unaffected. "Yeah. Thanks for backing me up in there. That guy had it in for me."

"I can't believe he was saying that shit to you." Another soft growl reverberates in my throat. "You shouldn't have had to turn out your pockets."

Wiping a few raindrops off her face, she flicks her hand and gives me a smile. "He needed the reassurance. I don't know what he saw on his security camera, but he must have assumed I just took that nail polish and didn't see me returning it or something. I don't know." She shrugs, licking her bottom lip before gazing across the street with a sigh.

"You know, there's another place on Fifth Street that sells great makeup. I know a lot of the girls go there. Can't remember the name of it, but it's got a great selection, and I think it's cheaper than the pharmacy back there."

"Oh yeah?" She glances back at me, a teasing smile growing on her face. "I didn't know you were into drag."

I snicker and shake my head. "My *girlfriend* is big on the beauty thing."

"Girlfriend?"

Her question stops me in my tracks, and I squeeze my eyes shut, muttering, "Ex-girlfriend."

"Right."

"Loves her makeup and polish and pretty clothes and shit."

Why are you still talking? Stop talking!

I clamp my lips together, my fingers curling into fists in my pockets as we silently walk side by side down the street.

"How long ago did you break up? Must be kinda recent." Her soft questions feel like horn blasts, and I grind my teeth together. She waits me out as she continues walking down the street, and when I don't say anything, she ends up giving me an easy out. "It's obviously still kinda fresh. We don't have to talk about it."

Her nose wrinkles when we get to the end of the shelter and have to walk into the rain again. It's still light enough to not be drowning us, but her boots splash into a puddle that's been forming over the past few days. It's been a wet week, and I'm so over this rain.

I usually don't mind it too much, but when I don't have an umbrella to offer the woman beside me, it becomes an irritation. Teah always hated getting her hair wet. Although... Blake doesn't seem to be as bothered.

Her damp curls are starting to frizz, but she just tucks a clump behind her ear and keeps moving forward.

"You got a boyfriend in Chicago?" I don't know what the fuck makes me ask.

She whips a look at me, her eyes rounding before she bursts out laughing.

"What?" I frown. "Why is that funny?"

"It's not. I just..." She shakes her head, still laughing like I'm fucking hilarious. "I don't have a boyfriend."

"Okaaay." I brush raindrops off my forehead. "What am I missing here?"

"Nothing." Wiping a hand under her eyes, she lets out another soft laugh before pulling herself together. "I just..." Licking her lips, she keeps her eyes across the street and finally says, "I'm too busy for a boyfriend."

"Right." I nod, still finding her reaction weird.

Turning back to me, she puts on a bright smile and shrugs. "No one wants to date a study nerd like me."

Yeah, right!

A study hottie like her. Guys are probably lining up around the block.

Fisting my hands in my pockets again, I resist the urge to reach out and touch her, pull her to a stop, cup those pretty cheeks and assure her that any guy would be lucky to have her.

Even just one date with this woman would make a guy's year.

I mean, come on.

She's one sexy siren.

Images of her naked body flash through me, and I force myself to move a step away from her.

She seems to notice, her eyebrows flickering with... aw, shit, is that a frown?

What's she thinking right now?

"Well, thanks for the assist, Newman." She gives my arm a soft slap. "I'll catch you later."

"Do you need a ride home?"

"Nope." She's already walking away from me, slipping her hands into her jacket pockets as she checks both sides of the street before darting across.

I watch her go, willing myself not to run after her, make sure she's okay. Wily wouldn't mind me getting her home safely. That'd be cool, right?

You have a PT session in twenty minutes. Do not run after that girl.

With an irritated frown, I spin back the way I came. I probably have time to go and finish buying those first-aid supplies, but after the way Kevin treated Blake, I'm inclined to shop elsewhere. They have the best supplies in town, but I'm pretty sure there's another pharmacy near the hospital that's well stocked. I'll drive out there tomorrow and get organized. Only one week to go until spring break.

All I need to do is get through my last assignment, two tests, some light football training... and then I'll be a free man.

Free to get back to nature and get my head on straight.

CHAPTER 9
BLAKE

Holy shit, that was close.

If Grady hadn't been there, I would have been totally busted.

But when he moved in front of me to argue with the store manager, it gave me the chance to slip that polish out of my pocket and tuck it behind the boxes of tissues on the shelf behind me.

Damn, what a thrill.

I've never been so close to being busted before.

Letting out a soft laugh, I shake my head, reliving the moment.

Oh man, the way Grady growled and told Kevin to get his hands off me...

Talk about sexy.

And sweet. No other guy has ever protected me that way before. Other than my brother, which is completely different.

Grady is so fire. Trying to play it cool when we walked out of the store took everything out of me.

The buzzing in my chest suddenly fizzles out, drowned by a bucket of cold reality.

Shit.

What if he hadn't been there?

Or what if he'd seen me pulling that polish out of my pocket?

The look on his face would have been...

My stomach sours as I then picture Wily's face if he ever found out that his little sister was a shoplifting thief.

I never thought I could do something like that, but I was out with my roomie. We were bored and she was restless, antsy. We were set to go to a party that night, but it was still three hours away. I'd made my morning classes but ditched the afternoon ones, not wanting to be reminded of the fact that I was failing like I never had before. I hadn't even bothered showing up for a test the week earlier, knowing I was bound to fail it. I hadn't done one minute of studying, so what was the point of putting myself through an hour of stress and confusion?

So, we were wandering around downtown Chicago, walking in and out of shops but not in the mood to buy anything.

Loitering in the makeup aisle, Cleo and I were giggling over different lipstick colors. She tried on a bright cherry red, then made me try a neon pink.

"We look like hookers." She giggled in the mirror, wiggling her eyebrows and making me laugh.

The color was awful on me, and I wiped it off with my finger, smearing a little across my cheek. She giggled again, then snatched the tube before I could put it back, shoving it into my pocket.

"What are you doing?" I laughed, going to put it back.

But she grabbed my wrist before I could.

"Take it," she dared me, her eyes sparking with challenge.

"What?" I whispered. "No way. I can't."

"Why not? It'll be fun." Her expression was so vibrant.

"It's stealing," I mouthed before glancing over my shoulder, feeling like a covert operative as I checked the coast was clear.

A thrill whistled through me.

No one in the aisle was watching us, but she leaned in close, her breath fanning across my face. "It's no big deal. Just do it. It's a rush."

"But I can afford to pay for it," I softly argued. "Even though I'd never buy this hideous color."

"It's not about the fucking money, Miss Trust Fund. It's about the thrill." She squeezed my wrist, leaning back to look me up and down. "Come on, baby. Don't be a pussy."

Her eyes continued to dance, and I couldn't deny that spark burning inside me.

I'd never done anything so daring. So dangerous.

And I wanted it.

I wanted that rush.

So, I lifted my chin, looked around us, and headed for the exit. Cleo curled her hand around my arm, and we strutted out of that store with my stolen lipstick.

And yeah, it was a rush.

Addictive.

Naughty.

I'd never done anything like it. And that one small act unlocked a gate.

Or maybe the hinge had been broken for a while, and I just hadn't been willing to act on it.

But meeting Cleo was the catalyst I needed.

She was the one who encouraged me to ditch class. She dared me to lift my first tube of lipstick, and that night, we celebrated like it was our last day on the planet.

Thanks to my monthly allowance from Mommy and Daddy, we lived it up. I got off-my-ass drunk and ended up making out with Cleo's friend Nico. He's Italian, and damn if his hands and lips aren't the best. He ended up being my first about two nights later, and it wasn't so bad. After that, I ping-ponged between him and Simon. It all depended on who was there. They didn't seem to mind sharing me, and I'm pretty sure they were hooking up on the side with Cleo and whoever else they were into. No one was a couple. Everything was casual, no strings attached, free love and all that shit.

Damn, when I think about it now, it makes the four of us sound like orgy-loving porn stars.

But I only hooked up with one guy at a time, and...

When I was lost in that drunken haze, partying it up... it didn't feel wrong.

It's not until you're sober, waking up half-naked in a bed you don't recognize, that you start to wonder if your life choices are all that great.

But that rush.

That rush is the best.

I miss it.

Shit, maybe I even miss Cleo.

No, you do not!

After what she did to me—what she's still trying to do to me—I've thought about buying a voodoo doll and sticking pins in its eyes. But that day I left… I think I was too numb to feel anything as I packed up my stuff and rented a storage unit. She just sat there on her bed, watching me, not saying shit.

I hated her in that moment.

But now I'm pining, like some loyal puppy dog.

Stop it! I hate you for doing that!

My insides coil.

She opened my eyes. Introduced me to a world of freedom and reckless fun.

It's an addictive rush, and I want it again.

Pulling out my phone for just a second, I think about texting her. I even find our last message exchange.

Rage fires through me, hot and fast.

Fuck her!

My mind jumps back to that first night out of the dorm. I was holed up in a hotel room, wondering what the fuck to do with myself.

I had no idea how I was going to tell my parents what had happened.

The university hadn't contacted them as far as I was aware, and I was just lying there, waiting for the impending explosion.

Hatred for Cleo burned bright. That bitch dumped me in it. She put all the blame on me, and I should have dragged her right down with me.

But for some reason, I didn't.

I still haven't figured out why.

She was just as guilty as I was.

Just as worthy of suspension as me.

But I let her get away with it.

Why the fuck did I do that?

Hating my weakness, I sat on that bed and deleted her number. And then I deleted Simon's and Nico's and every other contact I'd made in Chicago.

My chest was heaving by the time I was done. And in that moment, I had no idea Cleo would reach out to me again. Reach out to torture me.

Shoving my phone back into my pocket, I cross my arms, hunching over myself as the rain picks up and starts to fall in thick, heavy droplets.

That night in the hotel room, all I had left on my phone was my old life... and I couldn't reach out to anyone on that list.

Because none of them would get it.

I'd burned bridges with my high school besties, and they probably didn't want to know me anymore.

All that was left was my family. And they couldn't know. They could never know that their precious angel had become a complete fuckup.

But that's what I was.

And it's probably what I've always been. I was just really good at hiding it.

"Shit." I run a hand down my wet face, no doubt smearing my mascara. Who fucking cares.

I'm shaking. My whole body is vibrating with these restless tremors.

"I need a drink," I mutter.

I want to get rip-roaring wasted so I don't have to think about this shit anymore.

Fuck, I should never have thrown away my fake ID. It was in a moment of weakness when I was trying to find my old self again. I chopped it up into little pieces, then dropped to my knees on that hotel carpet and cried, instant regret taking me out.

I'm sure as shit regretting it again!

I just need a drink. A distraction. Something to numb this irritation.

The nail polish was supposed to be it, but that was a bust.

I should be grateful to Grady for saving my ass...

And I am.

But now I'm back to feeling like shit over what he'd think if he knew that I'd really done it. I'd taken that polish and had every intention of walking out the door with it.

I didn't even like that metallic blue. I wasn't going to wear it.

But it wasn't about the product. It was about the rush.

And I want that rush again.

I *burn* for it.

Crossing my arms, I stalk the streets of Nolan, not ready to head back to Football Frat but not knowing where else to go. I wander through the campus, my clothes getting more and more soaked as I check out the buildings and feel a small spark of interest. But it's quickly dimmed when I imagine the mind-numbing shittiness of becoming a study nerd again. I had no life. None.

And any kind of thrill?

I had no idea what that even was.

Not until I met Cleo. Not until I let her pull me off the rails.

Shit. How can I love and hate something in equal measure?

My phone buzzes with a text and I pull it out of my back pocket, reading Wily's message.

Shithead: Where you at, butt face? The rain's getting kind of heavy. Need a ride?

I glare at the screen, wishing I had an easy answer. I usually love how protective he is, but right now, it feels suffocating. I don't want a ride back to Football Frat. How do I face him right now?

My brain's a mess, and I don't have it in me to put on my good girl smile. I just need a little more time.

Guilt ratchets through me as I quickly type my response.

Found the library. Nirvana!! Don't expect me back anytime soon. Unless you need something.

It takes him less than a minute to reply.

Shithead: Haha! Study nerd! I'm all good here. Satch just arrived. Call me when you need a ride home and I'll send one of the guys to come get ya.

I send back a thumbs-up, already dreading that moment.

Spinning, I turn my back on the library and keep

walking. The darkness sets in as I aimlessly wander, and my sensible, logical brain is telling me to get back to the house already. I'm hungry, and walking around in the rainy darkness by myself is a terrible idea.

But I've wandered so long and so far now, I have no fucking idea where I am.

Slowing to a stop, I scan the neighborhood. I can tell by the cars parked in driveways and the unkempt lawns that I must be on a street that's mostly populated by college students.

Hearing a distant thud of music, I turn and walk toward it, curiosity getting the better of me.

I know that thud.

It's familiar.

It means a party.

It means fun.

It means a scratch for this restless itch I've been fighting all day.

It takes me two minutes to walk down the street, and I'm soon standing outside a house that's practically vibrating, the ground beneath my feet pulsing, the lights inside calling to me. Uncontrolled laughter, out-of-tune singing, shouts and whoops. It's all so familiar.

"Hey, sugar." A guy walks past me, his smile friendly as he heads up the path. Turning back, he points a thumb over his shoulder. "You coming?"

"Don't know anyone." I lift my chin at the house behind him.

"Doesn't matter." His smile grows even wider. "These parties are always for everyone. Come on. It'll be fun." Tipping his head toward the house, he beckons me through the front door.

I watch him step inside, shaking his wet hair like a dog and laughing when the girl closest to him lets out a squeal, then slaps his arm. He pulls her in for a kiss and she pushes him away, then laughs at something he said, raising her red Solo cup in the air and whooping before kissing his lips.

Uncertainty niggles, trying to warn me away as I check the street, left and right before my eyes land back on that front door. It's still hanging open, still beckoning me to enter.

That buzz starts to fire inside me again.

I need this.

Just one night to let loose, and then I can go back to playing pretend again.

There's no harm in that, right?

CHAPTER 10
GRADY

Trying to study when Blake Wilson keeps dancing in my brain is nearly impossible. Slamming back in my chair, I glare out the window. I left the curtain open, even though it's dark out, and my room is now a fishbowl. I can't even really see our neighbor's house. Right now, I'm looking at a reflection of my grumpy-ass face.

With the rain trickling down the glass, I look like I'm fucking crying.

Shit! Why won't she leave me alone?

I don't want to be into this girl at all.

But I can't stop thinking about that look of mild panic on her face before I intercepted the guy at the pharmacy. I didn't see it at first, too caught up in the fact that he was yelling at her, but the more I think about it, the more I realize she was freaking out. Being yelled at by anyone is unnerving. I'm grateful I was there, especially since she didn't do anything wrong.

A niggle stirs inside me that I don't even understand.

Shifting in my seat, I lean back over my laptop and try

to focus, but there she goes again, her laughter flittering between my ears. Why did she think having a boyfriend was so damn hilarious?

Is she not into guys?

Her heated look when we checked each other out in the bathroom... nah, she's into men. Or at least she's into me.

We have a connection. There's no denying it.

From what I can tell, it's simply pure lust, because I don't know this woman at all, so how can I possibly be romantically attracted to her, right?

I mean, I know what Wily's told me. He adores his sister. They grew up close. I don't really know what that's like. Owen and I never really saw eye to eye, unless we were playing football, and then when our parents got divorced, the divide turned into the fucking Grand Canyon. Jamar and Luis are so much younger than me, and even though they're great kids, I'm never gonna be super close to them.

But Blake and Wily... they're like best buds.

Which is why you can never go out with her.

Closing my eyes, I cup the back of my head with a heavy sigh.

I should be grateful for this unspoken rule. It'll no doubt keep me out of trouble.

Although, a fling with Blake might be exactly what you need right now. It'll help you get over Teah, right?

I growl, sitting up straight and hating myself for thinking that. I'm not using Blake like some rebound therapy. Fuck that!

Standing up, I kick my chair back and head for the

door. I need to get out of here and go for a run or have something to eat.

I don't fucking know.

I just need to move.

Slapping my laptop shut, I stalk to my door, grabbing my jacket off the hook and throwing it on. This is stupid. I don't even know where I'm going. Teah and Mac might be at Offside, so that's a no-go.

I could go to the library. Study there for a bit. Might be a nice change of scenery.

But I'll no doubt still carry Blake and her pretty face with me.

Damn, she's so fucking beautiful. Her big blue eyes, delicate features, and that waterfall of blonde hair.

Waterfall of hair? Man, would you shut the fuck up!

Closing my eyes, I try to inhale some sanity before trotting down the stairs and bumping into Wily, who's limping out of the living room with Satch tucked under his arm.

"You good, brother?" I move in to assist.

"Yeah, we're all good. Gonna get myself a sponge bath." Wily wiggles his eyebrows while Satch turns beet red.

And I'm most definitely out.

He laughs at the look on my face. "Don't worry. I don't want your help." He glances down at Satch, his heated gaze telling me enough.

This ain't no simple sponge bath. Those two are gonna have themselves a little naked time in the bathroom, and I don't want to know.

"I'll... leave you guys to it." I step back, steadying

Wily's arm when he takes another awkward step forward. "Do you need help getting there?"

"No, I'm good." Wily winces, slowly shuffling forward.

He is getting better, I can see that, but I'm guessing the healing process isn't fast enough for the guy. He's not supposed to put any weight on that leg for at least another week.

I watch him hobble down the hallway with Satch supporting him. I don't know how she's doing it. She's so tiny compared to that giant, but somehow they manage. Once they've disappeared into the bathroom, I move to put my shoes on. I still have no idea where I'm going, and I'm almost relieved when my phone starts ringing.

Standing back up, I abandon my Nikes in order to take a video call from...

"Hey, Dad." I grin at the camera. "What's up?"

"Grady Boy. How are you, kid?"

He'll forever call me kid, and I don't even care. It's always said with such warm affection that I can't even be mad at him.

"Yeah, I'm great," I lie, not wanting to dive into the torture that living in Football Frat currently is. I could definitely talk to my old man about it. I tend to tell him everything, but I know he's been worried about me since my breakup with Teah, and I don't want to get into it tonight. "How are things with you?"

He gives me an edgy smile. "They're really good, actually."

I frown. "What's up?"

"Well..." he starts, but is interrupted when his girlfriend takes a seat beside him. She passes him a mug of steaming... is that tea?... and he gives her an affectionate smile. "Thanks, baby."

Emma grins at me while Dad kisses her cheek. "Hi, Grady."

"Hey." I smile back at her because, despite the fact that she's fifteen years younger than my dad, making her closer in age to me than my old man, I really like her. She's been so good for him. "So, what's your news, guys? I know you're sitting on something."

Emma looks to Dad, her smile downright adorable as he gives me a cheesy grin and announces, "I'm moving in with this lovely lady."

"Really?" I let out a soft laugh. "About damn time."

Emma laughs. "We didn't want to rush it, but we found the cutest little place a couple of weeks ago, and we've decided to just go for it."

"So you're both moving?"

"Yeah, that wasn't the original plan, but this place is perfect for us, and we figured starting this next step with something fresh and new for us both was the right way to go."

"That's awesome." I smile at them. "I'm really happy for you guys."

"Thanks, kid." Dad winks at me, but then his smile fades. My gut twists. Is Mom giving him shit for this? Because she has no fucking say anymore. Like she can talk. She moved in with Emilio mere weeks after the divorce was finalized. Probably because she was already pregnant with Jamar. We just didn't know it at the time.

Anger roils through me until Dad's explanation captures my attention. "...and we realized that's the only weekend we're free. So I'm really sorry, but I won't be able to make it." He winces, and I finally catch up to what he's saying.

Well, shit.

"Bummer." I try to not make him feel bad, but it's impossible to hide my disappointment. I was really looking forward to hiking with the guy. He's my outdoor guru. The one who taught me everything I need to know about the wild—how to hunt, track, use plants for medicine and food. He taught me how to plan, navigate, where to look for danger, how to deal with animals, do first aid. The guy is a legend in the outdoors... and I really wanted to spend this time with him in one of our favorite spots.

"We're sorry." Emma cringes. "I feel so bad. Life's just gotten stupidly busy this month." Turning back to my father, she starts to try and fix it. "I could just move the stuff by myself. I could get Tony and Lauren to help me."

"No, baby. I don't want you to have to do it all." Dad puts down his drink so he can wrap his arm around her shoulders.

"I just feel bad."

"Don't," I assure her. "I still have Carson and Tyrell coming with me. We're gonna have a great time together. Unless you need me to delay my trip, and I can come and help you guys with the move."

"No way." Dad shakes his head. "You need to get into the forest for a few days. It'll do you the world of good."

"I can be there for you, though. I don't mind."

"Well, I do. Your spirit is yearning for nature, and I won't get in the way of that. I'm just sorry the timing is working out this way. I was looking forward to joining you. But I promise to be there next time."

"Thanks, Dad. I'll check my calendar so we can schedule something in."

"Sounds good." He rests his cheek against the top of Emma's head when she snuggles against him.

"Thanks for letting me have your old man." She gives me a wincing smile.

I laugh. "Anytime, Em. I know you'll look after him for me."

She smiles back. "Always. It's my pleasure." Leaning up, she gives him a sweet kiss on the lips, and I wrap up the call.

Shit, I'm surrounded by lovebirds at the moment. That would usually fuel my sappy, romantic heart.

But not right now.

I hate being single.

I miss having someone to snuggle with. Make plans with. Someone to call my own.

Fuck. I'm gutted that Dad can't make the hiking trip.

But I am genuinely happy for him and Emma. They've been dating for over two years now, and I thought she'd move in ages ago, but they've taken their sweet time, Dad no doubt being overly cautious after everything he went through with Mom.

I don't know if he'll ever marry Em, but at least they're moving in together.

Slipping my phone into my back pocket, I head back to the shoe rack. Maybe I'll just go for a walk around the block. The rain has eased up, the fresh air will clear my head, and—

Another phone starts ringing. I look over my shoulder. The sound is coming from the living room. It must be Wily's or Satch's. Do I take it to them?

Wandering into Wily's temporary bedroom, I notice the device lighting up on the coffee table and glance at the screen.

A hilarious picture of Blake making a face at the camera and the word Butt Face underneath makes me smile. These two are fucking hilarious. Picking up the phone, I smile down at her picture until I realize Blake is calling Wily.

And for reasons I can't explain, something in my chest hitches with worry.

I have no idea why I'm feeling this way, but I should take the phone to Wily.

Or answer it for him. He won't mind.

Clenching my jaw, I briefly war with indecision until I realize the call is about to cut off. I quickly swipe my thumb across the screen.

"Hey, Blake. It's Gra—"

"Sooooo." She breathes down the line, then lets out this giggle that turns into a groan.

I can hear thumping music in the background, a chaotic symphony of noise.

"Blake?" My instincts put me on instant alert. "Are you okay?"

"I feeeel weird." Her words are sloppy and barely coherent.

Shit. What the hell has happened to her?

"Where are you?" I walk into the entranceway, glancing down the hallway and figuring I should take this call to Wily.

"A party." Her breathy giggle is knotting my insides. She's totally wasted. Or worse, she's been roofied or some shit.

Fuck!

"What party? Where?"

"I don't know. I... Shhhhh." I can picture her lips pursing to make that sound, and then she whispers down the line, "Don't tell Wily."

I stop walking toward the bathroom, pausing in the archway of the dining room. "What? You called his number."

"Shit. Did I?" she slurs. "Wait, who's this?"

A heartbeat is pulsing in my stomach as I struggle to stay calm. Warning bells are blaring inside me as I grit out, "It's Grady."

"Ohhh! The hot one. He's got a sexy body." She laughs, but the sound is anything but funny because I know this girl is in some seriously deep shit right now. "Don't tell him I said that, though. I'm pretty sure the guy's afraid of me. Or just plain doesn't like me."

"That's not..." I close my eyes and dip my head. Even if I did take the time to explain that I've been desperately trying to avoid her because she turns me on like nothing else can, I'm not sure she'd register anything I was saying.

All I know is that I need to get to her.

Now.

"Blake, I need you to focus." I head back to the shoe rack. Wily doesn't need to hear this shit right now. It's not like he can jump into a car and wrestle his way into a party to find her.

But I can.

Snatching my sneakers, I start shoving them on.

"Where are you?" I ask in a clear, calm voice.

She sighs, and I wonder if she's looking around, trying to figure it out. "I'm at a party."

"Yeah, but where? Whose house are you at?"

"I don't fucking know." She groans again. "My head..."

"Blake."

She groans again.

"Blake. Focus. Stay with me, okay? I'm coming to find you, but you need to tell me where you are."

"I don't know!" she whines and sounds like she's about to start crying or something.

Fuck!

Closing my eyes, I try to think past the worry coursing through me. "Okay. It's okay. Just, uh..." My eyes snap open as a fresh idea pops into my head.

Whipping the phone away from my ear, I put her on speaker and then tap the screen, opening Wily's Find My app. Two names appear: Satch and Blake. Thank fuck for that.

"Blake, listen to me. I can see your location. Looks like you're at a house on Alpine Ave. Where are you in that house?"

"I don't know..." Her voice dribbles off, and I feel a surge of panic when she doesn't respond.

"Blake? Blake!"

"I don't... I..."

"Okay, listen carefully." I dig my keys out of the bowl by the front door. "Just look around you. What can you see?"

She groans again, and I will her to stay lucid so she can do this for me.

Fuck, Wily is going to lose it if something happens to her.

I should tell him what's going on, right?

And worry the shit out of him? No! Just go find her.

I can't afford the delay while he gets out of the bath anyway. I need to go.

Now.

If the urgency pulsing through me is anything to go by, I should have left five minutes ago.

"Blake? What can you see?" Trying to keep my voice calm is taking maximum effort.

"There's a wall and... I just... Who is this again?" She's struggling to get the words out. They're coming out of her in long, slurred syllables.

"It's Grady," I reply slowly. "Your brother's roommate."

"Oh, the hot one." She giggles, the sloppy sound making my insides sizzle with concern. "I picture him when I touch myself."

Wait. What?

I jolt upright, gaping at the front door for a second as that sizzle turns to something else entirely.

"But don't tell him I said that," she whispers.

A yearning shudder ripples through me.

Holy fuck.

Blake touching herself while thinking about me.

Now there's an image... that I really can't afford to get distracted by right now.

Clenching my jaw, I try to find out a little more information before leaving. "Tell me where you are in the house. What else is there other than *a wall*? Can you be more specific?"

"Paspefic. Spa-spefic. Sp—" She giggles again. "That word's hard."

"Blake." I close my eyes. "Please, come on. Help me out here. What can you see?"

"What can I see. I see… There's a cabinet. Whoooooa. It's so tall."

A tall cabinet. Okay, so maybe she's in like a living room or den or something?

"Is there anyone around you?"

"I—" There's a fumbling followed by a sharp clatter that makes me wince. I pull out my phone, bringing up Google Maps while she struggles to pick up her phone.

Shit, she's really in a bad way.

"Blake?"

"I'm Blake," she responds, her voice kind of raspy. "That's me."

"Okay, I'm coming to get you," I tell her, relief pumping through me as I punch in her location and see that I'll be there in seven minutes. Let's make it five. "Don't go anywhere with anyone, okay?"

"Okay." She sounds kind of sleepy now, and it kills me to end the call with her.

I want to keep her on the line while I drive to this party, but if I take Wily's phone, that's going to alert him to something being up, and she asked me not to tell him.

Frowning down at his phone, I ignore my gut and delete evidence of the phone call. It feels wrong, and I'm torn between respecting her wasted wishes and letting my roommate know what the fuck is going on.

But he'll just freak out, right?

Programming Blake's number into my phone, I then run out the door, trying to tell myself that I'm doing the right thing.

All I do know for sure is that I need to get to her fast.

I'll deal with the rest of this shit once I know she's safe.

CHAPTER 11
BLAKE

Shit, I feel weird.

My brain's a fuzzy mess, and yeah, I've been knocking back the shots, but this is different.

Something in the back of my muddy mind is warning me to get out.

But I can't find the door. All I could find was a dark corner in between a wall and this cabinet-bookshelf thing. I don't know what it is, but it's towering above me right now, like an ominous demon… or maybe it's keeping me safe and hidden.

I don't know.

I don't know anything.

My brain is scrambling to put two thoughts together.

I vaguely remembering stumbling into this spot, sinking down onto the floor. The shadows enveloped me, and I fumbled out my phone, not even knowing who I was dialing.

I just needed to get help.

Then some man with a deep voice answered.

He talked to me and told me to stay put. So I'm gonna do that.

Leaning my head back, I groan, my stomach roiling as I rest a shaky hand against my spinning head. The room is turning upside down, and I shut my eyes, trying to get off this ship.

The floor is tipping beneath me. Oh shit, I feel like I'm gonna puke or something.

I have to get out of here.

I'm gonna hurl chunks, and I don't want to get my dress dirty.

Wait, am I even wearing a dress?

I look down at myself, struggling to make sense of the jeans and shirt I'm in. I thought I was dressed up for a party. I came to a party, didn't I?

Where's my jacket?

Cleo wouldn't let me go in just jeans and a shirt. And my jacket. Did I have a jacket?

"Dress to impress, sweetheart." Mom's voice rings in my head.

"Make 'em hungry for it." Cleo smirks.

Wait. Who's Cleo?

I mumble her name, picturing a girl with purple-and-black hair. She has a neck tattoo—a bird, the wings stretching around her throat. Her smile is bright, her laughter kind of maniacal. She spins around my brain like a horror movie. A carousel of images attack me from all sides—moans of pleasure, puking, tucking lipstick into my pocket, laughing, drinking straight from the bottle, a loud clash of drums, stumbling, landing on a bed, hands on me, tongues, moans, ecstasy, headache, crying...

The chaotic kaleidoscope swirls inside me until my brain feels like it's going to explode.

I groan, clutching my head and struggling up to my feet.

I tip sideways, my shoulder slapping against the wall.

"Hey, you okay?" someone asks me. His voice is deep and soothing, his touch soft as he cups my face.

"Did you come to find me?" The words all blend together, and I can't understand what I'm saying.

The guy brushes his hand down my face, curling his fingers lightly around my neck. "I'll help you, sweet thing. You just come with me."

My head lolls to the side. It's too heavy for my skinny neck. I can't hold it up anymore.

An arm comes around my waist. It's strong and… and like a pincer.

It's too tight. Too strong. Too unrelenting.

I don't want it.

I try to pull away, but he holds me closer, his fingers digging into my side as he starts walking me away from the wall.

No! A sharp ping of terror jolts through me.

This is wrong. Something is wrong.

I push at him with floppy limbs that aren't working properly. "I don't want to go with you." I try to make my voice strong, but it's so soft, and he probably can't hear me above this music.

Ugh. It's thumping right through me. Pounding and painful.

My head is about to split open. I whimper, "No."

"It's okay, sugar. I've got you." His voice is sweet and coaxing, vaguely familiar, but something feels off.

This is wrong.

I push at him with rubbery arms, but he bats my hand away with a soft laugh. "You're okay. I've got you."

His fingers tighten around my waist again until I feel like he's gonna cut me in half. My floppy head lands on his shoulder, and I don't want it there.

"Stop," I whisper. "Lemme go."

He ignores me, leading us down a corridor.

I don't want this. I don't want this!

"It's okay," he croons. "You're safe with me."

"No, please," I whimper, wrestling in vain but achieving nothing.

"Blake!" someone shouts. "Get your fucking hands off her!"

There's a growl, and then the guy's hold on me loosens. I start to fall, gravity pulling me to the ground.

"Shit!" A hand catches my wrist, slowing my descent and softening the thump when I land on the floor.

I hear a grunt above me and open my eyes.

But all I can make out is a blur of bodies.

A woman screams.

"Stop!"

"Get off me!"

Knuckles crunching.

More grunts.

A tumble.

A crash.

Another scream.

I'm gonna be sick.

I rest my head on the floor, pushing my cheek into the cold wood, closing my eyes and willing the darkness to take me.

"Blake." Soft hands cup my cheek. "Open your eyes. Come on." Someone's lightly shaking me, then tapping my cheek.

I groan, forcing my eyes open.

"That's it." A Black man smiles down at me. He's handsome. There's something so familiar about him. "It's me. It's Grady. I'm getting you out of here, okay?"

His lip is bleeding.

Why is his lip bleeding?

I try to reach for it, but my arm is too heavy. It flops onto the floor, and I can't keep my eyes open anymore.

"No, come on. Stay with me, all right? Blake!"

Forcing my eyes back open, I watch him blur into a fuzzy blob as he pulls me into a sitting position, then wriggles his hands beneath my legs.

"Get the fuck back," he growls. "I'm not playin'! I will end any fucker who comes near her!"

"All right, chill man. Shit."

"Get out!" some woman snaps. "Just fucking get out. And you—take her out of here. I don't need this shit. You broke my favorite lamp!"

"Bill me," Grady mutters. With a soft grunt, he stands up, taking me with him. I rest my head on his shoulder.

This one feels right.

There's no fear in these arms.

And my eyes slide shut as I'm carried out of this wild, thumping place.

CHAPTER 12
GRADY

Fuck!

When I first got to the party, I raced through the door, frantically hunting for Blake. No one knew who the hell I was talking about, and even if they did, I doubt they would have been much help. The party was beyond chaotic by the time I arrived, drunken bodies gyrating around the room, manic cackling, the thumping bass. We've had our fair share of parties at Football Frat, but this one was wild.

Shouldering my way between bodies, I searched for a tall cabinet but couldn't see one anywhere. Finally, I popped out into a hallway. And that's when I saw her.

Well, I saw the back of her head as she was being led who knows where to do who knows what. She seemed to be pushing at the guy, trying to get away from him, but her body was too floppy to have an impact.

A primal rage tore through me as I shouted her name and wrenched that guy away from her. She nearly hit the ground, and I only just caught her arm. I couldn't stop her from hitting the floor, but I managed to soften her landing.

That was why I missed the fist launching at me.

It clipped me right in the fucking lip, and it still hurts.

I can taste the blood in my mouth as I carry Blake out of this damn house.

"What'd you take, huh?" I jostle her in my arms, too scared to let her fall asleep.

She's so out of it, I'm panicking that she's OD'd.

"Come on, Blake. Wake up."

With a groan, she opens her eyes and gives me a blurry-eyed stare before her heavy lids slid shut again.

"No, no, no." I hitch her higher in my arms, walking down to my Jeep as fast as I can.

I had to park a fucking block away and run to the house. I sprinted like my life depended on it.

Maybe *her* life did.

Fuck. What if I hadn't reached her in time?

What the hell was that creeper planning on doing with her?

I should have hit him harder.

My final blow knocked him backward. He smashed into a lamp on the side table before toppling to the floor, nursing his face with a groan.

It hurt my hand, but I don't give a flying fuck right now.

I just need to make sure Blake's okay.

"What'd you drink? Was it just alcohol? Huh? Or did you take something too?"

"I... I don't..." She groans and lurches sideways, rolling out of my arms.

"Whoa." I catch the back of her shirt but can't stop her from landing on the wet grass. "Blake?"

I crouch down beside her, brushing the hair off her face as she kneels on the ground, a trembling wreck.

"I'm gonna be..." Her words are lost as her body starts to convulse. She glances at me with wide eyes, like she's terrified, then lets out this weird gagging noise and starts to puke.

A spray hits my knee—thank fuck I'm in sweats—but most of it lands on the grass.

The stench is overwhelming, but I can handle it if it means she's getting this poison out of her. It won't cure the hangover she's gonna get. Whatever she's taken is pumping through her bloodstream, and she's gonna feel like total shit in the morning.

But she's with me now.

She's safe.

Scrubbing a hand down my face, I huff out a shaky breath as I gather up her hair. Brushing it over her shoulder, I then twist it around my fingers, holding it away from her face while she hurls chunks on the grass.

"What the hell were you thinking?" I whisper.

Watching her go through this is a weird kind of torture.

She's in obvious distress, and I can't do anything but let her ride it out. Her body continues to convulse, but she's out of puke, her stomach still jerking as she dry heaves, then tries to flop down onto her side.

I grab her arm before she falls, keeping her upright. She's trembling like she's got a fever, but when I rest my hand across her forehead, she's not burning up. Her body is just protesting the toxic shit that's been pumped into it.

"I feel sick," she blubbers, saliva dripping off her bottom lip.

"It's okay. You're gonna be okay." I slash my finger over her mouth and chin, then wipe her spittle off on the grass beside me. Rubbing her back for a minute, I give her a chance to reset before coaxing her to my Jeep.

After a few minutes, I think she's okay to move and am about to lift her back into my arms when she starts convulsing again and pukes once more.

Fuck, that smell is eye-watering.

"Did you mix your drugs?" I pinch my nose, gathering her hair back up again. I don't expect her to answer me. The last thing she needs right now is a lecture, but I'm trying to figure out if I need to take her to a hospital.

Her body jerks beneath mine. And just like before, her stomach is still spasming, but she's run out of puke.

Her head lolls back and she flops to the side, resting against me. Placing my hand on her forehead again, I cringe. She's clammy and cold, but at least her body isn't shaking as badly.

Wrapping my arm around her shoulders, I hold her close, taking this slow. She might need to puke again, and I don't want to be jostling her around.

Between the streetlights and the moon, I can see how pale her skin is. Brushing my lips across her forehead, I gently ask, "Have you ever partied before?"

"All the time." She whimpers. "But this is different. This feels different."

Her face buckles in distress, and the rage I felt when I saw that guy pulling her down the hallway has me ripping the phone from my pocket.

Roofies. Fucking roofies!

Someone slipped something into her drink. And because she was there alone, she had no backup. No one to keep an eye on her.

I dial 9-1-1, reporting a wild party as worry for any other girl in that house courses through me. I can't go back and check on them all. I need to take care of Blake.

"It's getting out of control," I tell the operator. "And I'm pretty sure there's underage drinking going on, plus I'm concerned there might be roofies floating around. The party needs breaking up. Now."

I stay on the line long enough to give the location, but I'm not sticking around to get interviewed by the cops. Blake's underage and doesn't need the trouble.

As soon as I hang up, I sweep her back into my arms and make a beeline for my Jeep. By the time I've got Blake buckled up in the passenger seat, I can hear the distant ring of sirens. Good. They're on their way.

"Here. Drink this." I hand her a bottle of water.

She takes a few reluctant sips, but I force her to take at least five more.

"You need to hydrate."

Her upper lip curls in protest, but I nudge the bottle back toward her.

"Drink."

She does as she's told before swiping the back of her hand across her mouth and resting her head back. Closing her eyes, she lets out an exhausted sigh. "Don't tell Wily," she slurs.

I grit my jaw, pulling away from the curb and heading in the opposite direction of the red and blue flashing lights. Two units pull up outside the party, and I glance in my rearview mirror, relieved things will get broken up quickly.

Wily should probably know about this shit, but... I don't want to get Blake in trouble.

"He can't know." She swivels her body to face me, but her eyes are still closed. Reaching out a floppy hand, she manages to rest it on my arm. "Not about the partying or getting kicked out."

Gripping the wheel, I glance at her. "Getting kicked out of where?"

"College," she mumbles, her chin dipping forward while I try to process what the fuck she just said.

Is she serious?

She got kicked out?

Her hand drops off my arm, landing with a thud on the center console.

"Blake?" I swerve up next to the curb, quickly pulling to a stop so I can check on her.

Lifting her chin, I check her vitals, not taking a full breath until I've figured out that she's just fallen asleep.

Her breaths hit the back of my hand in even puffs, and the pulse in her neck seems to be steady, but I'm gonna take her to the hospital, just to be sure.

Resting my head back with a sigh, I stay where I am for a second.

Shit. What a night.

Glancing back at Blake, I run my finger lightly down her cheek, tucking a wayward clump of curls back behind her ear.

She got kicked out of school?

What the hell?

Wily always talks about her being a star pupil. She

was valedictorian. A complete study nerd. He jokes about it all the time, but you can see how damn proud he is.

How's he gonna react when he finds out his sister's been expelled?

Do her parents know?

I doubt any of them know she's been partying... and whatever the fuck else she's been up to.

Shit.

Resting my head back, I stare out the windshield, wondering how I'm supposed to handle this.

I want to respect Blake's request and not dump her in it. This news is hers to share, not mine. But Wily's one of my best friends. I love the guy like a brother, and sitting on this is gonna kill me.

Letting out a long, heavy sigh, I lightly dab the cut on my lip and shake my head.

I should have fucking stayed up in my room and studied.

But if I had, I would have missed Blake's phone call.

And shit, I can't even think about where she'd be right now if I hadn't managed to find her.

Checking the road, I pull away from the curb and do the right thing... even though it sucks.

Going to the hospital will mean paperwork and possibly an interview with the police, making it that much harder to keep it from Wily.

Shit! Why do I want to hide this from him?

He should know.

Glancing at Blake again, I wage a silent war, trying to figure out which is worse: betraying her trust or hiding the truth from her brother.

Both options suck, but as I near the hospital, I know I can't take the first one.

It takes two hours to get Blake checked out. She wakes up in the middle of the exam and starts crying, blubbering incoherent answers to the sweet nurse who patiently talks her through the process. I stay by her side the whole time, answering what I can and holding her hand when a police officer shows up to take her statement. Her answers are muddy and vague, her skin turning scarlet when he asks her age. I quietly beg him to go easy on her.

"Please, Officer. I know she's underage, but she's had a really rough night."

He eyes me up and down, then points to my face. "Looks like you have too."

I dab my lip and softly murmur, "Some guy was trying to take her where she didn't want to go. I only just got there in time. If I'd known where she was, I would have gone sooner."

Clicking his tongue, he scribbles something else in his notebook while my heart starts to race the way it always does around authority like this. I've never once done anything wrong, but damn if they don't make me feel like a criminal just because my skin's a few shades too dark for their liking.

My teeth clench and I will my chin to stay up, because I am an innocent man.

"Can you describe the person you fought with?"

Closing my eyes, I try to picture him, but everything was such a blur. "Uh... the party was pretty chaotic, but from what I can remember, he was about six foot—a little taller than me. Caucasian. Light brown hair, kinda shaggy. Medium build. He was wearing jeans and a white shirt. I think it was white."

"And he'll have a fat lip too? Or a black eye or something?"

Smashing my teeth together, I give one quick nod but refuse to feel guilty for that. He was an asshole and deserved a punch in the face. "I was defending myself… and her." I rub my thumb over the back of Blake's hand and glance down at her. Her eyes are closed, her lips slightly parted. She's asleep again, oblivious to this conversation.

"You her boyfriend?"

"No, sir. She's my best friend's little sister."

"Where's he?" The officer frowns.

"He's with his girlfriend tonight, and I'm…" Looking down at Blake again, I give her slender fingers a light squeeze. "I'm trying to keep her out of trouble."

The man stops writing to study my face, and I dare to look him right in the eye. After a long pause, where I can't breathe, his lips finally twitch, and he starts nodding. "I take it he won't be too happy about his kid sister partying it up where she shouldn't be."

"No, sir." I shake my head.

"Okay, then." Flipping his notebook closed, I watch his lips form a thoughtful pout before he looks at the nurse, who's hovering nearby. "I've finished up here. Does she need to spend the night?"

"No. Test results are back, and she should be good to go home and sleep it off." Looking at me, the nurse rattles off some care instructions for the morning and I nod, absorbing each word like it's fresh information.

It's not. I've seen Carson through enough rough nights to know. Although I doubt he was ever roofied.

Those fucking assholes!

A blast of hot rage fires through me, and I call after the officer. "Any chance you're gonna find the guy who did this to her?"

He glances back over with a sad smile. "I wish I could say yes. It's going to be hard to prove who put the roofie in her drink, but we'll do our best. The information you've given me will be helpful." He points to Blake. "Just make sure she knows the danger she put herself in tonight."

I frown at him. "She didn't ask to be roofied. I'm not victim shaming her."

The officer frowns right back at me. "She went into a party, *alone*, obviously got drunk, and didn't watch herself. I'm not saying it's fair, but it is reality, and she needs to know not to put herself in a situation like that again." His lips form a thin line before his intense blue gaze is burning holes in my face. "She won't remember much in the morning, and it's up to you to make it clear for her. She needs to know that if you hadn't shown up, it's most likely she would have been raped tonight. You understand?"

I swallow, the reminder making my blood run cold. "Yes, sir." I lick my bottom lip and nod. "I will."

"Good." He turns, and with a heavy sigh, I watch him walk away before taking the discharge papers from the nurse and helping Blake to my Jeep.

Fuck, this night could have gone so much worse.

And it still could get worse if I can't get Blake inside without alerting her brother.

CHAPTER 13
BLAKE

I've been hungover before, but I'm pretty sure when I crack my eyes open, I'm experiencing death. Or pre-death. Or maybe it's just torture—this dull, aching torture that's radiating throughout my entire body. The kind that makes you wish for death.

Groaning, I slowly roll over, taking in my surroundings and realizing I'm not in my bedroom.

Oh shit!

Who the hell did I hook up with?

I bolt upright, instantly regretting the move.

My stomach roils while my head barks at me to be more fucking carefully.

Cradling my forehead, I squint at the room and... Hey, I know this place. I've been in here before.

Spying the corner of a little pink bed tucked behind a half wall, my eyes then track to the basket of toys and building blocks, then across to the drawers, framed pictures of Zander and Sienna littering the top. There's a big image of Zoey hanging on the wall above it, and...

Why am I in their converted garage?

For a harrowing microsecond, I have the ugly thought that Zander and I got up to something we shouldn't have and—

No, no. He's not a cheater, and I…

I was so fucking out of it last night, I can't remember a thing.

I don't know how I got in here.

I don't know whose T-shirt I'm wearing or where any of my clothes are.

Sniffing my hair, I grimace and can't even remember when I threw up, but I must have because I reek, and the taste in my mouth is vile.

My brain is dredging up memories from the day before.

There was nearly getting caught in the pharmacy. A shudder rolls through me until I remember the way Grady came to my aid. Shit. I would have been screwed without him.

Did I thank him?

I must have.

Please say I did.

We walked down the street for a little bit, and then I left him. I was antsy and…

A party.

I went to a party.

Some guy invited me in, and I walked through the front door, and it was all so familiar. It made me miss Cleo, and when those guys smiled at me, I walked straight toward them. There were some girls there, playing a drinking game, and they invited me to join. I can't remember what the game was, but we threw back shots, and I was laughing.

And...

And that's it.

I don't remember anything else, and now I'm here and... How did I get here?

"Shiiiiiit." I groan, running a hand through my hair and hoping like hell that I didn't call Wily.

He's never seen my party side. I've tried to keep all of that carefully hidden away. I need to maintain my sweet-girl persona when I'm around my family. They'd be so disappointed if they knew.

I mean, Wily knows I've got some sass. We hassle each other relentlessly, but I'm pretty sure he'd be gutted if he knew what I'd been getting up to in Chicago.

Fuck. I didn't give myself away last night, did I?

Dammit!

Shuffling to the edge of the bed, I swing my feet over and give myself a little minute, gripping the mattress as I sway and swallow.

Don't throw up. Don't throw up. Don't throw up.

I'm pretty sure if I tried, there'd be nothing left in me anyway. I feel empty. Depleted. Pathetically weak.

Glancing to my right, I notice a glass of water and some Advil.

Is that for me?

It must be.

Thank you, sweet Sienna!

I'm assuming she was the one who got me changed and tucked up in bed. Why'd she give me her bed? Seriously, I'm so confused right now.

Downing the meds and forcing myself to drink the

entire glass of water, I then wipe the drips off my bottom lip and slowly walk to the door.

Oh shit. I need to get my game face on before sneaking into Football Frat. I'm gonna try and make a beeline for the bathroom. I'm desperate for a shower. To wash off whatever I got up to last night.

I hate it when I can't remember.

It's so unnerving.

It's happened to me a couple of times before, and the worst was when I woke up naked next to Simon and had no fucking clue what we'd gotten up to the night before. Nico and Cleo were in the bed beside us, and I had no memory of how we'd ended up in that room or where the room even was.

Some seedy motel.

Clothes were scattered all over the floor, and we were all as naked as the day we were born.

We'd obviously gotten down and dirty, but I couldn't recall when or who I'd done it with, and… and I'd never felt so filthy in my entire life.

I tried to get back on track after that. I really did.

I pulled away from Cleo just a little and tried to focus on my studies, but I was so far behind on everything, catching up was impossible. And trying to avoid someone when you share a room—also impossible. Within a week, I was being pulled back to another party, and I had no willpower.

Shame shimmers through me, my shoulders twitching as I peek my head out the garage door and check that the coast is clear. All seems quiet as I count the cars in the driveway. Shit. Looks like everyone is home… and who does that camper van belong to?

I frown, wrapping my arms around myself as I shuffle toward the back door. I'm in bare feet, which is the stupidest idea ever because the ground is fucking freezing!

Rising to my tiptoes, I dart up the back steps and into the warmth of the house, hoping to sneak up to the bathroom, but of course luck decides to give me the finger.

The second I close the kitchen door and spin, I'm greeted with two curious sets of eyes.

Sienna and Zoey are sitting at the small kitchen table. Zoey's in her booster chair thingy, her face smeared with syrup as she messily devours her pancakes. Sienna's adjacent to her, smiling up at me while I bulge my eyes and try to tame my wild curls... as if she hasn't already seen me at my worst.

Her grin grows a little bigger. "It's okay. Wily's in the living room talking to my parents. You're clear."

I keep smoothing down my hair and force my good-girl smile into place, feeling pale and shaky as I pad across the kitchen floor.

"Good morning." Ugh, my voice sounds so croaky. "Hey, Zoey. How are you, kiddo?"

Zoey nods with a grin, holding up her breakfast. "Pancake!"

"I can see that." My stomach revolts at the sight of that sticky sweet mess, but I manage to keep my smile in place. I think. My teeth are clenched pretty tightly.

Sienna's watching me, mercifully not saying a thing, although her gaze feels like judge and jury. I dart my eyes at her, and she's not glaring or anything. Maybe it's just me who feels like I deserve a hammer loudly falling, smacking down on the wood with a clear verdict.

You messed up last night, and you should be ashamed of yourself.

Shit, I want to ask just how bad it was. Who brought me home?

But my courage fails me, especially when Zander saunters in. The second he spots me, his face lights with a teasing smirk. As he brushes past me, he softly whispers, "Morning, party girl."

I bulge my eyes at him, spitting out my usual defense. "I don't know what you're talking about."

"Oh, so you're gonna play it like that? Okay." He nods, moving around me to lift Sienna up so he can take a seat beneath her. She flops back onto his lap, feeding him a bite of pancake before grinning up at me.

I frown at their all-knowing expressions, hating how clueless I feel.

How bad was I? What did they see? Where did they find me?

Zander's playful smile starts to fade as he obviously waits for some kind of explanation on my part. Maybe an apology?

With a soft sigh, he gives me a pointed look. "You know you spent the night in *our* bed, right? And we had to creep up to the room you're sleeping in?"

I swallow and softly rasp, "W-why? Why didn't I just go up to my room?"

Sienna winces. "Not sure you could have made it up there."

"You smelled like a brewery and had puke all over your clothes," Zander adds, driving that knife all the way in.

Shit! I can feel myself going pale. I must look translucent right now. Or maybe just a dull shade of gray or that puke-green color.

"Grady didn't want to have to carry you up the stairs, right past the living room, and risk waking your brother," Sienna explains.

"It didn't help that you started singing sea shanties when he pulled into the driveway." Zander laughs. "That's why he came to us for help."

Grady helped me? How did he even know where I was?

I glance at Zoey, wondering how much of this she's absorbing. We probably shouldn't be talking about this in front of her, right? She might run and blab to my brother.

She probably doesn't even understand what you're talking about. Just wrap this up and get to the bathroom already!

"Thankfully, this little one was with my parents last night, so moving up to your room wasn't a big issue." Sienna gives me a reassuring smile, but I don't feel any better.

I'm so embarrassed.

Sea shanties?

Really?

And Grady had to carry me because I was so wasted I couldn't even walk?

I don't remember any of this!

Oh shit! Did he see me puke?

Humiliation washes through me in a wave so thick it nearly bowls me over.

I want to buckle under the pressure of it all, drop to my knees and wail my apologies before crawling into a dark corner and just sleeping the day away.

But I don't get that chance, because before I can say

anything else, a middle-aged couple with bright smiles and loud voices stroll into the kitchen.

"He is such an amazing young man," the woman is saying.

"Yeah. He's certainly coping well with what's happened," the man replies, smiling down at the woman before glancing up and noticing me. "Well, hello there!"

His voice is like a friendly boom box, but it still hurts my ears.

"Oh, you must be Blake," the woman gushes, pulling me into a hug before I can stop her. "Sweet girl. Wily's told us all about you. He's so proud of his baby sister."

The woman laughs right in my ear, and I pull out of the hug, fighting the urge to cry.

He shouldn't be proud of me.

I'm a fucking train wreck.

"Blake, these are my parents." Sienna starts the introductions, and I nod and smile the way I'm supposed to.

"You can call me Al." Her dad winks at me, laughing, then starting to sing some song I don't know.

"Dad, stop," Sienna softly complains. "She doesn't even know it."

That only makes her father sing louder, and she starts to laugh and roll her eyes. Zoey claps along, giggling at her grandpa when he crouches down and starts singing to her.

"Doooo, do-do, do, do," he sings. "Can you do that, lil' bug?"

"Do-do-do-do-do," she sings, and I back away from the cacophony, my head threatening to split right open.

My brain is pounding, its swollen edges bumping against my unforgiving skull.

I think I'm gonna be sick again.

"Need a coffee?" Zander points to the counter, indicating the mugs, but I shake my head.

What I need to do is get the hell out of this kitchen.

"I'm just gonna..." I point to the hallway, my slow-ass brain trying to figure out the quickest path to escape, but it soon gets blocked by my giant brother.

He fills up the frame, leaning on his crutches and smiling down at Zoey.

"How's my cowgirl?"

"Hey, Wywee!" She waves her sticky little fingers at him. "Pancake!"

"Oooo, yum. I'm gonna have to get me some of those? Are they a Grady special?"

"They are." Zander nods, wiggling his eyebrows.

"Then I'll have to get a whole stack."

I try not to react to the sound of Grady's name.

He brought me home last night.

He didn't tell Wily.

How did he know not to tell?

How did he know where I was?

"Hey, sis." Wily finally notices me, beaming brightly as he hobbles into the room. "Haven't seen you all morning."

"Oh yeah, I just..." My voice trails off when his eyes narrow at me.

"You okay? You're looking kind of pale."

I blink, scrambling to come up with a good excuse. "I didn't..." Sucking in a breath, I let it out in a rush, along with my lame-ass explanation. "Sleep very well last night. I've got a bit of a headache now." I rub my forehead.

Wily frowns, giving my chin a soft, affectionate little

nudge with his knuckles. "You're working too hard, sis. I didn't even hear you get home from the library last night. Did you Uber?"

"Uh-huh." I nod, my chest squeezing so tight it hurts to breathe.

"You should have called me. I could have sent one of the guys to come get you."

"I didn't want to be a bother." I cross my arms, my eyes darting to Zander, then flashing back to my big bro. Shit, is my face turning red?

"Look, why don't you take the day off and chill?" Wily rests his huge hand on my shoulder. "Stop studying every spare second and just relax."

"Yeah." I punch out a croaky laugh, glancing at Sienna, who's giving me a pained frown. "I'm gonna go... take a shower."

I move around my brother and make a beeline for the hallway, cringing when I hear him say, "What am I gonna do with her? She's working so hard to be here and look after me. How do I get her back to Chicago where she belongs?"

His questions make me shudder.

Shit! He has no idea, and I feel like crap keeping him in the dark this way.

But how am I ever supposed to tell him what a fuckup his perfect little sister has become?

No one can know about my academic suspension. I couldn't face it and decided to withdraw before shit really hit the fan. Like a coward, I quietly exited the school, and no one can ever know why.

This is my shame to bear.

But something is gonna have to come out eventually,

which means I need to fabricate a plausible story for why I'll never be returning to Chicago.

Reaching the top of the stairs, I walk into my room and gather up some fresh clothes, bundling them against me before spinning toward the bathroom.

But I don't even make it out my bedroom door...

Because a tall, sexy-ass Grady is blocking my way. His brown gaze is dark with concern... and a knowing look that makes my insides writhe.

Shit. I so cannot deal with this right now.

CHAPTER 14
GRADY

Blake is looking so pale. So fucking fragile, it's impossible not to worry about her.

Shit. She was a wreck when I brought her home last night.

As annoying as it was, hearing her start mumbling, then full-on singing "The Wellerman" was a huge relief. At least I knew she was on the mend. Her eyes were closed, her body floppy, but she was slur-singing that sea shanty like it was somehow keeping her alive.

Little weirdo.

My lips twitch before the memory starts to fade and that deep concern rides through me again.

"Morning." I keep my voice soft, assuming she has a monster headache.

"Hey," she croaks, her gaze darting away from mine, then suddenly pinging back up. Her blue eyes round as she chokes out, "What happened to your face?"

Lightly fingering my cut lip, I try to play it casual, not

wanting to scare her. I've got a feeling she doesn't remember much about last night.

Just tell her. Maybe a good scare is exactly what she needs.

It's tempting. Anything to warn her away from getting herself into that situation again has to be a good thing, right? And I told that police officer I would.

But my gut is telling me to play this gently, so I start with a shrug and murmur, "It collided with..."

"A fist," she whispers.

"You remember?" My eyes jump back to hers, searching her gaze... wincing when the truth starts to sink in.

"What did I do last night?" Her voice wobbles, then catches. "How did you know where I was?"

Resting my shoulder on the doorframe, I study her carefully as I softly explain. "You called Wily's phone... and he was in the bathroom, so I answered it. You didn't know where you were, and..." I shake my head, hating the scene I walked in on.

No wonder I couldn't fucking sleep last night.

The idea of what could have happened to her haunted me until the early hours. Even when I knew she was safe, that "what-if" game and all the scenarios that followed was a cruel companion as I tossed and turned in my bed.

"Blake, what you did last night was so fucking dangerous." My voice is coming out like a low growl, but I can't help it. "You just wandered into a stranger's party. Alone. What the shit?"

"I..." She shakes her head, then winces like the move hurts.

"When I got there, some guy was trying to drag you

down the hallway. Blake, you couldn't fight him off. You were trying, but you were too drugged up to defend yourself. He could have so easily..." I leave the sentence hanging, because I can't bring myself to say the word *rape*. It's too brutal. Too abhorrent.

And besides, she knows what I'm saying. I can tell by the way her skin blanches and she takes a step back from me, hugging her wad of clothes like a teddy bear. Or maybe a stress ball. Her fingers dig into the fabric, her knuckles white as she shakes her head.

"Did I get roofied?" she rasps.

"Yes." There's no point trying to sugarcoat this shit. She did. And maybe she wouldn't have if she'd had someone to keep an eye on her. If I'd been there, I would have watched her like a fucking hawk, but she knew *no one* in that house. She was easy prey.

Fuck!

"What made you do it?" I have to ask. I have to know why she'd be so reckless.

She shakes her head again, looking ready to puke.

Shit.

Letting out a soft sigh, I cup the back of my head and gaze at the floor. "Listen, I know you're going through a tough time right now. I don't know why you got kicked out of college, but it's obviously messing with you and—"

"What?" she snaps.

I glance up, taken aback by the venomous look on her face.

"Who told you that?"

"You did. Last night. When I was driving you to the hospital. After you'd puked your guts dry. You told me you—"

"No, I didn't," she snaps. "I wouldn't say something like that, because it's not true." Her cheeks flush, her words coming out in a quick staccato beat. "Like I would get kicked out of college. Are you insane? Don't you know what a study nerd I am?"

"No." I shake my head, trying to figure out how to play this. She's so obviously lying. Her arguments are thin and soaked in panic. But I can't just drop this, right? She's going through something right now, and she needs help. She obviously doesn't want to take this to her big brother, so maybe I can be the one to get her through it.

"You're so full of shit, Grady." Her voice is snappy.

My stomach tenses, but I stay calm. "Actually, I think it's you who is struggling right now. I don't know why you got kicked out—"

"I didn't get kicked out!"

I pause, taking in her flashing blue eyes and fierce expression.

Licking my lips, I lower my voice to a softer murmur. "You told me last night that—"

"When I was drunk or high or whatever the hell I was? Like you can trust anything that comes out of someone's mouth when they're in that state!"

"Would you chill?" I raise my hands as two white flags. "I'm trying to help you."

"Well, you're not helping me, are you? Not when you're standing there accusing me of being a little shit! Or getting kicked out of a school I worked really hard to get into!"

"I'm not accusing you of anything. I'm just telling you what you told me and saying I'm here if you need me."

"I don't need you!" Her eyes flash again, but it's

impossible not to notice the sheen quickly forming over them.

Shaking my head, I keep my voice low and easy. "You did last night. And you have no idea how grateful I am that I got there in time."

Her eyes glass a little more, and I know she's gonna start crying soon, but maybe that's exactly what she needs.

"You know you called Wily. I just happened to answer the phone."

"He doesn't know?" she squeaks.

"No, he doesn't."

"Not about the hospital or anything?"

"No. I haven't breathed a word."

She sniffs, lifting her chin but not meeting my gaze, and now I'm wondering if now's the best time to tell her about giving a statement to the police officer. Will that tip her over the edge?

Shit. One thing at a time.

Clearing my throat, I softly murmur, "I think you should tell him, though."

A crazy-sounding laugh bubbles out of her, and she glares at me like I've lost my fucking mind. "Oh really? What should I tell him? That I went to a party and got wasted and... and that I can't remember what else happened, but my hair smells like puke, you've got a fat lip, and I... what? Could have ended up doing who knows what with some guy I don't know if you hadn't arrived in time?" She slashes a rogue tear off her cheek with an angry growl. "You had to take me to the hospital, which means I must have been pretty out of it." A shudder runs through her, and she scoffs again. "I'm sure that would go over just great with my big bro. He'd just love to hear that his sweet, perfect little sister fucked up big-time last night!"

"Blake, that's not..." I shake my head and release a breath. "You don't have to tell him about last night, okay? I'm just saying that maybe you should tell him about the college thing and that you're going through a hard time."

"There is no college thing!" she snaps again. "And I'm fine!"

The way she's roaring at me is kind of contradicting the statement, but I'm wise enough not to point it out.

"You know what, Grady? I don't need your help, okay? And I don't appreciate you butting into my life and trying to play savior. I don't need saving, because my life is fine. It's perfect!"

"Obviously." I give her a deadpan stare.

With a little growl, she fists her bundle of clothes and barks, "Leave me alone!"

"I'm just here to help."

"Leave me *alone*!"

Raising my hands again, I back out of the doorway, and she storms past me, muttering something about me having a hero complex.

The little shit!

I glare at her back, shaking my head and trotting down the stairs as a door slams behind me. I really don't need this kind of drama in my life.

If she wants to be left alone, then fucking fine! She can solve her own damn problems.

"What was that about?" I'm not even at the bottom of the stairs when Wily appears, frowning up at me. "Was Blake just yelling at you?"

"I don't..." I shake my head, really not wanting to answer that.

"What happened to your lip?" Wily's deep voice is booming, and I wince, tensing as I wait for the rest of my roommates to appear.

Shit.

Zander knows everything, but I can't go spilling it all to Wily. Blake might be acting like a lying little turd blossom right now, but I'm not about to dump her in it.

With a sigh, I mumble out as much of the truth as I can. "I was at a party last night and this guy was harassing a girl there, and I couldn't stand by and do nothing. It got messy." I shrug.

"Shit, man." Wily's face buckles in concern. "Why'd you go to a party by yourself?"

I shrug, seriously not having an answer for that one.

Or at least an answer I can give him.

Leaning on his crutches, he gazes down at me, his intense stare fucking unnerving. "Is that why you were yelling at my sister, because you're in a foul mood over what happened to you last night?"

Forcing myself to look up and meet his gaze, I shake my head. "I wasn't yelling, man."

"She sounded pretty pissed off."

"She was," I admit.

"Why?" He grits out the question, and I have to remind myself that it's just brotherly concern talking. He's always been protective of her; it's obvious every time he opens his mouth to tell another story about "lil' Blakey."

Shit, he will not be able to cope with what happened to her last night. Even though nothing *did* happen to her, it could have… and if I'm struggling with it, he sure as shit will too.

"What's going on with you guys?"

"Nothing." I shake my head. "I just happened to cross her path this morning, and she was in a foul mood."

Wily's eyes narrow, and I want to tell him to fuck off and stop looking at me that way. I haven't done anything wrong!

But I hold my tongue, because I'm not about to stir up more drama.

Blake needs to tell her brother the truth.

She needs to tell *herself* the truth.

And I need to step the fuck back and not be a part of it.

"I gotta go." I move around Wily, grabbing my keys and mumbling, "Want to fit a workout in."

He doesn't question it, and I manage to slip out the door a free man.

Except I don't feel free.

I'm weighed down by a truth I can't share… and a disquiet I can't shake.

Blake's in trouble. My instinct is telling me to help her. But I have no idea how… and she doesn't want me to.

So what the fuck am I supposed to do?

CHAPTER 15
BLAKE

So, the last few days have sucked.

I spent most of the weekend recovering in my room... and avoiding my brother. Thankfully, Satch has been around to deal with all the stuff he needs, so I could play the hermit and use catching up on schoolwork as my excuse.

Every time I ventured downstairs for sustenance, Wily cornered me, asking if I was okay and why I yelled at Grady. He was worried about Grady's fat lip. Did I know anything about that?

I managed to deny, deny, deny!

But I think Wily's getting suspicious, and it's freaking me out.

Why oh why did I tell Grady I got kicked out of school? It's not even true. Although it *felt* like I got kicked out, I actually only got threatened with an academic suspension, because I was failing all of my classes and I'd royally fucked up. The school was beyond frustrated with me and threatening disciplinary action. I couldn't face any of it, so I told them I'd pack my bags and leave so they wouldn't have to worry about me anymore.

But I went and told Grady I got expelled.

Shit, I must have been so fucking out of it!

He took a fat lip for me. He took me to the hospital to make sure I was okay. He hasn't told me all the details, and I haven't asked, but I did slide an envelope of cash under his door last night to cover the initial hospital bill. Insurance will cover the rest, and I don't even want to think about how the fuck I'm going to explain a hospital visit to my parents, but hopefully it'll take weeks for the insurance company to notify them.

I have no idea how much Grady had to pay, but when I woke up this morning, the envelope was on my floor with a thank-you note and the leftover change.

Shit, he's so fucking nice… and I haven't even looked at him since I screamed, "Leave me alone!"

Yeah, that glorious moment on Saturday morning is burned into my brain—another scorching mark to add to my Wall of Shame.

Shit!

I have no idea who he fought with, but I know it was over me.

Wily mentioned something about Grady defending a girl at a party.

That was me.

He was defending me.

And how did I thank him?

I yelled in his face, and now I'm ignoring him because I'm too chickenshit to deal.

He even texted me on Saturday afternoon. I have no idea how he got my number, but his message was simple:

. . .

Here's my number in case you ever need me. Grady.

I mean, what the hell is his problem? Why does he feel so compelled to be nice to me?

I can't let that happen. He knows too much, and if I let my guard down, who knows what might come out.

I tried to deny everything he said I confessed, but I'm sure he saw right through my bullshit.

He totally did! You're not fooling anyone.

Except I am. Because Wily and my parents still think I'm their perfect little angel, and they're worried about me because I'm working too hard. Well, Wily's worried that I study too much. My parents keep piling on the pride, which is a stress all its own.

They are going to be so disappointed in me.

I've never done anything wrong before. I've always been the good girl, done my best, tried my hardest... gotten all the A+s and gold stars.

And now I'm practically a homeless loser. If it weren't for Wily's injury and the excuse of looking after him, where the hell would I be?

My monthly allowance, although decent, can only stretch so far, and it's being sucked dry right now.

I can't go home.

And Cleo got away with all our shit, so she's still in Chicago, happily playing college student while no doubt ruining someone else's life. It's not like I could stay with her, or Simon or Nico... I don't even *want* to be around them anyway.

And my friends from high school?

Yeah, I'm not admitting shit to them. They *are* perfect. I've been stalking their socials, and they're thriving at college.

But not me, right?

I had to lose the plot completely.

Shit!

My phone dings, my muscles tensing like they always do as I reach for my device.

No! Leave me the fuck alone!

Tears burn as I glare down at the screen—at another evil message from my ex-roommate. Another threat.

I wish I could just delete it without looking, but I can't risk that.

With a shaky thumb, I unlock my phone, and Cleo's message pops right up.

Cleo: Send another grand or these are going to Mommy and Daddy.

Below the text box is an image of me sprawled out on the ground, laughing my ass off. There's a spray can in my hand and blue paint all over my fingers.

With my heart in my throat, I flick to the next image and cringe at the brick wall where I messily painted the words *F is for fun, dickbag!*

Quickly deleting the two photos, I run trembling fingers over my forehead. What the hell was wrong with me?

That brick wall? Yep, it was the outside of Professor

Helliwell's apartment. He'd told me just that afternoon that "F is for failure, Miss Wilson." His stern voice had made my cheeks flare with heat, every eye in the class turning to stare at me while he told me off for not putting in any effort. "Maybe you should think about hitting the books or walking out the door! Because you're wasting my time!"

Beyond humiliated, I grabbed my bag, shoving my way down the row and storming out of the classroom. I got back to my room in tears, and Cleo found me, consoled me, then told me exactly how I should get my retribution.

At three o'clock in the morning, fueled on pure adrenaline, I'd left my mark.

And she had photographic proof of it. Proof that got me hauled into the dean's office. Proof that will ruin my life if she sends it to my parents.

With an irritated huff, I quickly transfer a thousand dollars from my savings account to the number she gave me a few weeks ago. It's dropped by nearly seven thousand dollars since I left our dorm room, and most of it has gone to keep Cleo quiet. I've been trying to top it up with my monthly allowance, but at this rate, I'm gonna be broke by the end of April.

Shit!

But those photos can't get out.

She has me over a barrel, and there's nothing I can do.

I text her back with a low growl.

Done. Now delete those fucking photos!

. . .

She replies a few minutes later.

Thanks. Photos gone. I'll be in touch again soon.

I shudder, hating to think what else she has stored on her phone. We got into so much shit together!

Dammit, dammit, dammit!

I have to get out of here. These walls are closing in. I need air. A space to breathe!

My insides sizzle, painful electric currents shooting through me as my chest starts to constrict. The air in my lungs is stifling. I push my hand against my chest, feeling my racing heart as a wave of dizziness whips around my head.

Jerking to my feet, I grab my jacket, desperate for escape. When I open my bedroom door, I listen for noises in the house and figure it's safe to head downstairs. I nearly make it to the back door in the kitchen when I hear Wily calling me.

"Hey, butt face, come say hi to Mom and Dad!" His voice is so cheerful. So oblivious.

I tense, digging my nails into my arms before forcing myself to turn around and walk back to the living room.

Game face on. Let's go. You're sweet, angelic Blake now, remember?

"I wish you wouldn't call her that, Wily. It's so vulgar," Mom's complaining.

"She calls me shithead. It's only fair."

Dad laughs while Mom continues to sigh and complain that she tried to teach us good manners but obviously failed miserably.

"Hey, Daddy." I put on my bright, cheerful voice. The one my father loves the best.

"My sweet girl." He beams at me through Wily's phone, then looks at Mom. "You didn't fail, sweetheart. These two are perfect."

Mom's lips twitch. "They are."

The pressure inside me blooms, pushing against my chest cavity and making my smile waver.

I force it back into place, playing along and sharing an eye roll with my brother.

"I was just telling them how well my recovery is coming along. The PT was really positive yesterday."

"Yeah, he was." I nod, happy to be focusing on my brother. "Wily's been doing all the exercises and not missing a beat."

"Well, he's motivated." Dad beams at him. "Proud of you, son. Your football career isn't over."

"Yeah, I know." Wily nods at our parents. "Everything's gonna work out."

I'm not sure he's 100 percent convinced of that, but it's what our parents need to hear, so he sells it the way he always does.

And I sell it the way I always do, having to work extra hard when Mom turns her attention to me and asks, "So, when are you heading back to Chicago?"

Shit, I hate that question so fucking much!

Blowing out a breath, I quickly spill the lie I've been refining. "I've been in touch with all of my professors, and they said because I'm keeping up with everything so well, they're happy for me to stay in Nolan and keep going with online studies."

"But what about exams?"

"Yeah, that part's a little trickier." I wince. "I might just fly back to Chicago for exam week. The test I missed last week, I can submit online. My professor figured out a way to help me do that."

Bullshit. Allllll bullshit.

"That was nice of him. Or her." Mom smiles, obviously relieved. "And I'm glad you're flying back for exam week, but don't you think you should head back earlier than that?"

I shrug. "I was always planning to be here until after spring break, and... it's nice hanging out with Wily and his roommates. I'm enjoying my time here."

Wily frowns up at me. "You're always studying up in your room or doing stuff to help me. How is that fun?"

"I get to have dinner with you guys and help Satch prepare meals and hang out with Sienna and Zoey sometimes. I'm not *always* studying." I roll my eyes and force out a laugh.

"She's studious." Mom stands up for me. "That's nothing to be ashamed of. We're proud of you, sweetie. You keep up that hard work. You won't regret it."

"Thanks, Mom." My smile is so forced my cheeks are starting to hurt.

"You've always been the smartest girl in the room." Dad winks at me.

I laugh and brush my hand through the air, batting his compliment away.

This pulsing pressure inside me is gonna blow. I can

feel it expanding, threatening to spew out of me in a volcanic, gassy eruption.

I'm not smart! I'm a loser with no control, and I've been systematically fucking up my life ever since I left home! Because I can't live up to your expectations anymore! It's too much. It's all just too much!

Resting my head on Wily's shoulder, I manage to keep that shit on lockdown and smile sweetly at my parents while they wrap up the call.

I say the "I love yous" I'm supposed to. I blow kisses. I make my parents laugh.

And then the call is over and I still can't breathe, because my big brother is right there.

Shit, I can't do this.

I can't breathe!

This weird clawing sensation is scratching my insides raw, and I end up bolting off the couch as if someone just stuck me with a hot poker.

"You okay?" Wily frowns up at me.

"Yeah, I just..." Letting out this weird cackle, I quickly clear my throat and grin down at my big bro. "I've got a hankering for Dr Pepper. I can't even explain it. I think I just need a sugar kick to get me through my afternoon study sesh. Are you good if I split and do a little shopping? I should be back in about—"

"Go." He waves his hand toward the door. "I'll be fine. Take as long as you need. I'm just gonna watch ESPN highlights and..." He sighs. "Finish reading that research I'm supposed to get through before Satch arrives for our tutoring session."

I snort and scoff. "More like make-out session."

"Hey, we work." His eyes sparkle as his lips form a

little smirk. "The making out is my reward for studying like a good boy."

"Uh-huh."

"So, if I get that research read and start my study notes, we'll get through it faster, and then we can..." His voice trails off as he scrambles for his laptop and the pile of pages next to it.

I help him get set up before walking out of the house and finally, *finally* inhaling my first full breath. Well, sort of. It feels shallow and does nothing to kill this antsy writhing in my stomach.

Bypassing Wily's truck, I walk into town, needing the exercise or fresh air or whatever. It's the first day of no rain we've had in ages, and I just want to enjoy the pale sunshine that's breaking through the clouds.

I need to move. To breathe.

My steps are clipped, my boots pock-pock-pocking on the concrete as I walk.

Keeping my head down, I try to wrestle my chaotic thoughts into line, but I seriously have no hope. They're swirling around me, and I'm caught in the middle of this impossible vortex.

What I wouldn't give to break free of all these lies and—

No! The lies are keeping you safe. The fallout is worse. It's so much worse. Just hold yourself together.

Until when?

How long do I have to keep this up for?

Until you have a plan.

A plan.

Yeah, that elusive thing I've been chasing ever since I left my dorm room for good.

I have no idea what kind of plan to concoct around this shitty situation. I've been batting ideas around, but nothing solid comes to me. Nothing sticks, because all of my ideas suck!

Storming across the street, I make it into town a torrid mess. My mood is foul, and I'm not sure where I'm going or what to do.

I don't feel like Dr Pepper. Or any kind of soda for that matter.

What I want is a drink. A real drink.

But I don't have my fake ID anymore. Dammit!

With a huff, I slow my pace, figuring I'll just wander around like I did on Friday, aimlessly trying to calm this storm in my chest.

No parties this time.

At least it's the middle of the day. I'm safe. There will be no raves, orgies, or drunken blowouts happening right now. Well, not easily accessible ones anyway, so I won't be tempted.

Although, a drink would be really nice right about now.

Just a little something to take the edge off. Not the reckless shots I did on Friday… and whatever else was put into my drink.

I shudder, not wanting to think about that.

But just a beer or two.

Or something to quell this storm inside me.

Looking up ahead, I take in my surroundings and notice a bottle shop across the street.

Don't do it.

The only way I can get something out of there is smuggled in my bag or tucked inside my jacket pocket.

It's not worth it.

Checking the street, I cross when there's a break in the traffic and ignore my sensible brain, swinging the door open and wandering in like I'm supposed to be there.

The guy behind the counter eyes me up, and I give him a bright smile. "Hi there."

He nods at me, obviously suspicious.

Bail now. This isn't going to work!

Turning left, I head down the next aisle, scanning bottles of spirits while heading toward the beer fridge against the wall.

I sniff, then scratch the side of my nose, checking for cameras and mirrors. I glance up at the big convex one on the wall, a bubbly eyeball reflecting everything back to the man behind the counter.

Crossing my arms, I walk a little farther until I'm pretty sure I'm out of view.

Eyeing up the bottles, I wander along until I get to the smaller ones. There's a half-pint of vodka right there that would easily fit into my bag.

Picking it up, I scan the label, then place it back on the shelf, turning away as if I'm not interested.

The bell above the door dings when a new customer comes in, and my insides do a little dance, hop-stepping it around my chest when the woman starts up a conversation.

"It's my husband's birthday next week, and I want to get him something special. He loves his scotch," she's saying while I take a step back to the smaller vodka bottles and pluck one off the shelf.

Slipping it into my bag, I glance around the aisle,

making sure my disinterested mask is firmly in place before heading toward the exit.

"We've got a really nice Macallan 18 Year Sherry Oak that he'd probably like." The man is smiling. I can hear it in his voice. "What's your budget?"

I make a beeline for the door, stoked that he's too distracted to notice me.

"Can you just give me a sec?" he says.

I'm two steps away from the door when a hand clamps around my arm. "I don't think so, kid."

"What?" I spin around, trying to wrench myself free of his viselike grip. "Get your hands off me."

"I'm sick of you guys strolling in here and thinking you can just take off with my liquor!" he growls, completely unperturbed by my protests.

"I don't have your liquor!" I shout back.

The old woman by the counter blinks at me in shocked surprise.

"I know you've got a bottle in your bag." He glares at me. "I'm not stupid." Yanking my arm, he drags me back toward the counter.

"Lemme go!" I snap.

"Not until I call the police. I'm sick of this happening."

My insides flail, dread pooling in my stomach.

"I'm so sorry about this, ma'am." He gives the woman an apologetic wince.

"No, it's quite all right. You deal with this. I can wait."

"No, no, no, wait! Please don't call the police," I rasp, pulling the bottle out of my bag and handing it to him. "Just take it back. I'll go, and I promise never to come in here again."

"Not a chance," he growls, forcing me into a seat before pulling out his phone and dialing.

"No, sir, please!" I lurch forward, trying to make a quick run for it, but he grabs my jacket, pulling me back down with a thump.

The older woman moves in front of me, her sweet face now puckered into a disapproving frown.

"Shame on you," she mutters softly, shaking her head and making me feel like shit.

Dammit!

"I'm sorry," I start to blubber. "Please, I'm sorry. Please, please, *please* don't call the cops." My voice hitches, panic racing through me so hard and fast I think I my pass out.

"You were trying to steal from me," the man growls.

"I know. I know. And that is so wrong, and I'm sorry." Tears burn my eyes. "I didn't mean to do it. I'm just having a really shitty week, and I'm sorry. I'll pay. I'll pay you anything."

He pauses, glaring down at me, his thumb hovering over his phone screen. Hope shimmers through my desperation, and I cling to it.

"Please." I sit up, blinking at my tears. "I'll give you any amount you want." I look at the woman. "I'll pay for your husband's present! Please, just... please don't send me to jail." I whimper, pressing the back of my hand against my mouth, my entire body shuddering as I imagine myself handcuffed in the back of a police car.

With a heavy sigh, the man drops his phone on the counter and crosses his arms. "I can't sell you alcohol. You're underage."

"I know," I squeak. "That's why I was trying to sneak out with it. I just needed something to take the edge off."

The woman scoffs. "Drinking your problems away won't solve anything, young lady."

I close my eyes, covering my face with my hands and letting out another pitiful whimper.

This has got to be my lowest point ever, right?

With an angry huff, the man takes his sweet time trying to decide what to do with me. Then he finally gives me an alternative... and for a split second, I wonder if going to jail is a better option.

"I'm not letting you just walk out of here. You need to call someone who is old enough to purchase this bottle. They are going to come down here and collect you, and you are going to explain to them what you did. Then they are going to pay me, and you are never going to step foot in this place again. Okay?"

With a soft sniff, I lower my hands and gape at him. "Call someone?"

"Yes." He gives me a firm nod, and my insides flail.

Who the hell am I going to call?

This cannot be happening right now.

Fear claws at me, panic working right alongside it.

I've never been caught before.

You nearly got caught the other day, you idiot! If it weren't for Grady, you'd be in this exact situation.

Shit. Where is he now?

Closing my eyes, I try to shake the question out of my head. Like he'd come and help me after the way I treated him.

I don't deserve Grady Newman's help.

But I have no idea who else I want right now.

He's the only one who actually knows the truth. Unless he blabbed about it to Zander and Sienna.

But no, I don't think he did.

Something tells me he's kept my worst secret to himself.

And that's why.

That's why he's the only person I can think of right now.

The only person I want walking through the door and saving me from...

Well, my own stupidity.

CHAPTER 16
GRADY

The sun is out today, promising a warm spring. Damn, bring it the fuck on. I'm not opposed to winter when the snow's all pretty and shit, but I am definitely a summer man. I like heat and sun.

And I'm so over the rain.

This has been the first fine day we've had in over a week. Everything is still wet, recovering after the constant deluge. It has worked in my favor, though. Thanks to the saturated field, Coach Jones has switched things around. Rather than having to be back early for spring training, he's giving us an extra couple of days so the fields have a chance to dry out. It does mean we'll have to sacrifice the last weekend of our break, but I don't mind. It means the boys and I can go hiking for five days now. That's gonna be awesome.

Squinting up at the partially cloudy sky, I let the sunbeams soak into my skin and rejuvenate me after what has got to be one of the most boring lectures ever. Professor Cho talks in monotone. I don't know how the fuck he got to where he is in the school. I guess it's his smarts, because dynamic he is most definitely not.

"Hey." Tyrell catches my attention, raising his chin as he jogs toward me and falls into step.

Our next class is together, and we wander toward the engineering building. Although he's a senior and I'm a junior, he's catching up on a class he missed last year, and I'm not complaining. I love studying with the guy. He and I vibe on a lot of the same shit, and he's the best study partner in the house.

"'Sup, man?" I ask him.

"Nothin' new." He glances past me at a huddle of giggling freshmen. They wander past, two of them eyeing us up, then blushing fiercely.

I share a quick glance with my buddy and shake my head.

He snickers.

We both know this is the closest we'll probably ever come to celebrity status.

Tyrell's not planning on going pro. I'm not sure why. He says it's because he's not good enough, but I think it's because he's not that interested in the pro lifestyle.

Me? I think I'm in the same boat as him. I've had plenty of agents calling me, but so far, I've stood my ground and told them I'm not interested.

I love playing football, but I'm smart enough to know that the NFL takes a select few, and even if you do get selected, it doesn't take much for your career to go belly-up. One injury and it could be over.

I want something more stable. Which is why I'm studying computer engineering. My chances of getting a decent job after college are that much higher in an area like that.

And besides, if I pursued football, it would take over my life. I want to be able to split my focus between career and the outdoors. I want weekends to go hiking. I don't need the fame and glory of being a pro athlete. Give me a forest and a waterfall any day.

"You pumped for spring break?" Tyrell nudges me with his elbow. "Hiking in the forest with Bear Grylls himself. It's gonna be awesome." My buddy laughs, and I shake my head.

"I'm not Bear Grylls, man. But I am stoked that we're getting to extend the trip by two days."

"You're the closest thing I'm ever gonna come to meeting the guy. You're like Black Bear."

I laugh. "Shut up, man."

"I'm serious. Last time we went into the forest, and you caught that fish with your bare hands, then built that fire and cooked it for us... City Boy here was impressed, okay?" He taps his chest. "I'm expecting more of that shit over spring break. You feel me?"

With a soft snicker, I murmur, "I'll try to deliver, man. Hey, did I tell you my dad can't make it anymore?"

"Really?" Tyrell's face drops. "Brah, I love that guy. Why can't he make it?"

"He and his girlfriend are finally moving in together, and it's the only time they're free to make the shift." Pride flares through me as I think about my ol' man and how much my friends all like him.

It's understandable. He's a good man.

And it does suck that he can't come, but...

"I'm looking forward to just getting away from everything. Having some guy time, you know? We don't really get that anymore."

"Tell me about it," Tyrell grumbles, bulging his eyes at me, then quickly wincing and shaking his head. "Sorry. I shouldn't complain. I love Sienna and Zoey. Nylah's pretty cool, and Satch seems like a sweetheart. But damn, they're all pairing off and leaving us in the dust."

"I was paired off." I frown. "But not anymore."

Teah floats through my mind, followed swiftly by flashes of Blake, which is a total mindfuck. I shake my head, trying to get her out of there. She hasn't looked at me once since she yelled in my face, and that's fine by me. I seriously do not need that kind of drama.

"Sorry, brah." Tyrell gives me another nudge. "I know that sucks for you. Heard she's hooking up with that Macalister guy. Must burn pretty bad."

"Yeah, man." I nod, then let out a derisive snort. "Women, right?"

Tyrell doesn't answer right away, and I glance up at him. He's nearly half a head taller than me. I'm the shortest guy in the house, and it used to bug the shit out of me, but I'm over it now. Carson's only got a quarter inch on me, and Zander's not far off that. But Tyrell and Wily are the giants of the group. I used to avoid standing next to them, but it is what it is.

So, I stare up at my friend, waiting for him to agree with me. Tell me that women *are* a pain in the ass, and we should be grateful not to have to deal with them.

But he doesn't say shit.

I frown at him when he glances at me, then looks away with a tut. "I know. I should avoid the drama, right?"

"But..." I keep going for him.

He sighs. "But… just between you and me?"

"Yeah, of course."

"Kind of wish I had someone." He makes a clicking noise with his tongue. "I'm watching all these guys pair off, and I'm like… damn, I want me a woman. Just someone who's on my side, you know? Someone to wake up with. Someone to make out with. Someone to share inside jokes and shit… I don't know." He shakes his head with a little huff.

I clear my throat, wishing I had something to say, but my tongue's stopped working.

Because I know exactly what he's saying. And I miss it. I don't want to admit that, but shit… I really miss it. I thought it was just Teah I missed, but it's more than that. I miss having a partner. A person who's just for me.

"I've been trying to put myself out there a bit, because I know that's what you're about to say. Can't meet nobody hanging out at Football Frat all the time. But… I can't seem to meet one I really want, you know?" Tyrell looks down the pathway as we slowly veer left. "After a date or two, I'm not feeling it. I don't want to lead them on, so I break it off."

"Maybe you need to give it more than just a date or two. It can take time to get to know someone. Fall for them."

"Nah, man. I want that cosmic chemistry thing. You know…" He taps his chest. "When you just *know.* If I ain't feeling that after a date or two, then it can't be the real deal."

I shrug, not sure I agree with him. It can't all be instant. Sometimes love grows slowly.

And other times your attraction takes you out at the knees.

Blake flashes through my head again, and I wonder if that's what Tyrell means. But it can't be, because I'm not in love with Blake. She's a pain in the ass! She might be a *gorgeous* pain in the ass, but I will not be falling for a girl like her. She's nothing but trouble, and I don't need that shit.

Nah, I want me another Teah.

Do you? Really? A nice boring relationship?

I was the boring one. Not her.

She never wanted to do any of the same things you did.

The thought hits me like a sledgehammer, and my insides rebel against it. Teah and I were great together. We lasted for ten whole months. That's not some bullshit thing—that was real. I loved her. I still love her.

Why?

My expression bunches into a frown as I wrestle for a swift answer. My thoughts should be flowing like honey as I list all the things I love about that strawberry blonde beauty, but my brain is fritzing out on me.

"Brah, you good?" Tyrell grabs my attention, and I quickly come up with an answer so I don't have to analyze my internal meltdown with him.

"Maybe you should sign up for one of those comprehensive dating apps. Not Tinder or anything, but one of those really in-depth ones, you know? Where you answer a bunch of questions and they find you your perfect match?"

I'm being serious, and it takes him a second to figure that out. At first, he laughs like I'm ridiculous. Then he suddenly stops and frowns down at me. "You for real?"

"Yeah, man. You should try it. I can help you sign up."

He cringes, shaking his head. "I don't know. I kinda hate that idea."

A weird-sounding snicker pops out of me, and I have to admit, "Me too."

Shaking his head, Tyrell shoves his hands into his jacket pockets. "I just want to meet someone naturally, you know?"

"Yeah, definitely." I scuff the concrete as I walk, then glance up at my buddy. "Although, that ain't gonna happen unless you go out to social places, you feel me?"

"Shit." Tyrell mutters some more, then looks up to the sky, squeezing his eyes shut. "God, help a brother out. Just make her magically appear in front of me." His eyes pop open and he scans the grass either side of the engineering building...

And there's not one chick in sight.

I have no idea how this is happening, but it's only guys: a group kicking a soccer ball around, another guy rushing up the building steps, and three more coming around the corner.

A girl's gonna come along any second now, I'm sure of it, but the fact that none were around when Tyrell opened his eyes is fucking hilarious.

I can't help it. I crack up laughing as Tyrell flicks up his hands and mutters, "What the fuck?"

Lightly shoving me for still laughing, he then ends up snickering along with me.

"I am doomed, brah. Fuckin' doomed."

"No, you're not," I say, trying to make him feel better, but how the hell would I know?

I'm not exactly the guy to talk to about romance anymore.

I'm just as single as he is.

Part of me wants to tell him to just embrace it. Being single is a damn sight easier than trying to keep a woman happy.

But I know that won't fly.

He hasn't had a girlfriend since moving here. He's dated and shit, but nothing serious.

And he's obviously ready for it.

But he's not gonna find it if he keeps going the way he is. I mean, sure, he'll attend parties at Football Frat and do some flirting in class, but he hardly ever comes to Offside with us. The guy's not exactly a socialite.

Maybe he just needs a little nudge.

"Hey, man, do you want to hit up Offside tonight? We could—" My phone starts ringing and I check my watch to see who it is, my eyebrows dipping when Blake's name appears.

Aw, shit. What does she want now?

I'm pretty sure she's not calling to apologize. The fact that she's iced me out completely speaks volumes.

So why is she calling, then?

She's in trouble.

The thought sends a chill right through me.

"You gonna get that?" Tyrell pauses at the bottom of the steps.

"Ah... yeah. I probably should." Pulling my phone out of my pocket, I reluctantly swipe my thumb over the screen. "I'll see you in there."

Tyrell nods and heads into the building while I walk

away from the stairs and force a genial tone. “Hey, Blake. What’s up?”

She doesn’t say anything, and now I’m wondering if this is a butt dial situation.

I’m kind of relieved to be honest. I don’t want to have to deal with any more of her shit.

But then she sniffs.

And I know that sound. It’s an “I’m fighting tears” kinda sniff.

Aw, shit.

I close my eyes. “Blake? You okay?”

She sniffs again, her voice wobbling when she finally speaks. “I need your help.”

“Okay.” Worry spikes through me, and I pick up my pace. I don’t even know where I’m going, but I’m breaking into a jog. “Where are you?”

She sucks in a shaky breath, then lets it out in a rush. “I’m at a bottle shop in town… and they’re threatening to call the cops unless someone comes down here to collect me.”

My steps falter, and I jolt to a stop on the grass. “What? Why?”

“Can you just come get me? Please.” She whimpers, and the sound does me in.

The sensible part of me wants to tell her to hang the fuck up and call her *brother*. Isn’t he the one who’s supposed to be saving her?

She called you, man. So get going.

Holding in my sigh, I squash down the myriad emotions battling for top position in my chest and start running again.

“Which bottle shop is it?”

There’s a pause and I hear a muffled, gruff voice in the background, then Blake’s shaky reply. “Liquor King. It’s on Maple.”

“I’ll be there as soon as I can,” I promise her.

CHAPTER 17
BLAKE

Calling Grady was fucking humiliating.

This entire thing has been fucking humiliating!

Mr. Liquor King marched me into a back room where he took my photo on a polaroid camera, then made me sit and wait.

"Don't touch anything." He pointed at me before he door slammed shut, the lock clicked, and I became his prisoner.

This has got to be me at my worst, right?

Not getting totally wasted at a stranger's party, then puking everywhere.

Not leaving college with my tail between my legs.

Not all the stupid shit I did in Chicago.

But this.

This moment right here.

Locked in a back room of a liquor store to avoid being carted off to a police station.

Fuck!

My insides are in chaos.

Why did I pick Grady to come get me? Why him?

He's probably talking to my brother right now, telling Wily all about how he's heading to the liquor store to collect me and coming up with a bunch of reasons why I'm being detained here.

They'll figure it out—they're not stupid. And then they'll have to decide what to do with me after that.

Fuck, fuck, fuck!

Wily's gonna hit the roof, and then he'll tell my parents, and they'll kill me for being an irresponsible little shit. And the truth is gonna come out, and I'll have to air my dirty laundry and face the consequences.

I can't!

I can't face them!

My parents will never speak to me again.

Because you'll be dead!

Ugh. If only it were that easy. They won't kill me. No, they'll lecture me and be so fucking disappointed in me. They'll be horrified, hurt, confused, and it's not like I can explain it to them, because I don't know why I jumped off the rails!

I don't get what possessed me to think Cleo was the best and why I followed her down that path. Why did I have to break free?

I don't know.

I don't fucking know!

My head is splitting, my temples pounding. Tears are burning my throat, my nose, my eyes. I don't want them to fall, but I'm not sure how much longer I can hold out.

I finally got busted, and there's no place to run.

A shaky whimper punches out of me, my chest concaving before I suck in a breath and can't hold back.

The first sob rips out of me, giving permission for the rest of them to follow. The stress is too much to handle, and I'm finally exploding.

My stomach convulses, a shudder running through my body as I pull my knees to my chest and blubber into my jeans.

I have no idea how long Grady's gonna take, or what the man's gonna tell him when he arrives. Shit! He'll work out that I tried to shoplift that nail polish at the pharmacy. That time he stood up for me when he really shouldn't have.

Panic sizzles through me, and I squeeze my legs even tighter.

I can't believe this is happening.

Really? You're surprised? You shouldn't be. You're a fucking train wreck right now!

Man, I really need to sort out my life.

I can't keep doing this.

No more shoplifting. That is it! I don't want that thrill anymore. It was fun to start with, but it's landed me in this shitty situation, and I can't be so reckless again.

You should stop drinking too. You know what could have happened to you at that party if Grady hadn't shown up. Think about it, dammit! THINK!

So I make myself.

I sit there in that hardback chair, bawling my eyes out and forcing myself to play out that scenario.

That guy probably would have raped me... or at least done shit to my body that I didn't want him to. And I would have been helpless to stop him.

A shudder runs through me, shaking my entire frame.

Shit.

"Blake." I whimper my name, hating myself for getting to this point. "You're such a fuckup. You have to stop." My voice cracks, and I press my lips against my knees.

Just stop.

But how?

What am I supposed to do?

I can't go back to Chicago.

I don't want to go home and admit all my sins.

So what do I do?

"He's here." The owner's voice jolts me upright. The door swings open, and my boots slap onto the concrete floor. When I don't immediately move, he gives me a pointed look. "Let's go."

With a thick swallow, I rise slowly from the chair, wondering why I'm not bolting out that door.

But I know what's waiting for me on the other side, and that's scary too.

Grady's gonna be so pissed off at me.

He probably hates the fact that I called him.

I'm an inconvenience. A pain in the ass.

Shit. I should have called someone else.

Who?

Wily? Like that was ever gonna happen.

Sniffing, I wipe the back of my hand across my cheek and meekly shuffle after the man. He's not saying anything, thank God, and I follow him out into the store, crossing my arms tight and keeping my head down.

"Okay. So, here's the deal." The man's voice makes me flinch. "You never come into my store again. I've taken your photo, and I will be pinning it to the wall with all the other sticky fingers who have come before you."

"What?" My head jolts up, my eyes wide.

When he took my photo earlier, I thought it was just for his own records, something to keep behind the counter, but—

He points to the wall behind the register, and I gape at the collage of images.

"No, please. I can't— You can't—"

"Blake." Grady's voice is a quiet rumble, and without meaning to, I look up and spot him. I'd planned to keep my eyes down and not make contact, but… there he is, standing on the other side of the counter.

He's so tall and strong, waiting there in his cargo pants and a Nolan U Cougars sweatshirt. Part of me wants to run into his arms right now. I want to rest my head against his chest, feel that strength wrap around me, and bawl like a freaking baby.

But he won't want me to do that.

I dare a proper look at his face, and yep… he definitely doesn't want me to do that.

Swallowing, I curl in on myself, my gaze shooting back to the safety of the floor.

"It's going up, and you're just gonna have to live with that. Actions have consequences," the man barks at me. "Now, your friend here has paid for the bottle you tried to lift and assured me that you won't be getting one drop of it. He's also promised me that you will not be walking into this place again."

I nod.

"I need to hear you say it."

After another thick swallow, I look up and mumble, "I won't be in here again. I'm sorry for the trouble I caused. And…"

"And?" His eyebrows rise.

"Thanks for not calling the cops." My voice drops to a raspy whisper.

The man grunts. "If it happens again, I won't hesitate." Lifting his chin, he gives me permission to leave.

Easing out around the counter, I close the gap between Grady and me. His handsome face is serious, and I wish I knew what he was thinking.

Is he disappointed? Or is he gonna yell at me and question me until I break?

Something sizzles through me, my defenses wanting to rise and lock into place.

If he yells at me, I'm gonna yell right back! I won't let him hurt me. I won't—

My bravado dies out as quickly as it rises.

He bailed me out. He came when I called.

There's no way I can get shitty with him. He's my frickin' savior!

"You okay?" he softly murmurs, resting his hand on my lower back and leading me out of the store.

I can't even nod.

Why is he being nice to me? Checking on me like I've been through hell and need comforting?

Well, I have. And I do!

But I don't deserve it.

Shit, I shouldn't have called him.

I should have just gone to jail and rotted away, because that's what my life is worth right now. Fucking rot!

As soon as we reach the intersection and pause at the crosswalk, I bolt right, around the corner, and take off running.

Grady doesn't need this shit.

"Blake!"

I shake my head, my boots pounding on the pavement as I try to make a break and…

I don't even know.

Where the hell can I run to anyway?

I've never been more lost in my entire life.

CHAPTER 18
GRADY

"Blake! Blake, stop!"

It's not hard for me to catch her. I'm used to putting on quick bursts of speed. She makes me sprint, but I reach her by the end of the block, just before she darts across the street.

Snagging her arm, I pull her to a stop.

She fights me for a second, letting out these gasping sobs and bending over.

I wrap my arm around her waist, plucking her off her feet and carrying her away from the prying eyes of people driving past.

Ducking into a side alley, I set her back down and turn her to face me.

"Hey." I crouch low, trying to look at her face, my hand resting lightly on her elbow.

"I'll pay you back, okay?" Her voice is shaking as she tucks her hair behind her ears. Her cheeks are pale, her eyes red-rimmed with smudges of black mascara under her lashes. She looks a wreck all over again, although this time there's a wild unpredictability about her. She's not wasted, she's—

"I'm sorry," she blurts, squeezing her eyes shut, her head shaking in quick, stiff movements as she clutches her biceps. Her arms are crossed over herself, creating a clear barrier. "Thank you… for bailing me out. You don't have to help me again, okay? You can… I won't be a problem."

"Hey," I whisper, running my hand from her elbow to her wrist and gently tugging. She's squeezing the shit out of herself right now, and she needs to relax.

She tenses, fighting my move, but I gently coax her to let go, wriggling my fingers under her palm until she releases her grip.

Her arm flops down and I hold her wrist, lightly rubbing the small slice of skin poking out from beneath her jacket.

"Blake." My voice sounds deeper and gruffer than I mean it to be, so I lick the edge of my mouth and try to whisper. "Blake, you need to talk to me."

"No, I don't." Her reply is clipped, and there she goes, shaking her head in those jerky movements again. She sniffs, looking away from me as she skims a finger under her eyes. Glancing down at her free hand, she winces, no doubt worried about the black streak across her fingers.

Yes, you look a wreck.

But you're still so fucking beautiful.

I clamp my lips together. Not about to let that shit out. It won't help one bit.

She needs support.

And right now, I'm the only one standing here. Because she called me.

I still don't know why, but I came, and I have to see this through.

"You have to tell someone what the hell is going on with you." I keep my tone soft but uncompromising. She's not allowed to just run away from this like it didn't happen. "If you don't want to talk to me, then who? Tell me who, and I'll take you to them right now."

She looks up at me, her eyes flooding with tears.

The fear in those blue orbs is fucking killing me, and I can't do anything but act on instinct.

Tugging on her wrist, I pull her against me, cupping the back of her head and cradling her into my chest.

She shudders, this silent sob racking through her before she lets out the softest whimper and curls her arms around my waist.

"It's gonna be okay," I whisper, holding her close.

I have no idea what's up, but I can promise her that.

It will be okay.

I will make it okay.

I don't know what that means or how it's gonna look, but I can't just turn my back on this pain-in-the-ass girl.

Any man with half a brain would be pawning her off to her brother.

That's exactly what I should be doing right now. Taking her to Football Frat and making her tell Wily the truth. I can get back to class and catch up with Tyrell, who agreed to take notes for me when I had to text him that I couldn't make it.

He'll want to know what's up, too, but I don't know what the hell I can tell him.

If I'm gonna get through this, I need Blake to tell me what's going on with her.

She'll need the support when she tells Wily, right?

Something's got her freaking out, and whatever she's hiding, having someone backing her up can't be a bad thing.

I may not have asked for this, but she's been shoved into my path, and I've got to hang on to her for a while.

Just until she's okay.

All I can hope is that she doesn't destroy me in the process, because her crying against me right now is doing my heart in.

CHAPTER 19
BLAKE

I have no idea how long I've been crying, but Grady's chest is a solid, safe wall. His arms around me are the exact cocoon I need to hide away and just let go.

The way he's cupping the back of my head and holding me close...

The way he's not saying anything, just being this unmoving anchor I can cling to...

Yeah, I could spend the rest of the day like this.

Except that I can't.

Pushing away from him on limbs that feel like cooked spaghetti, I stumble back. He catches my elbow, steadying me, and I glance up at him.

Shit. I should have stayed in his arms.

Those eyes of his are asking questions I don't want to answer.

Dipping my head, I lower my gaze, staring at the ground. It's safer than his gorgeous face. I really do love his face, you know?

It's so strong, his features carved from obsidian, with

clean lines yet lips that look soft and yielding. I bet they feel great. I bet they could decimate a girl's heart in a second. Or her senses, at least. I bet those masterful lips could send me right over the edge.

I steal a quick glance at them before darting my eyes back to the safety of the ground.

"Come on." He takes my elbow again, his voice soft and gruff. "Let's get out of here."

I let him lead me back down the street, because I can't argue with that sexy voice.

Seriously. What is wrong with me?

I should be running, but I'm letting him pull me to his car… his Jeep Wrangler. It's an older model and looks like it's seen a few years, been used to its full potential.

Crossing my arms, I wait on the curb while he unlocks and then opens the door for me. I'm starting to shake, and I don't even know why.

Shit, I hate crying.

I must look like a total wreck right now. I know I have mascara smudged on my face. I probably look ready for a Halloween party. I'll go as ghost girl.

Flipping down the visor, I check my reflection in the little mirror and grimace, quickly slapping it up again so I don't have to look. Swiping a finger under my eyes, I try to clean myself up, but I'm probably just making it all worse.

"Here." A small Kleenex packet appears in my lap.

Glancing to my left, I nod my thanks, my lips too heavy to form a smile.

This has got to be me at my worst.

Please let this be my worst!

Grady's still nice enough not to say anything as we drive out of Nolan. I have no idea where we're going, and

I don't even care. Wiping my face clean, I absorb the soft R & B music floating through the car. It's a Beyoncé song, I think. I don't know. I'm not really into music. I mean, I love dancing and getting a little wild, but—

Do you?

Do you really?

My shoulders slump.

I don't fucking know!

I don't know anything anymore!

The thought makes my chin bunch, tears threatening to take me out again.

Don't you dare!

I'm so done with crying today. I'm pretty sure I've clocked up enough tears to last me until Christmas.

Clenching my jaw, I battle the tingling in my nose, the swelling in my throat, and the burning in my eyes until we pull off the highway and head down a dirt road to what must be a trail entrance.

"Are we going hiking or something?"

Grady grins, his smile all things sexy when he glances at me. "Nah. There's just a great view I want you to see."

It takes another five minutes down this bumpy-ass road, but we eventually pull into a clearing and Grady parks his Jeep, overlooking a stunning vista. The valley stretches out before us, green and beautiful. It takes my breath away for a second, and I get out of the car, jumping down and wandering around the hood so I can get a better view.

"Wow," I whisper, leaning back against his Jeep and just soaking it in. "It's beautiful."

"Yeah. One of my favorite spots." Grady climbs up on the hood, his legs dangling as he drinks in the view. "Sky is clearing." He points to a big patch of blue between the scattered clouds.

Squinting up, he shades his eyes from the sun before looking back down at me.

I give him a twitchy smile.

"Come on." He holds out his hand to me, and I can do nothing but take it.

He helps me onto the hood, and I sit beside him, our legs kicking next to each other. We're like little kids on a park bench that's too big.

And right this second… it's the best feeling in the world.

Staring out at this vast valley below, the breeze tickling my blotchy, tender skin, the sun warming the top of my head… my insides find a calm I'm not used to feeling.

I don't even recognize it at first; it just slowly seeps through me, and after a few moments of silence, I become aware of this loosening in my chest. My shoulders start to relax, and with a soft sniff, I rest my head against Grady's shoulder and let out a long, slow breath.

"Think we could just stay here forever? Just like this?" I whisper.

Grady waits a beat, and then his soft, deep voice fills the void. "It'd be nice. But not possible." Gently hitching his shoulder, he encourages me to sit up so he can swivel and look at me. "Blake, you—"

"I know." Dipping my chin, I thread my fingers together, then figure the valley view will make things easier to get through, so I fix my eyes on a crop of trees and start talking, the way I know he wants me to.

I start with the first day I arrived in Chicago and just spill everything.

And I mean *everything*.

I have no idea what possesses me to tell him all my dirty little secrets. Maybe I feel like I owe him after rescuing me twice in less than a week. I don't know. But I haven't really shared any of the shit I've been going through with anyone, and I obviously have zero control once that door is unlocked, because it all comes out.

Even the shit I pulled with Cleo... and Simon and Nico. That weird-ass four-way relationship we shared together. How fucking screwed up that all was. How Cleo got me stealing and skipping class and...

Shit, I can't just lay all the blame on her.

I followed, didn't I?

Like a fucking sheep with zero brain cells!

"I don't even know how I let it happen," I admit with a shrug.

Grady hasn't said anything yet, and I'm too scared to look at him and check his reaction. He's probably horrified that Wily's sweet baby sister could fall so far.

"But I was so pissed off with that professor, and I had to get him back..." I shake my head and huff. "What the hell was I thinking? I'm lucky he didn't press charges. Thankfully, I managed to pay for the damage to be repaired, and he left it at that. It helped that I agreed to leave the school, just quietly walk out the door and never come back."

My shame hangs in the air for a minute before Grady eventually murmurs, "So you weren't officially kicked out?"

With a loud huff, I confess, "No. It just feels that way sometimes. But I knew the fallout for staying, for taking that academic suspension was…" I shake my head. "I couldn't handle it."

"So you took the fall, even though it was Cleo's idea?"

"Actually, I think it was Simon's. The spray paint belonged to Nico. And they stood around and cheered me on… Cleo taking photos." My expression crumples, my eyes burning so hot, I have to close them and try to speak past the lump in my throat. "I never thought she'd use them against me like this," I rasp.

There's a silent pause while he absorbs that, and then I hear his soft mutter. "What the fuck is wrong with her? She can't keep blackmailing you like this."

"Yeah, well, she is." I spit out the words, bitter resentment dripping off every syllable. "Cleo knows how to play the innocent victim to perfection. The dean believed her when she said she had no idea how reckless I'd been. She convinced him that if she'd known, she would have tried to stop me. But she took the fucking photos! And I… I couldn't even argue my side."

"Why not?"

I shrug, my voice dropping to a hoarse whisper. "I've thought about that a lot. And the only conclusion that makes any sense to me is…" I glance at him, then look back to the safety of the valley. "Maybe it was the out I didn't know I wanted. So I took all the blame. I owned that shit and withdrew so I didn't have to face it all." I sniff, wiping my nose with my sleeve.

"I take it Wily doesn't know *any* of this."

I shake my head.

"What about your parents?"

"They can't know." I turn to him, panic rounding over

me. "Please, they can never see those photos. No one can. No one!"

"Hey, it's okay." Grady's arm glides across my shoulder, running up to the back of my neck. He gives it a gentle squeeze.

I swallow, shaking my head. He's being way too nice to me. "I thought I'd feel free, you know? The day I moved out? I hadn't spoken to Cleo since she dumped me in it, and I couldn't even look at her as I carried my stuff out of the room. I ended up paying for a storage unit in Chicago. That's where my stuff is. And then I moved into a hotel. I know this makes me sound like a total bitch, but when I got the call that Wily was injured, I jumped all over that shit. I was relieved. It was the perfect excuse to get out of Chicago." Tears suddenly flood my eyes. "I don't want my brother to be hurt, I swear. But the timing couldn't have been better for me." My voice pitches, and I can't stop the flow of tears this time. "But I feel like such a horrible person for thinking that!"

"It's understandable. You were desperate. Wily will get it, you know? He's a good-hearted guy. He—"

"No!" I snatch Grady's wrist, squeezing it way too hard as I urgently tell him, "He can't know. No one can know! I shouldn't have even told you!" Panic splits me in half as I desperately beg him to keep his mouth shut. "Grady, you can't! You can't tell anyone this stuff."

"It's okay. Calm down."

"I won't calm down!" I bite back. "You have to promise me you won't say anything. To anyone! Grady, you can't. You can't tell."

"Blake." He touches my cheek, then ends up cupping both of them, gently forcing me to look at him. "It's okay."

"It's not okay," I blubber. "This whole thing is total shit."

"I know." He nods. "I know."

The calm, compassionate look in his eyes stills me.

Why isn't he mad? Why isn't he judging me?

"Just take a breath, okay?" He sucks in some air, showing me what to do. "Come on. Breathe."

I follow his next breath, copying his movement until the thundering in my heart has eased to something manageable.

"I'm not going to tell anyone," he assures me. "This is your story, and it's safe with me."

I close my eyes, releasing a heavy sigh.

His thumb rubs across my cheek in slow, gentle swipes, and I finally find the courage to open my eyes again and look at him.

"I won't tell," he promises again, then ruins it all by saying, "But I think you should."

Ripping my face out of his hold, I angle my body away from him and glare down at the valley.

"Blake—"

"No." I shake my head, feeling like a coward. "I can't."

"But—"

"You don't know what it's like being part of my family. Failure isn't an option, okay? Wily has to be perfect on the field, and I have to be perfect in the classroom. We know our roles, and we play them. We don't fuck up!" Leaning forward, I rest my elbows on my knees and cradle my head in my hands.

"Sounds like a lot of pressure," Grady softly murmurs.

"It is," I croak.

"Do you think that's why you let loose in college? The pressure just got to be too much, and you exploded?"

"Probably." My voice is barely audible, a mumble that would be unacceptable in my house. Mom hates mumblers.

"And the shoplifting? Was that all part of... breaking free?"

I sit back up with a sigh, hitching my shoulder. "I know, right? You think a little partying and carefree sex would be enough to sate me, but I needed an extra thrill. And what better way for a pampered rich girl to get that —by stealing stuff she doesn't actually need." I cringe, rubbing my forehead and hating myself a little more.

When I spell it all out like this, I seriously am the world's biggest idiot.

Grady's nice enough not to say it, but surely he's thinking it, so I feel compelled to explain. "It was such a rush. There was something so thrilling about the danger of nearly getting caught. And then that triumph when I got away with it. We thought we were motherfucking queens of the world." Shaking my head, I wish I could explain this better, but I can't. "Everything about my life up to that point had been so ordered. I was the good girl who did exactly what she was told. Always. I spent my life creating study timetables and goals, sticking to them, freaking out when I thought I might miss a deadline. I'd berate myself for getting less than an A+ on any test or assignment. Less than a 98 was a fail, you know?"

I glance at him and he nods, his closed-mouth smile small yet so understanding.

Seriously?

He's sexy *and* a sweetheart.

Yeah, my heart is officially screwed!

Covering my face again, I let out a screaming wail. It's a weird sound that probably scares the wildlife around me, but I can't keep it in anymore.

"It's okay to want to get out from under that pressure. It's too much for anyone," Grady states, filling the silence after my theatrical meltdown. "Maybe you just need to find some healthier ways to do it, you know?"

Dropping my hands, I look at him.

His lips twitch as he reaches up, tucking a reckless clump of hair behind my ear. "I can bail you out anytime, but there are more ways to have fun than being locked in the back room of Liquor King."

A watery laugh punches out of me, my stomach shaking as it quickly turns into a whimpering little sob.

Grady gives the back of my neck another gentle squeeze before running his palm down my spine.

He feels so good. So sure and steady.

"I'm so lost right now, Grady," I whisper. "And I can't find my way out, because I don't even know what my way is. I don't know what I want. I don't know how to settle this…" I tap my stomach. "This feeling inside me."

"You're gonna find it." His calm, easy voice almost makes me believe him. But it can't be that simple.

Nothing is ever simple.

Except the way that he's looking at me right now.

No expectations. No pressure.

Just a calm, quiet look that doesn't demand anything from me.

There's no judgment here. He's not silently telling me to put on a bright smile. I can be a wreck, and he's not gonna mind.

Reaching up, I brush my fingers down his cheek—a silent show of thanks.

My thumb skims along his lower lip, and I can see the remnants of the split lip he got defending me. Saving me.

"Thank you," I mouth, leaning forward before I can stop myself and pressing a soft kiss to the wound.

He stiffens against me, but I hold steady, not pulling away like he probably wants me to.

I'm being gentle, only applying the softest pressure... and I can't stop.

I'm right about his lips. They're supple and soft. My mouth can't help but explore, my tongue darting out to taste, to feel, to know.

The tip brushes his upper lip and he flinches, his body still rigid on the hood of his Jeep.

Pull away. Give the poor man some space!

But my hand curls around his neck and I add a little more pressure, molding our mouths together until my tongue is slipping between his lips again.

He tastes good.

Addictive.

I want his strong arms around me. I want to feel his hands curving around my body.

Please kiss me back! I silently beg him, swiping my tongue across his lips again.

And this time, he replies.

His tongue sweeps against mine—this beautiful, exquisite meeting that sends a delicious tingle right down my body.

Tipping my head, I deepen the kiss, hungry in a way I've never been before. I'm parched, starving in the desert, and he's my only source of water, sustenance... life!

With a soft whimper, I meet his tongue again, thrilled by the heady rush of this delicate dance. He's not thrusting his tongue down my throat; these are gentle licks, his lips only adding to the intoxication of the kiss.

This—

His mouth suddenly rips away from mine, his hands landing on my shoulders and pushing me back. There's nothing rough or annoyed about his movements, more just a determination to separate us.

"I can't," he puffs, shaking his head.

"What? You... you can't?" The disappointment is brutal—a burning hot poker right in the ego.

"You're Wily's sister."

"So?"

He gives me a pained frown, like how am I not getting this?

Scrubbing a hand over his head, he cups the back, his jaw clenching as he stares out at the valley, no doubt wishing he was a bird so he could soar right off the hood and get away from me.

Slumping back with a soft huff, I angle my body away from him. "It's some kind of bro code thing, isn't it?"

"Yep." He pops the *P*, and I give him a quick side-eye.

His face is bunched like he's concentrating on not looking at me... or touching me. "I can, um..." He clears his throat. "I can be your friend. I can listen to any of your secrets, and I'll keep 'em. If you need help figuring out your next move? I'm your guy." He turns to look at me, his expression so serious that he may as well be slamming the door shut on any future kissing. "But that's all I can offer. I can't..." He shakes his head again. "I respect Wily too much."

Frustration sizzles and burns. It's an effort to stop the rant bubbling in my mouth.

Fucking bro code! What the hell?

It's such bullshit!

Clenching my jaw, I glare at the forest to my left, homing in on a gnarly tree trunk and cursing the bark, because, well... I fucking can!

With a soft sigh, Grady lies back, stretching out on the hood of the car and resting a hand on his chest. He's gazing up at the sky, not saying a damn thing, and all I can do is stare down at him.

He won't look at me, and this muscle in his jaw keeps working—clench, unclench, clench, unclench.

Shit, he really is a good guy.

I should be grateful, not annoyed.

After another thick beat, I let out a long, slow sigh and lie back down beside him.

The sky above is a brilliant blue, making the white clouds pop, and I soak it in, focusing on the vastness of the beauty above me and trying to cool that sting of Grady's rejection.

And that's when a soft reminder filters into my brain.

Grady may have pulled away from the kiss.

But before he did... he totally kissed me back.

CHAPTER 20
GRADY

I kissed her back.

I totally did it.

Shit, I'm a lousy friend.

Wily is gonna kill me.

If he ever finds out.

The thought of keeping secrets from the guy sucks, but the fallout from telling him? He's trying to heal and focus on getting back to football; he doesn't need the added pressure of knowing what I did. Especially when it's not going to happen again.

Driving Blake back to Football Frat is a quiet affair. We've got a little Drake to keep us company, but we're not saying anything.

Man, I can't believe what she's been up to in Chicago. You never would have picked it by looking at her. She's got the angelic smile down pat. It makes me realize that she must have been wearing a mask this whole time, and she's been perfecting it her whole life. Being the girl everyone wants her to be… and they have no fucking idea.

I get why she doesn't what to confess everything to her family. They think she's a walking genius who never fails. They think she's perfect. Which is so unfair, because no one is, or ever could be.

The amount of pressure she must have been living with, it's a miracle she didn't crack in her teen years.

She's still *a teenager.*

She's nineteen now. She's an adult!

And she should technically know better, but if you've been perfect your whole life, there's bound to be a breaking point.

And man… did she break.

Tapping my finger on the steering wheel, I try to figure out how I'm supposed to help her through this.

Is she seriously going to keep lying and pretending to study while she's living with us?

The truth has to come out. She can't move on until the people who love her most find out about her downfall. And she'll never be set free from Cleo's blackmailing until she erases those threats by coming clean.

But she's kind of adamant about not saying a word. I won't betray her trust, but I'll need to keep working on her, letting her know that telling Wily will be painful, sure, but it'll ultimately release her from this burden. Then she can figure out what she wants to do with her life and move on.

Maybe Wily and I can head up to Chicago and pay Cleo a little visit. I grit my teeth, knowing that's a terrible idea, but what I wouldn't give to fix this for Blake. Set her free from this burden.

How can she ever forge ahead with her life when she's got this hanging over her?

"What do you want to do with your life?" I suddenly ask.

She flinches, my question obviously jolting her out of whatever reverie she's stuck in. "What?"

"I'm just trying to figure out what your next move might be. Are you gonna try to go to a new college or...?"

"I have no idea." She slumps back in the passenger seat, keeping her gaze out the window. "I'm so sick of studying. I just want a break from all that shit."

"Maybe you should go traveling. Your parents could afford to help you get overseas, couldn't they? You could explore the world, discover yourself."

"Yeah, right." She rolls her eyes. "They'd love that. Can you imagine? The second they find out I'm not going to be graduating, they will hit the roof." She scoffs. "They didn't mind Wily dropping out to pursue football, but Little Miss Brainiac here has to ace everything."

"Are you sure they really feel that way? What if you just talked to them and—"

"No. They won't understand where I'm coming from. They'll be so ashamed of my choices and..." She shakes her head, her voice starting to wobble all over again.

Shit. I need to wrap this up before we pull into the driveway.

"Hey, it's okay. We don't have to talk about it now. I'm just suggesting that when you do finally tell them... you have some future plans to counter what you're saying. If you can approach it with a 'this is what I want to do now' type thing, it might soften the blow."

Her lips twitch as she flashes me a smile of appreciation, but the look quickly falters.

"I wish I knew," she quietly mumbles.

It's hard not to keep checking on her as we close the distance to Football Frat. She's really quiet, but the closer we get to the house, the stronger her posture becomes. She checks the visor mirror, swiping her fingers under her eyes and pinching her cheeks, like she's putting on armor or something.

By the time I stop the car, her mask is fully in place, and she gives me a bright smile. "Thanks for coming to get me. Let me know how much I owe you."

"Blake, I—"

But she's already out the door, walking around the back of the Jeep and heading up the stairs.

I take a minute to steel myself, trying to put my own game face on before walking into the house.

I missed my class with Tyrell and the one after that.

Checking my watch, I figure there's no point trying to rush to the last half of my third class. I'll just have lunch here, maybe do some studying in my room, then head to practice.

I close the front door and hear voices in the kitchen, so I wander that direction to make myself a sandwich or something. Actually, a veggie omelet would go over nicely. Think I'll have that.

"I told you." Blake laughs. "I needed to get away from your sorry ass. There's only so much shithead I can take in a day."

"You are such a little turd," Wily teases her right back. "I'm fucking awesome to be around. Grady, tell her, man."

He points at me the second I walk into the room, and I force a grin.

"Yeah, you're all right."

"Fucking awesome. Those are the words you're meaning right now." He gives his sister a pointed look, and she just rolls her eyes.

"Whatever." She rests her hands on her hips and looks down at him. He's sitting at the kitchen table, his foot propped on a chair. "Do you need feeding?"

"Well, I was about to make myself something when you walked in and made me sit down."

"Because you were about to fall over." She flicks her arms up, brushing past me to get to the fridge.

"I was not," Wily mumbles, then glances up and winks at me.

Big shit. He's trying to get out of making food. The guy has always hated being in the kitchen. PB&Js are about the only thing he's capable of. Sure, he'll stand in here trying to look busy, but he's an expert at being just useless enough to get out of doing anything.

I cross to the fridge and stand behind Blake. "I was gonna make myself an omelet. You want one?"

She glances over her shoulder, her lips twitching as she steps to the side. "Sounds good. Thanks."

I swallow, trying not to fold at the sweet smell rising up my nose. I should not have stood so close to her. Damn, I can still feel her lips against mine. And her tongue. Holy fuck, that thing could make me do just about anything.

It took all my self-control to push her back earlier. If she hadn't listened to me and had gone in for another kiss, I wouldn't have been able to resist her.

You shouldn't have resisted her. It was just a kiss!

"Wily," I mutter under my breath. I can't do that to Wily.

"You good, man?" Wily says to my back.

Snatching out the carton of eggs, I spin and play the role I need to. "Yeah, brah. All good."

"Did class finish early for you today? Thought you'd eat on campus."

"Yeah, I just… felt like coming home. Cooking you lunch. You know how it is." I wink at him, forcing a grin and feeling like shit.

Blake's sitting at the table opposite her brother, looking sexy as sin, and I can't. I fucking can't go there with her.

I really want to, though.

Damn, this is gonna be hard.

She needs to tell the truth and get the hell out of Dodge or I'm not gonna survive this shit.

But I can't go dumping her in it, forcing her hand. That would be such a dick move when I promised to keep her secrets. So, I'm just gonna have to play this game of fucking charades and hope I don't screw it up.

"Hey, Blake, you want to get off your ass and help the guy out?" Wily nudges her with his good leg.

"You are such a hypocrite," she mutters.

"I'm wounded."

"You're full of shit," she counters, stalking to the fridge and yanking it open. The bottles rattle in protest, and I try not to check out her ass as she bends over and pulls bell peppers and a block of cheese out of the fridge.

"Grab the baby spinach and some mushrooms too," I direct her, then pass her a chopping block and knife.

She sets herself up at the kitchen table and gets to work, but not before placing a grater and the slab of cheese next to Wily. "I'm pretty sure you can't screw that up."

Wily laughs at her teasing, adjusting himself on the chair for a better angle.

We work in silence for a minute, until Wily starts humming tunes from the "Grease" soundtrack. He's off-key and it's fucking painful, so I cut that shit short as soon as I can.

"So, Blake, whatchu doin' for spring break?"

Why the hell I asked that, I have no idea.

Because right now, my brain is being crowded out by one thought. One very dangerous thought that I should seriously not suggest.

Don't do it. Don't you dare fucking do it!

"Not sure," she replies with a shrug. "Probably hanging out with this loser."

"You should head back to Chicago," he grumbles.

"I told you, I'm staying for spring break. I'll head back after that." Darting a look at me, she throws me a silent warning and pastes on a smile. "What are you doing?"

"I'm, uh… going hiking."

Don't it.

Don't fuckin' do it!

I turn to stare at her for a quick beat, then suddenly blurt, "Wanna come?"

You did it.

Yoooou idiot!

"Her?" Wily points at his sister, then cracks up laughing. "Hiking? With you guys? Are you kidding?" He's laughing so hard, he can barely get the words out.

"What is your problem?" Blake scowls at him, throwing a slice of bell pepper at his face.

He catches it, popping it into his mouth and munching loudly with this stupid grin on his face. "Blake. Come on. You in nature? That's not a thing."

"Why can't it be a thing?" she snaps.

"Because look at you." He waves a hand at her. "You're like a little bird, basically skin and bone. There's nothing to ya. You'd get blown off the trail by a stiff breeze."

I can feel a frown forming as I look between the siblings. "I'm sure she's not that fragile."

"Thank you, Grady." She gives her brother a pointed look, and I can practically see the steam coming out of her ears.

Wily rolls his eyes and looks at me. "Why do you even want her to come? I thought it was a guy's trip."

Oh shit. It's not like I can tell him that Blake needs to get away for a minute, to find herself, and what better way to do that than in nature. The outdoors speaks to the soul in ways nothing else can. I could plan a perfect hike on barely used trails that go deep into the forest. We'd be the only people on the planet for a little while, and it'd be so peaceful for her. So relaxing. Maybe if she could just get away from all this pressure and shit, her brain would have a minute to think. To come up with a way forward.

She needs this.

That's why I'm inviting her.

Clearing my throat, I try to play it cool. "It is a guys' trip, but Blake could be one of the guys for a few days, right?" I glance at her, knowing that I will *never* be able to think of her that way. Not after seeing her naked body in the bathroom. Not after the brief kiss we shared. Darting my gaze away, I force myself to look Wily in the eye. "She doesn't have to come. I just thought I'd throw it out there in case she was interested. I'm sure the others won't mind, and it'd give you an empty house, right? You and Satch could have some time together."

Wily's eyebrows perk up at that, and I start to question myself. Why the fuck am I trying to sell this?

Taking Blake on a hiking trip is a really dangerous idea.

The others will be around to check you. And besides, it's about her and what she needs, right?

The war continues to rage in my brain as I scramble eggs, then make up three separate omelets. It's not until I've placed them on the table and we've started eating that Blake finally says, "I'll come. Hiking sounds fun."

Wily snorts. "Lil' sis, you don't know what you're in for." Then his gaze hits me like a laser beam. "Choose a trail she can handle."

"I will, man." I force myself to look at him, nodding and raising my eyebrows so he knows I won't push her too hard. I even throw in a "we'll look after her" for good measure. Thank God I can say "we'll" and not "I'll," because I have to remember that. It's not just me and Blake on this trip. And that's exactly the way I need it to be.

"Maybe you should invite Nylah too. A little girl company for Blake?" Wily suggests.

I like that idea, but... "You sure her knee can handle it?"

"If you choose an easy trail." Wily scoops a forkful of eggs and veggies into his mouth, then talks around his food. "They could walk into a camping area, you could set them up, and they could chill there while you guys do some more challenging day hikes or something."

I nod, not minding that suggestion, but kind of hating the way he's demeaning Blake's ability. It's walking in the forest. Yeah, it can be tiring, but she's not some delicate petal on the verge of disintegrating. If he had any clue what she'd been up to in Chicago, he probably wouldn't be saying any of this shit.

Blake's got spirit... guts. She wouldn't have gotten into all that trouble in Chicago if she didn't.

I'm pretty sure if we threw her into the wild, she'd somehow come out on top.

And the more I think about it, the more I believe that's exactly what she needs.

Nature is gonna have all the answers, I just know it.

Glancing at the blue-eyed blonde with her pale skin and dainty features, I take in the smirk she's throwing Wily and know exactly what I'm gonna be asking the guys at practice this afternoon. Hopefully they won't mind adding another member to our spring break hiking team.

CHAPTER 21
GRADY

Staring down at my bed, I take in the neatly laid out supplies for the upcoming hiking trip. We're leaving in less than two days.

I have one more test to get through, and then it's on.

I've been gathering supplies all week and have mapped out the trails we'll be taking. The weather has been playing fair, and the forecast is telling me we're good to go. Although Nolan has taken another hit of rain, the area we're going to has managed to avoid the worst of it, and the conditions should be perfect for a really decent time.

I've ignored Wily's lame-ass suggestion and decided to combine two of my favorite trails. They intersect on the second day; we'll take the northern trail up to an awesome ridge with a view anyone in their right mind will be blown away by.

Like I'm gonna find some camping spot near the parking lot and set Blake up for the week. Whatever. That's not adventure.

Besides, Nylah can't even make it. She's got a thing with her grandmother... and much to my disappointment, Carson's decided to go with her.

He felt really torn over the whole thing, and Nylah felt bad too. I could tell when they came to talk to me about it. I wasn't gonna add any more fuel to their guilt fire and told them not to worry about it.

So we're down to Tyrell, Blake, and me. It'll be a good trio. Tyrell is awesome company. In fact, he's so nonthreatening that there's a chance Blake might open up to him too. Then she'll have two people in her corner when she finally tells Wily she's withdrawn from college, is being blackmailed by a girl she considered her best friend in Chicago, and has no idea what the future holds.

Thankfully, the guy's on board with Blake coming. He even helped her shop for some stuff online, although I wouldn't let them get any hiking boots that she hadn't actually tried on. So, on the weekend, Blake, Wily, and I drove down to Denver and checked out my favorite store. Managed to find her an awesome pair of boots on sale. She's been wearing them the past few days, breaking them in.

We also swung by her parents' place while we were in town, which was awkward as hell. If you'd been a fly on the wall, you probably wouldn't have even noticed. Everyone was all smiles and geniality, but I was sitting next to Blake on the couch, and her tension was palpable. Everyone else in the room seemed oblivious, too focused on Wily's knee injury and his recovery. We talked football most of the time, and Blake was probably on tenterhooks just waiting for them to bring up Chicago. And I found it impossible to relax because her parents are too much, if you ask me. Talk about pressure. It's all high performance, and the expectation for excellence was right in your face. No wonder Blake blew up when she left home. No wonder she doesn't want to admit anything.

Thankfully, we had to go before discussions could veer toward her. Wily wanted to get back to Satch, and Blake couldn't jump off that couch fast enough.

The drive back to Nolan was a quiet one. Wily ended up falling asleep in the back and Blake sat in the front, staring out the window, her face puckered into a frown. I couldn't risk talking to her about any of it in case Wily woke up, so I just had to drive his fancy-ass truck in pained silence.

Thank God we're getting away for a few days. Blake needs this break so badly.

Tyrell's been awesome, checking in if I need help with anything, but I'm pretty organized. I've done this enough times to pack in my sleep.

Scanning the contents of what I'll be carrying, I figure it'll weigh in at about forty-five pounds, which is a good weight for a multiday hike. Ultimately, I'd usually carry less, but I'm trying to compensate for Blake. Her pack will be as light as I can make it.

Thankfully, Tyrell's an ox, so between the two of us, we've got both tents and all the sleeping gear. Blake's just got her own clothes, plus some food supplies. I'm hoping to catch some fresh fish along the way, but you always have to plan for worst-case scenarios when going into the woods for a prolonged amount of time.

Having run through all the scenarios I can think of, I nod, happy with my supplies, and figure I can get packing.

I just want to check on Tyrell's stuff first.

Walking out of my room, I head across the hallway and tap twice on his door.

"Yeah, come in," he calls from inside.

Easing the door open, I peek inside and notice he's on the phone.

He beckons me with his fingers, but the move is distracted.

"Yeah, it's okay, Ma. Keep going..." He frowns. "What do you mean?"

I study his reaction.

Oh shit. Something's not good.

"Is it bad?" Scrubbing a hand down his face, he lets out a soft sigh. "I'm real sorry... Hey, it's okay. Don't cry. He's alive. He's gonna heal." Closing his eyes, his shoulders deflate, and my gut sinks.

Is this about his brother? Cyrus has Down syndrome, and it's been a lot of work for the family. Tyrell's really protective of him. They all are. That's why they moved to Texas, so he could attend a college there. I'm pretty sure his family is hoping that Tyrell will move down there after he graduates.

"Is Lacey home?" After a beat, he nods. "And Cyrus?" Dipping his chin, he cups the back of his head and sighs. "Yeah, no, I know. It's gonna disrupt his routine. Is there someone else who can— Yep... Yeah, I get it."

I'm pretty sure Tyrell ain't happy at all right now. About any of this.

Sliding my hands into my pockets, I wonder if I should leave him to it, but I'm guessing the guy might need to offload once this call ends, so I wander over to his desk and scan a packing list he's created for our spring break trip.

Snatching a pen out of the mug on his desk, I scribble down two items he forgot, then feel my insides shrivel.

"Yeah, Ma, it's okay. I'll come home."

Shit.

Clenching my jaw, I work on not letting my disappointment show when I spin to face him.

"I'll see you on Saturday... Yeah, love you too." Hanging up with a heavy sigh, he glances across at me and mutters, "Fuck."

"Uh-oh. What happened?"

"Dad had an accident at work. Shit."

"Damn, man. Is he okay?"

"Broken collarbone and concussion. He won't be driving for a while." His expression crumples. "And now Ma's all stressed because she's gonna have to take on extra shifts at work, and Cyrus's routine will be disrupted. She needs me down there to help work out the logistics and be there for Cy."

I raise my eyebrows. "You got people who'll be able to step up?"

"Yeah, we just have to convince Cyrus to go with them. He hates change. If I can be there to talk him around, it'll make things easier for everyone." Slipping his hands into his pockets, he stares at the ground, shaking his head. "He needs me."

"I know." I nod. "You're a good brother. A good son."

"I'm a grumpy-ass son." He clicks his tongue. "I was really looking forward to going hiking with you and Blake, man. I just need some time off, you know? And now I've gotta catch me a flight to Dallas and spend my week off trying to console my mother and take care of Dad and Cyrus while also making sure my rebellious sister doesn't do anything crazy." Gritting his jaw, he lets out another huff. "Makes me think I should have followed them to Texas."

"We'd miss you, brah. You belong here."

His lips twitch. "Yeah, I do. Just wish I didn't feel so guilty about it."

A heavy disappointment settles over the room, and I don't know what to say to ease it.

He winces at me. "Really sorry I can't make it."

"Me too."

Licking my bottom lip, I try to figure out my next play. Looks like the trip will be off now. It's not like I can go with just Blake. Wily would never let that happen anyway.

"You still gonna go?" Tyrell eyes me up before walking to his desk, taking a seat beside me and opening his laptop.

I think about it while he opens a new window and starts searching for cheap flights from Denver to Dallas. "Um..." Scratching my chin, I eventually murmur, "Yeah, I think I'll still go."

"Cool, man. Glad you won't be missing out."

"Yeah." I slap his shoulder, forcing out another laugh as I leave the room.

Of course I'm missing out.

I was looking forward to time with my bros. And one by one, they've fallen away thanks to girlfriends and family commitments.

Now it's just me.

And Blake.

No. I shake my head. It can't be that way.

It's just me. Going on my own and staying the hell out of temptation's way.

A solo hike will do me good.

I can shake off any stress, go at my own pace, and just enjoy the wild.

It's gonna be awesome.

So why the hell do I feel so gutted as I head down the stairs to find Blake and let her know she'll need to find something else to do over spring break?

CHAPTER 22
BLAKE

So we didn't mean to, but thanks to *Trollhunters*, Wily and I have been binge-watching all the shows we grew up on as kids. And now we're immersed in a hilarious *Looney Tunes* episode that Satch put us onto.

She's sitting beside my brother, all curled up against him and giggling away as Road Runner screeches to a halt next to a smoking Wile E. Coyote and goes, "Meep, meep," before disappearing down the road in a cloud of dust.

"This shit is ridiculous." Wily laughs before kissing Satch on the head. "I love it."

"Yay." She nestles her cheek back against his chest, still grinning.

Ugh, could these two get any cuter? Seriously, they're so sticky sweet, I can practically see sugar particles floating through the air.

They whisk past me, and I try my best not to be irritated by them.

I'm happy for my brother. He deserves a sweetheart care bear like Satch. I'm just annoyed because...

Shit, I don't even know why I'm annoyed.

Yes, you do. It's because the one you want isn't available.

Except that he is... if it weren't for the big, overly protective lug sitting next to you.

The cartoon wraps up with Road Runner once again triumphant, and I figure this is my cue to feign studying and disappear up to my room. But before I can even rise off the couch, Grady steps into the archway, and that flush of desire rockets right through me.

Shit. I can't even look at him without feeling something. This hiking trip is going to be interesting. It's lucky that Tyrell will be there. I'll just have to stick close to his side, I guess. Do my best to always keep him between Grady and me.

Although, that really doesn't sound like as much fun.

Oh man, why can't Grady and I just get it on the way we want to?

I force myself to look at his face and act as though nothing is bothering me... until I notice that something is definitely bothering *him*.

He gives me a half-hearted smile before raising his chin at Wily.

"Hey, Satch." He smiles at her, and she gives him a shy wave.

"Hi, Grady."

"How'd your test go this morning?"

"Yeah, good." She sits up, her confidence boosted by a safe topic like schoolwork. Blech! "I finished early but stayed for the full time." Her cheeks tinge pink, and

Wily's smiling at her, brushing his fingers through the ends of her hair while she speaks. "How did yours go?"

"It's tomorrow, but I think I'll pass. I've been studying my ass off in prep, so..." Grady nods. "It's my weakest subject this semester, but I'm feelin' okay about it. As long as the questions aren't any harder than my practice ones." He grins, and I take a mental snapshot of that smile.

"I love it when that happens." Satch grins back, then glances at me. "Have you finished all your online assessments?"

I nod, avoiding Grady's gaze. I can feel it all over me, and I can't go looking at him while I'm lying through my teeth. "Yep. All cleared away. I'm up-to-date on everything."

"Awesome." Satch grins. "Now you can really go and enjoy your time off camping. No school pressure hanging over you."

"Exactly." I look at Grady, desperate to move the topic away from school. "Did you just walk in here to bore us with school talk or...?"

Grady smirks at me, but his lips soon drop into a frown. "Looks like the hiking trip is off."

"What?" I ping up straight. "What do you mean? Why?"

I can't help noticing the disappointed look Wily and Satch are sharing right now.

Yeah, I'm sure they had big plans for this empty house.

Big naked plans.

Ew. I so don't want to think about my brother that way or what he might get up to with his girlfriend while they have the house to themselves.

Wily clears his throat. "What happened?"

Grady points his thumb over his shoulder. "Tyrell's family needs him, so he's heading back to Texas. Figure I'll just go on my own now."

Crossing my arms again, I glare at him. "Wait, so you're *uninviting* me?"

"Uh..." He whips his gaze to me, his brown eyes bulging just a little. "I figured you wouldn't want—"

"Why not? Should I be worried about hiking with just you?"

Oh, this is going to be fun!

Yes. Just Grady and me for like four whole days. Or is it five? I can't remember. I don't even care!

Grady, me, and a forest with no one else around. This could be my chance to finally convince him that—

"Of course you shouldn't be worried." He frowns at me, silently screaming *"What are you doing?"* but I just smirk right back at him.

Clenching his jaw, he looks at my brother for support.

And it turns out that miracles do actually happen, because Wily looks up at Grady with a shrug. "If she wants to go, why can't she?"

The running back's lips part for a second before he reins in his shocked expression.

Oh yes, baby.

This is happening!

It takes everything in me not to bounce over to Wily and kiss his big ol' cheek for being awesome.

With a swallow, Grady starts nodding and then croaks, "She can. I'm not saying she can't come, I just..."

His words trail off, because I don't think Wily's listening anymore. Satch turns to grin at him, and then he's touching her face... and now they're kissing like no one else is in the room.

Annnnd... I'm done.

Clearing my throat, I eye Grady up with a triumphant little grin.

He shakes his head at me like I've lost my ever-loving mind, so I walk toward him.

"It's settled, then. We're going hiking, Grady Newman. And I might be a newbie, but I'm sure you'll take *great care of me*." I pat his cheek, one pat per word, then give that sexy chin of his a little squeeze.

Wily is oblivious to my suggestive eyebrow wiggling because he's too busy sucking face with his girlfriend.

Grady stares at me, his brown gaze warning me away. Darting a look over my shoulder, he then puts on an unaffected smile, gritting out the words my brother needs to hear. "Yeah, it'll be great to have your company, Blake. Always love introducing people to the wilderness."

"He's like our very own Bear Grylls." Wily laughs before planting his mouth back on Satch's.

Okay, I'm really done now.

Making a disgusted face, I mutter, "Get a room, you guys."

"This is my room," Wily mumbles between kisses. "You can get out of it, if you like."

Glancing up with a cheesy grin, my brother silently tells us to get lost.

Rolling my eyes, I spin away, following Grady up the stairs.

His very fine ass is in line with my face, and it's taking everything in me not to give those toned butt cheeks a squeeze.

Save it for camping.

If he'll let me.

Surely he will.

It'll just be the two of us! No one has to know.

We can get the release we so desperately need and then—

Grady spins at the top of the stairs, crossing his arms and staring me down with an intense look that's... okay, it's a little unnerving.

"I know what you're thinking, and I can't be going there with you." His voice is gruff. "I already told you that."

Disappointment sears me, but I hide it behind my wide-eyed blink. "Going where? What are you thinking about right now, Grady? Where's that brain of yours at?" I tease him.

This sexy little growl reverberates in his throat, and a thrill of desire travels right through me.

Oh, he *is* going there.

With me.

Because we'd be insane not to take this opportunity.

It's obvious we both want each other.

A little fling in the forest isn't going to hurt anybody.

We'll both come back sated, and then he can get on with his life, and I can...

Okay, so I have no fucking idea what I'm going to do after spring break. I told everyone I'd be flying back to Chicago, but like hell that's happening.

But I'll have to fly somewhere. Maybe Grady can help me come up with the perfect place to escape to.

"You don't need to worry." I flick my finger lightly

under his chin, then wink at him. "We're gonna have fun, Flash."

His nickname floats off my lips, whistling between us like a promise.

Swanning around his rigid body, I throw caution to the wind and give that exquisite ass of his a playful tap before wandering to my room with a soft giggle.

CHAPTER 23
GRADY

I am in so much fucking trouble.

I should have just bailed on this whole hiking thing. But how was I supposed to do that without alerting Wily to the problem?

After Blake tapped my ass, then strutted to her room with those scintillating hips of hers, I scurried back downstairs to see if I could convince Wily what a terrible idea this is.

But he and Satch were fully immersed in their make-out session, and what was I supposed to say?

Oh yeah, so you asked why Blake couldn't come hiking with me. Here's the thing... She's hotter than the sun, and I've been dreaming about all the things I'd like to do to her luscious body... and now you want to put me alone with her in the middle of nowhere. That's why. That's why this trip should not be going ahead.

Yeah, that would have gone down a real treat.

All I could do was clomp back upstairs, taking them two at a time and forcing my brain into planning mode.

Things had to be rearranged now that it was just Blake and me.

I'd have to carry both tents. Man, it'd be so much easier to just take one, but I couldn't be doing that. Nope. No way.

In the end, I settled for a tent for her and a hammock for me.

I'll tie it between two trees and sleep under the stars, because I cannot share a tent with that luscious woman. My libido won't be able to take it.

For the past two days, I've been doing everything in my power to focus on the purpose of this trip. I'm gonna take Blake into the wild, show her how amazing it all fucking is, and hope that she can discover her purpose on this planet while we're out there.

That's it.

That's all.

It's done.

And I am still reminding myself of that as we wave goodbye to her tall, strong, could-kick-the-living-shit-out-of-me brother and his sweet girlfriend.

They now have the house to themselves, and they are more than excited about it.

Glancing right, I take in Blake and wish for just a second that she was Teah.

If Teah was still my girl, I'd be feeling completely different right now. I'd be driving her out into the forest, knowing exactly how spring break would be playing out. It would involve hiking adventures, dips in the lake, and a whole lotta lovemaking in the little tent I packed.

Are you kidding?

Teah came hiking with you one time, and she hated every

minute of it. You didn't get lucky because she was too pissed off, covered in mosquito bites and wailing to go home.

Yeah, okay, so that wasn't our best moment.

But still, if Blake was any other girl... if she was my girlfriend... then this would be a hell of a lot easier.

She's your friend. Your friend, your buddy, your pal.

Your very sexy pal.

Glancing at the skintight yoga pants she's sporting, I have to bite the inside of my cheek hard enough to remind myself that she is off-limits!

Blake turns to shoot me a smile, looking all excited as we head out of Nolan. She's pumped for this trip, and I have no idea if it's because she's genuinely excited to explore something new and be in nature, or if she's just relieved to be away from Wily and all the secrets she's carrying... or if it's because she's waiting to pounce.

Shit, how the hell am I going to resist her if she does?

This trip is the worst idea ever!

Forcing my brain back to the safety of practical planning, I run through my gear list and all the safety measures I've put in place. Success in the outdoors is all about planning ahead and anticipating any problems.

I love that part of it. Thinking things through, knowing I'm prepared for whatever nature has in store. The wild can be an unpredictable beast, but that's part of the appeal for me. Every hiking trip is different, and I love that rush of being surrounded by nature and knowing I have to survive it.

Unable to help myself, I steal a look at my hiking buddy. You know, she's actually been kinda helpful the past two days. She wanted to be part of the packing process and see all the stuff I'm carrying. She got annoyed when I overloaded my pack and made me transfer a few things to hers. We tested it out last night, and the weight seemed okay for her. She's obviously stronger than she looks, although I'll keep an eye on her as we're walking.

She's sharp, intelligent, and notices things I don't expect her to.

It doesn't take much to explain anything to her because she picks things up so fast. I get why Wily always boasts about her smarts.

He gave me the hard word last night, hobbling into the kitchen and cornering me just after I'd emptied the dishwasher.

No one else was around, and he took advantage of that fact and told it to me straight.

"I need your word that you're gonna take care of Blakey for me."

I nodded, my heart hitching.

"She's been working her ass off taking me to appointments, looking after me, *and* fitting in all her studying. It's stressing her out, even though she won't admit it," he grumbled. "That's why I want her to get away from it all."

"Yeah, well… uh, nature's great for that." I swallowed, then had to remind myself to stop acting so damn nervous. Squaring my shoulders, I looked him in the eye and promised, "She'll be safe, Wily. I'm totally prepared."

"Yeah, I know you are, but… you know, just…"

"Just what?"

"Make sure she has a good time."

My stomach dipped while my heart shot into my throat. My crazy-ass brain was breathily whispering, *Is he giving us permission to—*

No, you idiot! Shut up! And smooth out your fucking expression.

I nodded, clearing my throat. “She will.”

“She’s talking a big game, saying she can handle this hiking shit, but I don’t know, man. Don’t let her bravado cloud your judgment, okay? Watch her like a hawk, and don’t push her too hard.”

“I won’t,” I assure him.

“And if the weather packs in—”

“We’ll cut the trip short. I promise I won’t do anything dangerous.”

He grunted his approval, but that protective big brother look was still all over his face when he pointed at me. “I don’t want her coming back with blistered feet and aching muscles. So don’t—”

I cut him off with a laugh. “Bro, come on. That’s part of it.”

His eyes narrowed, his blue glare like a frickin’ laser beam. “Don’t push her too hard,” he repeated.

Nodding my understanding, I forced a smile and promised him, “I’ll take care of her.”

I would.

That wasn’t a hard promise to make.

He eyed me up like he was sussing me out, and I ended up frowning at him, because what the actual fuck. Of *course* I’d take care of her!

“And no arguing. I still don’t know what the fuck that was about the other day, but you don’t be yelling at my sister, got it?”

Working my jaw to the side, I nodded, resting my hands back on the counter. “Got it.”

“Good.” With a definitive nod, he slapped a hand on

my shoulder, a wide smile overtaking his face like he hadn't just been giving me the tenth degree.

The protective big brother was tucked away again, and Wily the Goofball was back.

"Hope you have the best time, brother."

After another friendly shoulder slap, he awkwardly turned away and hobbled back out of the kitchen, and I stood there, staring at the kitchen floor and hoping like hell I can get through this thing.

And I will.

And she will.

As long as I keep my focus on the right thing—introducing Blake to the wonders of the wild and giving her a chance to switch off from all the bullshit she's running from... and maybe even relax herself into a state of peace.

Hopefully from there, she can find the answers she's looking for.

CHAPTER 24
BLAKE

We drive for about two hours, leaving the highway, then meandering through roads that look as though they get used by like ten cars a year. I obviously know it's way more than that, but it feels like we're traveling in the middle of nowhere.

It's so stunning. I keep catching my breath as I stare at the mountains looming in the distance and the hilly landscape around us. The road is a snake in the landscape, winding back and forth through an ocean of pine trees. This is Colorado backcountry at its best, and I can't believe I'm about to hike through this wilderness.

I can't admit that I'm just a little nervous.

I'm mostly excited because I've never done anything like this before, and new adventures are fun.

I'm also excited because I finally have Grady all to myself.

Although, I highly doubt he's feeling the same way.

He's been tense and silent ever since we left, and this trip is going to royally suck if he doesn't chill the fuck out.

Seriously. Does he think I'm a rattlesnake or something?

I'm not about to pounce and inject him with venom. I just want to hang out... maybe get a little frisky, sure. There's nothing wrong with a spring break fling.

I just need to figure out a way to convince him of that.

Checking him out from the corner of my eye, I study the side of his gorgeous face, once again captured by those high cheekbones and the strong lines of his dark skin.

Mm! He's so freaking hot!

"Here we go," he mumbles, slowing his Jeep and pulling into a small gravel parking lot. There's one other vehicle, which looks to love the outdoors as much as Grady's Jeep does.

We park next to it, and then he cuts the engine and turns to look at me.

I smile at him, hoping to ease that tense frown off his face.

He stares at me for a beat before his lips twitch and he gruffly asks, "You ready for this?"

"You bet I am." Unbuckling, I jump out and walk around to the back of the Jeep.

We load up, Grady making sure my pack is sitting comfortably. I kind of love his close proximity as he adjusts straps and checks the pack's positioning.

"That feel okay?"

"Uh-huh."

"Make sure your hips are taking the bulk of the weight," he reminds me, checking the strap around my hips and giving it a jiggle until I confirm that I'm good to go.

My pigeon shoulders can manage this thing. I'm determined to make it so.

"Okay, then." Grady locks up the Jeep, then turns to glance down at me. "Time to show you my favorite place on earth." His lips stretch into a genuine smile, and I drink it in, grinning right back at him before spinning in my hiking boots and marching into the forest.

He sets a fair pace, and after twenty minutes, I'm struggling to keep up.

I don't want to complain and come across like some weak city girl, so I grit my teeth and keep going, totally understanding why my parents never introduced me to this activity.

Picturing my classy mother sweating it out on a dirty trail with insects buzzing about and nothing but the sight of endless tress nearly makes me laugh out loud. I may have grown up in Colorado, but my life has consisted of one luxury after another.

Mom's idea of a vacation is a two-story "cottage" by the lake or a three-bedroom suite on a cruise ship.

We've seen the world in style, and any vacation time we've spent in this fine state has been surrounded by country club pricks on the edge of a golf course with all the modern luxuries one could ask for.

This right here is new to me.

And although I'm already sweating and my muscles are asking me what the fuck I'm playing at… I'm loving it.

"You good?" Grady's stopped up ahead, waiting for me to catch up.

"Uh-huh." I reach him as fast as I can, and he narrows his eyes at me. "What?"

"You have to be honest with me when we're out here.

If you're struggling, you gotta tell me; otherwise, I don't know to adjust."

I make a face and reluctantly admit, "We're going a little fast. I want to keep up with you, but you're like... like the Flash."

He snickers.

"And I feel like a freaking princess who's never even broken a nail."

"You're not that precious." He gives my shoulder a playful nudge, then spins and starts walking a lot more slowly.

We meander along the trail for a while, and I tune in to the sounds of nature around me. Birds twitter; a woodpecker taps in the distance.

Wow. I'm not sure I've ever heard a woodpecker in real life before. That sounds so cool!

My boots crunch along packed dirt, dead pine needles, and rocks scattered before me.

"This trail seems pretty unused. Where are we?"

"We're on the Itsá Trail. It's not a very popular one, and I love it for that very reason."

"Why don't people like it?"

"Not sure. I think it's kind of out of the way, harder to find. Not too many people know about it."

"So how do you know about it, then?"

He glances back to flash me a smile. "My dad's been taking me out since before I can remember. We've hiked most of the state. Every vacation, he'd always take me someplace different. I think I was about fourteen or fifteen when he found this spot for us, and I fell in love with it. I don't even know what makes this place different to all the others. I guess it just speaks to my soul."

Okay, wow.

My insides tremble, and I gaze around the forest and instantly get it.

This place has a very special vibe. I can feel it too. There's an ancient type of magic or spirituality here. Its energy surrounds us, an invisible swirling mass that makes my heart pulse and my insides sing.

"It's really beautiful. I get why you love it."

He stops, turning to look at me, like he's double-checking that I actually mean it.

I nod. "I'm serious. I can feel the energy of this place. I get why it's your favorite."

His lips curl into a smile that warms his eyes as well, and I just want to stand here drinking him in. The dappled sunlight breaking through the trees is highlighting his handsome face and—

He turns away, continuing down the trail, and I try not to feel that burn of disappointment. We almost had a moment. I could feel it.

Wrestling my phone out of the front zipper pouch of my bag, I know I can no longer capture him just the way he was... but that shaft of light breaking through the trees is stunning.

Pausing on the trail, I line up the shot, catching Grady's back as he walks into the light. He's surrounded by trees, and it seriously looks like angels are smiling down on him or something.

"Nice," I murmur to myself, smiling at the screen and already imagining this picture blown up and framed on a wall. It's stunning.

"You coming?" Grady calls from ahead, and I pick up my pace, chasing after him as he teases me about being on my phone when I should be enjoying the view.

"I was taking a photo, dipshit." I snort, laughing when he turns to frown at me.

I grin back, and his lips start to twitch before he nods and keeps walking.

Happily following after him, I enjoy this slow pace, although it's probably taking us way longer to get to the first pit stop he planned. But I don't want to go any faster. I want to drink this all in.

It's so gorgeous.

We're like the only two people on the planet right now, and that's not overwhelming or scary at all.

It's comforting.

Peaceful.

Two hours disappear in a flash as I take in this nature like it's my personal brand of fuel. I snap a stupid number of photos, but I just can't help myself. There is so much to capture out here.

My shoulders start to ache, my calf muscles are cramping as we ascend a steep, rocky pathway, and my feet are complaining big-time.

But I'm struggling to remember a time that I felt this content.

This unburdened.

And I want to freaking drown in this feeling.

CHAPTER 25
GRADY

Blake seems happy. Her genuine smile is absolutely stunning. I'm not used to seeing her so unchecked. This smile isn't the one she puts on for Wily, and it's not the one I saw her use when she was talking to her parents yesterday. Their video chat was all about her parents questioning why she was taking this insane trip with me. They were obviously too busy, on the weekend we visited them, talking football with Wily to really let the news sink in, but now it has... and her mother wanted to know why on earth her daughter would choose to live like a savage for five whole days.

Blake had laughed at the comment, but it hadn't been a relaxed sound.

Not like the one she made when we spotted that squirrel racing up the tree.

A squirrel.

She's definitely seen one before, but obviously out here, in the wild, it's that much more spectacular.

The musical sound carried across the breeze, and I

turned back in time to see her pointing at that tree and grinning at me.

It was beautiful.

She's so stunningly beautiful, it's hard to concentrate around her.

Which is why I'm leading the way.

I have to be in front, because if I had to follow that luscious body of hers, I'm not sure I could do this.

I'm hyperaware of her behind me—listening to the sound of her boots, making sure her steps are steady and even. She hasn't faltered since I slowed the pace, and I can almost feel her relaxing the farther we get into this hike.

She seems to love it out here, and I can't even describe the effect that is having on me.

Showing people my favorite place is almost like a sacred affair, and when they don't get it, it's such a blow.

Teah never got it.

I think back to the one and only time I brought her out here. I'd planned for a weekend getaway, packed all the necessary supplies.

We lasted less than a day. We made it to the lake about an hour north of this position, and she was in the foulest, grumpiest mood I'd ever seen. Sweat was glistening on her skin—she was one sexy thing—but she wouldn't let me near her. She spent our lunch break complaining about the insects, perched on a rock and muttering about how much her feet hurt. I knew within a few minutes that there was no way she could cope with a night out here.

So, I suggested we go for a swim, then head back.

She was so relieved, she stripped off quickly and

jumped into the water, only to complain about how freezing it was, then grumbled her way back to the car, quickly giving up her pack before her shoulders hurt too much.

Needless to say, we drove back to Nolan in aggravated silence, and she didn't relax until I'd pulled up outside her sorority house.

"Sorry I didn't love it, Grady," she'd mumbled. "I guess hiking's just not my thing."

I gave her an understanding smile even though I didn't get it at all.

How I hadn't seen that as a big red flag is beyond me. I was too loved-up to do anything but forgive her.

We made amends the next morning, and I accepted the fact that I was with a woman who wouldn't share my passion for the outdoors. I could deal. We just wouldn't do that one thing together. I still had my bros and my dad to share that with, and it was enough.

But watching Blake get into this with me...

Yeah, there's something special about it.

Unhooking my water bottle, I slug back a drink, then dig out my trail mix.

"Want some?" I hand her the bag, and she takes it, greedily scarfing down a couple of handfuls before passing it back.

"Delicious," she murmurs around her mouthful. "What's in that?"

I glance down at the bag and list off the things I always put in there. "Cashews, almonds, peanut butter chips, raisins, dark chocolate chips, cranberries."

"So good. You make it yourself?"

"Uh-huh." I pop another handful in my mouth before

sealing the packet and zipping it back into the side pocket of my pack. "You still feeling all right?"

"Yeah." She hitches her pack on her shoulder, blowing a wayward curl off her cheek before grinning at me.

"We've got about two hours, maybe two and a half at the pace we're currently going, until we get to a place I thought we could camp tonight."

"Okay."

"You gonna be good? How's your body feeling?"

Resting her hands on either side of her slender waist, she nods. "Good. Yeah, I can keep going."

"You'll tell me if it gets too much, right? Because there's another spot we can go if—"

"Grady, I'm fine," she assures me. "I promise I'll tell you if I feel like my feet are about to fall off."

"Is your body hurting yet?"

"My legs are complaining, and getting up that hill made me feel like my lungs were about to explode, but that's my fault for not exercising on the regular."

My lips twitch. "And here I was thinking you were one of those gym bunnies or Pilates princesses."

She scoffs. "Yeah, right. I'm the study nerd who's allergic to sweat, didn't you know that?"

I gaze at her glistening skin and the red hue on her cheeks and can't help murmuring, "Could have fooled me. Sweat looks good on you, Wilson."

Her blue gaze lights with appreciation, and fuck, I shouldn't have said that. I don't know how I'm looking at her right now, but I'm probably giving away far too much.

Clearing my throat, I spin before I say anything else that's gonna get me in trouble.

"Sweat looks good on you too," she softly says behind me, and I pick up my pace, needing to create a little more space between us.

I slow it down after a couple of minutes when I can sense how hard she's trying to keep up with me.

Shit, she's fire.

And I'm gonna get so fucking burned in this forest.

Keep it together, man. You can do this!

"Ooo! What's that?" Her excited voice distracts me, and I happily launch into a detailed explanation of the wildlife she just saw scurrying away into the forest.

I've studied every animal out here, and it's easy to rattle off the facts as we plod along the trail.

The farther we go, the denser the surrounding trees and bush will get. The hike I planned and logged on the website is taking us into parts of these woods that are hardly ever touched. I feel safe doing it, because I've done it so many times before. I love choosing trails that are only touched by the seasoned hikers and hunters in the area.

Blake's gonna get a taste of what it really means to "go off-grid," and I'm stoked that I get to experience all of her firsts with her.

She seems so fascinated by what I'm telling her that I keep the conversation going and answer every one of her questions. She keeps saying how stunning and beautiful it all is, and holy shit, if I didn't like her before, I most definitely do now.

Pulling out her phone yet again, she ends up snapping a bunch more shots as we crest the next hill, then head down toward the lake. It takes us even longer than I expected, but I don't mind so much because none of the photos are selfies. This girl is all about capturing nature, adjusting aperture and fiddling with her phone app until she gets the lighting just right.

When we break out into a clearing that will be tonight's campsite, she actually gasps, running to the edge of the lake and taking what feels like a hundred shots. The mountains in the distance are highlighted by the early-afternoon sun, the snow on the peaks glistening, the blue-sky backdrop turning it into a picture-postcard view.

"Holy shit, this is amazing!" She glances back to gape at me. "Are you seeing this?"

"Yep." I grin and can't help stopping to watch her. I know this view by heart, but her, I'm still memorizing. I know I shouldn't, but I just can't help myself.

She's decked out in hiking attire, looking like a model for the REI catalog, and it's a freaking turn-on. Those skintight yoga pants with the clunky hiking boots? Yep, it totally does it for me.

Forcing my gaze away, I unclip my pack and let it slide off my shoulders as she finally slips her phone back into her pocket and steps toward me.

"I'm gonna run out of juice before the end of this hike, aren't I?" Her lips form a quick pout. "How am I gonna capture it all?"

"I've got a power bank you can use, but I'd also turn it off at night to save as much battery as you can."

"Okay." She grins, pulling out her phone again to take a quick shot of me.

"Don't waste your battery on me."

"It's not a waste." She gazes at the screen with a little smile that's both unnerving and enticing.

Shit, she thinks I'm hot.

The feeling is mutual, girl!

With a soft sigh, she turns back to stare at the lake again. "Seriously, this place is insane. I've never seen untouched beauty like it before."

"Yeah, it's one of my favorite spots."

"I can see why." She glances at me, her blue eyes bright with a smile that I can't turn away from.

So I just stand there as she unbuckles her pack. It thuds to the dirt because her arms are obviously too tired to catch it in time.

"Whoops. Sorry." She winces.

"No worries." I walk over to the pack, picking it up and stowing it next to mine. "Let's have some lunch, and then we can get to work setting up camp."

"Sure." Pulling the now thoroughly squished sandwiches out of her pack, I pass them to her, and we munch down the food I prepared when I first got up this morning.

For multiday hikes like this, you have to be organized, so I've mapped out our meals and snacks to ensure we have enough food to last us. I'll do some fishing this afternoon, and we can cook that over a campfire tonight, plus I have some overnight oats already soaking for tomorrow morning. I'll have to make sure I secure our packs properly and rig them up so we don't get bears sniffing out the food and visiting us in the night.

Figure I should probably go through safety procedures and warn Blake about all the potential threats and dangers we face on a trail like this, but I'll let her finish eating first.

One thing at a time, right?

"Ugh, I'm so sweaty." She pulls at the shirt sticking to her back.

"Yeah, you better get used to it. We've got plenty more to go."

She snickers, munching down another bite of her chicken salad sandwich like it's the best food she's ever had.

That's another thing I love about hiking. You appreciate the little things.

When your body's hurting and you've got sweat running into your eyeballs, there's nothing sweeter than a mouthful of plain old water.

When you've got nicks and bruises on your skin and your legs and back are screaming at you to stop already, there's nothing more delicious than a homemade chicken salad sandwich. You feel like freaking royalty biting into that thing because you've worked so hard to get it.

Damn, I really do love this shit.

Every time I come out here, I'm reminded of what brings me to life.

Don't get me wrong. I love being in class, filling my brain with stuff. And being out on a football field, making plays and scoring touchdowns with my team, that is golden.

But this right here... this is what I was put on the earth for.

I'm sure of it.

Which is why a part of me has been toying with the idea of switching from computer engineering to conservation engineering. Jobs in that field probably won't pay as well, but making nature a full-time part of my life could be so amazing. I have to do whatever I can to preserve places like this.

"What are you thinking about?" Blake places her sandwich crusts back into the wrapper.

"You don't eat your crusts?" I give her a pained frown.

"Never."

I tut and hold out my hand. "Give 'em to me. We're not wasting food."

She laughs and hands them over. "Sure, Mom."

"Can't believe you weren't made to eat your crusts as a kid. Come on, Wilson."

"What?" She laughs. "The crusts are..." She wrinkles her nose.

"They're what?" I munch through them, proving how delicious that are.

"There's nothing on them. It's just plain bread." Poking out her tongue, she shows me a taste of the prissy little princess she was no doubt raised to be.

I roll my eyes, holding back my teasing insults before telling her, "I was thinking about how I want to preserve this place and make sure it stays as fresh and beautiful and clean as it is right now."

"I love that." She smiles at me, before looking back over her shoulder. "And I understand why you want that. I've never seen anything like this before. It's so quiet and peaceful out here." Inhaling a deep breath, she holds it, then lets her shoulders sag as she releases it on a long sigh. "Just listen," she whispers, closing her eyes and looking all things delectable.

Her hair is golden in this light, her delicate features and porcelain skin raised to the sun as her lips curl into a smile I want to memorize.

I have to force myself to look away and only just manage to before her eyes slowly open. Dipping my chin, I ball the trash in my hand and slip it into my pack.

"Here." Throwing her the drink bottle off the side of her pack, I make her down at least five decent mouthfuls before we get to work assembling camp.

She has no idea how to pitch a tent or rig up a pack, so I walk her through each step. Thankfully, she picks things up really fast, and our little campsite is soon set up.

I'll build a fire before it gets dark, but we've got a few hours before that happens.

"We'll need to collect some kindling and firewood," I tell her. "Might as well set the fire up, and then we can light it just before the sun goes down."

"Sounds good." She starts searching the ground nearby. "So, what does kindling look like?"

"Come on, I'll show you." I tip my head, and she follows me into the nearby forest, where I pick up examples of the kindling and wood we want for this fire.

It doesn't take long before we're loaded up and returning to camp. We dump out supplies, and I show her how to build a fire, setting up the rocks and then stacking the kindling in a teepee formation. I can't help explaining the mechanics of how a fire works and am no doubt coming across like a mansplaining douchebag, but she doesn't stop me and doesn't seem to mind, soaking it all in like it's the most fascinating thing in the world.

"You can build the next one, if you like."

"Okay." She grins, flashing me those straight white teeth again and chipping away another piece of my resolve. “So...” She tips back on her heels. “What do we do now?”

“Well...” I look around, checking my watch and calculating the time until sundown. “We’ve got about two and a half hours left, so we can just chill here. I brought cards and travel chess, if you want to play a game.”

Her nose wrinkles.

“Or you could read a book. You packed your Kindle, right?”

“Yeah.” She crosses her arms, tapping her fingers like she’s agitated.

“Okay, what do you want to do, then?”

“I don’t know.” Bouncing from toe to toe, she gazes down at me.

I’m still crouched by the fire, trying to figure out how to entertain this woman... in ways that I’m actually allowed to. “We could—”

I cut myself off.

No, man. That is a terrible idea.

“We could what?” Her eyes dance with curious excitement, and because I am a world-class fool, I say it. I actually fucking say it.

“We could go swimming in the lake. There’s a rock face just around the corner we can jump off.”

Her face puckers. “Won’t it be freezing?”

“Yeah.” I bob my head. “This time of year, the water’s pretty cold, but it won’t kill us, and it’ll definitely freshen us up.” Standing tall, I brush my hands on the back of my pants, my lips twitching. “Plus... if you want a rush? Launching yourself off that rock face will probably do it for ya.”

Her eyes light to sparkling sapphires as she nods, then spins for the tent. "I'll go put my swimsuit on!"

Shit.

She looked at me like I was crazy when I mentioned packing a swimsuit. She didn't even have one and had to run into town to buy one. I should have told her we probably wouldn't use it, but I always pack swimwear unless it's the middle of winter. For a five-day hike, you have to freshen up, and I figured she wouldn't want to be skinny-dipping with me.

Or I knew I couldn't handle skinny-dipping with her, so I put it on the list. And now I'm closing my eyes, quietly berating myself for losing my head as I move to my hammock, digging out my bathing suit from my day bag and finding a spot behind a clump of trees to strip down and prepare myself for temptation city.

You are seriously such a fucking idiot!

CHAPTER 26
BLAKE

It takes me a minute to find my bikini. Thankfully, Grady made me pack all of my clothes into a separate bag that he pulled out of my pack before rigging it up so the bears can't get to it.

Bears. Holy shit! Bears!

That's thrilling enough, but now Grady's challenging me to jump off some rock face?

Who the fuck needs shoplifting, right?

I giggle to myself as I wrestle out of my yoga pants and slip my bikini on. A one-piece bathing suit would probably be far more practical for this kind of thing, but when I saw this one in the store, it was too cute to resist. So, a bikini it is.

I probably should have packed a rash guard or something too. Grady put it on the list as well, but I forgot to buy one when I was out shopping and didn't want to admit to him yet another thing he'd have to supply for me. I didn't think it'd matter anyway.

Adjusting the skinny straps of my bikini top, I then

make sure my boobs are properly tucked into the two flimsy triangles covering them before grabbing the world's smallest towel and flinging it over my shoulder. It's a quick-dry one and feels like it's made of fabric that will absorb nothing, but Grady loaned it to me, and apparently that's all that would fit in my pack.

He's right. My pack is stuffed to the gills, although it's like half the size of his, so no big surprises there.

Zipping my tent closed behind me, I then spin to find Grady gaping at me. His eyes are transfixed on my body like he's slipping into some state of catatonic shock.

It's hard to keep my smile in check.

Yep, that boy wants me so bad.

A sizzle races through me, but the second our eyes connect, he blinks and shakes his head, gruffly asking, "Where's your rash guard?"

"Uh..." I wince. "I forgot to buy one."

"But it was on your list." His gaze flicks down my body, his forehead wrinkling in irritation before his eyebrows start to rise again and he darts his eyes back to the dirt.

My lips won't stop twitching as I watch him awkwardly stroke the back of his head and try not to look at me.

Damn, he is loving this view. Talk about an ego boost.

I bite my lip, failing to hide my smile.

"The water's cold." He skims a hand down his own rash guard. It's sticking to his body like it was specially made for him, highlighting all of his delicious ridges and perfectly shaped torso.

"I'll be fine," I assure him, slightly distracted by the sexy sight in front of me.

"Suit yourself. Leave your towel on that rock over there." He points to a boulder near the edge of the lake, still doing everything in his power to avoid looking at me.

I do as I'm told, my heel catching on a stone as I walk over the dirt. "Ouch."

"Where are you sandals?"

"By the tent."

"You'll want to put them on." His voice is soft and gruff.

"But they're so ugly," I complain.

He lets out a dry laugh, then tells me off like a schoolteacher. "You've got to look after your feet. This trip will be over if you cut yourself up."

"Yeah, yeah, I get it." I force a smile and tiptoe back to the tent, avoiding sharp stones and spiky pinecones as best I can.

He waits patiently, staring out across the lake, his jaw clenching and unclenching, while I slip these monstrosities on. He made me buy them when I was picking out my hiking boots. I told him it was a waste of money because I would not be putting those things on my feet ever again.

"Screw fashion," he'd argued with me. "We're talking about practicality here."

And of course, he was right.

Smooshing down the Velcro, I get back to my feet. I probably look ridiculous in my sexy string bikini and a pair of freaking hiking sandals.

"Okay, I'm good. Let's go jump into the lake."

Clearing his throat, Grady spins and starts walking away. I watch his water shoes disappear down the path and wish I had a pair of those instead. They look way cooler. Why didn't he suggest I get those?

The hike only takes about two minutes and is a total breeze without the pack weighing me down. The only hard part is the steep incline at the end, where we have to literally scale a rock face before getting to the top of the small cliff.

I inch my way to the edge, my stomach pitching when I peer over the side.

"How far is that?" I whisper, clutching his arm so I don't lose my balance and tumble off.

His steady arm is so strong and sure; there's nothing weak or untrustworthy about this man. I can sense it. Wily always talks about how reliable Grady is. He's the one who keeps the house organized, together, running smoothly. And I get it. He's switched on, intelligent, sure of himself.

Even the rock-hard muscles in his forearm are assuring. I know that sounds weird, but it's true. Everything about him is solid. As stable as the rock I'm currently standing on.

"It's about fifteen feet."

I swallow, fear skittering through me. I've never been the best with heights, but I don't want to let that stop me right now.

I won't humiliate myself in front of Grady and chicken out.

"I'll go first, so you can see it's safe." His voice is a soft rumble, deep and reassuring.

Gently prying my hand off his arm, he steadies me by the elbow, then slowly lets go.

"Do I take off my shoes?" I glance down at my

sandals.

"No." He laughs. "Otherwise, you'll be hiking back up barefoot to get 'em. You can swim in those. You'll be fine."

"Okay." I nod. "I'm not the strongest swimmer."

"I'll be there." He smiles down at me, and I believe him without a doubt.

There's really nothing to fear here. As long as Grady's in that water below, waiting for me, I'll be fine.

I logically know this.

Trying to feel it is another story, but—

"Let's go!" Grady yells, releasing a loud whoop before launching himself off the cliff.

His arms are stretched out wide for a second, rotating in circles before he pulls them into his chest just before he hits the water. His body slices through the surface, straight as an arrow. He lands feet first and I hold my breath, my heart racing as I wait for him to surface.

His head soon pops out of the water, and he lets out another cry of victory before wiping his face and grinning up at me.

"Come on, girl. Show me what you've got!" He waves his arm at me to come on down, and shit, shit, shit! I don't know if I can do this.

Like hell you're climbing back down.

With a little huff, I shake my head.

"Wil-son!" he singsongs up to me. "You wanted a thrill, remember? This is your chance. It's a rush, I promise. And way healthier than taking something that doesn't belong to you."

I poke out my tongue at him. "Don't be an ass."

He laughs at me.

"I don't like heights!"

"Then this is perfect. You can overcome your fears." His expression softens, and even from this distance, I can tell if I really don't want to, he's not going to make me.

But I'll be so annoyed with myself. If I don't get my ass off this cliff, I'm gonna have to climb back down and shuffle my shamed self back to camp.

That can't happen.

It won't.

"It's okay, Blake. Just take a deep breath and trust that I'm right here. I won't let anything bad happen to you, okay? You're gonna be fine, and you're gonna love yourself for doing this."

"Okay, okay." I rub my forehead. "Just shut up for a second."

"Yes, ma'am." He gives me a little salute while I shake out my trembling fingers and pace along the edge for a second.

Do it, Blake. Just jump already.

"Okay," I call down to him. "I'm gonna do it."

"Yeah, you are."

His broad smile is so encouraging, I know I absolutely have to now. Dammit!

Sucking in a few deep breaths, I make fists with my hands and...

"Five," I whisper. "Four... Three..." I suck in another breath. "Two..." I squeak. "One!" I scream and run off the edge.

Another terrified scream punches out of me as I drop like a stone and plunge into the water. The freezing liquid assaults my senses, firing up my nose and needling my skin.

Kicking frantically, I propel myself to the surface, and as my head pops free, this feeling hits me like a blast.

I did it! I fucking did it!

This heady exhilaration fires through me as I spin in the water, seeking out Grady.

He's just behind me, grinning at me while I swim toward him and shout, "It's freezing in here!"

And I'm freaking right.

It is so cold. I feel like I've just jumped into the Arctic Circle.

Forcing my limbs to keep moving, I swim right up to Grady's side, warring between physically turning into an ice cube and the rush of adrenaline still pumping through me.

"Do you want to—" Grady's question turns to vapor, his eyes rounding as he swallows and stares down at me in the water.

I have no idea what his problem is until I glance down and notice that my string bikini has had a major malfunction.

Those two little triangles of fabric that are supposed to be covering my boobs?

Yeah, they're not covering anything important right now.

I may as well be topless.

CHAPTER 27
GRADY

Sweet Jesus, those tits are perfect.

There they are again, in all their beautiful glory. The curve of her milky white skin leading to those pink nipples... holy fuck, it's killing me. Those sweet nips are fully erect in this cold water, and I should seriously be looking away right now, but I'm fucking mesmerized.

I never should have agreed to take her camping.

I knew it was a mistake, but I ignored all the warnings, and now I'm right back where I was that night in the bathroom, unable to look away from her luscious body. That blue bikini should be illegal. I knew it the second she stepped out of the tent, but I still brought her up here.

I still coaxed her into jumping off that rock face, my idiot brain forgetting all logic.

I should have given her my rash guard. I should have—

Uh-oh.

Blake's looking at me, her gaze bright with mischief.

Trouble.

"Don't." I shake my head, warning her away from me, but she just laughs, untying her bikini top and bunching it in her fist. "Woman, you're gonna kill me."

This only makes her laugh again, the melodic sound floating right around my head.

She swims closer, her arms cutting through the water, and I quickly retreat, thrusting a wave of water at her.

It's such a dick move, brought on by a burst of panic.

It hits her square in the face, and she starts coughing and spluttering, wiping her eyes before flashing me a look that is so hella sexy, I am officially a dead man.

Wily is gonna skin me alive, then cook me over an open flame.

The smile on Blake's face when she recovers from my attack is all things dangerous, and I can't help a laugh when she shoves a wave of water right back at me.

I turn my head to dodge it, my ear filling with the cold liquid before I counterattack.

Her screams and laughter egg me on, and we battle it out, my legs kicking to keep me afloat as we drift farther out into the lake.

I don't even notice how far away the shore is until I catch a proper glimpse of Blake's face and...

Oh shit, her lips are blue.

Her jaw is trembling, her teeth clacking together as I stop splashing her and take in the fact that she's struggling to keep her limbs moving.

Fuck, she's freezing.

"We need to get you to shore." I cut through the water, reaching her quickly.

She nods, clamping her shaking jaws together. I can practically hear her teeth rattling.

"Here. Hold on to me." Grabbing her arm, I forget the fact that she's topless and pull her body against my back. She quakes against me, her body racked with cold shudders as it tries to counter the drop in temperature.

Shit, I should have been paying better attention.

I breaststroke to shore as fast as I can, my legs burning as I rush to get her warm and dry.

Why didn't I keep a better eye on her?

Uh... because she's half-naked, and you were trying not to look!

Plus, I was too caught up in the fun to notice how cold she was getting.

Fuck, fuck, fuck!

As soon as I reach the shallow water, I plant my feet and turn to wrap my arm around her waist. Her skin is covered in goose bumps, and she's shaking so badly, she can barely walk. Supporting her against me, I guide us to her quick-dry towel and wrap it around her shoulders. It's pretty small and doesn't even reach around her body.

Shit.

"You need to towel yourself dry." I rub her arms and back, working the towel over her body.

"O-o-okay." Her teeth are chattering so much, she almost doesn't get the word out. With quivering hands, she tries to pat herself dry, but she's never gonna warm up in time.

I need to get the fire going. I need to get her warm.

My brain starts running through all the first-aid courses I've sat through, and I whip off my rash guard, quickly toweling my chest before pulling her against me.

Skin on skin is the best way to warm her up. I start rubbing her back, holding her shaking body and trying to get that circulation going.

A sleeping bag. Get her into a sleeping bag.

Great idea. I can wrap her in that and hold her close until she starts to defrost. Then I'll get the fire going.

"Come on," I whisper against her wet hair, guiding her back toward the tent.

She stands beside me, shuddering and trembling as I unzip the tent and quickly open the sleeping bag she's already laid out. Unstrapping her saturated sandals, I support her weight as she steps out of them, then throw all caution to the wind.

"Can I take the rest of your bikini off?"

"Y-y-ye—" She gives up on the word and bobs her unsteady head.

Reaching for her bottoms, I turn my head away, forcing myself not to look as I pull the strings of her skimpy bikini. It lands on the ground with a wet thud.

And now she's naked. Fully naked, and I'm guiding her sexy, trembling body into the tent.

Her silky white butt cheek brushes against my arm as she crawls toward the sleeping bag.

"That's it. Lie down."

She curls into a ball, wrapping her arms around her legs, and I secure the bag around her, rubbing the outside of it as she continues to shudder and shake.

Shit. I really need to get in there with her.

Body warmth. It's the best thing I can offer.

Just do it, man! She needs you!

With a reluctant sigh, I step back out of the tent,

quickly whipping off my wet swimsuit and rushing over to my pile of clothes in the hammock. Yanking out my dry boxer briefs, I tug them on, then clamber back over the bristling pine needles and brush off the soles of my feet before crawling back into the tiny tent.

It's a two-person tent, but it's way more comfortable with only one. We take up the space pretty easily, and it's an awkward struggle to slip into the sleeping bag beside her. But I'm eventually in there, wrapping the padded material around us and pulling her against my bare chest.

Shit, she's cold.

Goose bumps ripple over my skin, but I hold her tight, squeezing her against me and willing my heat to transfer into her.

We're now two sardines, and I can already feel the warmth starting to permeate the cramped space.

"It's okay," I murmur, flattening her body against mine so that even our thighs are pressed together. "You'll get warm soon."

Pushing the sleeping bag against her back, I rub it vigorously, hoping the added friction will speed up this process.

She rests her freezing cheek against my shoulder, and slowly her jaw starts to relax. Her teeth stop chattering first, and then her torso starts to still.

The trembling that was jerking her stomach when I first slipped in beside her eases to the odd twitch, and I slow my frantic moves and just hold her still.

Thank fuck for that.

She's starting to thaw out, her frozen body heating

against mine. Her pert tits squish into my chest. Her silky thigh brushes against mine when she moves her leg and snuggles a little closer into me.

My heart rate spikes, my skin prickling with desire as the crisis is averted and I become hyperaware of all the things I've been desperately trying to avoid.

CHAPTER 28
BLAKE

Grady is so warm and solid.

His chest is like an electric blanket—all comfort and deliciousness. Despite his rock-hard muscles, there's still a softness to his skin. A solace.

The second he wrapped me up against him, I knew I was gonna be okay.

It was the weirdest thing; I didn't even feel the cold creeping over me. I was so busy caught up in that water fight that I didn't notice my insides quaking until my limbs started getting sluggish.

Then all of a sudden, it hit me.

I stopped throwing water at him and started seeking out the shoreline.

And it was miles away.

I'm not gonna make it. That was my first thought, right before my rescuer noticed that I was quickly shutting down.

Once again, Grady Newman stepped up and proved

himself. He swam me out of that water, dried me off, got naked with me. All to warm up my freezing body.

He's such a good man.

So freaking good.

I owe him so much.

This is the third time he's gotten me out of a jam, and I want to thank him.

Hugging his back, I cling to him and try to imbibe the words into his body. My cheek is pressed against his warm skin, and I close my eyes, willing him to feel my gratitude.

He's so strong and smart and capable.

I'm safe with this man.

And I don't know if I've ever felt like that before.

I mean, sure, my dad and Wily have always kept me safe, but this is different. I don't have to put on a show for Grady, because I told him all my shit, and he's still lying here keeping me warm.

He knows what a fucking wreck I am, and he still brought me to the most beautiful place in the world. He's sharing his heart and soul with me out here. He might not realize it, but I can see how much this land means to him, and he's letting me be a part of it.

I'm so overwhelmed by all the emotions rising and pulsing in my chest that I don't know what to do with them.

Part of me wants to scramble out of this sleeping bag and just run.

But that's never going to happen, because I don't know how I'm going to leave his side.

"You've stopped shaking," he whispers against my hair.

"Uh-huh." I nod, wishing he wasn't so observant. He's going to let me go in a second, and this will all be over.

But I don't want that.

I love Grady against me. He feels right. Good.

Not just in that safety, comfort way, but… now that my body's warming up, I'm starting to notice how good he feels in that sexy way.

The way that makes me want to thank him without words. I'll still be using my lips, but I won't be saying anything.

"I'll get a fire started, and we'll get you into some warm clothes. That'll help." Releasing me, he rolls onto his back, and I go with him, still not willing to let go. "Come on, Blake. I don't want you getting cold again, and I need to get this fire started."

I'll start a fire for you. I'll share some of this inferno raging in my body right now.

I wish I could say that to him, let him know just how much he affects me in all the right ways.

Tugging the sleeping back open, he exposes us to the cool air of the tent, and I know what I'm supposed to do. I'm supposed to slip off him and get my naked ass dressed. He'll no doubt be a perfect gentleman and avert his gaze while he leaves the tent in his boxer shorts and…

That's when I become fully aware of it.

I can't believe I didn't notice it before, but…

Shifting my hip, I confirm what I'm feeling and can't help my lips from twitching.

"Blake," he rasps, his voice strained as I gently grind myself against his erection.

And what an erection it is.

Holy shit, the boy is... well, he's got himself a magnum.

Unable to stop myself, I grind against it again, wanting to shift so that broad, hard length can tease the soft yearning between my legs. I'm so fucking hot for him right now, there's no way I can stop this.

He rolls onto his back, closing his eyes and gritting his jaw, and selfish bitch that I am, I roll right with him, lying over his body and nestling that impressive cock right between my legs. It's impossible not to moan as a spike of pleasure drives right through me.

"Please," he croaks. "You gotta move." It's taking so much effort for him to say those words to me, and I should seriously take pity on the guy and get off him.

So, I plant my hands on either side of his face. Straightening my arms, I stare down at him for a moment, my hair creating a curtain around us.

His brown eyes open, staring up at me. They're dark with intensity as he obviously fights this battle... that I cannot let him win.

Because he's being an idiot to deny this pull between us.

He won't let me kiss his lips. I know if I try, he'll pull away and tell me we can't, so I spin my body around before he can stop me and brush my lips along his torso, then lick a line from his belly button to the edge of his tented box briefs.

"Blake..." He breathes my name when I skim my finger into his waistband.

But he doesn't say no. He doesn't jolt away or beg me to stop.

So I pull the fabric down, exposing his length. My

eyes drink in this exquisite sight. It's so long, the soft umber skin taut, sticking up from a pocket of tight black curls. His powerful thighs flinch as I skim my fingers around the base.

"Blake..." Now he's rasping my name, and it's impossible to stop my lips from twitching.

He wants me.

It's so freaking obvious, and he needs to stop fighting this and just enjoy the ride.

Wrapping my fingers around his length, I give it a couple of delicate strokes, reveling in his croaky groans before suctioning my lips around his glistening head.

CHAPTER 29
GRADY

Holy shit.

I squeeze my eyes shut as an intense flash of something fucking awesome travels right through me. Her lips, her tongue, her...

The moan coming out of me is guttural and hoarse.

I pop my eyes open, willing myself to say what I'm supposed to: *We shouldn't. I'm not supposed to do this with you.*

But her pussy is right there, just above my face. Her knees are planted on either side of my head while her mouth works some kind of magic on my cock.

I have to tell her to stop. I really fucking have to, but... I'm too weak.

She feels so good, I can't even think straight.

Her tongue runs from the base of my dick back to my tip, and then she wraps her lips around me again and starts sucking. Stars scatter my vision and I groan, loving every second of this when I should be hating it.

I should be scrambling away, begging her to give me some space. But I can't.

I'm pretty sure my chest will cave in and I'll cease to exist if I pull my cock out of her mouth.

I haven't had anyone touch me since Teah. It's been months of drought, and I've been handling it, but this... this is too good.

I'm a selfish bastard, and I risk Wily's wrath if he ever finds out, but I cannot get off this train. I don't care if it takes me off a fucking cliff right now, I want to ride this until the end of the line.

Closing my eyes, I groan again, unable to contain myself as she sucks and licks, driving my nerves into a frenzy.

So good. So fucking good!

She whimpers, and my eyes open at the sound of appreciation. And there's her sweet pussy again. I can't help gazing up at it, open and exposed just above me. She obviously takes care to trim and keep things tidy down there. The crop of hair is shaped and short, barely covering her opening. The folds have a tempting sheen to them, and shit... she's wet for me.

I want to taste her.

I *need* to taste her.

And that's when my lips take over. They press into her inner thigh. It's so soft and silky. Skimming my fingers up either side of her leg, I round my hands over her perfect ass and give it a gentle squeeze as my lips travel north. My tongue peeks out, whispering a trail that makes her legs quiver as I work my way up to that sweet oasis. It's gleaming above me, begging for a taste, and I give in to every desire pulsing through me.

My tongue hits her clit, splaying across her sweet spot and eliciting a lengthy moan from her. I take that as permission to keep going and stroke another path from her clit to her opening.

Her mouth pops off my dick, and she lets out a breathy "Yeeees."

I smile, continuing to massage her with my tongue while she goes back to scattering stars with hers.

It's a heady rush. I've never sixty-nined in my life, and I'm wondering why the hell I haven't, because this is fucking awesome!

She tastes amazing, and the way her legs are trembling at my touch makes me even harder than I was before.

Her mouth is working me over with these piston movements that are gonna make me come, and I should probably start hunting out some tissues or—

Are you fucking kidding me?

Stop thinking and just pleasure her!

If I spurt all over this tent, we can clean it up later. Right now, I want to make sure she feels as good as I do.

Flicking my tongue down her center line, I squeeze her ass before moving my arm so I can slip a finger inside her.

She groans—a husky, sexy sound, her mouth slipping off me as I work her G-spot. She pumps me with her hand, giving me a slight reprieve from that sensation of wanting to explode in her mouth. I use the break to concentrate fully on her and play with her clit until she's mewling against my dick.

Panting breaths hit my sensitive skin as she rocks over me, then starts to whimper. "I'm coming. I'm coming."

Her voice rises and pitches, her pants turning into lusty wails that tell me just how much she's enjoying this.

Her body goes tense for a hot second, her pussy clamping around my finger... and then a delicious shudder runs right through as she finally gives in to the orgasm, her body vibrating over mine.

"So good," she whimpers. "So fucking good."

I grin, slipping my finger out of her and wondering what she's gonna do next.

Will she go back to sucking me off or...

Oh shit.

She's scrambling up my body with the speed of a striking snake.

"Blake," I rasp, but my voice evaporates the second she perches her sweet ass over my cock. Before I can stop her, she's guiding my rock-hard dick into a soft haven that feels so damn good I lose the ability to think, let alone warn her that we shouldn't be doing this.

CHAPTER 30
BLAKE

I know I should have asked.

I should have checked that he didn't mind me sliding myself over his very large cock. My inner walls stretched to accommodate him, this delicious, hot mix of pain and pleasure firing through me as I lowered myself to his hilt.

Oh damn, he feels so good.

My body was working on instinct, you see. I honestly don't think I could have stopped this. The physical drive pulsing through me took over, and I had to have him. I needed him inside me, piercing my most intimate self.

I've never experienced anyone this size before, and he's stretching me to my limit, but I am pumping him like I'll die if I don't.

I'm not facing him, so I have no idea if this is as good for him as it is for me, and I really should check.

I'm being a selfish bitch right now.

Grady grunts, the sound sending a burst of pleasure right through me. When his hands land on my hips, squeezing like he's only just in control, I can't help a triumphant grin.

Yes! He is so into this!

"Protection," he rasps, and I glance over my shoulder, quickly reading his dazed yet worried expression. "I'm not wearing anything."

"I'm on the pill." I puff and pant, riding him with short, fast jerks before slowing my pace and enjoying a few long, smooth strokes. "I'm clean," I throw in, just to assure him that he really doesn't have to worry.

I got tested before I left Chicago and haven't been with anyone else since.

"Me too." He groans, and I look back once more, watching his head tip back as he finally lets go and gives in to this.

Yes. We've been holding this on lockdown ever since we saw each other in that bathroom. And now, finally, we're getting that release we so desperately need.

Leaning forward, I rest my hands on his impressive thighs and pump his cock like a piston. I'm so wet, it's a smooth, slippery, mind-blowing ride.

My boobs are bouncing, the undulating rhythm adding a new layer of appeal. It's impossible not to moan, whimper, squeak, and make a myriad of other embarrassing noises as I lose myself in this man. He's all-consuming, my insides turning to liquid fire when his fingers trail down to my calves. He squeezes, explores, tantalizes with each soft brush, the perfect contrast to his powerful cock slicing into me, creating an entirely new and heady rush.

Another orgasm starts to build inside me and I run

with it, chasing that high as I lean back and sink right down on him.

His hands shoot back to my hips and he sits up, guiding my movements but still letting me be in charge. I've set the pace, and he's going with it.

His panting breaths hit my shoulder, his fingers digging into my skin.

He feels so amazing, I can't control this swell of power inside me. I come all over again, more erotic wails punching out of me as I surrender to this sensation.

He's so good. He's so, so, soooooo good.

I ride the wave of pleasure, still pumping him, my insides clenching around his dick and causing sounds to shoot out of him. Sounds that make me feel like a goddess. Sounds that warn me he'll be firing off any second now.

"Do you want me to..." He puffs. "Pull..." He groans. "Out?"

"No way," I quickly tell him, squeezing my breasts as I bounce on top of him.

His arms thread around me as he presses his lips into my back and lets out this guttural groan. I reach for his hands, guiding them to my boobs, and enjoy his squeezes as he holds on and rides to the end.

His grip on me tightens just before he lets out another grunt, then breathes a low, uncontrolled moan across my skin.

I can feel him coming inside me, and I match his noises with another keening wail that hopefully tells him just how amazing this feels.

He clings to me, his arms trembling just a little as he

slowly floats back to earth. His energy swirls around me. It's like he's high and unable to do anything but hold me until his body comes back online. I get it. I think I'm high too. High on dopamine and oxytocin.

Oh my fucking life, this is incredible.

My heart is still galloping like a spooked horse, and I'm pretty sure I'll never be able to walk again, but seriously... walking is so overrated, right?

This unchecked giggle rumbles inside me, rising up my throat and popping out into the air.

Finally recovered, Grady sags back down behind me with a heavy sigh. His hands slip off my boobs, and I feel instantly bereft of his hold on me.

Looking back over my shoulder, I smile at him, about to turn around and snuggle against him when I notice his expression.

He's looking kind of dark, staring at the side of the tent, his lips turning into a frown.

"What?" I whisper.

His jaw clenches as his expression crumples with what I think might be shame.

"We shouldn't have done that," he mutters.

He almost looks sick, and now I feel like total shit.

Anger spikes first—irritation that he's wanting to ruin this perfectly mind-blowing encounter—but then it's followed by a searing disappointment.

I want him to be celebrating with me, snuggling against me, securing me in his embrace and brushing his lips across my forehead.

But instead, he can't even look at me.

It hurts, bruises, maims.

And I don't know how to react.

All I can think to do is rise off him, ignoring the juices flowing down my leg as I scramble out of the tent fully naked and murder the soles of my feet as I head back to the freezing-cold lake to wash myself off.

CHAPTER 31
GRADY

Shit.

"Blake." I lamely call her name, but she doesn't stop.

I watch her lily-white ass crawl out of the tent, then drop my head back on the hard ground.

"Ouch," I grit out, rubbing the back of my scalp but knowing I deserve the pain.

I just betrayed one of my best friends.

I had mindless... mind-blowing... totally epic... sex with his sister.

He'll never forgive me for this.

Fuck!

Why couldn't I just control myself?

Because you've wanted her since the second you saw her naked.

And it was worth it, man. That was awesome!

It doesn't matter if it was awesome. It shouldn't have happened, and now I've gone and pissed her off by saying that.

Why did I have to open my mouth?

I couldn't have just quietly held on to my guilt for a little minute longer?

Instead, I had to say that shit while I was still inside her.

Shit, I'm in love with her pussy.

That felt so fucking good, I'm still struggling to think straight.

It's not until I hear a splash of water outside that I jerk up, pulled from my internal wailing by a warning alarm.

Is she getting back into that freezing-cold lake?

Wrestling my boxers back up, I ignore the sticky mess and scramble out of the tent, catching my back on the zipper and scratching my skin as I stand up too fast.

"Ow, shit," I mutter, quickly searching for her.

She's by the lake, ankle-deep in the water and splashing herself, cleaning up her inner thighs and looking like a goddess in the afternoon sunlight.

She's so beautiful.

I love her shape. Her curves. She's all smooth lines, her petite edges carved from alabaster.

Alabaster?

Seriously, dude. Pull yourself together!

Closing my eyes, I spin away from her and head to my pile of clothes from earlier today, wrestling them back on.

I can't think right now. I just have to do.

Shifting into practical mode, I try to rescue myself from the maelstrom that wants to wreak havoc on my brain, but it's an impossible task.

Lighting a fire does nothing to still the thoughts whipping through me.

I slept with Wily's sister.

No, I didn't. I just... screwed her. There was nothing

romantic about that encounter. It was horny and lusty. We may as well have been making a porn movie!

It wasn't that bad. You pleasured each other.

But I've... never done something like that before.

I'm all about the romance, the intimacy. I've never just had sex.

Until now.

Until that vixen brought out a side of me that I couldn't control.

I don't like it.

Okay, maybe I do, just a little bit.

Because it's everything Teah and I weren't.

What I just experienced in that tent was wild and unchecked. It was pure abandon, and I've never felt a rush like it.

I shouldn't be regretting that shit, but... I can't help it.

She's Wily's sister!

His baby sister!

The one he adores and would protect with his life.

Hearing a rustle behind me, I glance over my shoulder in time to see Blake picking her way back to the tent. She's on tiptoes, avoiding sharp rocks, her arms stretched wide to keep herself balanced. She's still totally naked, and my body responds to her on instinct. A flush of molten desire flows right through me, and I have to force myself to turn away, to focus back on the small flame I'm trying to coax.

Leaning forward, I gently blow on the fire. It moves and shifts under my soft commands and starts to catch on the rest of the kindling.

Blake is obviously watching me, I can sense it, but I

refuse to look and end up sagging with relief when she crawls back into the tent.

I hear her wrestling to get dressed with little grunts and muttered curses.

I get it. Dressing inside a space that small can be frustrating, but I know that's not what's really bothering her.

We should probably talk about it, but I don't know what to say.

All I know is that it can't happen again, and I have to show a lot more self-control. I'm not here to screw around with her. I'm here to help her find peace, and shoving my dick inside her is not going to do that.

Fuck. I'm such a selfish prick.

Scrubbing a hand down my face, I stare at the flames and promise myself to do better.

I have to. Because she deserves better. And so does Wily.

CHAPTER 32
BLAKE

So that burning disappointment beat out the anger. I really wish I could have just stayed mad, but after cursing up a storm wrestling my clothes back on, I was all worn out and just had to sit there in the tent, huffing and then staring down at the spot where Grady's ass had been.

I brush my fingers over it, lamenting his post-sex reaction.

Shit.

He wasn't as into it as me.

He didn't want it.

I forced myself on him, and now I feel like a dirty... I don't know... whore?

Fuck, I don't know what I am.

Trouble.

You're trouble.

And Grady deserves better than that.

Closing my eyes, I rest my head in my hands with a groan and just stay like that for I don't know how long. I wonder if I can just curl up and hide away from him for the rest of the night.

But my stomach is starting to grumble. I have no idea what time it is, but surely I deserve a snack after that water fight and sexy workout, right?

Cautiously crawling out of the tent, I spot Grady knee-deep in the lake. He's got some kind of fishing line thing dangling from his hand, and I watch in fascination as he waits, statue still in the water before doing a quick flick and pulling up a wriggling fish.

Holy shit, Wily's right—he's Bear freaking Grylls!

Carrying the fish back to the shoreline, he gathers up another one he's caught and glances up, going still when he spots me.

I swallow, rising to my feet and trying to play it cool. "So, I guess we're having fish for dinner?"

"Yeah." He eyes me up for a second before tipping his head. "Come on, I'll show you how to gut it."

Sounds gross, and my nose wrinkles in protest. But curiosity gets the better of me and I head to his side, watching as he talks me through how to gut the fish. He does the first one, then makes me do the second. I'm right, it's totally gross. Fish are slimy, and they smell.

But there's also this cool sense of achievement that comes from prepping my own dinner, and forty minutes later, when I'm picking bits of cooked white fish off the bone, I can't help smiling.

Grady taught me how to do all this, and I guess it was kind of like a peace offering. We won't talk about the sex again. I can sense it. We've just put it behind us and moved on. I'm guessing, in his mind, that he never wants it to happen again.

That hurts, because it was so good.

It felt pretty damn right to me, and I hate that it didn't to him.

Part of me wonders what I did wrong… other than not getting his full consent.

Yeah, that really was an assy move. I should have been more respectful, and I want to apologize. But if I raise it now, things will get all awkward between us again and… Ugh!

"Wanna play chess after dinner?" Grady asks.

I glance away from the flickering flames and stare across the fire at him. I still can't believe he packed a travel-sized chess set, but apparently, he takes it every time he goes camping.

"You know how to play?"

I nod. "Dad wanted me to join the chess club in middle school."

"Chess club?"

With a half-hearted shrug, I sigh. "What Daddy wanted, Blakey did."

He stares at me for a long beat, like he's taking the time to sense everything I'm not saying. His lips pull into a thoughtful pout as he swipes his fingers through the air. "We don't have to play if you don't like the game."

"Nah, it'll be my pleasure to kick your ass." My lips twitch as I suck another piece of fish out of my fingers.

His laughter is a joyous, surprising sound, booming in our quiet space and making me grin. "Oh, you're going down, girl."

"Bring it on, Newman." My voice is dry as I smirk across the flames at him.

His white teeth flash at me, his smile all things gorgeous.

Dipping my gaze, I focus back on my fish and how it's the most delicious seafood I've ever tasted.

Not that it's seafood.

Lake food.

It's the most delicious lake food I've ever had.

The thought makes me smile as I gaze around our little camping spot. The sun has pretty much set, the sky a very dark blue. It's the most amazing color, and I bet the stars tonight are going to be awe-inspiring.

"You done?" Grady stands up, walking over to me to dispose of the waste. He tells me about how we have to bury it away from our camp because of the wildlife. I trail after his flashlight beam and watch him work, then walk back to the camp with him.

He's a good teacher, and I'm picking everything up pretty fast.

I like the way he talks and moves.

I love the sound of his voice, so easy and soothing.

And his hands. I love the way they pick up chess pieces and move them around the board.

We play by lantern light, the soft beam casting shadows across our faces.

He's beautiful in all lights, and I find my gaze tracking toward him constantly. It's getting harder and harder to play it cool. The sounds of our sexy session keep popping into my brain, doused by the cold reality of his guilt afterward.

It makes playing chess a challenge, and he ends up winning.

"Checkmate." His lips quirk into a smile.

I gaze down at the magnetic board, seeing he's right and that I've got no way to outsmart him. My lips work to the side, and although it tastes like acid to say it, I force out the words I was trained to respond with "Congratulations. Good game."

I stretch out my hand to shake his, and the second his fingers curl around mine, my insides start yearning all over again.

"You really made me work for it." He seems impressed. "I'm looking forward to a rematch."

"So you can lose?"

"So I can beat you faster." He winks.

I laugh and shake my head. "Not gonna happen. I was distracted."

"Oh yeah?" He starts packing away the mini chess pieces. "Everything okay?"

Not really.

I let out a soft snort that hopefully conveys what I can't say.

He stills, his eyes tracking back to me. His shadowed gaze is so intense, I can't hold it.

Dipping my chin, I don't want to look into those eyes and figure out what he's thinking.

I don't want to know that he means more to me than I mean to him.

Or that—

"I had a really amazing day," he murmurs.

"You sure you enjoyed it?" I can't help the soft touch of skepticism tainting my words.

"Blake," he whispers, reaching for my hand and brushing his thumb over my knuckles. "Of course I did. I enjoyed *all* of it. Every second."

My eyes jump up to lock with his.

He means it. He actually means it.

"But you regret some," I have to whisper, because what's the point of hiding from the truth?

I'm stoked that he liked it; that part does ease the burning disappointment that's been eating at me. But it doesn't change the fact that he wished it hadn't happened.

His expression crumples, confirming what I already know. "You're Wily's little sister." He silently beseeches me to get it. "He'll kill me."

"He's my brother, not my boss." I sigh, whipping my hand out of his grasp.

Frustration bubbles up inside me, and I have to clamp my teeth together.

I don't want to get into a fight with him.

I'm so sick of tension and angst. I just want to feel calm and warm... the way I did when he held me.

Before I went and ruined it by jumping him.

You didn't ruin anything. That was amazing!

But the aftermath has been anything but.

Closing my eyes, I force myself to play it cool. I'm good at that, right? Saying and doing exactly what people need me to?

I muster a calming breath. "I get it, okay? I know you don't want to cross that line, and I'm sorry that I made you."

"I could have stopped you." Grady's voice is all rough and sexy, this soft growl that makes my insides twist with longing. "I didn't want you to stop. Even though it shouldn't have happened."

"Yeah." I nod, forcing my eyes back open and facing him.

His expression is kind of pained, still etched with remorse, and I really need him to stop feeling so guilty about this.

"Let's just... forget it ever happened, okay?" It's so freaking hard saying that. Just about as challenging as forcing a smile and putting on a cheerful tone. "Thanks for an amazing day, Grady. I'm really glad I'm doing this with you."

Keeping my smile in place, I turn back to the tent, grateful that I brushed my teeth right after dinner. Now I can just crawl right into that sleeping bag and try to get some sleep.

After all that's gone down today, it'll no doubt be an impossible task.

And I'm so right about that.

CHAPTER 33
GRADY

I couldn't sleep.

How the hell was I supposed to?

It wasn't that my hammock was uncomfortable. It wasn't that I was too cold or that mosquitoes were attacking me.

I was prepared, so none of that shit happened. And any other night, I probably would have slept like a log.

But I couldn't switch my mind off.

All I could think about was the fact that Blake was in that tent mere feet away from me.

All I could remember was exactly what went down in that tent.

I relived every second of it, over and over. Then my mind would travel to the rest of the day, and she consumed me as I pictured her jumping off those rocks, then splashing in the water. I heard her laughter and watched her excited face when she pointed out that squirrel or made us stop walking so she could hear the woodpecker in the distance.

Damn, she took over every corner of my brain. I'd gazed up through the trees, glimpsing the twinkling stars and willing myself to go to sleep.

I think I managed a couple hours just before dawn, but I woke up groggy, the sound of rustling brush alerting me to the fact that Blake was up and relieving herself behind a tree nearby.

Waiting until I knew she was decent, I got myself up and did the same, trekking a good minute or so away so she didn't have to hear me pee.

By the time I got back, she was up and dressed, stuffing the sleeping bag into the pouch and obviously getting ready to move on. I'd shared the itinerary with her, and she was clearly set on sticking to that plan.

Good.

Walking is just what we both need.

While she repacked, I got the packs down from their perch and unearthed the overnight oats, sprinkling a few raisins on the top plus a drizzle of honey. I always keep those mini ones you get in hotels, and my dad and Emma collect them for me too. Licking the last of the honey out of the plastic wrapper, I stow my trash in the side pouch of my bag before holding out a plastic bowl and spoon to Blake.

"Here you go." I clear the morning croak out of my throat and smile at her. "Breakfast of champions."

She gives the food a dubious frown, stirring in the fruit and honey before giving it a tentative taste.

"Hm. Not bad," she murmurs, scooping in a bigger mouthful.

"Slow-release carbs. They'll keep us going, especially since the first part of today's trail has an incline."

She looks over her shoulder at the direction I'm pointing, then turns to face the water. "We can't just stay here?"

"Well, we can." I nod, disappointed. "I mean, I planned a loop for us to take over the five days, but if you want, we can just do some day hikes here and back again."

I won't get to show you some of my favorite spots, but maybe that's a good thing. It's not like you're my girlfriend and I'm trying to share a massive part of my life with you.

I remind myself, yet again, that I'm doing this for her. So if she wants to set up camp here, then—

"No, it's okay. You're right. Sticking to the loop will be fun. I don't want to mess up your planning."

"I can be flexible." I watch her carefully, making sure she's not just saying this to appease me. But her blue gaze brushes over mine and she gives me an honest-looking smile.

"I'm gonna miss this beautiful spot, but I'm also excited about seeing what else you wanna show me."

"There's plenty more beauty to come," I promise her.

Her smile grows, and I take a mental snapshot before dipping my chin and begging my libido to calm the fuck down.

The sound of her erotic moans dance in my brain, her undulating ass as she rose and sank on my cock yesterday. Fuck, that was hot.

My dick twitches just thinking about it, and I shovel down the last of my oats, willing my brain to behave its damn self.

"Let's get packed up and go," I end up snapping as I rise from my spot and stalk around the fire.

I made sure it was fully out last night and didn't bother reviving it this morning. Yes, it's cold, but we're gonna be moving soon, and that will get our blood flowing. This spot is kind of sheltered, the sun hidden behind a bank of trees. But as soon as we reach the top of the ridge, we'll be hiking under clear blue skies and heating up fast.

Without a word, I take our bowls to the lake and clean them off. Blake follows me, her delicious scent pure torture. Clenching my jaw, I keep fighting my battle and hand her the dishes for drying. She does it, and then I'm teaching her how to pack away the tent, talking her through it while I roll up my hammock. I have to help her with the final folding, but as usual, she's picked things up faster than I thought she would.

Her instincts are spot-on, and I love that about her.

You love a lot about her.

Don't remind me!

"You good?" I adjust the belt around my waist and check that hers is sitting right before daring a look at her face.

She nods, her expression closed. Blank.

It makes my insides jittery, and I'm really missing the playful, mischievous girl that lurks beneath the surface, waiting to bounce out and surprise me without warning.

"Okay, well, uh..." I point at the trail ahead and start walking.

The silence is fucking killing me. I can't go the whole day like this. Despite my grumpy demeanor, I force myself to talk, to ask, to peel back the layers keeping her trapped in this "I have to be perfect" world.

She reluctantly tells me a few stories from her childhood, then starts to relax and open up, filling our morning hike with tales about Wily and her growing up together, the pranks they'd pull on their cousins, the dares they'd give each other to do.

She fractured her arm when she tried to learn skateboarding, then got told off by her parents for being so reckless.

"My talents lie in the classroom, apparently," she muttered before continuing on about all the clubs and student councils she's been a part of.

Geez, she was pretty damn busy in high school. It still surprises me that she didn't lose her head then. But under the watchful gaze of her parents, she probably didn't even think to get a little crazy.

"Every Friday night was football, of course." I can practically hear her eye roll and spin to catch the tail end of it.

"You don't like football?"

"Of course I like it." She flicks her hands up. "I'm a Wilson, so I have to be obsessed with it. Didn't you know?"

I snicker and shake my head. "I'm pretty sure your dad has never missed one Cougars game."

"I assure you, he hasn't. There was one time Mom had to get her appendix out—emergency surgery—and Dad watched the game on his phone. Honestly, he's a lost cause."

"I take it you're thoroughly over the sport."

"I was never really into it, to be honest. If I'm gonna spend a few hours watching something, I want it to be a movie or..." She stretches her arm wide, indicating the vista on our right.

We reached the top of the ridge about an hour ago and have been hiking west. The trail's pretty flat and easy. It's a nice reprieve after that climb we puffed our way through. Blake kept on telling stories, though, stopping for breaks and sips of water before forcing her body to keep going.

She'll be aching tonight, but I know she can handle it. She's not some delicate petal.

I pause to study her smile, stoked by how much she's loving this view. She really appreciates it, and that means so much to me. I don't even understand why. I guess it's just nice to be with someone who totally gets it.

My insides simmer and squirm, so I look away from her, drinking in the stunning vista. "My dad loves this spot."

Blake turns to watch me, her nose wrinkling as she shades her eyes from the sun. "You and your dad seem close."

"Yep." I nod. "We're real tight."

"What about your mom?"

I pause, trying to figure out what I'm supposed to say. I end up expelling a sigh, and she nods.

"So it's like that." She saunters toward me, her hiking boots clomping along the dirt. "Come on, then. Spill the tea, baby."

With a soft snicker, I'm about to shake my head, but she gives me this arched-brow look that says it all: *I just spent the last two hours spilling my family history. It's your turn, buddy.*

And so I do.

I tell her about Dad's indiscretion and Mom's hardline over the whole thing.

I tell her about the rift between my brother and the relationship I'm trying to maintain with my half-brothers.

I tell her about Dad's girlfriend and how much I like her.

"But you only put up with your stepdad?"

I shrug. "I don't have that much to do with him. He focuses mainly on his kids, leaves Mom to focus on hers."

"Blended families always sound so tricky."

"Yeah, they are," I mumble, trying to come up with happier topics. This is such a downer. It's darkening my mood again, and just as we're walking out of the sunlight and back into the forest.

Perfect timing, right?

Opening up to her is making me feel too vulnerable. We're getting too deep, too personal. Her insightful comments are wearing away at my resolve like sandpaper. It's thinning my protective exterior, making her more than just a sexy hiking buddy. I mean, of course she's more than that, but do I honestly want to become good friends with this girl? Do I want to confide in her?

Hell no! That'll only make this a thousand times harder!

Gritting my teeth, I pick up my pace, desperate to create a little more distance. Slamming my feet down with purpose, I glance over my shoulder to check she's still following me and completely miss the broken tree branch that's poking out onto the trail.

"Ah! Fuck!" I can't help shouting, agitation firing through me at the hot pain lancing my forearm.

"Are you okay?" Blake starts running; I can hear her crashing down the trail.

Quickly moving, I push the branch out of her way so she doesn't get jabbed, too, before slapping my hand over the wound.

"What happened?" Her skin is pale, her eyes large with worry.

"Branch just got me," I grit out. "No big deal."

"Well, let me look." She reaches for my wrist, holding it steady and trying to move my other hand.

"It's fine. I can deal with it."

"At least let me help." She unbuckles her pack, dropping it at her feet and rummaging around for the first-aid kit. I gave it to her after our *you can't carry all the weight* argument.

Pulling it free, she rips it open and starts plucking through it, clearly having no idea what she's doing.

"Give it to me," I growl, yanking the small red bag out of her hands.

"You don't have to be a dick about it," she grumbles. "Just tell me what you need, and I'll pass it to you."

"I've got it." I crouch down, placing the bag on the ground and picking out the things I need.

"Can I hold that for you?" She steps close, her thigh brushing my shoulder as she leans down to steady my arm.

Shit, she smells so good.

This is dangerous.

She's too close. Her leg is pressing against my arm. I can't concentrate when she's this near.

Fuck. I'm losing my mind around this woman!

What is happening to me?

"I'm good, Blake. Just give me some space."

"But it looks sore." She hisses, studying the ragged wound.

It's really not that bad, just a surface scratch, but I still need to sterilize it and maybe just wrap it until we get to our campsite.

"Here. Let me." Taking the alcohol wipe off me, she rips open the packet and starts wiping down my wound.

It burns and stings, and now her hair is tickling my face as she leans over me.

All I want to do is fist those luscious curls and swivel her to face me. I want to press my mouth against hers, drinking her in, kissing her until we both can't breathe.

"I got it!" I snap, my tortured brain instantly regretting my harsh tone.

Blake steps back, frowning down at me. "I'm trying to help."

"Yeah, well you're not!"

Why am I still yelling at her? This isn't her fault.

Letting out a short huff, I'm about to apologize when she growls, bunching her fists and snarling at me. "Fine! You grumpy asshole! Look after your own fucking injury, then!"

Snatching her pack, she wrestles it back onto her shoulders, making a right mess of the straps and ties.

With short screeches and snappy grunts, she soon has it hitched onto her back, her face red from exertion and her eyes bright with two words: *Shut up!*

I don't say a fucking thing.

She stomps away from me in all her fuming glory, and I race to get myself patched up. I forgo the bandage and slap a few haphazard Band-Aids over the wound so I don't smear blood everywhere. Shoving everything into the first-aid kit, I chase after her when she gets out of sight.

Shit! Doing the right thing by my teammate is fucking hard.

I don't want to betray him, but I'm not sure how much more of this I can take.

CHAPTER 34
BLAKE

This hiking trip is the worst fucking idea ever!

Why the hell did I want to come?

If I'd known Grady was going to be a grumpy ass, allergic to my touch, I would have just stayed at Football Frat.

And put up with Wily and Satch's disappointment? Not to mention the plethora of answers they want over your college education.

"Grrr!" I stomp my foot, my anger rising when I hear Grady coming up behind me.

Screw him. I am not talking to him for the rest of the day.

He can take his fucking itinerary and shove it up his ass!

I hope his arm's okay.

Shit, if anything happens to him out here and I have to be in charge... yeah, I'm not gonna manage that. I love this forest so much, and I see how instinctual it would be to survive out here. Everything he's taught me so far has been very natural and common sense-ish. But if he got badly injured and I had to take the lead?

My pace slows just thinking about it, and I move to the edge of the trail, letting him pass me.

"You good?" he murmurs, lightly touching my elbow.

I ease away from his touch, refusing to look at him.

He holds his place, eyeing me for a beat until he figures out that I am not saying a damn word. His sigh tells me so.

"We'll stop for lunch soon. There's a clearing up ahead."

I don't respond, standing my ground until he's moved off and I can just follow right behind him.

Okay, so maybe I'm dampening the mood a little, but he yelled at me first. I was trying to be nice, and it pissed him off, so I'll ice him out and see what that does to his mood.

I'm just being logical, right?

Anger spikes through me again, knotting my stomach and stealing my hunger.

When we sit down to eat and he passes me a bag of veggie sticks, I glare up at him, silently indicating that I'm not hungry.

"You gotta eat. You need to keep your energy up."

With an irritated huff, I snatch the food off him and force it down.

He munches on some cheese and crackers, and then we silently do a swap before he hands me a stick of jerky to finish up with.

I shake my head, my nose wrinkling at the disgusting-looking piece of dehydrated meat.

"It's protein. You need it." He waggles it up and down.

"Take the jerky, Blake." When I don't move, he grabs my hand and slaps the stick into my palm. "Fine. Eat it as you walk."

Ugh, this is shit!

I cannot do this anymore. Yes, it's been less than thirty-six hours, but I don't care. He's being a dick! And I'm not spending my spring break in this vortex of irritation.

"I want to go."

He pauses mid-chew, studying me carefully before finishing his mouthful. "Go where? Back to Football Frat?"

I nod, one decisive movement as I pull my shoulders back and lift my chin. "I'm not staying here with your grumpy ass anymore. I have better ways to spend my time."

My voice is so short and snippy. Ugh. I sound like my mother when she's pissed off with the world.

Wincing, I keep my eyes averted, even when he lets out a heavy sigh.

Although my head is angled away from him, I can sense him running a hand down his face. After a long, painful beat, he finally murmurs, "There's this... spectacular rock face I wanted to show you. It's one of the highlights."

I sniff, my insides jumping at the idea. If he thinks that's a highlight, what has everything else been before this?

Spectacular.

Who the hell uses that word?

Shit, it must be so freaking pretty.

Clenching my teeth, I stay statue still when he lays

out the rest of the plan. "Let me at least show you that. Then we'll cut through the forest and get a few hours in before we lose the light. It'll just be one more night, and then I'll take you home in the morning, okay?"

With a thick swallow, I bob my head again, desperately trying to ignore the burn of discomfort spreading through my chest.

He's giving me what I asked for.

I should be feeling elated. Not like this. Most definitely not like this.

CHAPTER 35
GRADY

Well, I've gone and fucked this up, haven't I?

I completely failed her.

And all because she's too damn sexy and hard to be around.

I'm a selfish asshole. Who's trying to do right by my friend... and hurting his sister in the process. No matter what I do, I can't win.

Glancing over my shoulder, I check that she's still following only a few paces behind me.

She is, her face so fucking beautiful in this early-afternoon sunlight. The dappled shadows dance across her skin, the points the light is touching giving her an ethereal glow.

Spinning back around before she can catch me staring, I don't say a word, quietly leading her up to the lookout point I know she's going to love.

She seems to really gel with the nature out here, which is why it sucks that she wants to leave.

The thing is, I don't think she wants to leave. She just wants to get away from me.

Because you're being a grumpy asshole!

Shit!

Running a hand down my face, I berate myself some more, then start mapping out how I'm gonna get her back to civilization.

Checking the time, I break down the hours we have until sunset. If we spend a half hour or so at one of my favorite views in the world, then we can head back down the hillside and reach the bottom of the valley just before dark. We might be pitching her tent at dusk, but I've got two headlamps. I don't want to be hiking in the dark, so we'll have to push to get to the place I'm thinking of.

Wrestling the GPS out of the side pouch, I check the topographical map and work out the quickest route.

"What are you doing?" she asks, nearly bumping into me when I stop.

"Just planning out the rest of today," I mumble.

She sighs and goes around me, walking ahead on the trail. I let her go because there are no intersections. This path leads straight to the lookout point.

Giving her some space, I figure out the rest of our plans while she stomps ahead in obvious frustration.

Ignoring the sizzle of whatever the fuck I'm feeling, I figure if we camp in the valley tonight, then we can hike out first thing and reach the parking lot by the afternoon. I'm looking at the most direct route there is. It's not as pretty, and there's a steep climb in the middle, but she wants to go back, right? And I'll get her there the fastest way possible.

Huffing, I shove the GPS away, feeling like shit.

I don't want to go!

But we obviously can't stay here together, and I can't send her off on her own, so it looks like my spring break has been thoroughly shat on, and I've only got myself to blame.

Because I couldn't say no to her sweet ass, and now I'm smothered in guilt and longing and...

FUCK!

"Holy shit!" Blake's voice rises from in front of me, and although it doesn't sound like she's distressed, I pick up my pace anyway.

Breaking into a jog, I negotiate the trail with ease and pop out onto the huge slab of rock that juts out from the side of the mountain and overlooks a stunning view of the valley below and the mountains stretching out as far as we can see.

The landscape cascades down to a river that winds its way through the northern valley. It's breathtaking. Wildflowers are starting to pepper the hills in the near distance, and snow is capping the mountain peaks beyond.

"This is so beautiful," Blake murmurs in obvious wonder while snapping a bunch of photos on her phone.

I love how in awe she is.

I love how much she appreciates this.

My heart swells and pulses—a mixture of pain and desire and rage at how unfair it is that I'm finally starting to get over Teah... and the girl who's helping make that happen is the one I'm not allowed to have.

Why does she have to be Wily's sister?

Why can't she just be some random girl I met in a drugstore or something?

A random girl you helped after she got busted for shoplifting.

I close my eyes, not wanting to think about that. She said she'd never do it again. I think that scare was the exact kick start she needed. And this hike. This week was supposed to be the next step in her journey.

And you went and fucked it up.

Dammit.

Clenching my jaw, I internally argue that she started it, but that's no excuse. I could have stopped her at any second, but I gave in to temptation, and we had each other like the consequences didn't matter.

Just stop thinking about it!

A growl rumbles in my chest and I shake my head, begging myself to snap out of this angsty mood.

Look at the view. Just enjoy the view!

Unclipping my pack, I slip it off my shoulders and walk closer to the edge. Gazing down at the river below us, I go still, the sounds of nature starting to amplify as I take a moment to listen.

I love this place so much.

It fills my soul every time.

The thump of Blake's pack hitting the ground makes me jolt, and I glance over my shoulder, the view I've been admiring taking on a different edge when she steps into it. Her blonde ponytail is dancing in the breeze, those reckless curls flicking across her shoulders as she sighs and smiles at the landscape.

Wow.

She's just so… wow.

I can't breathe as she moves in beside me, planting her feet next to mine and looking content.

Don't say anything. Don't ruin this moment for her.

Watching her out of the corner of my eye, I slip my hands into my pockets and try to keep my raging emotions on lockdown. She's so close I can smell her again, that sweet citrusy scent blending with hints of sweat and pine and…

My insides clench as another wave of desire flushes through me.

I take a quick step sideways, creating a wider gap between us.

She glances at me, her eyebrows dipping in confusion, and I hide what I was trying to do with a smile, quickly pointing at her phone.

"Do you want me to take a picture with you in it?"

She glances down at her hand, waving the device and shaking her head. "I don't want to ruin the shot."

"Are you kidding me?" I step forward, taking the phone off her before she can say any more bullshit. "You'll be enhancing the photo."

Stepping back, I snap a few shots of her admiring the view before ordering her to turn around.

She puts on that fake smile of hers and then strikes a few poses. My lips start to twitch as she gets more and more ridiculous with each one. It starts with simple peace signs and quickly escalates. Everything from Marilyn Monroe's white dress image to Betty Boop's little butt-sticking-out routine.

And the only reason I know that is because Emma's

got a poster at her place. Which will no doubt be moving into her new house with Dad, and I'll see it every time I go back to visit.

Man, they'd love Blake.

Stop it. They're never gonna meet her. They have no excuse to ever meet her!

The thoughts sour my mood, and I cut the photo shoot short.

"Yeah, got a bunch. I'm sure your family will love them." I pass her phone back and her nose wrinkles, her lips dropping into a pout at the mention of her family.

Maybe it's just dawning on her that heading back early is going to have her facing Wily and the truth that much faster.

But I'm not about to convince her otherwise; she needs to get that shit off her chest. And I need to get some distance from this woman before I do something stupid again.

My eyes trail down her lush body before I can stop them, and I'm back to picturing her naked ass perched on top of me again.

"We should go," I mutter, turning for my pack.

"No, it's so pretty. I want to stay."

"I thought you wanted to go?" I bite back before I can stop myself.

She pauses for a thick, painful beat, her eyes narrowing into a hot glare. "I only said that because you're being an ass. Are you gonna keep that up and drag me away from this stunning view before I'm ready?"

"If you wanna go back to Nolan tomorrow, we have to start hiking now or you'll end up having to suffer my company for two nights, not one. And if we want to get to the camping spot before dark, then we need to get going now." I flick my arms wide. "So, what the fuck do you want, Blake?"

"You!" she snaps. "But that's not an option now, is it?"

Her words stun me silent for a second and I just blink at her, taking in her raging expression and fiery blue gaze.

"You don't think I want it to be an option?" I huff. "You're so fucking sexy I can barely contain myself around you!"

"Then why are you fighting it so hard!" She stomps toward me, getting all up in my face. "You're ruining this for both of us with your stubborn ass and gorgeous face and hot body and—"

"It's not my body that's the problem!" My volume rises to match hers. "You're the vixen here. You're the one who's irresistible. You think it's easy for me to stand here watching you while fighting every temptation in my head?"

"Then stop fighting!"

"Oh, so you want me to betray your brother, is that it?"

"No! I want you to want me as badly as I want you!"

"I do!" I shout, snatching her face and planting my lips on hers.

It's a hungry kiss. A desperate one.

I shouldn't be doing it, but the idea of her thinking I don't want her is killing me.

She has to know.

My lips cover hers, my tongue diving into her mouth when she opens it and lets me in. Fisting my shirt, she yanks us together, her arm wrapping around my neck as our urgent kiss turns into a frantic mess.

Lifting her off the ground, my body takes over as I finally surrender to this battle and stop thinking.

My brain switches off with a definitive click, and I let my body do all the work. My hands squeeze her ass as I dip my head, changing the angle of the kiss and relishing the way her tongue slides against mine, an erotic, deep connection before she goes back to quick, desperate licks.

Her whimpers fill my chest, my heart thundering as she grinds her sweet center along my already rigid cock. I walk us to the closest tree, leaning her back against it so I can explore her luscious legs, trailing my hand down one of them before heading back to squeeze her perfect ass again. My hungry lips devour her jaw, sucking a path down to her neck. She tips her head back, giving me better access while she squeezes my shoulders and moans.

Her skin tastes like salty sweat and that citrusy stuff she puts on it. It's an erotic blend of delicious, and I can't stop. I won't stop.

"Take me. Take me right fucking here. Please." She's begging, her sweet voice knocking out my senses, her frantic fingers tugging at my shirt, making me act on impulse.

I place her on her feet, helping her yank off my clothing.

My shirt drops to the sunbaked rock, followed quickly by hers. The cute cotton bra she's wearing is blue with white daisies all over it and… it's gone.

Thrown on the ground beside our shirts. I reach for those sweet tits while she makes quick work of my pants. Peppering her face, her neck, her shoulders with kisses, I don't protest as she pulls out my cock and starts pumping it with her eager hand.

Fuck, that feels so good.

I groan against her throat, my hands gliding over her hips and into the top of her yoga pants. Pulling them down in one swift move, I yank them to her thighs, wishing I could remove them altogether. But it'll take too long to lose the hiking boots, and she's pleading again, doing my soul in with her soft whimpers.

"Please, Grady," she moans. "Please."

She spins around, resting her hands on the trunk of the tree and poking out her ass for me.

Shit, I want to face her, plunge right into her and watch her eyes glaze over, but practicality and fucking hiking boots demand this position, so I step in behind her, running my fingers between her legs and checking how wet she is.

I don't want to hurt her and... fuck, she's so wet. My fingers explore her glistening edges, dipping inside her warmth for a moment. She cries out, her nails scraping against the tree as she rests her forehead on the back of her hand.

"You want this?" I whisper, then lean forward, pressing my lips to her shoulder.

"Yes." She moans the word more than says it, and I give her what she's been waiting for.

Lining up my cock, I steady her hips, then spear her in one swift move.

Her cry of pleasure rockets right through me, and I'm blinded by every sensation traveling through my body. Her tight, wet pussy clutches me, drawing me in and demanding instant friction.

I deliver, pumping into her in fast, smooth strokes.

The energy between us demands it. This isn't some slow, languid coupling. This is all passion and heat and speed.

This is animalistic instincts.

Our basic human nature overriding all common sense.

CHAPTER 36
BLAKE

Grady's dick is a fucking work of art. I love it inside me, splitting me in half, taking over my senses with each thrust and plunge.

He feels so good, I've forgotten how to breathe.

My mouth pops open as I take each heady thrust, my body absorbing his urgent energy and spiking with pleasure.

He's moving deep and fast, almost a little rough, and I fucking love it.

"Yes," I pant. "Yes."

A white heat starts spreading through me, the flames firing from my core and spreading down my legs. I tip my hips back, taking more of him, wanting to feel his cock all the way to my center.

"Ah!" I cry out again, lightly biting the back of my hand while a cool breeze kisses my exposed skin.

Grady's hands glide up around my body, cupping my breasts and giving them a squeeze as he continues to pound into me.

My body is overrun, those flames turning to sizzling electricity.

He grunts, obviously enjoying the ride as much as I am. His puffy breaths against my shoulder are magic, and when he moves back and starts working my G-spot with his glorious cock, I'm quickly sent over the edge, orgasming with riotous wails. He plunges back into me—a deep, long thrust—stretching out this mind-bending ride.

Yes. Yes. Yes!

I want him to come inside me. I want my body to do for him what his has done for me.

Moving my hips back, I meet each of his frantic thrusts, my lips curling into a smile when I glance over my shoulder in time to see him fully let go.

His mouth pops open, his face scrunching in perfect abandon as the high takes him out. Snatching my hips, he groans, his movements turning jerky and frantic as his fingers dig into my flesh and his cock fires off inside my body.

Closing my eyes, I groan right along with him, taking the full force of his final thrust—my body vibrating with it... with him.

Leaning forward, he secures our sweaty bodies together, holding my breasts and pressing his lips to my naked shoulder. He's trembling, and I can feel his heart thundering against my back.

Finally, I sag against the tree, the electric storm running through my body starting to fade.

"Oh shit." He puffs and pants, resting his forehead between my shoulder blades. "Shit. That was... That was..."

"Don't you dare regret this," I warn him.

He goes still, holding my hips like he needs them to balance. He doesn't say anything while he catches his breath, and I close my eyes again, hating that he probably *is* regretting this.

Which is a total travesty, because that sex was amazing.

Fast and frantic and...

It was more than amazing!

I've never felt a connection like this to someone. And I don't want to go back to the way things were before he kissed me.

Gently slipping out of me, Grady gives my ass a soft pat and turns away. I shuffle around, hiking up my pants and ignoring the squelchy mess running down my inner thigh.

"Look," I snap at his back, then close my eyes with a sigh. "Grady." I soften my voice to a whisper, opening my eyes, and am relieved to see him looking at me.

He's hitched his pants but hasn't done up the fly yet. His cock is tucked back into his pants, still a little hard and tenting his boxer briefs.

I force my eyes away from it and look at his face instead. His beautiful, strong face.

He's standing there staring at me, so stoic, yet there's an obvious battle raging within him.

"Grady," I repeat. "Please don't ruin this moment. It was amazing and mind-blowing, and I wanted it." Letting out another soft sigh, I flick my hand at him. "I want you. Over and over. I want you."

Closing his eyes, he dips his chin and nods. "I want you too."

Moving toward him, I rest my hand on his chest and coax his eyes back open with a soft kiss to his chin. Cupping his cheek, I rub my thumb along his cheekbone. "I get that you don't want to hurt Wily, but we obviously can't resist each other. And I'm not ready to go back yet, so let's just have a torrid forest affair."

His hands move to my hips, resting there like that's where they belong. His brown eyes search my face, his expression skeptical when he whispers, "An affair?"

"Yes." I grin up at him. "It would be exciting, you know? I've never had an affair, but the idea of a few days of passionate, hot sex to get it out of our systems sounds pretty damn good to me."

"A fling."

"Yes. And then when we get back to Nolan, things can return to normal."

His forehead wrinkles into a frown, and I reach up to smooth the lines away.

"It's just the two of us here, Grady. No one has to know."

"I'll know."

"It'll be our little secret. Wily will never find out, and it won't hurt him because this is just a snapshot in time." I grin, beseeching him with my hopefully persuasive gaze. "Let's just give in to this and stop fighting. I like having sex with you, and you obviously like having it with me, right?"

His lips twitch as he gives me an emphatic nod.

"So let's just have each other already." Reaching up, I press my lips to his, waiting for the response I am so desperate for.

He's no doubt thinking this through, and I am going

to keep my mouth on his while he does that, because I need him to say—

“Fine,” he mumbles, his hand cupping the back of my neck as he slides his tongue into my mouth and makes my fucking day!

CHAPTER 37
GRADY

An affair. A fling. A secret romance with an expiration date.

It's not my style.

But something about it is so enticing, *because* it's not my style.

I thought Teah and I were endgame, and what a fucking disaster that turned out to be. So the idea of just giving myself over to this forest fling with Blake actually feels pretty damn good.

It means I can't think about the outside world for a second.

For the rest of this week, there is no Wily. There is no football, no school, nothing.

It's just me, Blake, and the wild.

So rather than rushing her away from this amazing view, I linger, kissing her until we're struggling to breathe, then spinning her around and pulling her back against me. We stand there, drinking in the view, and I let myself hold her the way I've been wanting to for weeks.

We end up swaying, our bodies merging with the gentle breeze as we stand in silence, letting the sounds of nature grow around us.

Damn, I could stay here forever.

But we've still got another hour or so of hiking and then setting up camp. It'd be great to do that before the darkness sets in, so I force myself to let her go.

"Come on, Bee. We've got to get moving." I reach down for our shirts while she laughs at me.

"Bee? Where did that come from?"

"I don't know." I watch her secure her bra, then slip her clothes back on before I reach for her pack and slide it up her shoulders.

"Too lazy to say my full name? One whole syllable? You're right, that is a lot of effort." She grins at me when I move around her, checking her straps are still good.

With a soft snicker, I reach for my own pack and hitch it up my shoulders. "I can keep calling you Blake or Wilson if you want me to." My waist belt closes with a click. "But I'm liking Bee for you."

Her lips curl into the sweetest smile as she whispers, "I'm liking it too."

"So, come on, then, Bee." I hold out my hand. "Let's go."

With a melodic laugh, she takes my hand, and I pull her back into the forest. The trail gets narrow pretty fast, and I have to let her go, but all that ugly tension between us has disappeared and we're now hiking along, happily playing the alphabet game, which she started.

The topic is book titles, and we're smashing through it. I love that she knows all the classics. She's obviously well-read, just like me. I don't actually love the classics, though; I prefer political thrillers, espionage, stuff like that.

"What are you into reading?" I ask after she comes up with *The Zookeeper's Wife.* We decided "the" and "a" didn't count for the game.

"Um..." I turn to watch her scratch her cheek, then blow away a curl that's tickling her. "I'll pretty much read anything. I really enjoy biographies and autobiographies."

"Yeah, me too." I nod. "Have you read Michelle Obama's?"

"Yes!" Her voice rises with enthusiasm. "That woman is freaking amazing!"

"I know, right?" I smile. "I also love *A Long Walk to Freedom.*"

"Nelson Mandela. What a legend," she agrees. "And I also enjoyed *I Am Malala.* Have you read that one?"

"No, but I've heard of it." I wince. "Makes me so fucking grateful to be born and raised where I am. I mean, sure, it sucks being a Black man in this country sometimes. But the stuff women have to face in some of those countries... Just horrific."

She goes quiet, and I turn back to glance at her, noticing her pinched expression.

"What?"

"I hate that things can suck for you. This is *your* country, and you should feel the same sense of freedom I do. It makes me feel incredibly white and rich and privileged, and I'm so sorry."

"Hey." I stop and turn to face her. "That's not your fault. You didn't choose to be born into what you are, just like I didn't choose. We have to take what we get and make the most of it. And you've never made me feel less than."

"Because you're not." Her eyebrows rise. "Holy shit, Grady, you are a million times better than me. I'm the lucky one here just to be with you. Black doesn't mean less. *Ever.*" She's so emphatic. "There are a hell of a lot more shitty white people in the world than there are any other color."

I let out a soft laugh. "You might be right about that. But look, there are just a lot of shitty people, period." I smile at her, capturing that wayward curl and tucking it behind her ear. "And I'm not better than you."

Her blue eyes look up at me, dark with intensity. "Have you ever been pulled over unfairly? Treated like a criminal when you're so obviously not?" Her face puckers with worry.

"I doubt there's a single Black man who hasn't." I watch her expression turn to one of horror. "But we deal with it, and we keep on working toward a better future, you know? It's like what Martin Luther King Jr. said. 'The arc of the moral universe is long, but it bends toward justice.' I have to believe that things will get better. That's what keeps me going on the days when I get really angry."

"It sucks," she mutters, clearly annoyed. "Things like that should never happen."

"No, they should not," I agree, reaching for her hand, gazing down at the stark contrast of our black and white skin.

I can't even tell you why, but I've always been attracted to white girls. Is that safe for me? Not always. There have been more times than I can count where a white guy has given me a look, muttered a comment under his breath or to my face. I've always done my best to ignore it. As far as I'm concerned, people are people. Skin is skin. Who gives a fuck if it's a different color?

"Come on." I give her hand a little tug. "We need to keep moving."

She follows me without complaint, and we walk in silence for a while. The birds are twittering a late-afternoon song, the volume increasing as they obviously have their daily meeting to discuss whatever it is they got up to.

I grin at the sound, picking up my pace a little. The camping spot is just up ahead, and I want to get us set up and ready before nightfall.

As soon as we reach the grove, I slip my pack off and start instructing Blake on where we should pitch the tent. She follows my orders, although she starts doing some stuff before I tell her to. So after twenty minutes, I stop acting like the boss and we just work together as a team.

She sets up the tent with relative ease, which is pretty impressive considering she's only done it once before, and I was helping her the whole time.

"Nice." I grin at her, and she smiles right back with a look of genuine pride and pleasure.

She's stoked with herself, and I know this because she pings to her feet and snaps a bunch of pictures of our little camping setup before heading into the woods.

"Just gonna find some kindling."

"Cool," I call from my spot where I'm tying up the packs. We've got everything out that we need for the night... I hope.

An hour later, the fire is set, a trail of smoke wafting

on the breeze, and I'm frying up the two fish I caught from the river.

Blake stares at the flames, her lips twitching as she watches me. "You're like Bear Grylls."

I roll my eyes but can't help laughing. "Tyrell called me Black Bear the other day. Said I'm America's version of the guy."

"Black Bear," she muses, her nose wrinkling. "I kinda love it."

I grin at her across the flames. "Gonna start calling me that now, are ya?"

She shrugs, her lips tipping up into a sexy little grin. "A bee and a bear? Sounds like a perfect pair to me."

Yeah, me too.

A wave of heat courses through me when I catch her eye and know exactly how we're gonna be spending our night.

This time, I'm gonna face her. I'm gonna study her expression as she comes. I'm gonna feel those luscious legs wrap around my hips.

If she wants that, of course.

Dude, look at her face. She's already thinking about it.

Biting my lips together, I turn the fish a little fast, willing it to cook through in record time.

I burn my tongue scarfing it down, noticing her doing the same. Watching her lick those greasy fingertips sets my body on fire in a whole new way, and I rush through the cleanup, catching her against me when we're finally done.

Her tongue is warm in my mouth, tasting minty. She's just brushed her teeth, washing away the fish and leaving her addictive tongue fresh and beautiful for me.

Fisting the back of my hair, she wraps her legs around me, squeezing her thighs and already grinding.

I manage to pull back enough to whisper, "I want to take it slow."

She frowns down at me. "Meaning?"

"I want to taste every inch of your skin." I kiss her neck as I walk us toward the tent. "I want to savor you, Bee. Let me take my time."

"Savor me," she purrs against my cheek. "Think I'm loving the sound of that."

CHAPTER 38
BLAKE

So it turns out that Grady's version of "savoring" is the most erotic, mind-blowing thing that has ever happened to me. Keeping to his word, he kissed what felt like every inch of my skin. He went down on me with slow, languid licks but pulled back just before I came, mumbling something about wanting to make it last.

It was sweet torture, and I loved every second of it.

He took his time sampling each of my breasts, sending me right to the edge with his masterful tongue, and then he stroked my pussy, inside, outside, his fingers working me until I begged him for release.

"Don't stop," I rasped. "Don't you dare stop. Let me come. Pleeeease."

His soft laughter against my neck was hot and beautiful, his mouth trailing down to my nipples, sucking one of them into his mouth while he circled my clit and finally took me right over the edge.

Scraping my nails across his shoulders, I writhed beneath his touch, my body igniting in a way it never had before. He captured my wailing moans, sucking them into his mouth while he slipped his fingers inside me, then cupped my trembling pussy.

"You want me?"

"I need you," I whispered, out of breath and ready to beg all over again.

And he took me. He slipped into me, slow and smooth, his brown eyes beautiful in the soft lantern light. I stared up at him, feeling that connection on a deeper level. He was seeing my pleasure, drinking it in, grinding into me, his rock-hard body gyrating over me. I ran my hands up and down his back, loving every inch of his body.

Tucking his hand under my knee, he encouraged me to wrap my legs around him, and I did, digging my heels into his steely ass cheeks and riding this languid wave.

I was enjoying this liquid pace, his smooth, easy strokes, and my body ignited all over again—a slow burn that built and rose, cresting over me as I whimpered and strained beneath him.

He moaned his approval, tucking his forehead against my cheek and rising right along with me. When he came, it was quiet and gentle; then he held me close, his arms wrapping under my shoulders, his lips pressing into the crook of my neck.

And that's how we stayed, locked against each other. I lightly stroked the back of his head, staring at the tent walls and reeling.

I'd never had sex like that before. It was so intimate, so tender... and it was making something in my chest glow. It was an addictive feeling—I knew that in my core. Thank God we still had three more days to go, because this man inside me, he was something special. I knew it the second we saw each other in that bathroom. The connection between us was undeniable then, and it's shifting to something entirely new now.

I don't know how I'm supposed to let him go at the end of this, so I just cling a little tighter and force myself not to spoil this perfect moment with words.

I wake the next morning, the rising sun making the walls of the tent glow. Grady's arm is still around me, heavy on my waist, and I can't help my instant smile. We're both naked, our bodies stuck together with a mixture of sweat and all the other juices we made together throughout the night.

Three times.

It was impressive, and my body definitely feels it.

But in all the good, right ways a body should feel when it's completely sated.

Determined to make the next three days count, I roll over, kissing him awake and finding out what the plan is. He mumbles it in his sleepy, morning voice, and I can't help that kick of excitement.

I love being out here in nature.

I love being with my bear.

And the next two days fly by as we hike and talk and laugh together.

We eat snacks and lunch in perfect spots, overlooking breathtaking vistas or surrounded by towering trees. He points out wildlife, and I wish for a long-range lens so I can capture the mountain lion in the distance and the bear we saw when we neared the river.

He kept me safe, and we crouched behind a boulder, watching the bear lumber along. I whispered how I'd give anything for a decent camera, and once it was safe to keep moving, we spent the next few hours talking about photography and the posters on his bedroom wall. He tells me about all the national parks he's visited, and I pine for the same.

I pine for a lot of things as we hike these woods, desperately trying to ignore the growing warning in the back of my brain.

It's nearly over.

Reality will be on you tomorrow, and there's nothing you can do to stop it.

I try to ignore the thought, but those three words keep ringing in my brain on repeat.

It's nearly over. It's nearly over.

Paradise is about to come to an end, and I'd give anything to just stay out here in the wild...

Just a bee and a bear—the perfect pair.

CHAPTER 39
GRADY

It's nearly over, and I'm trying to hide how gutted that makes me feel.

This is our last night, and I don't want to waste a second of it.

Closing my eyes, I try to absorb every touch, taste, and feel of this moment.

We're lying naked in my hammock, Blake tucked by my side, her bare body stretched out against mine as we lightly swing between two trees.

Yeah, this is heaven.

If this were a movie, a montage would be playing about now, showing off our last three days in all its splendor—laughter, wonder, sex... so much sex. We've skinny-dipped in lakes and swimming holes, we've played chess by the fire (she's beaten me three times, and we're now tied with an even number of wins—fuck, I love how smart she is). Blake has taken a million photos of nature; she can't get enough of it, and watching her awe at the simplest things is a thing of beauty. We've laughed, we've talked for hours. Set free from outside pressure, we've been able to talk about anything and everything. And she's easy to talk to. She's funny and smart. She has a wicked sense of humor, and she gets my sarcastic little quips and one-liners. She doesn't mind me talking about my love of the forest and what I want to do with my future. She walked beside me whenever the track was wide enough, asking me questions about my engineering degree and actually listening to the answers, encouraging me to pursue what I want rather than sticking to the safest bet.

She then told me how much she's always loved photography but could never pursue it because it wasn't academic enough.

"It's a hobby, and I was only allowed to fit it in when I had the time, which was never because I've been so busy doing all the other shit that only smart people do." She rolled her eyes over that one.

And now she's rolling her eyes again at me, her cute smile coming into play. Damn, I can't get enough of that smile.

Gently brushing my finger down her cheek, I grin. "You know, you've got this barely there dimple right here." I brush the spot again. "It only shows when you're doing your 'I want to be unimpressed, but I secretly think you're cute' smile."

She laughs. "That's a very specific smile."

"It's one of my favorites."

She beams up at me, biting her bottom lip and filling my chest to overflowing. It's hard to breathe around her sometimes... yet I've never felt more relaxed.

Splaying her hand over my pec, she nestles her head back on my shoulder, and we continue to swing as the world grows dark around us. We had an early dinner because we were hungry after our dip in the lake... and the sex that followed. We took each other on the shoreline—her beneath me on the edge of the water, her legs wrapped around my body as I plunged into her, sending us over the edge. I didn't want it over too fast and tried to slow things down, but it's hard with her. She's addictive and sweet, and I love her body so fucking much.

She came while I was inside her, spasming around my cock and making me follow quickly after. Her cries are still ringing in my ear, and I want to take her all over again, but I need to let her rest too. I don't want to hurt her sweet pussy. We've been doing it every chance we can get, like we know the clock is ticking on this thing and we don't want to waste a second of our time.

"I could stay out here forever," she murmurs, her lips tickling my skin as she talks against me.

"I know, right?" I glide my finger over her shoulder, painting circles on her soft, smooth skin.

Her leg inches up my thigh, her pussy pressing into me. I love lying naked with her. She fits so perfectly against me.

Shit... I don't know how I'm gonna let her go tomorrow.

"Hey, look, the first star." I try to distract myself from that melancholy feeling, not wanting to think about the fact that we'll be hiking out of here in the morning.

She looks up, gazing at the twinkling dot. We have a small window of sky above us, the trees creating a frame, and as the night sky darkens, that patch is going to be peppered with stars. It's going to be beautiful, and I wonder if we should hike back to the lake so we can get a decent view before tucking ourselves into the tent for our final night together.

Shit, I don't want to go!

I'm not ready for this to end.

As if she can sense what I'm thinking, Blake kisses a line from my pec to my neck, obviously trying to distract me.

Shuffling around, she rolls on top of me, the hammock swinging in protest.

I softly chuckle, realigning her hips so she's centered, her sweet tits pressing into my chest.

I pull the blanket up so it's covering her back and protecting her from any bugs. We smell like insect repellent, but it's worth it. She's already been bitten a few times over the past few days, and I don't want her getting any more.

"How am I going to leave this place?" she whispers, running her finger from the edge of my eye to the tip of my chin before leaning forward to kiss me.

I trail my hand up her spine, then cup the back of her head, holding her in place so I can kiss her longer, deeper... and not have to answer that question.

"I can't do it," she murmurs against my mouth. "I can't go back."

"Yes, you can." I force myself to say what she needs to hear. Holding her face, I encourage her to look at me. In the fading light, I can still make out her face, but the darkness is stealing the details. "You're strong enough to face anything. You're smart and brave... and you can do this. You can face whatever is waiting for you back in Nolan and with your parents in Denver. You can do this."

"I don't want to." Her words catch, and she sucks in a shaky breath. "I don't want to face it all. I just want to stay here with you."

My lips twitch in appreciation. It's impossible not to smile. Oh man, I want that too! These past few days have been perfect, and I don't know how I'm gonna go back either.

But one of us needs to be strong, right?

"Wily loves you, and so do your parents. Sure, they might be disappointed or annoyed, but they're going to get over it. And this is your chance to come clean and figure out what you want for *you*, not because you need to be the best at what your parents want. What do *you* want? What sets you on fire? This is your chance to pursue that, to fight for it and find out what makes you happy."

"You make me happy," she mumbles, then quickly kisses me before I can tell her that I'm not an option.

Our clock runs out tomorrow, the second we get back to Nolan.

I wish it didn't have to be that way, but I don't know if Wily will get what we've done out here. Maybe after Blake spills her news? Maybe once she's confessed all and fought to pursue what she wants... then maybe she can fight for me too.

But not yet.

This has to be what we said it would be—a short-term thing.

As her tongue glides into my mouth and our bodies start to heat with that familiar flame, I hold her tighter against me and force myself not to think beyond this hammock, our little campsite, and this forest.

Right now, there can be nothing outside this space. No person, no place, no thing.

It's just us, cocooned in this little oasis.

Blake starts to rock against me, my cock responding the way it's been doing all week, and I know what's coming.

"You sure?" I murmur between kisses.

"Yes. You want to?"

"Of course I do," I mumble against her neck. "Just want to make sure you're not too sore or anything."

"Boy, you're mine tonight, and I'm having you."

"I don't want to hurt you," I argue, sucking her shoulder and swallowing down a moan.

"You can't hurt me, Grady," she whispers before nibbling my earlobe, then rising so I can suckle her sweet tits the way she likes me to.

The hammock rocks and sways, adding a new layer to our lovemaking that we haven't experienced yet. It's kind of funny, and we end up laughing when she goes to line us up and the hammock starts swinging wildly. Her tits bounce, and I hold them steady until she sinks onto me and I lose the ability to do anything but grip her hips and let her ride me.

We find our rhythm easily, and our grunts and cries of pleasure are swallowed up by the darkness and the woods beyond. We are the only two people on the planet right now.

Adam and Eve. Making each other come under the stars.

My thumb teases her clit, and she slows her moves to

long, languid glides that tease my cock into a frenzy. I want to explode inside this woman, but I hold off, waiting until she's come. I love letting her go first. I love hearing those whimpers and uncontrolled cries. I love her pussy clutching me, her knees squeezing around me when she falls apart.

"I'm coming," she whimpers, bouncing on top of me. I keep working her clit, loving the way her tits gyrate in the open air. The breeze is playing with her hair, brushing it across her shoulders. "I'm coming," she squeaks, and I lightly fist the back of her hair, wrapping the loose tendrils around my fingers when she leans forward and wails against my cheek.

And just like all those other times, her sweet pussy grabs ahold of me, spasming around my cock and making my eyes roll back in my head.

Holy fuck, that feels good.

Her lips find mine and we drink from each other—two thirsty souls. Locked in a tongue tango, she continues to ride me, and I moan into her mouth, the orgasm building fast and furious. Blue fire spreads from my center to my toes and fingertips. I thrust deep, slapping my hands on her hips and pulling her down on top of me.

She envelops me, taking out every one of my senses until there is only her. Only us.

I come inside her sweet body, leaving a part of myself like I've done every other time.

And she takes it, seems to relish it, like I'm something special.

Resting her hands on my chest, I feel the quivering vibrations running through her, so I pull her down to lie against me. Her head tucks into the side of my neck, and I hold her, because that's all I can do.

There are no words, just panting breaths as we absorb each other, our thundering heartbeats blending into one rhythm.

Our rhythm.

Shit, I never want it to stop.

CHAPTER 40
BLAKE

I've just had the best time of my life, and walking out of this forest is killing me.

Grady told me this morning, as we packed up the tent for the last time, that it'd take about four hours to get back to the parking lot. He specially planned this route, knowing my lack of experience and turning what he could have probably done in two days into a five-day trek with short hikes and lots of downtime.

Shoving our love oasis (aka the hammock) back into its little bag sucked. And then I almost cried as I watched him roll up the tent.

I fought tears as we ate our overnight oats. I had to quietly sniffle my way through teeth brushing and the final checking of our gear.

I've been hiking behind him in silence ever since we walked away from last night's spot.

We made love under the stars. I gazed up at those tiny diamonds in the sky while he came inside me for the last time. I've never had so much sex in such a short space of time, and I'm sore and achy. But it's been worth it. His dick is glorious. His entire body on me, in me, around me... it's all perfect. I haven't been able to get enough of the way he feels, thinks, sounds. I love his laughter. It's deep and rich, and he isn't one to laugh at every little thing, so when he does, I know he means it... and that makes it even more special.

I've never felt this way around someone before, and the thought that it'll all be over in an hour or so kills me.

Grady's stolen my heart, and as much as I want to beg him for it back, I also want him to keep it. I'm not sure I'll ever find better.

Damn his loyalty to my brother.

Why does a stupid bro code even have to exist?

Can't we just be together, and Wily can get the fuck over himself!

I tried that argument last night, just as we were drifting off to sleep. Grady was tucked behind me, spooning me in his perfect shell, and all he said was "It has to be this way" before squeezing me tighter and kissing my naked shoulder.

He held me like that all night.

I barely got any sleep, drifting in and out while my heart mourned the loss that's coming.

"You okay?"

Glancing up, I notice Grady's stopped ahead of me. I didn't realize my pace had slowed so much. I wish I could ask him for another foot rub. If I drop to my knees and beg to just camp here for the rest of the year, would he agree to it?

Nope. Look at his face. He's set on this decision. He won't betray his friend.

I could argue that he *has* betrayed his friend, but that will contradict my reasoning for having this fling in the first place. He only agreed to it because no one would ever find out.

Forcing a smile, I nod and pick up my pace, my body complaining, like it knows this is about to end and it doesn't have to soldier on anymore.

"Just think about that hot shower or bath you're gonna take as soon as we get back." He's trying to encourage me, but his voice is lacking a cheerful edge.

He knows as well as I do that a hot shower can't be half as good as two naked bodies in a freezing-cold lake. It'll never beat stargazing and strip poker. It can't be better than disappearing into a forest and listening to a symphony of insects and birds, the rustling of leaves as the breeze blows through the trees.

Nothing can beat this.

Not a fucking hot shower.

Not easy access to hot food.

Nothing.

I feel like I'm walking out of heaven, back into a nightmare of choices and confessions.

Keep walking. You have to keep moving forward.

Lifting one concrete foot after the other, I trek after Grady until we've nearly reached the parking lot.

I can tell we're almost there because his steps have slowed too. He's shuffling along like a tortoise, and I'm soon right behind him, snatching his hand and gripping it like my life will be in jeopardy if I let go.

Through the trees, I spot the edge of a red Jeep and quickly yank on Grady's hand. He stutters to a stop, spinning to face me.

He silently asks me what's wrong, and my throat swells, turning my words into a raspy whisper. "Thank you."

"For what?"

My eyes fill with tears, a smile curling my lips as I sniff and look around us. "For bringing me to this amazing place. For always looking after me. For helping me at the liquor store. For rescuing me at that party." A shudder makes my spine twitch. "If you hadn't come..." My voice catches. Why the hell am I saying all this now?

Why am I bringing up the fact that I'm a trainwreck?

Because reality is knocking on your door! You're about to head straight back into it, and you're fucking terrified!

"Hey." He steps into my space, cupping my cheek and gazing down at me like he actually gives a shit. A genuine one. This man cares about me, and I can feel it all the way to my core. "I'll always be here for you, okay? That won't change when we get back to Nolan. You can always call me for help."

"But not more." The words are so quiet, I'm not sure he can even hear them.

His brown eyes search my face, his forehead wrinkling with a look of... desperation, maybe?

And then his lips are on mine—covering them, owning them.

I rise to my tiptoes, gripping his bag straps and hauling him against me. We stumble back together, falling off the trail and against a thick tree trunk, where he steadies me, lashing his tongue against mine and drinking, taking, devouring every last piece of my soul.

I give it to him freely.

It's all his because this man is...

He can't be everything. Don't you fucking think that! He's not yours. This is over!

Yet, I keep kissing him.

I take back as much as I'm giving, knowing this is the end of our road.

Knowing my life will never be the same again.

CHAPTER 41
GRADY

Fisting the back of Blake's messy ponytail, I curl my fingers through her luscious locks and drink from her mouth like I'll die of thirst if I don't.

I've been wrestling all fucking morning, wondering if I can somehow make this work.

What if we got back to Nolan and walked into the house holding hands?

What if I walked right up to Wily and told it to him straight?

"Your sister is the best sex I've ever had. She's fun and smart, and I love spending time with her."

But do you love her?

The question trips me up every time.

Do I?

After only a week? That's too soon, too fast.

Teah still beats in my chest cavity. She was the girl I thought I'd marry, and the bruises from her sudden breakup are still tender.

But Blake's filled a hole.

She's made me forget and given me this week of joy and freedom.

But that's not reality.

And what the fuck will Wily say if he knows I went and did all this with his sister and I'm telling him after the fact?

That will not fly with him. I know it.

He'll want my head on a platter... and maybe that's exactly where it deserves to be.

I've gone behind my friend's back. And I thought that was okay, just so I could get this physical temptation out of my system. But Blake's becoming more.

She's chipping away.

She's—

Ripping her mouth off mine, she pushes me back, and I'm forced to let her go, to release her hair and create some space between us.

It's only then that I hear the sound of chatter on the trail up ahead.

Straightening my pack and adjusting the semi that has quickly grown in my pants, I force a smile and move forward, turning back to the parking lot just ahead.

The group catches up to us quickly, and we share the standard greetings.

"How's it going? Good conditions on the trail?"

"Yeah, it's been a great few days."

"You make it up to Crystal Peak?"

"Yeah, just in time for sunset. It was awesome." I smile and nod, then force my legs forward.

Blake wishes them a good time, and my chest deflates as the parking lot comes into view and I spot my Jeep waiting for us.

Shit. It's over.

Glancing back, I catch Blake's stoic expression. She walks past me, heading straight for the Jeep, and for a second, I wonder if I should stop her. Shit, if I had more supplies, I'd drag her right back into the forest again.

But I have to be practical, right?

I've got football training and... she's got decisions to make, a future to carve out for herself.

I can't go screwing with that.

What kind of selfish asshole would I be?

I brought her out here to find peace. I think she's got that now. She's had healthy fun, adventure, and good times. She's hopefully broken free of that burning angst inside her to steal and be reckless.

Now it's time for her to face up to her family and tell them what she really wants.

Maybe she'll pursue this photography thing. That could be cool.

I try to bolster my spirits with images of her chasing something that makes her happy.

What we just had together is going to be a memory I'll cherish.

But that's all it can be, right?

CHAPTER 42
BLAKE

Grady and I meandered back to Nolan, stopping at a diner for something to eat and spending a few hours there.

I felt kind of sorry for the waitress who was serving us, because we no doubt smelled like sweaty armpit, having spent five days in the forest. Sure, we bathed in the lake, but that's not the same. My hair is greasy; I need to shave my legs and pits. I'm the messiest I've ever been, and I laughed myself silly as we drew out our meal playing Mad Libs and Heads Up on Grady's phone.

When his battery died, we switched to mine and turned what was supposed to be a quick snack into a three-course meal.

We were still playing pretend, I guess, unwilling to fully return to reality.

When my phone buzzes with a message from Wily, my heart crumples into a little ball.

. . .

Shithead: Where are you? Can't get Grady on his phone. Are you okay? Why aren't you home yet?

"What is it?" Grady sits forward, his dark eyebrows dipping in concern.

I sigh and spin my device to face him.

He reads the screen and slumps back in his seat. "Shit. We better go."

"Yeah." I nod, forcing my eyes away from him. I don't want to see how easy it is for him to end this fling.

Clearing my throat, I quickly reply to my big brother, then slip my phone away and wriggle out of the booth before anything more can be said.

I pay before Grady can, and he gripes at me.

"What? It's not like this is a date, right?" I snap.

His jaw works to the side, and he mutters, "We could have at least split the bill."

Ugh! I hate that idea!

I'm not sure why it feels like a slap to the face, but it does, so I spin on my heel and march my dirty boots out of the diner at a fast clip.

He catches me easily, because of course he does. He's Flash, right? Quick and strong and agile and… my bear.

My brain tortures me with images of his naked body. He's the hottest guy I've ever been with, and I'll never get over him. I know it as I buckle myself into the Jeep and we head for Nolan.

We don't say anything, and it's like a bucket of cold water has been poured over us.

Not just one bucket, multiple buckets.

We're driving back to Football Frat in a metaphorical rainstorm, and neither of us can break the silence.

There's not even music playing.

All I can hear is the hum of the engine. All I can feel is the thrumming in my chest.

Part of me wants to start yelling and ranting.

I'm pissed off at myself for even suggesting this fling idea. What the hell was I thinking?

I should have just controlled my raging libido and left him alone like he wanted me to.

And missed out on everything you shared?

Forget it!

But what's the alternative?

Fessing up to my big brother.

That's gonna go down like a glass of warm sick. He may not be my keeper or my boss, but there are rules, and I made Grady break them. I forced myself all over the guy, and if Wily finds out, Grady's the one who will pay the price.

I can't keep doing this. Breaking rules and hurting people.

Grady's good. He doesn't deserve all my shit.

I won't put him in Wily's line of fire.

This just has to be over. They'll be sweet memories I can cling to on those days and nights my brain's about ready to explode as I try to figure out how to tell the people I love that I've let them all down in the worst way possible.

My stomach clenches, my entire body seizing up as I picture how that's all gonna play out.

Fuck! Not tonight. I can't face that tonight!

We reach Nolan, and Grady glances at me. I quickly look away from him, keeping my eyes out the window as we drive through this university town. It's pretty here. I've always liked Nolan, but I didn't want to attend here and end up in my brother's shadow.

Besides, Chicago was a better choice for the things I wanted to pursue.

At least the things my parents thought I should want.

What am I going to do now?

The urge to throw myself out of this car and just start running is overwhelming.

I can't do this! I can't face this!

Take me back to the forest!

The words are screaming through my brain as Grady pulls into the driveway.

He cuts the engine, and I know I should reach for the handle and open the door, but I can't move.

Grady turns to me. I can't really see his face in this light, but I can sense his intensity and stop breathing while I wait for him to speak.

"Thank you," he finally whispers.

I want to ask for more—*thank you for what? Be specific!* —but the opportunity is stolen away when the front door opens and Wily hobbles out onto the porch.

"Hey, guys!" He waves, his smile bright and dopey and all things lovable.

He has no idea, and if he finds out what we got up to this week, that smile will disappear. He'll stop grinning at me like I'm his sweet little sister. He'll be disappointed, hurt, betrayed. And he'll be so angry at Grady.

I look to the man beside me, hoping for a short pep talk, even a quick hand squeeze, but he's already pushing the door open, raising his hand with a cheerful grin. "Hey, man."

"Welcome home," Wily booms, stretching his arms wide.

Satch appears behind him, tucking herself beneath his arm, and he pulls her close, kissing the top of her head, but obviously looking for me.

"Where's my lil' sis? You didn't leave her in the forest, did ya?"

"Yeah, right." Grady forces out a laugh. "I value my life, man."

Shoving the door open, I order my stiff limbs out the door and wander around the Jeep.

Time to put on a show.

I can still do that, right?

I've had a lifetime of practice; five days of finally being myself for the first time won't erase that, will it?

"Hey, shithead!" I wave at my brother, forcing my lips to move in the right direction.

"How was it?" He's eyeing me with obvious interest, no doubt looking for cracks as if to prove himself right, that I couldn't handle a five-day hike.

"Amazing!" I brighten my voice, which isn't too hard, to be honest. It *was* fucking amazing. Every second of it.

"You're not too sore?"

"My body might be aching a little." I force myself to wander up the path and climb those front steps. "And I smell like a sewer, but other than that, I am just fine, thank you very much."

Wily's expression is comically skeptical, and he silently checks in with Grady.

He's unloading the Jeep, his biceps curling as he takes both packs with ease.

Shit, I love his arms.

I picture my skinny white fingers trailing over his dark skin as he moved inside me and have to snap my eyes shut for a second.

"She did great. You wouldn't know she was a first-timer." He sounds like he actually means it, and I glance over my shoulder, my lips twitching before smiling down at him.

He winks at me, then looks at my brother.

Wily glances between us and my body stiffens, making me trip on the top step.

"Whoa." He reaches forward to grab my arm, then hisses as he obviously twinges his knee.

"Careful," I snap.

"You be careful," he snaps right back as I flick his hand off my arm and steady myself.

"How's he been?" I ignore my brother's frown and look at his girlfriend.

She tucks herself back against his side and rests her hand on his stomach. "He's been mostly good." He whips an injured look at her, and she giggles. "You know you like to push it. You just need to be patient."

"I don't wanna be patient. I want to get on with my life already." He starts hobbling back into the house, and I sense Grady right behind me as he pauses at the top of the front steps.

I want to turn and burrow myself against him.

I want his arms around me again.

But that's not going to happen, is it?

It can't.

So I dutifully ignore every instinct in my body and follow Wily and Satch inside.

Once my brother is settled back on the couch, he sniffs the air and wrinkles his nose at me. "You're right. You do smell like a sewer."

"Wily!" Satch tells him off while I snicker and shake my head, giving him the finger.

He grins back at me, his smile wide and adoring... and I'm reminded why I can't tell him the truth.

Because if he knows what I let myself become in Chicago, he'll never look at me like that again. If he knows what I forced one of his best friends to do in the forest, he'll never speak to me again.

Shit.

"You okay?" His expression buckles, and I quickly school my face, forcing those lips of mine back into a smile.

"Yeah, I'm good. I'm just desperate for a shower."

Grady moves past me, carrying our packs upstairs and calling over his shoulder, "You go first. I want to unpack my gear anyway. If I don't do it the second I get home, it takes me over a week."

I watch his very fine ass disappear up the stairwell and glance back into the living room, hoping my cheeks aren't as red and hot as the rest of my body feels.

Shit, I'm gonna give myself away if I'm not careful.

Get that mask back in place! You're not in the forest anymore, sweet thing.

"I'm showering."

"Enjoy the hot water." Satch grins at me.

"Believe me, I will." I overexaggerate my words and bulge my eyes the way they're expecting me to.

I score two laughs, the way I need to, then hike my butt upstairs and straight into the bathroom.

The second that hot spray hits me, I start to cry, the way my body has been begging to ever since I woke up this morning.

CHAPTER 43
GRADY

I heard Blake crying in the shower. I didn't mean to; I just realized she went into the bathroom without a towel; so I went to leave one outside the door for her.

This soft whimper reached me, and I pressed my ear against the wood, my heart cracking in half as I listened to her keening wail.

Shit, it took everything in me not to open that door and step right into the tub with her.

I wanted to wrap my arms around her, cocoon her against me like I'd been doing for the last few days.

Truth be fucking damned, I was about to risk every consequence in order to go in there and comfort her, but I was stopped by Zander.

"Hey, you're back."

I whip away from the door like I've just been struck by a bolt of lightning.

He snickers at me, obviously surprised by my reaction. "You okay?"

"What are you doing up here?" I scrub a hand over the back of my head.

His face buckles with confusion as he points his thumb over his shoulder. "Saw your Jeep and wanted to come see how it was. Blake behave herself, or was she a nightmare?"

I force out a laugh, shuffling away from the bathroom door and then trying to explain myself. "Just bringing her a fresh towel." I point to the one I placed on the floor and my best friend nods, still obviously waiting for a coherent answer. "Yeah, it was good." My head starts to bob as I walk toward my room.

Zander follows me, and I stick with the facts. Simple truths that don't hurt to say.

I quickly run through the hike I mapped out, mentioning how I taught Blake to pitch a tent, fish… then adding that she beat me at chess.

"Really?" Zander's eyebrows rise as he perches on the edge of my desk, sliding his hands into his pockets.

"Yeah, she's good, man. Real smart."

"But you're a chess king."

I shrug. "So is she."

"Huh. Looks like you've met your match." Zander glances at something on my desk, and thank fuck, because I can't hide the emotion I'm feeling right now.

Shit, I want to tell him.

But I can't.

I won't put him in that position.

"Did she handle the hiking okay?"

"Yeah. Didn't complain once. She seemed to really love the outdoors. Think she's found her happy place, you know?"

Zander glances back at me. “So, you think it’s helped her shake off this angst or whatever she’s battling?”

I nod, not knowing how much to share. Those aren’t my secrets to tell. They’re Blake’s, and hopefully she’ll have the courage to share them soon. She’s running out of time and excuses to stay in Nolan. She’s gonna have to come clean about Chicago before they find out another way. If Cleo ends up sending those photos to her parents… yeah, I don’t think Blake will survive that, especially if she hasn’t given them a heads-up.

Anger toward her ex-roommate fires through me hot and fast. Being away in the forest, I was able to forget about all the things hanging over her. But now that we’re back, it’s hitting me full force.

“Well, it was nice of you to do that for her.” Zander stands up, having no fucking idea.

I didn’t do anything for her. I gave in to temptation, and I took.

Fuck, I’m such a shitty friend.

“You seem tired. We can catch up more over the weekend. Although, I’m sure the coaches will be working us hard. You ready for spring training?”

I’m honestly not sure, though focusing on football for a while will probably be a nice reprieve.

Giving him a pained frown, I apologize for being so morose. “Sorry. Once I’m clean, I’ll probably feel better.”

“It’s cool, man.” He flicks his hand at me. “Five days in the forest would do my head in. If you want to come down and use our shower, you’re welcome to. Sienna and Zoey are on a video chat with her parents. They won’t mind if you use our bathroom.”

“Thanks, man, but I’ll just wait.” I shake out my pack,

having emptied it completely, then fold it away for storing at the top of my closet.

He stops by my door, his eyebrows buckling. "You sure you're okay?"

"Yeah, yeah, I'm great." I clear the tickle from my throat and force myself to face him. "How was your thing? Have a good time?"

His lips twitch, his shoulder hitching. "I think there's a chance you had more fun than me."

"Really?" I rest my hand against the closet door frame. "What do you mean? Did something bad happen?"

"No, it was just very family intense, and Zoey was unsettled for some reason." He lets out a weary laugh. "I would have given anything to just be away with my woman for a couple of nights in the middle of nowhere, you know?"

"I take it you didn't get any while you were away?"

He snorts and shakes his head.

I give him a pained wince. "If you ever need a babysitter, just let me know. You two obviously need a night to yourselves. We can make that happen."

"Yeah, thanks." He raises his hand at me. "I'm gonna have to take you up on that, man."

"Done."

He raises his chin in gratitude before heading out the door.

I listen for the shower and hear that it's stopped, which means the bathroom might be free.

Taking my time, I gather my clean clothes and towel, giving Blake a chance to get back to her room without me walking in on her again. It's been established that when it comes to her, I basically have zero control, so it's best that I give her space.

By the time I get to the bathroom, it's empty, and I can't help the slice of disappointment that takes me out.

But it's okay. This is the way it should be, right?

I rinse off pretty fast, soaping every inch of me until I smell like African Storm shower gel. I manage to wash the last of the suds off my body just before I lose the hot water. Jumping out before the cold spikes get me, I towel off, my mind consumed with thoughts of Blake... and the tears I heard before Zander interrupted me.

When I ease out of the bathroom, a towel securely wrapped around my waist, I stare across the hall at Blake's bedroom door.

I have no idea if she's in there or downstairs, putting on the show Wily's expecting.

Or maybe she's tucked up in bed, pretending to study.

Or maybe she's curled up in a little ball, whimpering against her knees.

Fuck, I hate that image the most.

Padding across the wooden floor, I pause outside her door and gently knock before thought can stop me.

My heart starts to drum a wicked beat when I listen to her shuffling behind the wood.

And then the handle is turning and her face appears, all wide-eyed and blotchy.

Her eyes. Damn, I can't get enough of them.

They're all glassy and are such a vibrant blue, they look like a crystal-clear lake on a cloudless day. Her tear-streaked face begs to be touched, kissed, comforted.

"I know I shouldn't be standing here right now," I croak, straining for noises in the house.

Her supple lips part, her eyes trailing down my body and turning my insides to molten lava.

Walk away before you do something insane!

"But I just wanted to make sure you were okay."

A creak on the stairs makes us both flinch.

"Catch you guys later," Carson mumbles as he climbs the stairs, Nylah giggling beside him.

"Stop. You are not keeping me up all night."

"Kitty Cat, you know that is exactly what I'll be doing."

Her laughter grows, then turns into a squeal, and I act without thinking, quickly ducking into Blake's room before I get caught outside her door.

The second the wood shuts behind me, I realize my error. I should have gone to my room. I could have dashed down there before they saw me, but no, I had to step into the pit of temptation.

Spinning around, I spot Blake leaning against the door, staring at me.

All I can do is drink her in.

She's wearing a pair of pajama bottoms that hang low on her hips and show off her flat stomach. The material is covered in cartoon hearts, and the flimsy top that goes with them has a massive heart across the front. I can make out the shape of her boobs—her puckered nipples—and have to force my eyes to the floor.

Her cute toes are curling into the rug and... shit, I have to get out of here.

"Please," she whispers. "Please don't go."

Glancing back up at her desperate frown, I swallow, knowing there's no way in hell I'm walking out of this room.

I can't.

I can't leave her like this.

And it's not because I don't want to. I physically don't think I can, which means we need to come clean about this shit.

But not tonight.

Not right now when she looks so vulnerable, so raw, so real.

My feet shift before I can stop them, and she meets me halfway, crashing into my body and cupping the back of my head. I kiss her slow. It's smooth and familiar, our tongues knowing this dance.

It's the easiest thing in the world, my hands gliding over hers, dipping into the back of her pajamas bottoms and palming her sweet ass.

She rises on her tiptoes, her tits rubbing against me through the thin fabric. Grinding her hips into my growing erection, I relent to her soft whimpers and lift her off the floor.

Her legs wrap around me like she's home, and I walk us back to her bed. We've never done it on a bed, never experienced a soft mattress, the comforts of home.

As her body sinks into the fluffy duvet cover, I can't help a smile. She deserves this—comfort and warmth, soft tenderness.

Taking my time, I ignore all the risks that wait for me outside that door and slowly peel the clothes from her body.

Whipping my towel off, I let it drop to the floor so I can move more freely. I'm used to being naked around this woman. We spent the week acting like naturalists, living without the constrictions of clothing, and it feels so right to pull her pajamas off, to throw them to the floor and relish her naked skin.

Kneeling between her legs, I kiss and tease her clit, loving the way her body moves and gyrates. Her neck cranes back, her teeth sinking into her bottom lip as she tries to stay quiet.

When I slip my fingers inside her, she lets out a soft moan, and I reach up, covering her mouth with my hand. "Shhh," I remind her, and she nods, writhing beneath my touch.

Trailing my hand back down her body, I pause, enjoying her perfect tits before focusing back on what I'm doing between her legs.

When she finally comes, her pussy is wet, my fingers slick as I trail them down her leg and lay myself over her.

Studying her face, I silently ask for permission, and the heated smile she gives me injects a dose of liquid gold into my veins.

Covering her lips with mine, I kiss her deep, her tongue shredding me while her fingers scrape down my back.

"Please," she whispers into my ear. "Now, Grady. I need you now."

I suck the bottom of her chin, then trail kisses along her jawline, not wanting my lips to leave her skin. She tastes divine, all clean and fresh. She's shaved and preened, and her body is a delicious wonderland.

"Grady." She softly whines my name, her hips rising to find me, seeking out the thing she wants most.

Grabbing my dick, I line us up and slowly ease into her.

I don't even want to take it fast. There's no place for

frantic thrusting in this moment. I just want to take her slow and easy, like I did beside the lake, like I did that first night we shared the tent together. I don't want to rush this thing because I know it might be our last.

Last night was supposed to be that, but now we're here all over again, unable to resist.

Shit, if Wily could walk up those stairs…

If he heard one whisper of what we're doing…

But I can't stop.

Then tell him! Fight for this girl!

Her fingers dig into my shoulders as I rock into her, moving back and forth in easy, gentle thrusts.

My lips continue to pepper her with kisses, the tip of my tongue painting lines from her shoulder to her ear. Shifting her leg, I bury myself a little deeper, loving the way her body responds to me.

"Yes, Bear. Yes." She breathes the words against my skin, and I dip my head, nestling our foreheads together as I continue to move and slide, move and slide within her.

She's clutching me, her inner walls a soft oasis that is slowly getting hotter.

The fire that I love so much builds and burns until the inferno within me is raging.

I'm yours, Blake Wilson. Fuck, I am all yours.

Her soft gasp hits my skin, my heart spasming when that orgasm builds inside me, slow at first and then quickly rushing through me like a storm.

I'm blinded, my hips wanting to thrust and plunge and take, but I force myself to move slow and gentle, using every ounce of control I have to take care of her.

My throat swells, my lips parting when I can't control

that physical takeover anymore. The build escalates to a mind-reeling explosion, and I'm soon letting loose inside her, my thrusts turning short and uneven as I leave a piece of my soul in this woman.

She didn't even have to fight for it.

I'm a weak man, unable to contain myself around her.

Which means I can't just pretend like nothing has happened between us.

We have to tell Wily the truth.

We just need to figure out the best way how.

CHAPTER 44
BLAKE

I wake up with a moan, reaching back behind me, then spinning when I notice the bed is empty.

My gut twists into a sad, uncomfortable knot.

That empty mattress beside me is horrible and depressing and… when the fuck did Grady sneak out?

I must have been completely passed out, because I didn't even hear him.

With a little huff, I tuck my wayward curls behind my ear and flop back down onto my pillow.

Of course he snuck out. Be logical about this. He wasn't supposed to be there.

Grrr. My brain is right, and this is so annoying.

He belongs beside me. As we made love last night, I felt it. He felt it. I could tell by the look in his eyes after he came and gazed down at me like I was something special.

The tender kiss he gave me just before he lay down beside me and pulled me into his arms…

It was all so meant to be, which means he can't go sneaking out in the middle of the night!

Throwing back the covers with a huff, I grab my pajamas off the floor and slip them back on. The wood is cold beneath my feet when I hit the bare floorboards in the hallway, and I rise to my tiptoes, sneaking down the hallway.

Glancing over my shoulder, I pause outside Grady's room. I don't want to risk knocking and alerting anyone to the fact that I'm here. Everyone should be asleep anyway. It's like five in the morning.

With a wince, I ease the door open, my face bunching at the creak. Going still, I listen for any other movements in the house and don't relax until three full beats of silence greet me.

Releasing my breath, I slip into Grady's room and close his door, padding through the dark and slipping into his bed. It's warm and delicious, his hot body working like an electric blanket, and I smile as I pull the covers around myself and snuggle up against him.

He's still kind of sleepy and murmurs something unintelligible as I tuck myself into his back.

"Your feet are freezing, woman," he complains.

"Sorry." I giggle, sliding them up his leg until he snatches my thigh and keeps me in place.

He's still half-asleep as he rolls me over and spoons me from behind. I lie in blissful drowsiness until I feel him tense behind me.

"What are you doing in my bed?"

Aw crap, he's fully awake.

Glancing over my shoulder, I give him a sweet smile and innocently blink. "Good morning."

He groans, rolling onto his back and whisper-barking, "Your brother is going to kill me."

I shuffle around, hiding my face in the crook of his neck before gently kissing that soft skin just beneath his morning whiskers.

"I'm serious, Blake. If any of the guys see you sneaking out of here..."

"You snuck out of my room," I argue.

"At two in the morning when everyone was asleep."

"Everyone is still asleep. It's only five fifteen."

"And everyone will be getting up for practice in like ten minutes. How are you planning on leaving without being spotted?"

My head pops up, and I stare at the doorway. "I'll think of something. It's all about timing. Why don't I just wait in here until after you've left?"

He gives me a doubtful snort, and I whip a surprised look at him.

"What? I've been sneaking around all year. I'm good at this. And everyone will think I'm in my room. Seriously, stop making such a big deal and just let me snuggle."

The way his eyebrows wrinkle tells me he doesn't really want to hear that I'm an expert sneak, so I drop my head with a sigh, resting my forehead against his shoulder.

"Look..." His hand glides up my back, settling between my shoulder blades. "I can't believe I'm saying this, but... maybe we should just come clean."

An alarming terror I was not expecting jolts through me, and my head pops back off his body again. "What?"

He opens his mouth to reply but then ends up giving me a helpless shrug.

So I arch my eyebrow at him, silently demanding an explanation.

"I don't know what else to do. The whole 'this thing being over as soon as we got back' isn't gonna work for us. We couldn't even go two hours."

I squeeze my eyes shut. "You know, it's really your fault."

"My fault?" His whispers increase just a little in volume, and I open my eyes in time to see him frowning at me.

"Yeah, well..." I draw a circle on his bare shoulder. "If you weren't so divine, then it'd be easy just to let you go, but you had to be... be..."

"Be what?"

"Perfect." I bulge my eyes at him. "Inside and out."

He shakes his head. "I'm not perfect, Blake. Please don't put that on me. I'm a shitty friend who went behind your brother's back. That doesn't make me perfect. Far from it."

Brushing my thumb across his bottom lip, I give him a sad smile. "Compared to me, you're perfect. I'm the shitty sister who's been lying to her brother, the horrible daughter who's been lying to her parents. I'm..." I shake my head as well.

Cupping my face, he holds me steady, his face becoming clearer by the second as I adjust to the darkness in his room. "Let's end this charade. Let's just come out with the truth and face the consequences."

Consequences?

He makes it sound like this simple thing.

Consequences!

One word. Four syllables.

And it's the most terrifying sound in all the world.

Fear clutches me, but worse than it's ever clutched me before. It's like there's this vise around my throat, choking me, flattening my chest.

The air in my lungs is turning into toxic gas. I can't inhale.

Why can't I inhale?

I start scratching at my collarbone, whimpering as I claw at my pajama top.

This charade has been keeping me sane, and now he's telling me to just shed it.

Shed it and face the *consequences.*

"Hey. Hey, it's okay." Grady notices my sudden surge of panic, but his calm voice can't cut through the haze clouding my vision.

I can't breathe. Why can't I breathe?

This tightness in my chest is unbearable. It's like there's a concrete cinder block squishing my lungs into pancakes.

"Blake, look at me." Grady quickly shifts, freeing his arm from around my side and taking my face in both his hands. "Blake," he whispers, his voice urgent as he tries to cut through whatever the hell I'm going battling.

What is this?

I've never had this before.

Is it a panic attack?

Why is everything so blurry?

How can I go from calmly lying beside him to this!

"Bee. Baby." He's still calling to me, his calloused thumbs rubbing my cheeks. "Breathe. Just breathe. Inhale. You can do it."

A short burst of air rushes into me.

"Good. And again."

I suck in a little more, my vision starting to clear.

"And again. Breathe again. You can do it."

"I... I..." Shaking my head, I try to speak, but—

"Breathe." He leans in close, saying it with such authority that I have no choice but to take a full breath.

It hits my lungs and I blink, my eyes glassing over as he comes into full focus. "What's happening to me?"

"You're having a panic attack, but you're going to be okay." His voice is so smooth and even, so calm and steady. I cling to it, to him, my hands reaching for his solid arms.

Clutching his wrists, I hold on and whimper.

"Keep breathing," he instructs me, and I do. I take a breath and then another until finally... slowly... I return to myself.

My skin feels clammy and hot, my heart racing erratically, but that sensation is starting to ebb. I can breathe again. Loosening the pincer grip on his wrists, I run my hands down his arms but can't let go.

Not just yet.

That sucked.

Holy shit, that sucked so bad.

"Hey," Grady whispers.

My eyes dart to his. "Why did that just happen?"

"I don't know." His voice is low and gravelly, his expression pained. "We were talking about telling your family the truth."

He's saying it carefully, like he's worried he might trigger me all over again.

But I've been wrestling with this for months. Why the sudden attack now?

Because it's so close. It's so near. If you want to be with Grady, you can't hide from this anymore. You have no way out but the truth, and that scares the shit out of you!

Closing my eyes, I suck in a shaky breath, my entire body shuddering.

"Blake, you told me, and you survived it just fine."

I keep my eyes shut, unwilling to look at him, even though he's trying to encourage me.

"Your family loves you."

"You don't understand." My voice is soft and raspy. "They'll be so let down."

"It'll be worse if they find out another way. It has to come from you."

"I can't," I whimper, shuddering again as I relive that horrible moment as the word *consequences* bounced inside my brain. "Don't make me do it, Grady. Please."

Curling my arms around his shoulders, I cling to his solid body, feeling weak and pathetic. But I don't know what else to do.

I thought I was stronger than this, but I'm obviously not.

I can live in a lie. I've been doing it most of my life.

The truth is too big and terrifying.

I can't face what's waiting for me on the other side of these horrible conversations.

I just can't do it!

CHAPTER 45
GRADY

It's been three days since Blake's panic attack, and I still can't stop thinking about it.

Holy shit, that was intense.

Seeing her lose it on my bed, that terrified look on her face when she thought she couldn't breathe...

I've never watched anyone succumb to a panic attack before, and it was horrible, made a million times worse by the fact that I really care about this woman, and watching her suffer fucking killed me.

I want to help her, but how do I convince her to come clean?

Sure, telling her family the truth is going to be really hard, but once it's out there, she can start moving on. Part of her issue is that she's held out for so long that the problem feels too big. But it won't start getting better until she does the right thing.

Same goes for you, man. You need to talk to Wily.

But I need a green light from Blake before I do that. It's her secret, too, and I won't send her into a spiral just to clear my conscience. But we can't keep sneaking around either. Which is why I've been resisting every instinct in my body and trying to stay clear of her.

When I walked past her bedroom door last night, I didn't sneak in the way I wanted to.

Sleeping without her sucks, but thankfully football training has been intense, so I come home totally shattered.

We've barely interacted, as I've been so busy with this truncated training schedule and catching up on homework that I haven't had time to see anyone. And Blake's been out of sight every time I've gotten home.

Wily's complaining about her being a study whore, and I wanted to punch him for using that word in reference to her. It was only a joke, but it still got my back up. She's no whore. And the fact that I couldn't warn him of that killed me as well.

But she's not my girlfriend.

She's my teammate's little sister, the girl I had a fling with in the forest. The one I can't stop thinking about.

Dammit.

When I get home tonight, I'm gonna have to talk to her. We can't keep going like this. I miss her. Part of me just wants to take her and disappear back into the wild. She was so happy and carefree there. No pressure, no demands. She could just be herself. We both could, and I want that back.

I want to see her unchecked smile, not that measured shit she pulls out around Wily and everybody else. I want to hear her laughing, see her dancing, watch her face when she's overcome with awe or wonder.

Man, has Wily ever seen that side of her? Has she ever let anyone in?

Or has that privilege been mine alone?

The thought forms a quick lump in my throat.

Yeah, we really can't keep going like this.

I gotta come clean. I have to convince *her* to come clean... if she'll let me talk to her. She's kind of been hiding away since she lost it on my bed. I hated that I had to get up and leave her for football practice. I have no idea how long she stayed in my room after I left the house, but she was back in hers by the time I got home, and she barely looked at me over dinner. Is she embarrassed about the panic attack?

She doesn't need to be. The fact that she can fall apart around me is a compliment in some ways. She trusts me enough to be her raw and real self. That's a huge privilege.

I want to honor that and respect her.

But I have to convince her to stop sitting on all these lies. She'll never be truly free—neither of us will—until the truth comes out.

But which truth should she spill first?

Which one is less scary for her?

Telling her brother about me... or the shit she got up to in Chicago... or the roofie scare... or the liquor store incident?

Shit, she's got a lot to confess.

I know which one I'd prefer, but I'm not gonna be a selfish prick about it.

"Hey." Carson snaps his fingers in front of my face. "You need me to drive, man?"

Coming to with a quick blink, I notice that the crosswalk I paused for is now clear. Accelerating over the zebra stripes, I ignore Carson's frown, clenching my jaw and refusing to engage.

But he won't let me get away with it.

"You good, man? You seem... off."

"I'm fine."

He snickers. "Soooo freaked out, insecure, neurotic, and emotional."

"What?" I glance at him.

"*The Italian Job*. You know. The movie? I'm fine? But fine actually means... ach..." He flicks a hand through the air. "Don't worry about it." He shakes his head and mutters something about needing Nylah.

I have no idea what the hell he's talking about, so I keep my mouth shut. I'm not really in the mood to engage. The coaches ran us hard at practice, and I was into it, because I need to burn off this angst, but it's also made me sore and... okay, I'm grumpy.

Better get my shit together before we reach Football Frat, because I have to talk to Blake today. I just have to.

Carson rests his foot up on my dash. I fucking hate it when he does that, but I don't want to get into it with him, so I grip the wheel and pick up speed. We make it home a couple of minutes later, and I slam out of the Jeep, stalking for the front door.

"Dude, what's got your panties in a twist?" Zander laughs at me as he hops out of his SUV and spots me on the lawn.

"Nothing!" I bark, taking the stairs two at a time.

I can sense the guys looking at each other, trying to figure what's up with me now.

Hopefully they assume it's got something to do with Teah so I don't have to tell them what's really going on.

They'll all find out soon enough, but Wily has to be the first to know. It's the only way that's fair.

"I've already told you this!" Blake's raised voice hits me the second I open the door.

Dumping my bag and kicking off my shoes, I don't even think. I bolt down to the kitchen, my muscles coiled tight as I listen to her distress.

"Why do you keep pushing this?"

"Because you told us you were going back to Chicago after spring break. Classes start again tomorrow. Why aren't you on a plane?" Wily's towering over her, holding out his phone like he's recording this shit.

What the fuck is he doing?

Blake looks so small beside him, her cheeks pale, her eyes wide and a little wild.

I try to catch her attention behind Wily's back, waving my hand at her.

She darts me a quick look, her headshake subtle but oh so clear.

I am not allowed to say a fucking word.

Dammit!

I'm here. She should just do it now. I'll support her, protect her as best I can.

I make a move to enter the kitchen fully, but she bulges her eyes at me, then glances at the screen, putting on a smile.

"I really don't want to argue about this." Her voice is sweet but strained. "Why won't you all let this go?"

My eyebrows dip together, and it's not until I hear a

female voice coming out of the phone that I suddenly realize she and Wily are talking to somebody else.

"Blake, we can't let this go." It's her mom. "You're not sticking to your plan, and we're confused. Concerned. We know you've found college a breeze this year, but that doesn't mean you can just slack off. You should be aiming for top grades in every single subject."

Blake closes her eyes, looking sick for a second, and I wish I could step forward and defend her, explain the situation *for* her, but I doubt that's gonna fly. I'm nobody to this family, and I can't go blurting that I'm more than just an acquaintance to Blake. If they knew what we got up to in the forest, I can only imagine what her parents would say... let alone Wily.

Shit, this is bad.

"If you don't get your butt back to Chicago, I'm driving up to Nolan and will take you to the airport myself." Her dad's voice comes out of the phone, and Blake's eyes ping open—wide and bright and etched with fear.

Part of me wills her to say it, to just shout out the truth and be done with it all.

But she bites her lips together, refusing to look at me when I try to stare her down. I know she can sense my gaze on her, but she won't connect because she already knows what I'm going to try and convey.

Her muscles coil tight as she crosses her arms, her fingers digging in just above her elbows, like she's holding her slender little body together. She's so fine-boned. Like a fragile bird. But I know how strong she can be. She was so tough in the forest, never complained about aching muscles. She just soldiered on.

But right now?

She looks on the verge of breaking, and I'm starting to worry that she'll have another panic attack.

Dropping my gaze, I lean against the doorframe and clench my jaw. I should walk away and give them some privacy, but like hell I'm moving right now. I'm gonna be here if she needs me.

"Come on, Blakey." Wily gives her shoulder a little nudge with his fist.

She sways on her feet, glaring up at her brother. I'm wondering if the dynamic is usually them against the olds, but he's siding with her parents right now, and she's feeling pretty alone over this whole thing.

"Would you guys stop ganging up on me!" She flicks her arms wide. "I have a plan here."

"What plan?" her mother demands. "Explain it to us."

She huffs, and I can only imagine how fast her pulse must be racing right now. "Can't you just trust me?"

"You should be back in Chicago, Blake." Her dad's voice is firm. "Your finals are going to be here before you know it, and Wily doesn't need you anymore. Enough is enough!"

She flinches, her expression crumpling for a second before she pulls it back into line.

Wily steps forward with a softer approach. "Hey…" He rests his big hand on her delicate shoulder. "Is there something else stopping you from going? Is everything okay in Chicago?"

She shakes him off, her eyes darting across to mine. I silently beg her to spill. This is the moment. This is—

"Of course it is," she lies. "Chicago's great. I just…" With a little shrug, she gives her brother a half smile, then looks at the phone screen. Her smile is growing more plastic by the second, and my insides coil. "I've just been enjoying hanging out in Nolan. Believe it or not, I actually like spending time with this shithead." She points her thumb at Wily while her father booms with laughter and her mother groans.

"Language, Blake!"

Her dad laughs over top of her mother's reprimand, like he couldn't be prouder that his children are more than just siblings... they're friends.

I can't see all of Wily's face from where I'm standing, but I bet he's grinning—that smile he gets when he talks about his sister. He really does adore her... and he's gonna be gutted when he finds out the truth.

"Because I've been able to do both," Blake goes on to explain, "I just figured I'd stay here for as long as I could."

"I think it's safe to say that your time's up, sweetheart." Her dad's tone leaves no room for argument.

"I know, Daddy." She puts on her good-girl smile just for him.

"Now, we've let you have your fun over spring break," her mother starts saying. "We let you go off and be in the wild."

Let her?

She's nineteen, for fuck's sake. She doesn't need anyone's permission.

"And we're glad you had so much fun. But it's time to get back into the swing of things. You have classes to ace, exams to get top marks on. You really need to get back to reality."

Blake's lips tremble as she forces them into yet another fake smile. "You're right. I'll go up and start looking at flights now."

"That's my girl," her dad says while my shoulders slump.

Shit. She bailed.

Shaking my head with a frown, I quietly turn and walk away. Looks like the truth is gonna have to wait for another day.

I mean, what the fuck does she honestly think she's gonna do? Fly back to Chicago and live out of a hotel again, wasting her days *pretending* to go to school?

She's just made things harder for herself, and I don't know if I can get her out of this hole she keeps digging. I want to help her so badly, but I can't if she won't let me.

CHAPTER 46
BLAKE

Mercifully, this hideous video call with my parents wraps up a few minutes after I agree to book my flight back to Chicago.

My heart is hammering as I duck out of the kitchen and head upstairs. All I can see as I ascend is the disappointed look on Grady's face. It's killing me.

He's pissed off that I won't tell the truth.

No, he's let down, and I hate that more than anything. I'd rather he be annoyed. It's easier to deal with.

No, it's not. None of these emotions are easy to deal with!

This is exactly what I've been so afraid of facing with my brother and parents. I didn't mind so much when I annoyed Grady before, but now he really means something to me, and the idea of me letting him down is too much.

My heart kicks out of place, picking up another notch until my breaths start getting too shallow. It hurts to inhale and—

No, no, no! I won't give in to another panic attack. I won't do it.

Pausing at the top of the stairs, I grip the railing and sway on my feet. Closing my eyes, I force air in through my nose.

My entire body feels on the verge of snapping—muscles so tense I can't even move.

What the hell am I supposed to do?

Tell the truth!

But how? If I let the first part out, the rest will have to follow, and my family will never look at me the same again. All of Mom and Dad's pride will vanish in an instant, and then what's left? If I'm not their shining star... what am I?

Nothing.

My heart rate kicks up another notch and I grip the railing, my chest vibrating as I expel these shaky, shallow breaths.

A toilet flushes behind the bathroom door, and I flinch. I don't know who is in there, but they can't see me like this.

Dashing away from the top of the stairs, I should head to my room and bolt the door behind me, but I think I'll lose my mind pacing in that space, so I find my feet rushing to Grady's door instead.

Why?

I can't even answer that.

I have no idea why I head for his door, but I do.

Shouldering it open, I burst in there and find him sitting on the edge of his bed with his head in his hands.

He looks up as soon as he hears me, and our eyes connect for a thick beat.

"Don't hate me," I rasp, then suck in a sharp breath.

Rising to his feet, his brown gaze drinks me in—soft and kind—and the second he's within reach, I fold myself into his arms.

"I could never hate you," he whispers, cupping the back of my head. "I just want to help you."

"Why can't I do it?" I squeak, clinging to the back of his hoodie. "Why am I such a coward?"

"It's okay," he murmurs, brushing his lips across the side of my face. "You're not a coward. You're brave and strong and smart. You can do this, Bee. And I'll do it with you. We can go down there together, right now."

My body stiffens. Everything in me is coiled so tight that I feel like I'm about to break.

"Take me away from here," I beg him. "Let's just go back to the forest. I felt safe there and unhindered. No one was judging me or demanding anything of me. I was free. I want to be free again." My voice starts to pitch, and I'm going to start crying in a second. The tears are brewing, building, threatening to start and never stop.

"You can be free now." Grady pulls back, holding my face in his hands. "All you have to do is tell the truth. Get this over with, and then you can move on."

I'm shaking my head, and he must think I'm such a stubborn little shit.

"I can't just steal you away, baby. As much as I'd love to go back to the forest with you, that would be a really big mistake. You need to face this. And the longer you leave it, the worse it becomes. It's growing into a mountain so big you can't climb it anymore. Please, I'm begging you... just rip off the Band-Aid and deal with this."

His face right now.

He so desperately wants me to come clean, because he cares about me. Maybe.

Or because he's the kind of guy who likes to do the right thing.

I've been doing the right thing my whole life... until I got to Chicago and fucked everything up.

But I don't want to go back to that rigid path I was walking before.

I want my own life that isn't controlled by my parents or Cleo!

I just want to be free to do whatever the fuck I want!

Staring up at Grady's gorgeous face, I drink him in.

I want him.

I want to have him without the shackles of secrecy.

Tears burn the back of my throat as I circle back around to the fact that he's right. If I want all those things, I have to tell the truth.

I just wish it wasn't so damn scary!

Grady's smile turns soft and tender, his thumb brushing over my cheek, and I swear I've never loved a boy until now. I mean, I guess I started falling for him in the forest, but that look on his face, his willingness to fight for me, to help set me free...

I love him.

And maybe after this shitstorm is over, I'll have the chance to tell him.

But for now...

Lurching forward, I plant my mouth on his, needing this connection, needing to draw from his strength.

With my courage flailing, I sweep my tongue into his mouth, clinging to him as his arms circle around me. It's like he knows what I'm trying to do and is delivering like the champ he is.

Fueling me with his fortitude and bravery, he pours everything into this kiss, claiming yet another piece of my soul. I sign it over without hesitation. He can have it. He can have *all* of it.

And once it's his, I'll find the strength to pull away. To walk back downstairs and take on my first fight. I'll start with Wily, then—

"What the fuck!" A roar comes from Grady's doorway, and I rip my mouth from his, turning with wide, horrified eyes to find my brother towering in the space, his face mottled with rage.

Oh shit.

The battle's been brought to me.

And I'm so not ready.

CHAPTER 47
GRADY

Oh shitballs.

Wily looks about ready to end me as he glares over the top of Blake's head and yells, "Get your hands off my sister!"

"Wily." She steps forward, her voice all out of breath and wispy. "What are you doing upstairs? Is your knee okay?"

He ignores her, still eyeballing me with a venomous frown. "What the fuck are you doing in here with her?"

"Wily, calm down." Blake steps into his space, resting her hand on his chest.

"She's a virgin!" he bellows, and the room goes still.

Blake swallows, closing her eyes and cringing. Wily glances down, noticing her expression, and the color drains from his face.

There's a thick, awkward beat, and then he smacks his crutch down and thunders, "You stole my sister's V-card?"

Stepping around his sister, he limps forward with his other crutch and gives me a forceful shove.

I let him do it, stumbling back and catching myself before I topple onto my bed.

"No!" Blake darts forward, snatching his arm. "Stop it! He didn't steal anything!"

"Well, what am I supposed to think?" Wily turns on her. "You're making out in here, and you've just spent five days in the forest together. Something has definitely been off with you. Is this it?" He turns back to me, his eyes flashing with a look that makes me feel like the shittiest friend on the planet. "You've been screwing around together behind my back?"

"Wily, we were gonna tell—" Blake starts, but he ignores her once again, his dark glare focused solely on me.

Clenching his jaw, he grits out, "Look me in the eye and tell me you haven't slept with her."

Straightening with a resigned sigh, I keep my gaze level and my voice even, confessing the truth without hesitation. "I can't do that, man."

He takes a second to absorb my words, and then his anger is firing up again, turning his face red as he barks, "Are you out of your fucking mind? I am gonna kill you!"

I stand my ground, figuring I'll give him the first punch for free, maybe even the second as well. I deserve it. I went behind his back. What kind of shitty-ass friend does that?

"You took something from her that she can't get back!" He points at his sister before that accusing finger swings back to me. "And when you're still in love with Teah too! Don't deny it! I know you still have feelings for her, the way you've been moping around for months. And now you're just screwing my sister like you're over it? Bullshit!"

I don't even know how to respond to that. With a slow blink, I'm trying to figure out my best response when Blake steps in front of him, slapping her hands on his chest.

"Would you stop? He didn't take my virginity!"

"He just told me you were sleeping together." His eyes hit her like laser beams, his scowl intimidating as hell, but she's looking right up at it, not backing down.

"Wily." She closes her eyes and huffs, her tone coming out much softer when she explains again, "He didn't take my V-card, okay?"

It takes him another beat... and then he finally gets what she's saying.

And the way his expression drops to one of shock and confusion... shit, it's kind of heartbreaking.

"What?" he whispers. "When?"

She bulges her eyes at him. "Are you kidding me? I'm not talking about my sex life with you."

"Yes, you are," he growls. "Who? When?"

She closes her eyes again, and I'm waiting for her to reiterate her point. Her sex life is her own business—she doesn't have to share shit if she doesn't want to.

But then she ends up muttering, "About six months ago. It was just some guy at college. You don't know him."

"You lost it to *just some guy*?" This news is slaying poor Wily. "Was he your boyfriend?"

"No. I mean..." She scratches her forehead, squeezing her eyes shut. "Sometimes. Maybe."

"What the fuck does that mean?" he snaps, and I doubt he's gonna be okay with that weird-ass group thing she had going in Chicago. Even I struggled to wrap my head around it.

I step forward to try and back her up, but that only causes Wily to growl like a dog.

Pausing before I can reach Blake, I raise my hands and step back. Her shoulders slump, agony ripping through my chest at the pale, dejected look on her face.

"I don't... I don't know what it means." She sighs, crossing her arms and staring at the floor.

"How could you not tell me this?" Wily's voice has dropped to a gruff whisper, all the fire going out of him. Shit, he looks... wounded. "I tell you everything."

Those four little words drop into the room as a shattered whisper, and the pained look on Wily's face is killing me. I can only imagine what it's doing to Blake.

She looks destroyed when she raises her head and stares at her brother. Her face crumples in regret, remorse... Shit, she's gonna cry.

Wily just shakes his head, stumbling backward out of my room. Catching himself on his crutch, he balances against the wall before staring at his sister one last time, then limping away.

"Wily. Wait..." Blake's voice trembles, tears glassing over her eyes. "I'm... Wily! I'm sorry." Her chest starts to hitch as she watches her brother slowly disappear down the hall. Rushing to my doorway, she calls after him. "I'm sorry!"

He ignores her, and I want to tell him to stop already. Hear her out.

But he's hurting right now.

"Wily?" Satch's voice calls from the bottom of the stairs, and then she's thundering up them. I can hear her awkward rush. She stumbles on one of the steps, then appears at the top. I can't see all of her from this angle, but I can hear the worry in her voice. "What's going on? Why are you up there? Are you okay?"

"I had to check something." Wily voice is dead and sad.

Blake sucks in a shaky breath, and Satch's head pops into view. She looks confused, her eyebrows wrinkling as she tries to figure out what's going on.

"I'm going to my room." Wily sounds so gutted.

"Up here?"

He must nod, because Satch disappears from sight, no doubt moving to comfort him.

Blake stays where she is, gripping the doorframe, her knuckles turning white... and that's when I notice her heaving chest. Breaths are punching out of her in shaky bursts as she bends over and lets out a whimper.

"It's okay. Just breathe." I lurch forward, rubbing her back as those punchy breaths turn to shaky sobs.

"He hates me."

"He doesn't hate you."

"He's never going to talk to me again."

"Yes, he will. He loves you. He's just hurting. He needs time to process."

She looks up, her blue eyes wild and bright with tears. "I hurt him."

I want to shake my head and tell her she didn't, but I can't... because that's not the truth.

All I can give her is a pained frown. "*We* hurt him. But we're going to make it right, okay?"

She shakes her head, standing tall and ducking out

from under my touch. “How? He hasn’t even heard the worst of it yet.”

“Blake.”

“No,” she whimpers, moving away from me.

I want to reach out and tug her back, but she’s shaking her head, stumbling down the hallway and into her room.

The door slams shut behind her, and as much as I want to demand she let me in to make her feel better, something in my gut is telling me to stay put.

I need to give her some space.

Fuck, we all probably need space right now.

Wily’s not ready for my apology, but while I’m waiting, I may as well construct a good one.

Shit, I’m gonna need help with this.

Heading for the stairwell, I race down it, jumping off the last step and heading for the garage at the back of the house.

I need Zander.

CHAPTER 48
BLAKE

I cry until my eyes are swollen and aching. I've run out of tissues, and the floor is covered in balled-up wads of snot and tears. My sweater sleeve is grimy, and my head is pounding.

When there's a gentle knock at my door, I assume it's Grady, and I'm not sure if I can handle his comfort. He'll be so sweet and forgiving… and I don't deserve it.

"I'm… busy," I squeak.

My visitor obviously takes that as a cue to open the door, and I glare at the wood until Satch's head appears. Her sweet face tells me she's not mad… just sad… and I dip my chin, unable to look at her.

"Hi," she whispers, easing into my room. "You doing okay?"

I shake my head. There's no point trying to lie when I obviously look like shit.

I'm wrecked, and I doubt even layers of makeup could hide that fact.

Satch shuffles into the room, fidgeting with her fingers before shaking out her hands and straightening her cardigan.

Glancing at the ribbed fabric, I watch the way it sits on her wide curves. When I first met her, I thought she was a bit of a weirdo. She dresses like a woman from the 1950s, but she's so sweet and shy and I just couldn't judge her for it. I mean, no one should judge her. She's all things kind, and I'm the asshole for thinking my sense of fashion was better than hers.

I'm not better.

Nothing about me is better.

No matter what I wear or how well I do in school, nothing about me is better than Elizabeth Satchwell, because she's the genuine article. And my brother deserves someone just like that.

Sucking in a breath, I clench my jaw to try and ward off the next batch of tears.

"Wily, um..." She licks her lips, and I tense at the sound of my brother's name.

"Wily never wants to speak to you again. Can you move out, please?"

"Wily wants me to tell you that he's disowning you."

"Wily needs you to know that you've let him down, and he's not sure he'll ever get over it."

"He's pretty cut up." She bites her bottom lip. "But he'd really love to talk to you."

"What?" My head jolts up. "No, he wouldn't."

"Yeah." Satch nods, obviously surprised by my reaction. "He would have come here himself, but I wouldn't let him. He needs to rest up his knee after climbing those stairs." Her eyebrows dip. "He shouldn't have done that. The doctor and PT said he's got another week before he can move up to his room."

I swallow, guilt slamming me when I realize he broke the rules because I was acting sketchy. Shit. I made him hurt his knee too!

"So, would you be willing to come to his room?" She points over her shoulder.

"And tell him what?"

She shrugs. "The truth. He just needs you to tell him what's been going on. He's really worried about you."

"I hurt him," I whisper.

Satch bites her lip and slowly nods. "This might help heal things."

I scoff, shaking my head. "I doubt it." My expression crumples, tears taking me out before I can stop them. "He's gonna hate me even more when he finds out what I've done."

"Oh. Um..." Satch bounces on her toes before moving to my bed. Taking a seat beside me, she wraps her arm around my shoulders and pulls me close. "It can't be all that bad."

"It is," I wail.

She rubs my back, cradling me against her until the worst of my sobs have passed.

Wiping tears off my cheeks with her thumbs, she moves her head until I have no choice but to look into her kind eyes. Her smile is gentle and sweet.

"Wily could never hate you. He loves you so much. You're his baby sister. His best friend. He's hurt because you didn't tell him a really important thing that happened in your life. And he's hurt because you went behind his back with Grady. If you don't tell him... whatever else it is you've been hiding, it'll only make things worse." Her pale eyebrows form a wonky line over her eyes. "Please, Blake. He needs you. He'll be destroyed if he loses his relationship with you. You're his little butt face."

I let out a shaky, watery laugh, fresh tears lining my lashes as I sniff and try to find the courage to go with her.

Just go! Get it over with!

Satch gets off the bed, awkwardly standing and straightening her clothes before holding out her hand. I reluctantly take it and let her drag me down to Wily's room.

He's sitting on his bed, staring at the wall with this glum look on his face.

His leg is propped up on a stack of pillows, his arms crossed over his broad chest. Even injured, he looks big and strong and a little intimidating.

He's your brother! The one you used to run to, remember?

Sucking in a breath, I force myself to stand at the end of his bed while Satch takes a seat beside him. Threading her fingers through his, she runs comforting circles over the back of his hand while nodding at me.

Oh shit.

This is it.

I open my mouth, not even sure where to start with this big confession, but Wily speaks before I can.

"What were you thinking?" he snaps. "Going behind my back with one of my teammates? Don't you know there's a bro code? I can't believe that asshole broke it!"

"Don't call him that," I quickly bite back. "He didn't

want to, but I just kept throwing myself at him. The poor guy didn't stand a chance. It's my fault, okay? Not his."

"He should have known better," Wily grits out. "It's not good enough."

"Oh, come on," I whine. "Don't make him sound like some villain. He's a good guy. We just got caught up while we were away, and... and then I kissed him again here, and that's what you saw."

His eyes narrow. "You didn't just get caught up; you were full-on sleeping together."

I shrug, unable to argue with that point.

"Is that all it is? Just sex?"

I open my mouth to respond, but I can't, because I honestly don't know. Wily's accusations about Grady still being in love with Teah haven't stopped ringing inside my head. I've just been too distracted over hurting my brother to really soak it all in.

Maybe that's why Grady was so hesitant to get something started with me. Maybe it was more about her and less about my brother.

Shit.

My insides shrivel, my knees wanting to buckle as I stand here quaking at the end of Wily's bed.

I lock them into place and clench my jaw to stop my teeth from chattering.

"You know, it's a good thing you're going back to Chicago. I really appreciate all you did to help me, but I'm okay now, and you need to get back to your life, you know?" He huffs. "I'd love to tell you to keep me posted on how things are going, but you obviously don't want that kind of relationship with me anymore."

"That's not true." I close my eyes.

"How could you not tell me you lost your V-card? That's huge. I told you all about my first time."

"Wily." Squeezing my eyes shut even tighter, I pinch the bridge of my nose. "It's embarrassing talking about it."

"We used to tell each other everything! Even the humiliating stuff! That's what made our relationship so damn special. You're always the one I go to first when shit is happening."

"Not anymore. Not now that you've got Satch." I point to his girlfriend.

"Don't you dare use her to justify what is going on right now! Yes, she's shifted things between us slightly, but you lost your V-card before Satch even came into my life. With *some guy* who might maybe be your boyfriend and sometimes not. What does that even mean?" He flicks his hand up in obvious frustration. "Have you been sleeping around up there? Have you turned into some kind of party girl? You told me you weren't into that scene, which means you outright lied to me. It wasn't just an omission—you *lied to me!*"

I flinch as his voice rises to a thunderous shout.

"Wily." Satch tries to soothe him, her voice like a silken breeze.

He instantly relaxes back against his pillows, the thunder replaced with a gray, depressive kind of fog that's killing me.

"Seriously, sis, you should just go book your flight and get out of here. I think that's best for everyone."

"I can't go back to Chicago," I mumble.

"What?" He whips his head up to look at me.

"I can't go back to Chicago!" I shout. "I don't go to school there anymore!"

There's a horrible, thick beat that weighs a million tons. My legs finally give out and I slump onto the end of his bed, facing away from him.

"Why? Wha— What?" Wily stutters.

With a thick swallow, I talk to the carpet, because it's easier than facing him. "I was going to get an academic suspension and… some disciplinary action. It was just easier for me to withdraw and pay for the damages. Leave quietly, you know?"

"Pay for the damages?"

I hunch my shoulders, trying to make myself as small as possible.

"What happened?" His voice pitches. "What did you do?"

Closing my eyes, I fight the bile surging up my throat and finally… *finally* mumble out my sins. I start with the worst and work my way backward, telling him about Cleo and Nico, Simon, and all the shit we pulled.

"I don't know why I did it," I finish, daring a glance over my shoulder.

He looks shredded, gaping at me like he doesn't even know me anymore.

"And now Cleo's threatening to send photos of me to Mom and Dad unless I keep paying her." I wince, my expression buckling. "And they're really horrible photos, Wily. They can't see them. They can't." I hiccup out the last two words, my stomach convulsing.

Slumping forward, I rest my elbows on my knees and whimper into my hands.

"What are the photos of?"

"You don't want to know."

"Yeah, I do," he grits out, and I force myself to tell him.

"Just me being a drunken idiot, dancing on this table... topless." I wince. "Me and Nico getting it on." Hot bile surges up my throat, but I swallow it back down. "There's another one of me giving Simon a—" I cut myself off. I can't say it. Dammit, if I'd known Cleo was capturing that shit, I would have stopped.

"Blake." Wily's whisper is broken.

I sniff and force out the rest before I lose my nerve. "There are, uh... a few of me shoplifting. I mean, I guess I could argue that I paid for it later, but she snapped me slipping stuff into my bag, so yeah... it's so obviously me being a little shit. And the last one she threatened me with was evidence of..." I lick a tear off the side of my mouth. "Of the spray-painting. I'm holding the can and everything. It's..." I shake my head while my brother hisses.

I turn in time to see his gutted disappointment.

It kills me.

"I can't..." I shake my head, begging him not to judge me, but what right do I have to ask that?

I deserve to be judged!

I've fucked up so badly!

And now he knows. The one person I looked up to all my life. The one who adored me because I was his sweet little sister now knows.

And I can't handle that look on his face.

Sucking in a shaky breath, I lurch off the end of his bed and rush out his door.

"Blake!" he calls, but I can't turn back.

I don't want to hear what he has to say.

I need to get out of here. Hide away.

Something!

Grady. Where are you? I need you to take me away from here. Please!

CHAPTER 49
GRADY

Zander's garage feels hot and stuffy, but I think that's just me.

As I stare across the room at Zoey, snuggled up on her mama's lap, fast asleep, bundled under a blanket and looking as peaceful as ever… I know it's just me.

I'm the one with the leg jackknifing while Zander calmly looks at me from his perch on the arm of the two-seater.

Pressed against the other side of the sofa, I avert my gaze from Zoey's cute little face and Sienna's pained smile. Her compassion is killing me.

When I first walked in here, they were on the bed together, gazing down at Zoey with these adoring smiles. Their whispered words were going over their daughter's head, and I felt like the worst intruder. I started backing out of the garage immediately, but Zander waved me in.

"I don't want to wake her," I whispered.

"She can sleep through a fireworks display." Sienna grinned at me. "Don't worry about it."

She might have been saying that, but she's still kept her voice low this whole time... and when her expression started to fold as she took me in.

"Are you okay?" Zander asked for the both of them, and before I could stop myself, I slumped my butt on the edge of their couch and fessed up with zero coercion on their part. The guilt just tumbled right out of me, splattering all over their floor until they were both blinking at me in surprise.

"So, what are you gonna do?" Zander crosses his arms, his expression serious.

Yeah, I know! I know! I broke the bro code!

Leaning forward, I rest my elbow on my bobbing knee and shake my head.

Then I sigh.

"Fuck," I mutter. "I need to go talk to Wily. If he'll let me. You should have seen his face, brah."

I look at Zander. I have no idea what my face is doing, but it must be pretty pained by the way his forehead is wrinkling.

"I screwed this up so badly."

"Do you love her?" Sienna's question makes my head pop up. I blink at her, not sure what to say. "Or was this just wild sex in the woods?" Her lips twitch.

I let out a breathy laugh and shake my head. "It wasn't just that," I assure them both. "I mean, we thought it would just be a fling, you know? And then we'd come back to Nolan and pretend it never happened. But..." I shake my head. "I couldn't do it."

"So, you do love her." Sienna's face brightens.

I wince, rubbing my forehead. "It's been a week."

"So? People fall in love that quickly all the time."

"I don't know if I'm ready for that again. I mean, that breakup with Teah was brutal and—"

"You're still not over her, are you?"

"I..." My shoulders shrug before I can stop them. "No. Yes. I mean... I..." Squeezing my eyes shut, I force myself to think it through.

Am I still in love with Teah the way Wily thinks I am?

Images of our time together flash through my head—the ease of how we got together. Everything was so uncomplicated. We never fought... not until nearer the end. We just... got along from Day One. It was comfortable.

And boring.

She said you were boring.

My mind quickly jumps to Blake—the complete opposite of boring. She's had me on my toes from Day One. It's been stressful... and exciting. Being in the forest with her was... magic.

"You're obviously torn." Zander reaches over, squeezing my shoulder. "And until you figure it out, you guys should probably cool off, you know? For Wily's sake."

I wince, rubbing my forehead.

"I mean, if you really love her... if this is something that you can see going long term, then I'd fight for it, man. Wily will come around. He's got a good heart. He's just been thunder-punched, and he needs a minute to process that. You know how protective he is of Blake. Those two are tight."

"Yeah," I murmur, unwilling to share just how much Blake's been hiding from him.

But she let you in. She trusts you.

I can't go bailing on her now. She needs me... and I want to be there for her.

Because you love her. You're just scared to admit it.

Working my jaw to the side, I shake the thought from my mind.

I'm not scared.

I'm being cautious.

I can't go handing my heart away only to have it broken again. What if Blake turns around and decides I'm boring too?

What if she doesn't love me back?

"Grady?" I hear a voice in the driveway and ping to my feet.

Looking out the tinted windows of the garage, I spot Blake hovering near my Jeep. She looks fragile and cold, her face a puffy, blotchy mess.

Opening the door, I quickly beckon her into the garage. "Blake. C'mere."

The second she spots me, her face floods with relief. Her blonde curls fly out behind her as she runs toward me, throwing herself at me.

I wrap my arm around her waist, lifting her off her feet and carrying her into Zander and Sienna's space.

Taking a seat on the couch, I pull her onto my lap, and she burrows against me, stealing a cautious look at Sienna and Zander before softly whispering to me.

"I told him. He knows everything now."

Shit. I know how much that cost her.

Kissing her forehead, I rub circles on her back. "How'd he take it?"

She shakes her head, gently sniffing as she nestles her forehead into the crook of my neck.

Her tears are silent—soft and slow—as she snuggles against me.

All I can be is a solid wall to hold her steady.

There are no words right now.

Just quiet pain.

And I try to absorb as much of it as I can while composing the ultimate apology to my roommate.

Even if he can't forgive me, I have to convince him to forgive his little sister.

CHAPTER 50
BLAKE

Nothing is resolved by the time we go to bed.

I'm still not ready to face my brother and that disgusted, shocked, *who the hell are you* look on his face, so I sneak up to my room, feigning a migraine, and desperately try to get some sleep.

It doesn't work.

All I want is Grady's arms around me and for this to all be over. But I doubt sneaking to his room tonight is a good idea.

Is Wily right?

Is Grady still in love with his ex-girlfriend?

Am I just a fling that he's trying to get out of his system?

The thought sits horrible and heavy in my chest, making it hard to breathe again. I do my best not to panic but end up sitting up, kicking the covers off me, and pacing the room while I try to regulate my heartbeat.

It's about two in the morning, and I'm close to losing

my mind when my phone buzzes with a series of texts and photographs.

Frowning, I snatch the device off the nightstand, wondering why my Do Not Disturb isn't on, then feel my heart plummet into my stomach.

Cleo's name is splattered all over my screen.

Cleo: Gimme more money. Or I'm sending these to your parents.

Fresh images pop up, ones I didn't even know were taken. There's a photo of me making out with Cleo. It was a dare, and I figured a little kissing wouldn't hurt anyone. We didn't take it further than that, but I have vague memories of Nico and Simon cheering us on.

My parents won't see it that way. The skimpy outfit I'm wearing, my tongue in another girl's mouth? They won't get that it was just a little college fun.

Because it wasn't fun. You felt so incredibly uncomfortable, don't you remember?

I played it off like it was my idea, but Cleo launched herself at me first.

The next image is me flashing the camera, my boobs on full display as I pull my shirt wide and let the camera see it all. My tongue is sticking out, and I have this wild, crazy look on my face.

That was at the heavy metal concert. I can't even remember the name of the band. It was loud, crashing music that made my eardrums bleed, but I pretended that I loved it.

I swallow, feeling sick as another memory crashes through me, Simon pouring beer all over my chest, then licking it off. He thought it was the funniest thing in the world.

And yep… there's the photo.

I'm laughing, totally intoxicated and barely aware of what I'm doing.

Shit. I was such a fool.

I thought my parents had me locked in this prison of academia and perfect appearances, but all I did was walk straight out of one cell and into another. I wasn't happy leading this reckless life. I was terrified the whole time. Worried I'd get busted.

And I did.

I got myself into the worst kind of trouble, and it didn't end when I got to Nolan.

Whoops. Forgot to mention those indiscretions to Wily. Better add it to the list.

Shit. There's so much to confess.

My stomach starts to hurt as I plunk myself onto the edge of the bed, perching my heels on the frame and staring at those photos.

Cleo will send these to my parents if I don't pay her off.

She's obviously got a stockpile, and I will continue to be her prisoner until she runs out of them. Who knows if she's even deleting them each time I pay her?

Probably not. She's smarter than that.

I'm the stupid one who let her play me because I needed to become something else.

Letting out a shaky breath, I flick through those images, one after another. They're so awful. If my parents see these with no explanation attached, they'll be wrecked.

They'll be wrecked either way. You're not their little angel anymore.

And Cleo knows it, because I told her everything. She knows I'm a trust fund baby and that my family is loaded. She knows about my monthly allowance, which is more than what she earns in a year. Her bitter tone rings through my head.

That's why she's coming after me. Because she knows I'll pay up.

Shit, she owns me.

And until I take her greatest threat away… she will *always* own me.

A cold shudder runs through my body. I'm so spent after my harrowing afternoon confession, but I'll never be truly free until I endure one more.

"I really want to be free," I whisper, my mind going back to the forest… to Grady.

I was free there.

I was happy.

I was… *me*.

"But they don't know me." I think about my family—my brother… my parents.

How were they ever supposed to when I kept putting on a show the way I did?

Am I seriously going to keep spending the rest of my life doing that?

Letting Cleo have this hold over me?

Letting myself be ruled by my parents' expectations?

I may not know exactly what I want right now—but I do know that I don't want that.

They're gonna be horrified either way, but maybe if they hear the truth from me first, it'll be easier for them to handle.

Just like... maybe if Grady and I had talked to Wily first, rather than him catching us, it would have been less traumatic for him.

Sniffing, I slash a tear off my cheek, and before another panic attack sets in for real, I dial my father's number.

"Hello?" His voice is groggy, but the second he hears my pitiful whimper, he's alert and saying my name. "Blakey? Bean, what's wrong?"

"Is that Blake? Is she okay?" Mom's voice pitches. "What's the matter?"

"I don't know. She hasn't said anything yet?"

"Well, why not? Why is she calling us so late? Oh my gosh, is Wily okay?" Her voice quakes, panic obviously nipping at her.

"Calm down, Joanne. We need to let her speak. Blake, talk to me."

I suck in a shaky breath, my chest shuddering when I release it. "I have to tell you guys something."

"Is Wily okay?" Mom's voice comes through loud and clear. She must have grabbed the phone off Dad and put it on speaker.

"Yeah," I whisper. "He's fine. Everything's good with him."

"Oh, thank God. I thought you were calling with some kind of knee emergency." I can picture Mom patting her chest, then looking at the time. "Why aren't you asleep? What are you doing calling us at this hour?"

"I, um..." With another sniff, I will my courage not to

fail me. "I know I should have waited until morning, but I was worried that I'd chicken out. And then I was worried Wily might call you. And then..." My eyes fill with tears. "I mean now... I'm freaking out that you might get an email from someone named Cleo."

"Cleo." Dad's voice is gruff, confused. "Who's Cleo?"

"She was my roommate."

"No, your roommate's Claire. We met her."

"Yeah." I let out a short, choking laugh. "That was Cleo pretending to be Claire."

There's a thick pause, and I can picture my parents looking at each other in confusion.

"We lied to you," I confess in a tiny voice. "I've been lying to you for months."

"Wh-what?" Mom sounds thunderstruck, and I force myself to keep going.

"Cleo's not the sweet, good girl we led you to believe. She's a total party animal, and she pulled me into her world. I let her."

They take a second to absorb that.

"So..." Dad clears his throat. "So, you've been going to parties? Drinking? You're underage."

I sigh. "Yeah. I've been... I've been getting up to a lot of things I shouldn't have."

The stone-cold silence that follows that statement is harrowing. It's tempting to hang up and get rid of my phone, but that won't change the inevitable, right? I still have to get this shit out in the open.

"Okay." Mom clears her throat before I can keep talking. "So, you're telling us that the allowance we've been depositing into your account each month has been going toward illegal substances and a fake ID?"

I cringe and bob my head, even though they can't see me.

"You've been wasting your time and money," she snaps. "How are you maintaining your grades?"

"I'm... I'm not."

"So, you're failing?" Dad barks.

"Yes," I whisper. "And then... I withdrew."

"What?" He obviously didn't hear me, and I'm forced to say it again.

Clearing my throat, I suck in a breath and hit my parents with news I know will shatter them. "They were going to give me an academic suspension because I haven't been attending classes regularly, and then I... I did something." I suck in a sharp breath. "I spray-painted a professor's house, and they caught me. I had no recourse, so I offered to pay for damages and withdraw from the school. I'm no longer a student. Anywhere."

"Oh... my..." Mom's voice pitches, and the rest of her sentence is lost to a soft wail.

"You..." Dad can't comprehend it either. "You... you did what? You... Blake, I can't believe this."

"It's all true, Dad."

They don't say anything after that, and I haven't even told them about the shoplifting and Grady having to pick me up from the liquor store. Or how he had to take me to the hospital.

Shit. Grady.

Do I mention him too?

And what about the photos Cleo is threatening to send? Shit, I *have* to tell them about that.

Swallowing down what's left of my tattered pride...

Pride? Are you kidding? You shed your dignity months ago. Just own it and move the fuck on!

Closing my eyes, I quickly rush out the rest. "Cleo's threatening to send you some very upsetting photos unless I pay her off. I've been doing it ever since I left Chicago. and I realized tonight that if I don't stop now, she'll drain me dry. I can't keep letting her have this hold over me. So..." I huff. "If you get an email from Cleo or Claire or whatever the hell she plans on calling herself, please ignore it. It'll only upset you. And if you can't and you have to look, I'm sorry. Okay? I'm sorry I couldn't keep being the perfect little angel you thought I was. I'm sorry I lost my mind and went completely crazy. I've let you down. I know I've let you down, and I can't take it back. I'm sorry." I whimper the last two words.

They're still not saying anything, and I have to take it for what it is.

I'm not their golden girl anymore.

They can't boast about me to their friends. I'm now the kid they have to avoid talking about at dinner parties.

I knew this would happen.

This is what I was so damn afraid of.

If I'm not their perfect performing monkey, then they have no need for me.

Covering my mouth, I wait for them to say something. *Anything.*

But all I get is a weeping sniff from Mom and a stony silence from Dad.

After a full minute, I can't take it anymore.

So, before they can find the right words to say, I hang up.

I want to turn my phone off, but before I can do that, I have to send one last text to Cleo.

Send whatever the fuck you want. We're done. You can't own me anymore. Never contact me again.

As soon as the message goes through, I block her number, then switch off my phone.

It's done.

I'm finally free of her.

And quite possibly my parents, although that part feels awful.

I knew I risked their disappointment, and that kept me silent all this time.

But who knows what they're thinking or saying to each other right now.

I'm not their little angel anymore. That much I know for a fact.

I don't know what the hell I am.

CHAPTER 51
GRADY

It's the first day back after spring break, and I'm toast.

After my forest fling, an intense four days of truncated spring training, and then the truth explosion that went off in Football Frat, I've returned to classes anything but refreshed.

Shit, it's hard to concentrate when all I can think about is Blake and how to fix things between her and Wily.

She was still asleep when I left this morning. So was Wily.

From what I can tell, things are still pretty frosty between them, and I'm not sure how to fix it.

I really need to—

I stutter to a stop when I round the corner and find Teah waiting outside Athletes Hall. There's a little spot in the sunshine where she used to stand and wait for me.

And now she's waiting for Mac.

My stomach sinks and I clench my jaw, looking away from her pretty face. She'll always be beautiful. She puts in the effort to be just so, and I always appreciated that about her. I love her style. She's got a great sense of fashion and knows exactly how to highlight her best features.

Blake's like that, too, although she seems to do it with way less thought.

An image of her makeup-free with her blonde curls in a messy ponytail hits me. She was so raw and unchecked in the forest... and she was fucking gorgeous.

Swallowing, I move forward, knowing I'll cross paths with Teah and having to be okay with it. I need some lunch if I'm gonna get through afternoon classes and a weights session.

Teah glances up from her phone just as I pass her.

"Hey, Grady." Her smile is instant, like she's forgotten we've broken up.

Shit, it'd be so natural to pull her against me and kiss her hello.

But she's not my girl anymore.

"How are you?"

"Uh... yeah." I shrug.

Her nose wrinkles, her eyes telling me she knows I'm anything but good.

I glance away from her. Damn, it's all so familiar. She knows me better than anyone, because I let her all the way in.

"How was your spring break?" she asks, her voice cautious, like she can tell it wasn't great.

Well, she's wrong.

"It was amazing." I force a smile. "Went hiking and had..." My voice softens. "I had the best time."

"I bet you did." She grins. "You and the forest have always been one."

My lips twitch before rising into a genuine smile. "Yeah."

"Well, I'm glad that part went well. How was the rest of it, though?" She touches my arm. "Are you okay?"

I nod, then for some reason end up spilling, "Things are a bit rough at Football Frat."

"Oh no, what happened?"

"Wily's pissed off with me."

She blinks in surprise, her glossy lips parting. "I heard about his injury. That's awful. But… why is he mad at you?"

I wince. "Because he saw me making out with his sister."

"What?" She laughs. "You didn't. Grady Newman. Bro code!"

"I know." I cringe, pinching the bridge of my nose. "I know."

"Unless…" She lets the word hang until I look at her again. "She means something to you. Like, you didn't just break bro code because you were horny, and there's more to it."

Licking my lips, I nod. I have to, because there is more to it. Sure, Blake makes me hornier than I've ever been, but there's definitely more to it.

"Oooo… how hard are you falling?"

Okay, talking about this with my ex is too weird. All I can do is shrug and try to get out of this conversation.

She catches my eye, and I give her a pained smile before looking away again. "You still with Mac?"

"Yep." Her voice goes quiet.

I purse my lips, still hating the fact that she moved on with someone who is so completely opposite to me.

"I swear I never cheated on you, Grady."

"Yeah, I know." I swallow, this antsy, restless feeling starting to eat at me.

I can't even explain it.

Talking to Teah like this is so familiar and easy. Our relationship was always drama-free. No irate brothers. No secrets. We were just us. My mom and dad and Emma all adored her. Her parents liked me.

Easy.

Easy, easy, easy.

But—

"Well, I better get going." Teah points past me, and I turn to see Mac sauntering out of Athletes Hall. He's staring at me with an intensity that's off-putting. What does he think I'm trying to do? Steal her away? That's not my style.

"Hey." Teah's smile is all loved-up and gooey as she rushes past me and straight into his arms. He lifts her off her feet, his lips twitching when she wraps her arms around his neck.

He looks at me again, his *she's mine* vibes impossible to miss.

Yeah, I get it buddy. You won.

Turning away from the lovefest, I head inside, my mind overtaken with the feel of Blake in my arms.

Have I won too?

Being in the forest with Blake was perfect. We were caught in our own little world, but that's not reality, and I'm not sure how I'm gonna win Wily over or what to do about Blake.

Should I fight for her?

Wily's not gonna be okay with some lame-ass fling. I need to commit to Blake. Which means I need to commit to helping her and taking on all the shit she's going through right now.

I want to be with her. I love being with her... when it's just us and the world's not trying to disrupt what we're doing.

Damn, I wish I could just disappear back into the forest the way she wants to. That would be fucking perfect.

But it's not life. We can't become hermits just because we don't want to face the conflict.

Her future is so uncertain. She needs to tell her parents the truth. She needs to figure out what she's going to do with her life.

Do I really want to throw myself into the middle of it all?

And now I'm back to worrying that if I do... she'll figure out that I'm not the best choice. Just like Teah did, she'll work out that I'm too boring and set in my ways.

She'll realize she wants something better—someone more exciting—and I'll be left alone all over again.

Shit. I don't know what the fuck to do.

CHAPTER 52
BLAKE

I stayed in my room all day, only sneaking out for a small amount of sustenance when my stomach was growling so badly I couldn't stand it.

I crept down the stairs and stole into the pantry, making it back up to my room without encountering my brother. Thank God for that.

He tried to connect with me earlier in the day, knocked on my door and called my name. I couldn't face him, not after that horrible phone call with my parents, so I pretended to be asleep.

Having spent most of the night awake, it wasn't hard to play dead. I'm seriously exhausted. Wily watched me pretending to sleep for so long, I think I did actually drift off for a while there.

I woke up with a growling stomach, did a sneaky food snatch, then retreated to my room and have spent the rest of the day glancing at my phone while trying to watch movies off my laptop.

I still haven't turned my phone back on since texting Cleo a proverbial "fuck you." And I'm too scared to do it. There's probably a message on there from my parents, and I don't want to face them right now either.

It's a miracle they haven't driven up from Denver to see me. Maybe they still will.

A flush of tension runs through my body as I imagine that scenario—their ashen faces, their deep disappointment.

Ugh. I can't face it!

I just want to hide away from the world until I feel like I can breathe again. Is that really such a bad thing? I told the truth like I was supposed to, and it's been a complete shit show! Let me wallow, for fuck's sake!

Although, wallowing is killing me.

My body is aching from being in bed all day. My head is pounding from lack of sleep and fresh air. This room is making me claustrophobic, but leaving it only means angst and drama and—

The sound of a Jeep pulling into the driveway catches my attention. Rushing to the window, I peer out and spot Grady hopping out with his bag.

Closing my eyes in relief, I press my forehead against the glass and bite my bottom lip.

Thank God he's back.

It's been the longest day ever, and I need a hug, some reassurance that I can survive all of this.

Rushing to get dressed, I throw my stinky pajamas into the laundry hamper and spray on my best-smelling deodorant. I then pull on my favorite pair of yoga pants and the baggy sweatshirt Wily gave me when he left for college. I used to steal it all the time because it was so big and comfy. He ended up giving it to me the day we dropped him off at Nolan U, and I nearly cried. He grinned down at me, gave me the biggest hug, and told me, "I'm only ever a phone call away. And you better call me, butt face."

"I will," I promised, knowing we'd stay in touch because we told each other everything.

Until I started fucking up my life and keeping secrets.

Shit.

The sweatshirt flops down to my mid-thighs as I run fingers through my tatty hair.

Seriously?

Glancing in the mirror, I gape at my horrid reflection. I look like a ghost with red-rimmed eyes and scarecrow hair.

Quickly snatching my makeup bag, I do some hasty work, tidying myself up. I keep the look natural, because going overboard would be so damn obvious. I just want to take the edge off by covering the gray bags under my eyes and running a pick comb through my hair.

Fifteen minutes later, I'm looking at least presentable and ready for a Grady hug.

I hope he's up for talking to me. He was so sweet yesterday afternoon when we hung out with Sienna and Zander. They were pretty nice about it all, although it's clear they want things amended with Wily as soon as possible.

Shit, I really need to talk to him.

Maybe after I hug Grady and ask about his day, he'll come with me to see Wily. I'm not sure what we'll say to him, but maybe if we present a united front to show Wily that we're not just messing around here...

I mean, I think we're not, right?

I really care about Grady. I think I might be falling in love with him.

The thought of having to end things just because my brother is pissed off... well, that's not fair.

Grady and I aren't over, are we?

Unless he's still in love with Teah.

My stomach coils as I stare at my reflection in the mirror.

Either way, I still want to see him. I still need to hug him and assure myself that I haven't lost everything. That I haven't destroyed every relationship in my life.

Please, not Grady. Don't let me lose him too!

Rushing for the door, I fling it open and listen out for where he might be in the house.

I hear voices downstairs and tiptoe to the landing, figuring out that Grady and my brother are talking in the living room.

Shit!

Holding my breath, I creep down the top few steps and lean against the wall so I can hear what they're saying.

"...I shouldn't have done what I did. It was wrong to go behind your back," Grady's saying. "I should have told you that I was starting to catch feelings for your sister before I left for the forest. I really tried to fight it, man. I swear I did. I thought I was strong enough to resist her, but—"

Wily growls. "I don't want to know the details."

"I never disrespected her if that's what you're worried about."

"Of course I'm not! You're the most respectful guy I

know. I'm just pissed off that you kept secrets from me. I'm pissed off that she let you in on all her shit before telling me about it."

Grady doesn't say anything, because what is he supposed to say? None of that was his fault. I mean, sure, he encouraged me to open up, but he didn't know Wily would be so offended.

Wily sighs. "I guess I should expect it. Blake and I can't be best friends forever."

"Yes, you can. She was just afraid of telling you because she knew you'd be disappointed in her. She was worried you were going to hate her."

Wily doesn't say anything, and my stomach squeezes into a tight ball. I'm desperate for him to deny all of that.

"I could never hate her. She's my sister."

But he's not saying it! Why isn't he saying it?

"I know this sucks, man. Watching her suffer is killing me too," Grady murmurs. At least I think that's what he's saying. It's hard to catch everything when he's talking so quietly.

Wily mumbles something back, and I frown, walking a little farther down the stairs.

"...broke the bro code, and there's no excuse for that."

Another huff from my brother. "I just need to know that you're not using her as some kind of rebound to get over Teah. I—"

A phone starts ringing, cutting off Wily and making my heart stop. I need to know too!

Answer him, Grady. Assure him. Assure me*!*

The phone rings until it cuts off, and then Grady lets out a sigh, obviously about to answer him when the phone starts ringing again.

"Oh, just fucking take the call," Wily growls.

My face scrunches as I swallow down my own growl. Stupid fucking phone call!

"Hey, Bella. What's up?"

Who's Bella?

With a confused little humph, I walk down a few more steps, then stop when Grady's voice pitches.

"What?" It's impossible to miss his shocked panic, and I race down the stairs before I can think about it.

Instinct has me rushing to check on him, and my gut plummets when I take in his ashen expression.

"When?" His voice gets sharp. "At the hospital?... Yeah, I'm on my way."

He hangs up, sees me standing in the archway of the living room, and his brown eyes darken with intensity, his jaw clenching.

"Are you okay?" I whisper, my heart thudding erratically at the silent agony pulsing out of him.

Wily whips a look at me, runs his eyes down what I'm wearing, then turns back to check on Grady. "Dude, what's up?" He grabs for his crutches.

Grady holds up his hand to stop him. "Teah's been in a car accident. That was one of her sisters from the sorority. They're freaking out. Thought I should know."

"Is she okay?" Wily's obvious concern makes me realize what a part of the Football Frat family Teah used to be.

"I'm not sure, man. It sounds pretty bad. She's in the hospital." Grady looks so torn up right now. "I need to go check on her."

"I'll come." Wily struggles to stand.

“No. I’ll go,” I tell my brother, then turn to the side table where Grady keeps his keys.

He needs me right now, and I can’t care that we’re going to see his ex-girlfriend. Grady looks too cut up to be able to drive, so I will take him. And I’ll make sure he gets through this… no matter what it costs me.

CHAPTER 53
GRADY

Teah's in the hospital.

It's bad.

Bella was crying on the phone. She hadn't made it to the hospital yet, but she needed me to know.

And I have to be there for her.

She may not be my woman anymore, but the idea of Teah dying kinda kills me.

She better be okay.

I have to find out what happened.

Car accident.

Was she driving?

Or was it Mac?

Fuck, if he injured her, I will end that fucker!

Anger overrides the worry coursing through me, and by the time Blake pulls into the hospital parking lot, my muscles are vibrating.

She didn't say anything on the way over, and I'm grateful. I can't talk anyway. The only sound in the car was the Maps instructions. The man's voice directed us to the hospital the quickest way possible. Blake sped the entire way there. She wasn't reckless, just fast and efficient, and the second she cuts the engine, I'm out the door.

Racing into the emergency room, I head for the desk and am about to ask where Teah is when someone calls my name.

"Grady, over here."

I spin and find Teah's father beckoning me over.

"Hey." Walking around the chairs, I join him by the vending machine. He looks pale and gaunt, the look in his eyes freaking me out.

"Is she okay?"

"She's gonna make it, but she's pretty banged up." He blinks, his eyes glassing over. "Broken arm, cracked ribs, stitches from the glass. Concussion."

My insides spasm as I picture the impact that must have caused such trauma. "Any internal injuries?"

"They don't think so, but they're monitoring her. She'll be in here for a few days." His eyes flick past me, his brow wrinkling with confusion when I feel Blake's hand slip into mine.

I glance down, giving her fingers a light squeeze. What am I supposed to say right now? Introduce her to my ex's father?

"Hi. I'm Blake." She gives him a sympathetic smile. "I'm sorry this is happening."

"Me too," the man mutters, not bothering to introduce himself before leading the way down a series of corridors.

Blake is tense beside me, and now I feel rude for not making proper introductions, but I doubt this man even cares who she is when his daughter is stuck in a hospital with multiple injuries.

We turn left and I spot Teah's mother, who's crying into her hands and shouting, "He needs to get out! I want him out!"

"Natalie?" Mr. Rogers rushes forward. "What's going on?"

"He's in there!" She points to a hospital room door. "And he's refusing to leave! I couldn't stand the sight of him, so I had to wait out here, but you have to make him go, Colin! He needs to go!"

"Who?" I ask, releasing Blake's hand and darting to the door so I can see what's going on.

Peering through the glass, I spot Mac leaning over Teah's body. He has a banged-up face and a bandaged hand. But the worst part is... the look on his face. He's staring down at her with an expression of pure guilt. She's out of it, completely unaware of his presence, and seeing her so pale, bruises mottling her freckled skin... it makes something inside me snap.

"Was he driving the car?" I growl, glancing at her parents and knowing the answer before they can respond.

I knew he was no good for her!

Pushing the door open, I rush into the room and grab him by the back of the collar.

"You fucker," I whisper-bark, yanking him away from the bed.

"Get your hands off me," he snarls, going for a punch.

I block it, flicking his arm away and noticing the wince of pain. He's injured, no doubt beat up by the car accident. But he's not lying in a hospital with broken bones, is he?

Not letting go of his collar, I respect Mr. and Mrs. Rogers's wishes and haul him out of the room.

"Get off me!" he shouts, but I won't let up.

As soon as we're free of Teah's room, her mother rushes back in there as I shove Mac against the wall.

"You're supposed to look after her!" I push him back when he tries to move.

"It wasn't my fault! It was a fucking accident! You think I want to see her this way?" He wrestles against me, fisting my sweater and tussling with me in the hall.

He's taller than me, but I'm fucking stronger, and I have him pinned on the floor in a second.

"You stay away from her," I warn him. "You're no fucking good for her!"

"I know!" he shouts back, his expression crumpling like this is pure torture. "I thought she was dead." His whispered words are broken, his eyes glassing like he's reliving the horror show all over again. "I thought she was dead."

"Grady." A soft hand lands on my shoulder, giving me a squeeze. "Let him go."

Glancing up, I notice Blake. She's staring down at Mac like she can feel his pain.

I want to snap at her to not give him any sympathy. He doesn't deserve it. I know about this guy. He's wild and reckless. He would have been speeding. He put Teah in danger!

"I want him out of here," Mr. Rogers barks. He's talking to someone down the hallway, and the scuffling of feet tells me it's security. "Get him out of my sight."

"I'm not leaving her," Mac growls from the floor, and I tighten my grip on him. "Get your fucking hands off me." His blue eyes burn with intensity, his thin lips forming a scowl. I glare at the piercing in his bottom lip, then take in the black bruising around his eyes. He must have broken his nose. There's still blood on his shirt.

Fuck. I can hear the screeching of tires and crunching of metal.

I want to know exactly what happened.

But I also don't.

Because picturing Teah's body being slammed and crunched that way, her neck snapping back as her bones cracked and broke... Shit. How much pain was she in?

"We've got him." A security guard taps me on the shoulder.

"I'm not leaving her," Mac tries again. "Don't touch me." He wrestles against the guards, and it takes two of them to drag him down the corridor, his shouts echoing off the walls. "I'm not leaving her! She needs me! She needs me!"

CHAPTER 54
BLAKE

The man's cries are haunting, filling the hospital with his fear and desperation.

I don't know who he is. I'm guessing Teah's boyfriend from what Grady was saying.

He seems to really care about her. That look of devastation on his face when he thought she was dead was kind of harrowing.

But man... Grady wasn't having it.

I've never seen him so angry before.

He's still in love with her.

It's obvious.

And it's taking everything in me to keep my emotions in check.

Leaning back against the hospital wall, I watch Grady calm Teah's father. His voice is so soft and soothing. I love it. I love how deep it is.

I watch his lips move but can't hear what he's saying.

Keeping my distance seems like the right thing to do. A moment later, Teah's mother comes out of the room.

She's crying, tears trickling down her face as she steps into Grady's embrace.

He comforts her, too, and it's becoming clearer by the second.

He's part of this family.

He belongs with them.

Teah may have broken it off, but it's clear her parents would much rather have their daughter with Grady than the guy with all the piercings.

Grady Newman is the stable one. The sensible choice.

He's *my* choice, but that's not up to me now, is it?

Biting my lips together, I shuffle quietly down the hallway.

Grady's still caught up in conversation and doesn't notice me slip away.

That's a good thing.

It's probably best that I quietly disappear into the ether and let him get on with his life.

It's better this way.

For him.

He deserves uncomplicated and easy.

All I've brought him is lies and secrecy and drama. I've potentially destroyed one of his closest friendships, forced him into situations he didn't want to be in. He got a fat lip rescuing me from a party I shouldn't have been at.

I even made him sleep with me when he didn't really want to.

What kind of bitch does that?

He deserves better than me.

So I'm just gonna go. The only person who can figure

out my life is me, and I shouldn't be pulling Grady into that just because I'm too weak to deal.

Slipping out of the hospital, I realize I'm still holding Grady's keys, so I walk back to reception and quickly explain the situation. The woman behind the desk seems annoyed at having an extra job given to her, but I write a note and tell her that he'll come looking for them, so she doesn't even have to move from her chair.

She rolls her eyes and lets me do it. Then I dart out of the hospital and nearly bump into Teah's boyfriend.

He's waiting outside, leaning against the hospital wall and smoking a cigarette. He looks agitated. His face bunches into a harsh scowl as he blows a stream of smoke into the air.

Yeah, he really is the opposite of Grady.

No wonder Teah's parents want him gone. He's got *wild bad boy* written all over him.

I gaze at him for a second, trying to figure out his story. Is he as lost as me? Was Teah helping him find his way home? Has she been the same beacon Grady's been for me?

Obviously sensing my gaze, his head turns in my direction, and I quickly spin away, not wanting to connect with him.

Our two sorry asses standing in this parking lot pitying ourselves isn't going to achieve anything.

I kind of have to admire the guy for not leaving, though.

He may have been kicked out of the hospital, but I've got a feeling he's gonna stand guard outside its walls until they let him back in. Even if it takes all night.

A cold breeze whips across my body and I cross my

arms, hunching my shoulders and walking down to the main road. I don't have my phone on me, so I can't order an Uber. All I can do is walk and hope I'm going in the right direction.

Thankfully, I end up passing a taxi around the other side of the hospital, and I'm able to wave it down. He drives me back to Football Frat, then has to wait for me while I run inside and get money for him. He's really nice about it, so I give him an extra-large tip.

When I go back inside, I pause in the entryway, listening for voices.

I didn't hear any when I rushed in, and I can't hear any now.

But the door was unlocked.

"Wily?" I call quietly, kind of relieved when he doesn't answer me.

Creeping up the stairs, I tiptoe to his bedroom door and press my ear against it.

A soft moan reaches me and I cringe, stepping back from the wood and not wanting to picture what must be going on in there right now.

"Yes, baby. That's good. You feel so good." Wily's voice is only mildly muffled by the door, and I shudder.

Yeah, I *really* don't want to know what he and Satch are doing in there.

So I rush back to my room and close the door behind me.

The second it clicks, I'm swamped with that horrible sense of claustrophobia again. I can't stay in this space. I can't hide under the covers. I can't be here when Grady finally gets back.

I don't want to see that look of regret on his face as he

takes my hand and softly tells me that he's so sorry, but his heart belongs to Teah. He thought he could get over her, but he can't move on.

She needs him more than ever now, and there's no space for me in his life anymore.

I get it.

I really do.

She's easy. I'm complicated.

"I should go," I whisper, gazing around the guest room before jumping into action and snatching my clothes off the floor. Bundling them into my bag, I work at a furious pace, gathering up my stuff.

Darting into the bathroom, I grab my toothbrush but leave my shampoo in the shower. I can restock when I get to where I'm going.

Where's that?

How the hell should I know!

My insides swirl into chaos as I dart down the stairs, fishing Wily's keys out of the bowl. I'll get his truck back to him somehow. He's not supposed to be driving it right now anyway. It'll just be a few days. Once I'm settled, I'll call and let him know, and we can work out logistics.

Stop acting like a crazy person!

I ignore common sense and rush to his truck, throwing my bags in the back. My laptop case topples and falls onto the floor, but I leave it, wanting to get out of here before someone sees me.

Revving the engine, I back out of the driveway and narrowly miss clipping a car parked on the road. Shit, this truck is huge!

Sucking in a breath that's too shallow, I steel myself and press down on the accelerator.

I have no idea where I'm going.

It can't be Denver—my parents don't want to see me right now.

It can't be Chicago.

Maybe LA? I do love the beaches.

Or maybe New York.

I shake my head, barely conscious of my direction as I weave out of Nolan.

That's all I know for sure.

I have to get out of Nolan.

CHAPTER 55
GRADY

It takes me a good long minute to help calm Mrs. Rogers down. She's distraught, and for some reason, she's clinging to me and not her irate husband, who is still pacing behind us, muttering foul-mouthed insults about Finn Macalister.

Okay, maybe I do know why she wants to hold me instead.

She eventually stops blubbering, leaving a massive tearstain on my shirt, then tells me I should go sit with Teah for a bit.

Patting my arm, she ushers me into the room, ignoring my offers to get her coffee.

"Colin will look after me. You go. Be with our girl." The vulnerable look on her face makes it impossible to argue, and if I'm honest, I don't want to.

I just need to see Teah properly, with my own two eyes, and assure myself that she's going to make it.

Quietly stepping into the room, I move around the

bed, watching her face carefully and trying not to disturb her. It kills me to see her like this. She may not be my girlfriend anymore, but I'll always care about her. We shared nearly a whole year together. The intensity of the summer after we got together was like a year in two months, and by the time we got back to college, we were already into the settled stage. Shit, if she'd asked me to move in with her, I would have said yes in a heartbeat. But she wanted to stay with her sorority girls, and I love Football Frat.

So we spent nights at each other's places. We met up most days for a coffee or a meal together. When I wasn't caught up with football, I was with her. We'd study together, party together… I thought we were endgame.

But that was never in the cards for her.

I wasn't her one.

And maybe she's not yours.

As I take a seat beside her and gently brush my fingers down her arm, I think of Blake.

She left while I was hugging Mrs. Rogers. I'm assuming she's just gone to the bathroom, or maybe she's hunting down some drinks for us. It was good of her to come with me. I'm grateful for her support, and as soon as I'm done with Teah, I'll go and find her.

Just a few minutes to gather myself, and then I'll check on Blake and figure out what to do. It's probably best that we leave. Now that Mac's gone, Teah's parents can relax. I'll check with security again before I go, make sure he doesn't try and come back to her room again. I'm hoping he's left the hospital altogether. Maybe he's walking the streets, hopefully berating himself and finding the guts to break up with her. For her own good.

"Mm-hmm." Teah makes a soft noise, and I glance up to see her eyes fluttering open.

She winces, touching her forehead with trembling fingers.

"Hey," I whisper. "You okay? Do you need more pain meds or…?"

With a confused frown, she turns to me and blinks like she's trying to clear her vision. "Grady? What are you doing here?"

"I heard what happened. Had to come make sure you were okay." I reach for her hand, but she recoils from my touch, looking around the room.

"Where's Mac?"

"He left."

"What?" Her eyes flood, her lips trembling as she sucks in a breath. "He left?"

Aw man, I so wish I could play this off that it was his choice. She can do so much better than him.

But I can't lie to her.

So, against my better judgment, I softly explain, "He was asked to leave. Your parents didn't want him here."

"That's not their decision." She tries to sit up, causing herself obvious pain.

Lurching from my chair, I gently lower her back to the pillow. "Take it easy."

"I want Mac. I need Mac!" she shouts at me. "Why'd you make him leave?"

"Teah, he hurt you."

"No, he didn't!" Her voice pitches.

"Teah—"

"No, stop!" She squeezes her eyes shut, her face

scrunching in obvious pain before she whispers, "I need Mac."

"Okay. Okay," I soothe her, gently rubbing her arm. "Just stay calm. Rest. We'll... find him." I have to grit out the last two words, hating that he's the only comfort she wants.

Sucking in a shaky breath, she rests her head back and blinks at the ceiling. A slow tear trickles out of the side of her eye, and I suddenly feel like I don't belong here. I shouldn't have come. Who am I in her life now?

No one.

I'm the ex.

She doesn't want me, she wants *him*.

Slumping back in my seat, I play with my bottom lip as I stare at her. I should go look for her man, but I just need a second.

This request will cause an argument with her parents. I'll have to battle through that, then find him.

Shit, poor Blake. Should I just send her back to Football Frat, or will she want to help me scour Nolan for the man Teah truly wants?

"I'm sorry."

The soft statement has me sitting up with a jolt. What the hell is she apologizing for?

Teah's head slowly turns on the pillow. "It's nice that you came to check on me. I should be saying thank you, not demanding someone else."

I flick my hand through the air, silently forgiving her.

"I could always rely on you, Grady Newman."

I stand so that I can inch a little closer to her. Resting my arm on the back of her bed, I lean over her and give her a closed-mouth smile. "I'm a reliable guy."

Reliable and boring.

"Yeah, you are." Her voice is so weak, her eyes glassy with exhaustion.

"But I'm not the one you want."

She gazes up at me, her expression crumpling with remorse. "I know you're the sensible choice. My parents couldn't believe it when I broke it off. They thought I was going to marry you."

I swallow and, for some reason, admit, "I thought that too."

Her lips pull into a pained smile. "I never meant to hurt you."

I want to tell her that she didn't, but that would be a lie. Instead, I settle for "You were ready to move on."

"I shouldn't have called you boring." Her weak voices trembles. "That was mean."

Clearing my throat, I force another closed-mouth smile when she glances up at me.

"I felt really bad about our breakup, and I felt kind of guilty for... falling for Mac so fast."

Working my jaw to the side, I lean back. She can still see me, but I need a little distance between us.

"I can't even explain it." Her voice is wispy, and I can see sleep tugging at her again, but she seems determined to keep going. "It's like this cosmic energy. Our eyes connected, and I was... gone. I couldn't get him out of my head no matter how hard I tried."

Images of Blake flash through me.

"It was like I had no control. I had to give in to my feelings for him or perish." Her laughter is soft and sleepy. "He's the one, Grady. And even though you'll always hold a special place in my heart..." Her words start to tumble together as her eyes slip shut. "He owns it. Just like I own his." She goes silent for a beat, and I'm pretty sure she's fallen asleep until her eyes blink back open and she stares right at me. "I need him. Please, find Mac. I just want Mac."

And then she's gone again, her last effort to get what she wants draining her completely.

Bending over her, I reassure myself that she's still breathing before lightly pressing my lips to her forehead.

I get it now.

I understand that feeling of cosmic energy and no control.

That's exactly what I feel around Blake.

And sure, when I first met Teah, I was drawn to her. We were friends. We had a blast together, and then that friendship turned into something more.

It was fun and easy and comfortable...

But it wasn't cosmic.

It wasn't all-consuming.

Not like it is for her and Mac.

Not like it is for me and Blake.

An urgency to see her suddenly overwhelms me, and I dart out of the hospital room, scanning the corridor.

She's not back yet. Dammit.

Glancing over my shoulder, I spot Teah's parents down by the nurse's station.

I'll go have a quick chat with them, let them know that Teah needs Mac. Hopefully they'll relent for the sake of their daughter.

And then I gotta go.

I gotta find Blake and get out of here.

I need to tell Wily that this thing with his sister is no rebound—it's the real deal. I'm gonna fight for her. Whatever it takes. Whatever I have to do.

I am going to make it clear that Teah may always have a small piece of my heart, but it now beats for Blake.

CHAPTER 56
BLAKE

It's stupid.

I'm stupid.

I *know* this, yet still I drive through the night, negotiating these winding roads in Wily's big-ass truck. The built-in navigation system takes me to the parking lot I left only a few days ago.

I park in exactly the same spot Grady did and stare out at the darkness.

Hiking into the forest at this time of night is insane.

I'd be an idiot to do it, but my logical brain can shut the hell up, because I *need* to get into this forest right now.

I knew myself in this place.

I liked myself in this place.

And I have to get back there.

Jumping down, I grab the flashlight out of Wily's glove compartment. My phone is still off, and the battery has probably died now anyway, so I won't bother taking it.

Emptying my smallest bag, I throw a water bottle in

there and grab a protein bar from Wily's stash. He's always got supplies in the back of his truck, and I don't hesitate to steal from them.

I'll replace it when I get back.

I'm not planning on going far.

I'll just hike to that first spot Grady and I found. It only took a few hours. I'll head there, find a perch on that rock we jumped off, and lie back to watch the stars.

Grabbing my jacket out of the back, I tie it around my waist.

See. I'm being sensible.

Slamming the door shut with a huff, I pocket the keys in the zip-up pouch of my yoga pants and start my trek.

The trees loom around me, and despite the darkness, I feel an instant sense of peace. This is what I need. To be shrouded by nature. To walk in a place where no one can judge me or reject me.

I'm free out here.

"I'm free!" I shout, my voice getting swallowed by the dark forest.

I shiver but let out a laugh, sweeping my flashlight beam across the empty space.

"I! Am! Freeeee!"

My words fly into the sky, and I can't help another giggle… that quickly dries up in my mouth.

Free to do what?

Become what?

Moving forward, I keep my pace steady, following my beam of light along the trail. I can't remember exactly where we went last time because I was simply following Grady, but I'm hoping it'll be instinctual.

The path is relatively clear before me, and when I get

to a fork in the road, I feel good about heading left, so I follow my gut and start ascending the slope. My sneakers aren't as good as my hiking boots, but I ignore the thought and keep pushing, welcoming the burn in my thighs as I continue to disappear into this wilderness.

The ground's a little soft here, which I don't remember, my sneakers sinking into the mud, but I keep pressing on.

It's kind of weird that I'm wanting to get lost in order to find myself, but I just know that if I can make it to that perch on the rocks... if I can lie there staring up at the stars... answers will come to me.

I don't have to say or do anything for anyone else in this moment.

There are zero expectations, and maybe from that place, I'll finally figure out exactly what I want.

CHAPTER 57
GRADY

"I'm telling you, it's all she wants." I look between Teah's parents.

Her mother's face scrunches in disbelief. "But he's so awful. All pierced and pale and rough around the edges."

I shrug. "She loves him. And you raised her right, so she must love him for a reason."

I can't believe I'm advocating for this guy, but Teah needs him, and so I'll do it for her.

Mr. Rogers lets out a disgusted scoff. "He's nothing but trouble. Look at where she is right now. It's all his fault."

My insides knot. Shit, what if he's right? What if it wasn't an accident? What if Mac is totally to blame?

Then he'll go down for that, and it won't be your problem.

Right now, Teah wants Mac, so help her.

For some bizarre reason, I feel compelled to make that happen. There's this urgency firing through me that I don't understand, but I need to wrap this up.

Teah wants to wake up and find Mac by her bedside,

so the sooner I can make that happen, the sooner I can go.

Checking my watch, I look at the time and cringe. Shit. I've been here for hours. And I still don't know where Blake is.

Why hasn't she come back already?

I need to find her... if I can just wrap up this conversation.

"Look, I know you love her and you care deeply about her welfare, but she's old enough to make her own decisions, and she wants Mac. Denying her access is only going to drive a wedge between you. Surely you can see that."

"Of course we can." Her father glares at me. "Why are you standing up for this idiot?"

"I'm not." I raise my eyebrows. "I'm standing up for Teah. She loves him... and I think it's genuine. She's not trying to rebel or break free. She doesn't have to. You guys have a great relationship. She's just... in love."

"Why can't she still be in love with you?" Mrs. Rogers whines. "I much prefer you."

My lips twitch and I nod my thanks but get back to the point as quickly as I can.

"I've seen families suffer from lies and secrecy. If you don't let Mac be part of Teah's life, you'll be forcing her to go behind your backs. And that's only going to cause more pain. Things will go better if you accept what she wants."

They both look sick, swallowing hard before glancing at each other.

"Who knows, maybe she'll get bored with him the

way she got bored of me." I'm trying to be encouraging, but it sounds horrible when I say it like that.

The truth is, the way she was talking about him, the look on her face... I don't think she'll ever get over him.

I don't remember her ever calling me "the one."

She loved me. I believe that.

But if I'd proposed my senior year, the way I was planning to? Would she have said yes?

I honestly don't know.

"Let me go find Mac. Please. She's hurting and upset. I think having him around will keep her calm. She was gutted when she woke up and found me instead of him. Don't make her go through that again."

Her father huffs. "Fine."

"Colin." Mrs. Rogers looks up in surprise. "Are you sure?"

"What else are we supposed to do, Nat? I won't lose my daughter over this."

I lightly slap his arm, congratulating his decision before hightailing it down the corridor.

I'm scanning for Blake the whole time, and my stomach pinches when I get to the waiting room and can't see her.

Has she left?

Running out into the parking lot, I spot my Jeep behind the pillar and am relieved to see she must still be here. She's got my keys, and she wouldn't have taken off with those.

Spinning back toward the entrance, I'm about to go and see if someone can page for her on the PA system when I notice a guy standing against the edge of the building.

His hands are in his pockets, and he's got his head leaned back against the wall, his eyes closed.

"Macalister?" I move toward him.

His head pops off the wall and he narrows his eyes at me, his guard instantly going up. I can practically see it forming, his expression hardening, his shoulders flinging back like he's tensing for a fight.

I raise my hands to show him I'm not about to start one.

"What the fuck do you want?" he seethes.

His complexion looks so pale in the moonlight. He really is a vampire. Those angular features and high cheekbones. He would have been perfect in the *Twilight* series. Teah made me watch them, and she couldn't stop gushing over the amazing Edward Cullen. I was Team Jacob, all the way. He was the sensible choice. The obvious one.

But of course Teah's heart belonged to the vampire.

This is just real life mirroring fiction.

And that cosmic connection she was talking about... the one Edward and Bella shared... I can see it.

"Have you been out here the whole time?" I raise my chin at the wall behind Mac.

He nods. "Told you I'm not leaving her."

"Yeah." My lips twitch and I raise my eyebrows, tipping my head. Guess he does have some good in him if he's willing to stand out here all night. "You love her?"

I have to ask.

He narrows his eyes at me like it's none of my damn business, but then he lets out a huff. "Not really into all that romantic shit, but..." He shakes his head, then clicks his tongue. "She got me."

"So that's a yes, then."

"It's a yes." His reply is gruff, and is that a blush I'm seeing under the hospital lights?

I lick my lips, and with a soft sigh, I finally give myself the closure I've been waiting for.

"She only wants you, man." I raise my chin toward the hospital doors. "You should go in there."

"Yeah, right." He snickers. "You trying to get me arrested?"

"I'm serious. If she wakes up again and finds you not there..." I shake my head.

He straightens. "She woke up? You spoke to her? Is she okay?"

I nod. "She will be... as long as you're there."

And he bolts for the door.

The glass slides open to let him in, and I watch him disappear through the waiting room, charging past surprised patients waiting to be seen and hauling ass down to his woman.

Damn, I hope they let him in, because I'm not going down there to check.

I need to find Blake.

Wandering back in through the entrance, I scan the waiting room one more time before I spot a hand waving at me from behind the glass.

With a frown, I point at myself and she nods, beckoning me over.

"Uh... hi." I stop against the desk, and she gives me a pointed look before slapping my keys and a note down.

"She left these for you."

My eyebrows dip together as I pocket my keys and open the note.

. . .

You're busy, and I'll only get in the way. Here are your keys. Take care, Grady.

And that's it.

Reading the note again, I can't help this pinching sensation in my gut when I read those three words at the end again.

Take care, Grady.

There's something farewell-ish about them, and it's making me uneasy.

Pulling out my phone, I try to call her, but it goes straight to voicemail.

"Shit," I mutter under my breath, then dial Wily as I walk to my Jeep.

"Hey." His tone is clipped and I roll my eyes, wishing he wasn't still pissed off with me. I have some major damage control to do. Dammit. "How's Teah?"

"Yeah, she's pretty banged up, but she's gonna be okay," I mumble. "Is Blake with you?"

"What?" His tone sharpens. "I thought she was with you."

I pause by my Jeep and have to confess, "She left. Must have caught an Uber back to Football Frat or something. I tried to call her, but her phone went straight to voicemail. You sure she's not in her room?"

Wily growls. “You better not have lost my sister.”

“I’ll go check her room.” Satch’s sweet voice filters down to me, and I hop into the Jeep, starting the engine and waiting for her to come back and say, “Yep, she’s in there.”

Setting my phone in the cradle, I reverse out of my spot and start heading toward the exit, only slamming on my brakes when Satch walks back into hearing distance and destroys my night.

“She’s gone.”

“What?” Wily whispers. “What do you mean?”

“All her stuff. It’s gone. Her room is... empty.”

CHAPTER 58
BLAKE

Okay, so I think I must have gone the wrong way, because I do not remember a climb this steep. Not on the first day anyway.

By the time I reach the top, I'm breathing like a rhino, my limbs are screaming at me to stop already, and my palms are covered in scratches from having to grab onto branches in order to keep myself upright.

A fine sheen of sweat is coating my skin, and every time a cold breeze whistles between the trees, I can't help a shiver.

Pausing at the top, I rest my hands on my knees and suck in lungfuls of air.

Despite the fact that I've made an error, I'm still feeling okay.

I'll just find a spot nearby to spend the night, and then I'll hike out the way I came in when it's daylight. It'll be a million times easier when I'm not relying solely on a small beam of light.

A beam that seems to be fading fast.

Shit. Spare batteries. Those would be handy about now. Wriggling the bag off my back, I pull out my water bottle and slug some back. I wonder if I should put the jacket on too. But, as soon as I get moving again, I'll warm up.

Tightening the jacket around my waist, I stow the bottle away and grip the bag in my fist, sweeping the beam of light around me. It's barely reaching past the closest trees now, the darkness beyond just a touch unsettling.

Grady would have remembered spare batteries.

I huff at my own stupidity and force myself up straight.

There's no point standing here feeling sorry for myself.

If I can get out from under these trees, the moonlight can help me along… and I think I see a patch of it up ahead.

Tightening my grip on the bag, I surge forward, determined not to make this night my biggest disaster.

I'll find my thinking spot.

I'll think.

And then in the morning, the sun will rise and I'll return to Wily's truck, confident and secure in what I'm going to do moving forward.

Are you kidding me? You are gonna have no idea!

Shut up! This will work!

I berate myself, anger firing through as I stomp over tree roots and leave the edge of the trail. I can see a patch of light up ahead, and I'm sure it's this bright because it's shining on a slab of rock.

That rock will be my bed for the night.

It's not like I'm planning on sleeping. I just want to stare up at the night sky and find frickin' peace. Is that too much to ask?

Moving around a tree trunk, my feeble beam of light highlights what I think is my way forward and I head toward it, totally missing the tree root that trips me up.

I stumble, no doubt looking like a comical cartoon as I lose my balance and try to correct myself. My arms flail, and I plant my foot on what I think is solid ground, but the rock rolls beneath me. I let out this weird squawk when my ankle turns.

And now I'm stumbling to my right, then letting out a feral scream as the ground disappears and I hit nothing but air. The bag—which I really should have put back on properly—tumbles out of my hand, bouncing away from me, but I'm too busy shouting, "No!" and reaching up to slow my descent to even lament the loss.

"Shit, shit, shit!" I scream again, my body sliding down the rock, then landing with a bone-crunching thud. "Ahhh!" My wail echoes across the black space in front of me.

I reach for my leg. I have no idea what I've twisted or broken, but the pain is blinding.

Patting the ground around me, I try to feel for the flashlight, but it's gone as well.

All I have left now is a pale moonlight that isn't enough to truly show me where I am.

My chest heaves, breaths punching out of me as I try to think through this haze of pain.

Breathe.

Figure out where you are.

You'll need to climb back up. The thought is harrowing, my brain sizzling with panic.

Breathe!

I suck in a breath, snapping my eyes shut as I grip my knee, trying to ignore the pulsing pain in my leg.

Breathe.

Think.

"Think, Blake," I whisper. "Think."

Sucking in another breath, I force my logical brain into action and take it one step at a time.

First, I need to figure out how precarious my situation really is.

Cautiously feeling around me, I run my hands over the dirt and debris until I reach a ledge.

I gasp, pinging away from what I have to assume is a sudden drop.

Okay, so no leaning to the right, then.

Using my non-aching leg to check my left side, I quickly discover an edge there too.

Holy shit.

I must have landed on a small shelf sticking out from a rock face or something. Scrambling back, my butt hits a wall of rock, and I push into it, needing to reassure myself with the solid surface.

Fear is trying to choke me. My chest starts heaving as the reality of all this really kicks in.

I'm gonna die.

I'm gonna fall off this rock face and plummet to the ground.

Pushing my back into the cold wall behind, I try to control the shaky breaths spurting out of me, but I have no chance in hell.

A panic attack is rounding over me, and there's nothing I can do to stop it.

This is it.

I thought I'd done the most idiotic things I possibly could, but I was wrong.

No one knows where I am.

I've busted my ankle.

And I'm in the most precarious position I've ever been in.

There's no saving me from this.

So the panic may as well just go ahead and eat me whole.

CHAPTER 59
GRADY

I haul ass back to Football Frat, breaking the speed limit and even running a red light. It's late, the streets are basically empty, and if Nolan does in fact have a traffic camera in that particular intersection, then I'll pay the fucking fine.

All I care about is getting back and confirming with my own eyes something I know in my gut is true.

Parking haphazardly by the curb, I jump out and run across the front lawn. I don't know why I didn't park in the driveway; my brain obviously thought the curb would be quicker.

Bolting up the stairs two at a time, I shoulder the front door open and don't bother greeting anybody.

"Grady!" Zander calls to me from the living room, and I hear footsteps behind me, but I don't stop moving until I'm standing in the doorway of the room Blake has been occupying.

It's empty.

All her stuff is gone.

I gaze down at her unmade bed, the only evidence that she was even in here this morning.

Shit.

Slumping back against the doorframe, I try to figure out what the fuck happened and why the hell she left without even saying goodbye.

"Come on," Zander softly coaxes me out of the doorway. "We're all downstairs."

"Why'd she go?" I frown at him. "*Where'd* she go?"

"That's what we're trying to figure out."

Following my friend back downstairs, my mind starts racing to think logically, to problem-solve this so I can fucking find her!

She left the hospital.

Did she walk back to Football Frat or catch an Uber?

Her phone is obviously off if it's not even ringing before going to voicemail. Or maybe the battery's dead, which means maybe she couldn't catch an Uber and she's still walking home from the hospital. At this time of night. Fuck!

What was she wearing?

I think back and picture a massive hoodie. Maybe yoga pants.

Is she warm enough?

It might be spring, but the temperatures can still fluctuate. At night it can get down to thirty degrees at this time of year. Her skinny little body can't handle that temperature. Not in a hoodie and yoga pants. She needs a jacket. A beanie.

My heart starts racing until I hear Zander's voice cut through the noise in my chaotic brain.

"She's taken Wily's truck. At least that's what we're

assuming." Zander turns at the bottom of the steps. "It's not in the driveway and his keys are gone, so she must have left with it."

"Did anyone hear her go?"

Zander gives a pained frown, scratching the back of his head. "Nah. The only people here were Wily and Satch. They've been in his room all evening and were potentially... preoccupied... when she left." He raises his eyebrows, and I feel sick.

She was sneaking out while they were getting it on.

Sneaking out while I was trying to deal with this Teah situation.

Fuck!

What was she thinking?

Why didn't she wait for me?

I step into the living room. Wily's assembled the troops, and everyone is there, even Sienna, who has a baby monitor clutched in her hand and a worried look on her face. She's in her pajamas, Elmo's red face grinning at me from the material around her legs. She's sporting a massive Nolan U hoodie, which must belong to Zander. Next to her is Nylah, who is anxiously watching Wily as he talks to his parents on speakerphone.

"I can't believe this," his mother frets. "Why would she just leave without saying anything to anyone?"

"She's probably catching a red-eye back to Chicago," his father mumbles, and Wily stifles a groan while Mrs. Wilson balks.

"After everything she told us last night? Of course she's not going back there! She better not be," Mrs. Wilson growls. "If I ever get my hands on that Cleo girl, I'm going to ring her neck!"

Oh wow. She told them. She told them everything.

Is that why she freaked out and left?

When did she call them?

"Can't you track her phone or something?" Mr. Wilson barks, clearly rattled.

Wrenching the phone out of my back pocket, I pull up the Find My app, which I set up after the liquor store incident, and try to do just that, but she's not showing up anywhere.

Because her phone's off, dumbass.

Dammit!

Where the fuck is she?

"I'm sure she's fine, Mr. and Mrs. Wilson." Zander is trying to bring a little calm into this clusterfuck, but I don't think it's going to work. Something is wrong. I can feel it in my gut. "She's probably driving down to Denver as we speak. That's why we're calling, just to make sure she got there safely." He shares a worried frown with Wily, who looks about ready to break the phone in his hand.

His fear is palpable, and it's hard not to feed off it.

Blake has obviously never done this kind of thing before, and after everything that's gone down in the last few days...

Shit, please be okay, baby. Please!

"But she's not here!" Mrs. Wilson wails. "Where is she, David?"

"I don't know." He sounds pretty cut up. "We should have tried harder to talk to her today. We shouldn't have given her space. We should have driven up there and seen her. Dammit! I'm coming up."

"No, Dad. We need you to stay in case she shows up." Wily clenches his jaw. "Please, just stay put, okay?"

After an awkward beat, his father finally huffs in consent. "Fine. We'll wait. But you keep us posted, okay? After everything she told us yesterday, who knows what she might get up to." He sounds rattled and pissed off, and I can't help glaring at the phone as Wily says goodbye and hangs up.

As soon as he drops the device on the couch, he spins to bark at me. "Why'd she take off? What the fuck did you do? She was at the hospital, and then she just disappears? What the hell happened!"

"I don't know!" I raise my hands to shut him up and stop him stalking toward me. He's limping, and Satch is trying to pass him his crutch, but we seriously don't have time for this shit!

"What happened at the hospital?" He glares at me.

"I. Don't. Know," I repeat emphatically. "I was dealing with Teah's parents and her boyfriend, who security had to drag out of the hospital, and when I turned to check on Blake, she wasn't there. I assumed she'd gone to the bathroom. Teah's mom wanted me to go sit with Teah for a minute, and I did. We talked, and then I left. I was expecting Blake to be waiting for me, but she wasn't. I don't know why, okay?" My voice starts to pitch. "All I do know is that we have to find her, and I don't have time to stand here arguing with you!" Pulling the keys out of my pocket, I turn for the front door. "I'm going out to look for her. You can beat on me later."

Zander steps in front of Wily before he can reach me. "He's right, man. Just calm down. None of this is helping Blake."

I glance over my shoulder in time to see Wily's shoulders slump.

Shit, he looks destroyed right now.

"We need to split up and start searching around any places we think she might go. Any guesses?" Zander asks.

"The library," Wily mutters at the same time I grumble, "A party."

His eyes snap to mine, and shit, the gutted confusion on his face says it all. Yet again, it's occurring to him how much his sister has changed. How much he doesn't know her. And it's brutal.

"I'm sorry, man," I mumble, feeling his pain. "But you need to put whatever hurt you're feeling aside, because we have to find her." My voice cracks and I blink, wrestling with this onslaught of emotion I was not expecting.

If something's happened to her...

If she's wasted at a party or someone's doing something to her...

My imagination tortures me, blurring my vision for a second.

Sucking in a sharp breath, I look back at her brother and rasp, "I need to find her."

His eyebrows rise for a brief second, like he's surprised by the intense emotion I'm battling, but doesn't he get it?

I care about Blake.

She's my... cosmic match.

My chest spasms and I rush out the front door. I can't go losing her now. Not when I've just figured it out.

CHAPTER 60
BLAKE

I survived the panic attack.

I don't know how. I thought I was going to pass out from lack of oxygen. Or maybe my heart was going to explode. But somehow, I managed to keep breathing. Somehow, I managed to push my back into the rock and lock my body into position until that wave of dizzying nausea passed and I could inhale a full breath again.

I feel sick now.

Drained.

But I'm too afraid to close my eyes and fall asleep.

What if my limp body slips off this shelf?

I'm not ready to die.

The thought makes my insides hitch, and once they start trembling, they won't stop. It's fucking freezing up here.

Checking my watch, I light up the little screen and wince at the crack across the glass.

Shit.

The time is still showing, though, and it's one thirty in

the morning. The temperatures are only going to keep falling and...

My jacket.

Feeling around my waist, I let out a surprised, choking laugh when I notice my jacket survived the fall. Carefully untying it, I inch it around my body, my ankle whining in protest.

I hiss but refuse to straighten my leg. If I do that, my foot will be dangling off the side of this little shelf, and that's too much.

I have no idea how high up I am or how steep the drop is. But my imagination is filling in the blanks, and it's terrifying. So I keep my extremities as close to my body as I can while wrestling the jacket out from under my butt and around my torso.

Rather than putting it on, I use it as a blanket, wrapping it around myself and bunching it under my chin. My teeth are starting to chatter. This is going to be a fucking long night.

Glancing up at the night sky, I try not to get freaked out by the vast expanse and instead focus on the twinkling stars. I home in on a cluster of three and stare at them until they blur.

Closing my eyes, I feel that edge of exhaustion tugging at me. The adrenaline is fading from my body, but—

I snap my eyes open, willing another injection of that stuff to course through my veins.

I can't rest. I can't relax.

"Stay awake," I order myself. "You have to stay awake."

A cold breeze whistles over my face, and even though it makes me shiver, I welcome it. I need it to keep me alert. Sleep is not an option on this precarious shelf. I have to keep my wits about me and stay still.

Tightening my grip around my legs, I pull the jacket even closer to my chest and start whispering under my breath. I play the alphabet game because it used to calm me as a kid.

"Pick a topic, sis," Wily would tell me.

Wily. Shit, I miss him. I've screwed up so badly. I lost him without even meaning to, and it's never gonna be the same again.

I'm not his sweet little sister anymore, the one he's determined to protect.

I'm the lying delinquent who had to withdraw from college. The girl who got herself arrested. The one who lost her V-card because Cleo dared her to do it, and Nico had never done a virgin before.

Shit, I'm such a fucking loser.

Why would Wily want to be related to me?

Tears flood my eyes as my little pity party goes into full swing.

"No," I whisper. "A topic. Pick a topic!" I growl at myself, then start with an easy one. "Boys' names." Swallowing, I lick my lips, then instantly wish I hadn't. The breeze is so much colder against my wet skin. With a grimace, I clench my jaw and mutter, "A... Adam. B... Barry. C... um... Carson." My eyebrows rise as I think about Wily's grumpy-ass friend. "D... Donovan. E... Edward. F..." I blink, my brain starting to hurt and telling me to shut up.

Just let me sleep!

No!

F... let's go!

"F..." I close my eyes, then force them back open. "Frank. G..." My stomach twists, this pain in my chest making me believe for just a moment that souls are a physical thing. Because my soul is aching as I whisper the word "Grady."

I'd give anything to have him here with me right now.

He'd know exactly what to do.

Exactly how to help me.

And he would. In his calm, sweet way, he would once again get me out of trouble. Even though he'd rather be with Teah. Sweet, simple, uncomplicated Teah.

Who thought he was boring.

My insides writhe with anger for a moment, but then logical thought overrides the emotion.

"She'll wake up and realize that she was wrong." My voice is slow and kind of slurred as I whisper to the stars. "She'll wake up and he'll be there, telling her she's strong and she can make it. Being the perfect boyfriend."

My eyes feel heavy as they once again flood with tears.

I wanted him to be *my* perfect boyfriend, but why would he want a train wreck like me?

"I'm such a mess."

So stop being one. You know how to do that.

"But I don't want to go back to the way things were. I don't want to be an intense study nerd again. I want a life. I want to enjoy my life."

So do it. Enjoy it.

I nearly ask how, but I already know how. Enjoying life means doing the things you love, right?

So... what do I love?

"Grady," I whisper, my lips rising into a sad smile. "I love being with Grady."

But that's not an option anymore, so what else? What else, Blake? Stay awake. Stay alert and THINK about it.

Blinking, I shake my head, trying to wake myself up and force my brain to comply.

What do I love?

What do I love?

"Nature," I whisper. "I loved hiking with Grady."

But it wasn't just about Grady. It was about being in the woods. Watching... hearing... nature around me. I loved photographing it and studying it. I loved standing still and submerging myself, like I was becoming one with the forest.

That worked for me.

I felt joy like I'd never experienced it.

That's why I came back here tonight. I was hankering for that feeling again.

A cloud, which was covering the moon, glides away, allowing a shaft of light to flood my little spot here on the edge of this cliff. I stare up at the pale orb in the sky, my lips parting as that sense of wonder takes me out again.

Being out here, even in this precarious state... it's... it's where I belong.

Not in a library surrounded by books, but out here. I want to be out here!

Which means I need to stop fucking up my life and make it happen.

Inspired, my brain starts calculating all the ways it could happen. What kind of jobs work in nature? What kind of training would I need to do?

The minutes tick by as I work out a plan in my head.

My chest starts to thrum as images of me hiking through the forest with a kick-ass camera flood me. I see myself snapping images, selling them to nature-loving websites. Maybe I could even start my own company? I could learn all there is to know about photography and selling photographs. Coffee table books, large prints—there's so much potential, right?

And maybe I could tie that in with conservation, the way Grady wants to do with his engineering. Maybe showing people how truly amazing and beautiful this world is could inspire them to get out into it, to preserve it, to...

I start to smile, more ideas exploding in my brain as an excitement I've never felt before starts to buzz through me.

I want that. I want that life.

So go get it.

I swallow, the thought of telling my parents making me shudder.

Seriously, you're still afraid? Look at where you are right now!

The thought makes me stiffen, and then this weird laugh pops out of my mouth. I'm basically facing down death. There's a serious chance I won't get found and this is the end of the line for me... and I'm still shuddering at the thought of telling the truth?

I am so screwed in the head.

Another laugh pops out of me, but it quickly turns into a tearful little wail.

Shit, if I do survive this, I have to get the fuck over myself.

I have to stop bullshitting my way through life and stop striving for people's approval.

The only approval I really need is my own.

I need to stop making decisions out of fear and start making them based on what lights me up and gets me excited.

I have to get my life together, and I need to tell my parents that it's my turn to start making the big decisions. They think they're supporting me by constantly giving me advice, pushing me, demanding certain standards, but all it's done is pressured me to the point of exploding into a reckless idiot child.

"I want to do photography." I test it out, picturing them in front of me as I lay out my plans. "And I want to stay in Nolan. I love it there. I'm not a big-city girl. I never have been. I just didn't realize it until I had the opportunity to be somewhere small-town." Gripping my legs a little tighter, I battle my chattering teeth and quaking insides to keep telling them all the things I want to do.

"And I want to be with Grady," I finish, my bravado dying the second his name slips off my lips.

That's not really up to me, is it?

I may want him, but he's probably already back with Teah.

And I need to get on with my life and just hope that one day, he'll come back to me... or I'll find someone else who is exactly like him.

CHAPTER 61
GRADY

The longer I drive around Nolan, the worse I feel. I've hit up all the usual party spots and shoved my way through crowds, calling her name and showing her picture to people who had no idea who she was.

"Haven't seen her."

"Nope."

"Who's she?"

By the time I leave my third party, I am beyond frustrated.

Zander calls me with his latest update as I slam back into my Jeep.

"Tyrell and I have walked around campus. There's no sign of her. Carson and Nylah didn't see her in Offside; they even checked the bathrooms. Satch and Wily said the library is closed already and they didn't see her around it... and Sienna's searched the house from top to bottom. She's not here, man." Zander sighs. "Fuck, I don't even know if she's in Nolan anymore. But we'll drive past that all-night diner on Main before heading back to Football Frat."

"Unless you think there's somewhere else we should check," Tyrell calls out.

I shake my head, irritation sizzling through me as I stay parked alongside the curb and slam the steering wheel. "Fuck!"

"I know. I'm sorry, brah."

Closing my eyes, I end the call and rest my forehead against the wheel. Where the hell could she be?

Maybe she didn't leave the hospital. Could she be hiding out in that massive building?

Then why'd she leave the note?

And Wily's truck is missing. She's taken his truck, and she's gone somewhere.

Shit! Why would she just take off?

"Think, dammit!"

Starting the engine, I head for the hospital, for no other reason than I don't know what else to do.

"Siri, call St. Vincent's Memorial Hospital."

My phone does as it's told, and I get through to reception faster than I thought I would.

"St. Vincent's emergency room. How may I help you?"

"Yeah, hi. I was there earlier this evening and my... girlfriend... had to leave early. She left me my car keys and a note. Do you remember that?"

There's a pause, and I can feel the woman's confusion before she slowly answers me. "I'm sorry, sir, but my shift only started three hours ago. What time was this?"

"Uh..." I glance at my watch. "Yeah, shit, it would have been way before that."

"I'm just looking around my desk, and I can't see a note or car keys."

"No, that's okay. Don't worry about it." I hang up after a quick goodbye and slam my wheel again, pausing at a red light and forcing myself to stop being so fucking emotional and use my logical brain.

I tap my finger on the wheel as I try to go back to the beginning and run things through.

We got to the hospital. She was with me.

I had to deal with Mac, then Teah's parents and… she must have walked out at some point during that exchange. The last time I remember seeing her was when she touched my shoulder and told me to let Mac go. Then security came, Mrs. Wilson was crying, and she wanted me to go see Teah.

Blake must have walked to reception, given them my keys and the note.

As soon as I make it through the intersection, I pull over and scramble to tug the note out of my pocket.

You're busy, and I'll only get in the way. Here are your keys. Take care, Grady.

"I'll only get in the way." I read the words aloud a few times, and a horrible, ugly thought starts to form and grow and…

Fuck! Did she think she was getting in the way of me and Teah?

Did she think…?

"Fuck!" I shout again, balling up the note in my hand and forcing myself to think the way she might have been.

After the blowup with her brother, she's running on the assumption that Wily hates her. She's obviously confessed all to her parents, and that mustn't have gone well by her parents' reaction on the phone before. And now she's running on the false assumption that I'm trying to get back with Teah.

Maybe.

Shit. I can so understand why her brain went there.

I hate myself for giving her that impression. I was just so pissed with Mac for putting Teah in danger. I've been worried about her with him. It's been eating at me ever since the first time I saw them together; then the accident happened, and it all came bubbling out of me.

Snapping my eyes shut, I focus back on Blake, shoving my guilt aside for another time.

Right now, all that matters is finding her and making sure she's okay.

So... she's feeling rejected, alone... ashamed after that shit with her parents.

"What would she do?" I whisper, my brain lighting with an idea. "Disappear."

Hasn't she been begging me ever since we got back to take her into the forest and disappear? It was always said in jest, but the underlying tone was clear. She wants to run away from her problems.

"Would she do that?" I stare out my windshield, gripping the wheel and wondering if she would seriously drive back to the forest.

Looking at my watch, I wince, hoping like hell she isn't that reckless.

But fuck it. I have to check. What other options do I have right now?

Squealing away from the curb, I head out of Nolan, speeding to the forest as fast as I can get there.

It's a two-hour drive, and it's getting close to dawn by the time I pull into the parking lot and spot Wily's truck.

"Thank God," I whisper under my breath, then feel my insides disintegrate.

Oh shit.

She went into the forest. No doubt unprepared, just stormed into those woods in the dark. Who knows where the fuck she's ended up.

"No," I whisper, jumping out my door and running around to check Wily's truck. It's been here for hours. The metal is cold, the windows frosted over from the dropping temperatures throughout the night.

She's out there in it.

I spin, eyeing the start of the trail and feeling my gut plummet. Which way did she go?

Yanking out my phone, I call Wily. "I've found your truck. It's in the parking lot."

"Is she there? Is she okay?" Wily sounds wired, like he's been pacing all night...or ever since I called to let him know where I was heading.

I wince. "She's not in it. I think she's gone into the forest."

"Fuck!" he barks. "How long ago?"

"I don't know, man. But I'm gonna go in and start looking for her. If I don't find any tracks within the first thirty minutes, I'll call in search and rescue. It's fucking freezing out here, and she's completely unprepared." Fear starts choking me. She's unprepared. And there are so many dangers in this wood—animals for one. What if she's been mauled by a bear? Attacked by a wolf pack? Pounced on by a mountain lion?

My brain starts short-circuiting as I picture her wounded, all alone, bleeding out on the forest floor.

"Shit, Wily!" I run a hand through my hair, breaths punching out of me. "Shit!"

"Hey, dude." Wily quickly switches roles with me, his voice easing me out of this sudden, blinding panic. "Chill. I need you to stay calm. I need you to find her, okay? Promise me that you'll find her."

"I have to," I choke out. "Because I'm gonna lose my shit if I don't. Wily, she's got to be okay." Images of me stumbling over her frozen body make my heart rate spike.

"She will be." Wily's only saying what I need to hear, but he can't hide the underlying fear lacing his tone. "She'll be okay, but only if you stop freaking out and go do your thing. Go find my sister, Grady."

I swallow, nodding and sucking in a breath as I let that sizzling terror rip through me, then force my body around to the back of my Jeep.

"If I haven't heard from you in an hour, *I'm* calling search and rescue," he tells me.

"Yeah, okay. Reception might be a little sketchy once I get into the forest, but I'll do my best to keep you posted." We say a quick goodbye, and I hang up before pulling out my emergency supplies.

I go through them, quickly repacking my smaller daypack and taking the essentials for this situation. The guys always hassle me about having a backup for my backup. Well, it's for moments like this!

I don't know what I'm gonna find, but I remind myself that Blake can survive a night. It'll take temperatures much colder than this for a body to freeze. She'll probably be dehydrated and suffering mild hypothermia, but she'll still be alive.

As long as an animal hasn't gotten to her first... but if she's making enough noise as she moves around, they'll probably keep their distance anyway.

"She has to be alive," I tell myself, willing the statement to calm me, forcing my brain to conjure up images of me finding her sleeping peacefully just off the trail, or stargazing by the lake where we spent our first night.

"But she might be injured." I have to be prepared for any scenario, right?

Placing my first-aid kit at the top of my bag, I then throw in an extra bottle of water, forcing my brain away from more wildlife nightmares.

Mountain lions, black bears, coyotes. Does she know how to deal with those?

Shit, shit, shit!

Fear is taking out my barely there calm like machine-gun fire.

I've never felt like this before.

The thought of losing her is fucking killing me.

Because you're in love with her. You found your cosmic match, and you just didn't realize it!

Snatching the bear spray, I slip it into my pocket as a final precaution, then close up my Jeep and catch my reflection in the glass.

"You!" I point to myself. "Calm down and go find her."

Clenching my jaw, I suck a few deep breaths in

through my nose, then turn and start running. Shouting her name, I head down the most likely trail and scour the ground for dainty shoe prints.

CHAPTER 62
BLAKE

I'm so cold I can barely think straight. My muscles are so exhausted from shivering that they've lost all power, and I'm struggling to keep my eyes open.

Every time I drift off and my head starts to tip, I jolt awake, a flush of adrenaline running through my body.

"Stay awake." My speech is way more slurred than it was last night.

The longer I'm out here, the drowsier I become, and I can feel the danger nipping at the edges of my brain.

I'm in trouble.

Big trouble.

My face feels frozen, and even though I want to cry, I'm not sure I can.

Everything is so cold.

I'm gonna die up here on this lonely little ledge.

And all I can think about is Grady.

It's so sad that our perfect forest escape couldn't become something more. It's all so complicated, and Wily's so mad, and my parents are so ashamed of me.

Even if all that wasn't in the way... Grady's in love with Teah, and there's no place for me.

Our bubble was popped the second we left the forest, and my heart is breaking.

I fell in love with him between these trees.

I fell in love with him as we watched the sun lighting up these rocks.

I blink, staring at the golden glow warming the rock face in front of me. It's so beautiful. Dawn is here. A new day. A fresh start.

Or a fresh end in my case.

Shit, I don't want to die.

I whimper, tucking in my chin as a fresh set of shivers rush over me. It's like my body is instinctively fighting, putting in a last-ditch effort because I don't want this to be over.

"I just want to make things right," I whisper, thinking of my brother, my parents... Grady.

Grady.

Grady.

"Blake!"

I can hear his voice in my head, calling to me even though he's miles away.

"Blake!"

He'll be at the hospital, yet I can still hear him so close.

"Blake! Where are you?"

My forehead wrinkles in confusion, my eyes blinking as I hold my breath and wait.

"Blaaaake!" His voice carries across the air, over my head and...

He's close.

He's...

"Grady?" I scream, my throat aching as I force the word out of me as loud as I can manage. I hold my breath and don't hear anything, so I try again. "Grady!"

"Blake!" There's a scrambling, a rustling above me, and a fresh shot of adrenaline punches through my veins.

"I'm here! I'm here!" I shout, my body screaming at me when I try to move.

"Blake! I'm coming!"

"I'm here!" I shout once more for good measure and strain to look up the rock, willing him to appear. To...

There he is. His face pops into view above me. I crane my neck back and drink him in, confirming that he's not just an apparition my delirious brain is trying to conjure.

"Bee," he rasps, and my chest deflates with relief, a watery laugh punching out of me that quickly turns into a sobbing wail.

He has never been more beautiful.

Even as his expression crumples in concern, I soak him in. I want to proclaim my love right here and now, but my throat is aching, my mouth dry and swollen.

With a thick swallow, Grady takes in my precarious position and is doing a shitty job at hiding how horrified he is. "How the hell did you get down there?"

My chin bunches, my voice quaking as I try to make a joke. "Never hike in the dark on a trail you don't know. Hiking 101."

He tips his head with a frown, obviously calculating how he's gonna get me out of this.

And all I can do is gaze up at him, softly whimpering. "You came looking for me."

"Of course I did." His eyes dart to mine.

I want to ask why he's not with Teah, but I don't want to bring her name up right now. I just want to soak him in.

He found me.

I'm not gonna die anymore.

"Just give me a second, okay? I'm not going anywhere." His face disappears, and I can't help another whimper, but then his voice carries down to me and I cling to it. "I've found her… Yeah… I don't know yet…" He huffs. "Look, I gotta go, but she's alive and I'm bringing her home, okay?… Yeah… *yes, Wily…* Yes, I promise. Now I gotta go… I gotta go!"

And then he's above me again, flashing me a quick smile before he starts studying my position and the surrounding terrain.

"How'd you find me?" I croak as he cautiously starts making his way down the side of the steep embankment. "Be careful," I quickly warn him.

He pauses to stabilize his footing, then looks at me with a grateful grin. "You left tracks everywhere, baby," he calls down to me. "Thanks for doing that."

My laughter is once again watery and completely hysterical. Yeah, I really am losing it.

But I'm not gonna die! I think there's a serious place for hysterical laughter in this moment.

He pauses on a safe spot above me, his face that much closer.

I stare up at him, my belly still rumbling with this ridiculous laughter as I drink him in, studying every line and angle of his worried expression.

"Are you injured?" His brown gaze is rich with concern.

I sniff, forcing my arms out from the jacket cocoon I've been shivering in. Pointing to my leg, I indicate the problem. "I think I've hurt my ankle pretty good. I don't know if it's broken. I haven't exactly been able to assess it."

"Okay." He nods. "We're gonna get you out of here."

"Be careful," I warn him again as he inches closer. "It's really slippery."

"Yeah." He keeps looking around me, no doubt tracking the safest path to reach me.

He can't make it down this far.

I'm gonna have to stand up, spin around, and reach for him.

The idea is terrifying. Now that the sun has risen, I can see exactly where I am on this rock face, and it's a miracle I didn't plummet to my death.

Sucking in a sharp breath, I try not to look down as I ignore the pain in my ankle and start to shuffle myself around.

"Slowly." Grady's voice catches. I can tell he's trying to stay cool and calm for my sake, but did his heart just jackknife the way mine did when my foot nearly slipped off the edge?

My hands are shaking as I place them on the ground and very slowly turn my body around. I'm now on my knees, facing the rock and cautiously trying to straighten myself up.

He can't reach me unless I put in some effort, and there's no way I'm risking his life for mine.

I don't want him coming any farther away from the ledge he's on.

"That's it. Nice and slow. Nice and—"

A gasp flies out of me as the jacket slips off my shoulders, tumbling down the edge and showing me exactly what's gonna happen to my body if I don't take care.

My breath catches, my heart about ready to explode as I rest my head against the cold rock face and beg my body to work for me.

"I know you're hurting, baby." Grady coaxes me to look up at him. "But you can do this."

I snap my eyes in his direction to see him lying on his stomach, positioning himself perfectly so he can reach down for me. His big, strong hand is stretched out just above me.

All I have to do is take it.

"Take my hand." He wiggles his fingers. "Use the wall to balance yourself and rise up on your good leg. You can do it."

Clenching my trembling jaw, I slither up the wall, waves of fear-filled nausea surging through me.

My legs protest as I put weight on them, my bum ankle stabbing me with a sharp complaint.

I hiss and lift my foot off the ground, the sudden movement making me flail, then lose my balance.

"Blake!" Grady's shout is overrun by the terrified scream popping out of my mouth as gravity does its best to end me.

CHAPTER 63
GRADY

My heart catapults into my throat as I thrust my hand forward and just manage to snatch her wrist.

She's still screaming, and I swear I think her mind is tricking her into believing she's falling to her death.

"Blake!" I shout, ignoring the strain on my arm. My iron grip on her wrist is locked in place, but I need her to stop struggling. "Blake! Look at me!"

She stills, her blue eyes wild with fear as she glances up.

"I've got you," I assure her. "I've got you, baby. See?"

I squeeze her wrist and notice the cloud of terror starting to clear from her eyes.

"That's it." I smile down at her, the strain on my arm starting to hurt, but like fuck I'm showing her that. Trying to keep my voice as smooth and easy as possible, I keep talking her out of this panic. "I know you're scared, but I'm not letting you go. You're not gonna fall, okay? I've got you."

She starts to nod.

"All I need you to do is stay calm and help me pull you up, okay?"

She nods again, her vision obviously clear enough to see and understand everything I'm saying.

"Gimme your other hand. Reach up. That's it. Reach, reach, reach." I snag her other hand and grunt, using all my strength to drag her up the rock face.

She digs her knees in, half climbing as I tug and wrestle her out of this precarious position. As soon as she's beside me, I grip her hips and lift her up the steep incline, pushing her up the last part until she's crawling onto the flat ground above us.

Ragged sobs are punching out of her, and I quickly scramble up, crawling behind her until I can reach her again. My hand lands on her back and she quickly spins to face me, launching herself at me with such speed that I lose my balance and topple onto my butt.

Wrapping her legs around me, she clings tight, whimpering against my neck. "I thought I was gonna die."

I hold her tight, wanting to promise that I'd never let that happen, but I can't find my voice. For a split second there, I thought I'd lost her, and my heart is still trying to find its way back into my chest cavity. Cupping the back of her head, I close my eyes and fight the surge of emotion powering through me.

"I don't want to die," she rasps, her lips resting against my neck.

"You're not allowed to, Bee." I squeeze her tighter. "You have to stay with me."

My words take a second to sink in, but I can tell the moment they do, because she eases away from me, her tearstained face coming into view as she takes me in with a surprised blink.

My fingers are dirty, but I touch her face anyway, resting my digits lightly on her pale skin and smiling at her. She's so beautiful. I just want time to stand still for a minute so I can drink her in.

"You're my cosmic..." My smile grows as I try to find the right words to erase that confused look on her face and explain what I mean. "You're my... you're..." Her frown only gets deeper, and I end up just saying it, because it's what I fucking mean. "I love you, Blake."

She jerks back a little farther, and I reach for her waist, worried she's about to take off on me. She looks like a scared jackrabbit.

Shit. Does she not feel the same way?

That cosmic thing. I thought we were on the same page here.

Pain rockets through me before I can talk myself out of it, and I end up saying in a whisper, "Why did you take off? I was looking for you all night. I've been worried sick."

"But..." She shakes her head, trying to speak past her chattering teeth. "Y-you didn't want me at the h-hospital."

"When did I say that?" I frown. "I came out to find you and—"

"You're s-still in love with Teah." Her voice is so sure, so resigned as a shudder ripples through her. "There's no r-room for me, so I-I left."

"No, baby. No." Reaching for her face again, I rush to clear the air between us. "I love *you*, and talking to Teah last night made me realize how much I do."

Her lips part, her blue eyes wide with surprise as she gapes at me.

"She's always gonna be part of my history. And yeah, she owns a little piece of my heart, but Bee... you own the biggest chunk by far. I'm gone for you, baby. I'm yours..."

Her expression crumples like she's about to start crying.

And now the nerves are kicking in as I lamely mumble, "I mean, if you want me. I'm yours if you want me." Shit, I hate this stab of insecurity.

Reaching for my face, she cups my cheeks, her smile warming with tender affection and cooling the spray of hot nerves firing through me. "Y-you love me?"

I nod, trailing my hands back to her hips and giving them a light squeeze. "You make it too easy."

She shakes her head. "I'm a tr-tr...train wreck, Grady."

I shrug. "You're my train wreck."

Her watery laugh is music to my ears, but not as sweet as the sound that follows. "I love you too." She sucks in a breath, giving me a watery smile. "Since the second I s-saw you shirtless in that b-bathroom... I've been f-falling, and you've just kept m-making it h-h-harder and h-harder not to."

I pull her closer, rubbing her arms and trying to warm her up.

"I thought if we j-j-just had a mindless fling, I could get you out of my s-system. But I c-can't. And I don't even w-want to."

My heart relaxes, letting out a contented sigh and finally sinking back behind my rib cage where it belongs.

She loves me. She fucking loves me.

Thank God for that.

"C'mere." I coax her against me, cupping the back of her neck and melding out mouths together.

She sinks into the kiss on a sweet sigh, and I brush our tongues together, reveling in her touch, letting that mind-numbing fear eke out of me.

She's in my arms.

She's safe.

She loves me.

Shit, I never want to let her go. But as we sink a little deeper into the kiss, I become hyperaware of her quivering muscles. She's been out all night in these freezing-cold conditions, adrenaline pumping through her, and she's gonna crash soon. In fact, I think it's already starting. I need to get her warm and hydrated. I need to check on her ankle.

So stop kissing her and do that!

Just one more.

I swipe my tongue against hers, holding her tight for one last squeeze before finding the willpower to do the right thing.

"I need to get you warm and hydrated, baby."

"Yeah." She keeps kissing me, peppering my chin with her shivering lips.

Pulling away from her, I wrestle out of my jacket and wrap it around her, rubbing some warmth back into her limbs.

Taking off my beanie, I nestle it over her curls, pulling it down past her ears.

"Now let me check out this ankle." I ease her off my lap, keeping a firm hold on her arm until she's settled safely on the ground beside me. Taking the time to do up the jacket and making sure she's snug, I then take a quick look at her ankle.

Now that I'm out of my relieved haze, I'm starting to think logically and feeling that pressure of getting her back to my Jeep as fast as possible.

Gently pushing up Blake's pant leg, I frown down at the swelling, shifting her sock so I can press the tender skin. She winces as I gently prod it and go through the first-aid checklist in my head. I keep an eye on her reaction, my stomach clenching at the obvious pain slicing through her.

"Yeah, it's definitely busted," I murmur, dragging my bag toward me and taking out the first-aid kit. Handing her a water bottle, I help her take a few sips before asking, "Can you wiggle your toes?"

She gives it a try, but I can't see because I've chosen to keep her sneaker on. With the threat of hypothermia lingering, I need to keep her extremities as warm as possible.

"Yeah, I think so," she squeaks, wincing again.

"Good, that means the chances of a breakage are slim. I'm guessing it's a bad sprain." Digging a bandage out of the kit, I wrap it around her ankle and sneaker, securing her foot as firmly as I can before checking out the rest of her.

She's got a few nicks and bruises, her hands scratched up from her trek through the forest. I brush my fingers lightly over the superficial wounds and resist the urge to tell her off for being so reckless. We can deal with that later, but I am *making* her promise to never do this to herself—or me—again.

"I know it was stupid," she whispers, carefully watching my face.

I glance up, forcing a closed-mouth smile. She doesn't need me adding to her regret right now, so I lean forward with a soft kiss and murmur, "You're safe now. Let's get you home."

She lets out a soft snort. "Home? Where's that?"

Resting my forearm on my bent leg, I give her a gentle smile and tell it to her straight. "It's with me."

CHAPTER 64
BLAKE

Those three little words, said with such conviction, send a warm smile whistling through me. My lips curl at the corners as he hands me a couple of pain meds. I take them without complaint, my chest still buzzing as everything he's said to me starts to sink in for real.

He loves me

My home is with him.

When he stands and holds out his hand to me, I take it without hesitation.

Helping me up, Grady's strong arm then comes around my waist and steadies me. It's going to be a long hike back to the parking lot, but I can do this. I've still got the shakes and am feeling kind of wrecked, but a few more pulls from his water bottle boost my determination, and I cling to his shoulder as he supports me along the track.

It's narrow and steep, and at one point, I have to drop to my ass and do a butt-shuffle routine to make it down to the bottom of the hill.

Grady coaches me through every step, quietly encouraging me and steadying my body whenever it's practical.

Once we reach flat ground, it gets a million times easier, and even though the trail is awkward walking side by side like this, Grady keeps a steady hold on me. He's so strong, so calm, so quietly determined.

"I would give you a piggyback, but I don't want to jostle your ankle. I know it's slower this way, but I think it's less painful for you."

Exhaustion is eating at me, and I can't even find the energy to respond.

He glances down at my face. I can practically hear his brain running through a quick assessment, and when I stumble over my next step, he stops and winces.

"Think you can handle it if I do give you a ride? You're flaking on me, girl, and I'm starting to worry about hypothermia."

I give him a slow blink—silent permission to do whatever the hell he wants. I can't think anymore. I just need him to act.

Treating me like cracked porcelain, he leans me against a tree trunk, arranging his pack to sit over his chest before crouching down and coaxing me onto his back.

He's right about the pain in my ankle; it spikes and snips at me with every swing of my foot, but I'm too tired to care. He's walking at a quick clip, and I close my eyes against the discomfort, gripping his shoulders and trying to keep my head upright.

I feel like everything inside me is getting slower, and by the time we reach the parking lot, I'm hoping he'll offer to let me lie in the back of his Jeep and sleep my way home.

But the screeching of tires has me looking up, and there's my brother, struggling out of the passenger side of Zander's SUV.

"Blake!" he calls, pausing in obvious frustration to take a crutch off Satch, then hobbling toward me.

She's smiling, her eyes all glassy and tearful as she watches her big-ass boyfriend lumber toward us.

Grady gently lowers me, checking my face, his forehead creasing with worry. "Hang in there, baby."

"I'm okay," I whisper, feeling anything but.

"Blake, thank God," Wily whispers, pulling me against him as soon as I'm within range. "Don't you ever fucking scare me like that again, you little shit." He's laughing... or maybe crying, I can't tell.

All I know is that he's crushing me to his chest like I matter.

"Careful with her, man," Grady starts complaining. "She's got a busted ankle. Let her breathe, for fuck's sake."

Wily lurches back, steadying me with his arm and studying my face. "She's really pale."

"We need to get her to the hospital. She's dehydrated and cold, and that ankle needs looking at."

Grady gently nudges my brother away from me and swoops me into his arms. "Come on, baby."

"I'm coming with you guys." Wily hobbles beside us, then turns to look for his girlfriend. "Satch?"

"Yeah, I'm right here." She runs up behind him, nearly tripping in her haste. He reaches out an arm to steady her, and she shoots him a grateful smile before following us to Grady's Jeep.

"Let's take my truck. It's got more room." Wily glances at me. "Tell me you didn't lose my keys, butt face."

I pat the deep pocket on the side of my yoga pants, relief washing through me. Finally, I didn't screw something up.

"I didn't lose your keys, shithead," I softly mumble and am rewarded with a deep laugh from my brother.

"I'm driving," Satch announces, surprising everyone, and helps me wrestle the keys out of my pocket.

Grady doesn't complain, looking at Tyrell and ordering him to drive his Jeep back to Football Frat.

Holding out his hands to catch, Tyrell takes the keys Wily digs out of Grady's backpack, and then we fuss around the cars for a few minutes, deciding who's gonna sit where.

Wily and Grady get into a short bickering match until Satch asks if Wily can please sit in the front with her.

"I'll feel better if you're beside me." She glances at Grady, and I don't miss the little wink she shoots him.

Thankfully, Wily is already moving for the front, and I get to sit in the back with my legs stretched out and my throbbing foot resting on Grady's lap.

He's still treating me like a delicate petal, and I don't mind so much.

It's nice to be treated with such tenderness, and I soak it in, resting my head against the back of the seat and looking at him until I can't keep my eyes open anymore.

With the heat blasting and danger no longer an imminent threat, I drift into a thick doze that makes me feel groggy and hungover when I'm shaken awake what feels like only a few minutes later.

"We're here, Bee." Grady's voice is soft and gruff.

I force my eyes open and give him a bleary blink.

When did he get over there?

He's standing behind me now, on the ground, lifting me out of Wily's truck.

I whimper when my foot catches on the side of the seat.

"Sorry." He winces, securing me in his arms and walking into the emergency room.

I didn't expect to be back here so soon.

Yeah, well, maybe if you hadn't acted like an insane person, you wouldn't be.

The weight of what I did is hitting me hard now, and I can't even look the receptionist in the eye as Grady and Wily check me in.

They take me straight through, nurses fussing around me as they get an IV into my arm. Zander must have called ahead, because they were obviously expecting me. Before I know what's happening, my dirty clothes have been stripped away and I'm wrapped in a heated blanket that is all things delicious.

It feels so good, I just want to close my eyes and drift into oblivion, but the voices around me won't let that happen.

Satch is helping to fill in all the forms while I rest. Grady stands beside me, absently brushing his fingers through the top of my hair.

It feels so good.

"Have you let your parents know?" Grady asks over me, and I turn my head to take in my brother. He's found a chair and has his leg propped up in Satch's lap.

Shit. All this running around can't have been good for him.

Closing my eyes, I silently berate myself for being so thoughtless. So self-absorbed.

"Yeah." Wily's voice is rough and gravelly, kind of distracted. I open my eyes to see him pointing to the form and answering Satch's question. "I called them as soon as I heard from you. We were already on our way to you by then. I couldn't just sit around at home. When you called to tell us you'd found her tracks, we piled into the car to come after ya."

My lips curl into a grateful smile.

So much care.

So much concern.

For me.

"Mom was freaking out and wanting to call every emergency service provider there was. I'm pretty sure she was seconds away from hiring a helicopter to start the search herself, but I told her to stay put. She hasn't slept all night, and Blake doesn't need Mom's fussing on top of everything else. I'll call them as soon as she's been checked, give them another update." He looks right at me then, his blue gaze intense. "Be warned, they're coming later today. I don't think anything can stop that from happening."

I wince, my gut clenching at the thought of having to face them.

"Hey..." Wily lightly squeezes my uninjured leg. "It's gonna be okay."

Closing my eyes, I softly mumble, "I can't think about it right now."

"Okay."

He lets me be after that, quietly murmuring to his girlfriend while Grady keeps running soothing lines over the top of my head and brushing gentle kisses across my forehead.

I keep my eyes shut, my body drifting in and out as the medical staff tend to me and deal with my ankle.

Thankfully, it's not broken, but it's a bad sprain, so I'll be sporting a walking boot for a week or two. And they want to keep me overnight to make sure I'm fully rehydrated and stable.

Shit. I really don't want to spend my entire day and night in here, but sleep takes me out before I can complain.

I wake up alone a few hours later, my gut twisting as I gaze around the darkened space. The curtains have been drawn for me, and I don't like it.

I don't want to lie here in the dark.

All by myself.

My chest starts to rise and fall in rapid succession, and when the door opens, I actually let out a terrified squeak before I see that it's my brother.

"You okay?" He limps toward the bed.

"Yeah, I just..." Looking around, I rest my hand on my forehead and force a breath. "Where's Grady?"

"The guy was dead on his feet, so Satch took him home. He was complaining big-time, but he's no use to anyone if he keels over. I'm sure he'll be back soon." Wily's forcing a smile. I can tell.

Eyeing him up, I watch him hobble around the bed, then plunk into a chair.

"Are you all right?" I quietly check.

"Yeah, I scored me some sleep when you were out of it. The nurse let me lie in one of the spare beds."

I nod, gratitude pulsing through me. He didn't leave me, which means maybe he doesn't hate me.

My eyes dart back to his, and that fake smile he's wearing turns a little sad.

"I'm sorry," I whisper. "I shouldn't have taken off like that. I shouldn't have scared you. I shouldn't have... lied to you." I bite my lips together, my scratchy throat swelling as emotion takes me out. "I've been a horrible sister."

"No, you haven't. You just..." He shakes his head. "I'm not mad at you, Blakey. It just hurts to know you're pulling away from me."

"I didn't mean to," I rush out. "I guess I was just afraid to tell you the truth, because I wasn't sure you'd understand. I thought you might judge me and... and..." My head starts shaking just the way his did. "I don't know what I thought."

"You didn't think I'd understand?" He leans forward with a pained frown. "We grew up in the same house, sis. I know the pressure."

"But you didn't buckle under it. I did."

"I wasn't being forced to do things I wasn't into. I *love* football, so the pressure didn't matter so much to me. I felt supported. You obviously felt..." He waves his hand at me, letting me plug the gap.

"I felt..." I lick my bottom lip, wincing at the dried, peeling skin. "I felt trapped, like I was locked in a strait-jacket and if I tried to get out, everyone would be so disappointed."

"So you lost the plot."

I swallow, nodding because that's all I can do.

He lets out a heavy sigh, linking his fingers together and looking pained. "It kills me that I couldn't be there for you. That Cleo bitch, I have some words for that chick. And those assholes who treated you like their personal sex toy? I wouldn't mind breaking a few of their limbs for ya."

I let out a dry laugh. "It's not worth it. *They're* not worth it."

"But you are." He looks at me, silently begging me to believe it. "And if you'd told me, I would have been there for you in a heartbeat."

My heart cracks right down the middle at the look on his face. Deep down, I knew he would. I could have called him at any time, but I was too ashamed. And I didn't want him having to deal with my mess.

"I couldn't ask you to do that. You can't be my guardian forever."

"Yes, I can." He's so adamant that a wispy laugh bubbles out of me, but it quickly dies off.

"I have to forge my own life away from this family."

"What?" He sits up straight, looking utterly horrified.

"No, I mean, I'll always be part of this family, but I need to figure out what I want outside of it. All my decisions before Chicago were based on what I thought you guys wanted for me. But I need to break away from that." I give him a pained smile, imploring him to get what I'm saying. "I need to be Blake. Not 'Blake, Wily's little sister' or 'Blake, valedictorian.' Not 'Blake, David and Joanne's daughter.' And not 'Blake, the smartest girl in the room.'" I spit out the last few words, then huff. "I don't know what I am, but I think I'm starting to figure it out."

Those words give me a sense of hope. It's soft and a little uncertain, but I cling to it like a promise.

Wily shuffles in his seat, adjusting his leg before frowning at me. He looks all injured and wounded by what I just said, and I wish I could have worded it better.

"So you don't want to talk to me about stuff anymore?" His voice is small and vulnerable.

It's a relief to be able to smile and reassure him. "Of course I do. You're my best friend. But I don't need you to be my watchdog anymore. And I have to stop trying to be the perfect little sister. I can't make you proud all the time. And if I'd realized that, I would have come to you sooner, before I really fucked things up for myself."

"I never asked you to be perfect."

"I know." I wince, my expression crumpling as I rub my aching forehead.

"Hey." Wily leans forward, straining to reach me. I throw him a bone and stretch out my arm, letting him take my hand. "I love you, sis. Always. No matter what."

"I love you too." It's easy to say because it's so freaking true.

He gives me a kind smile, then tuts and pulls a comical face. "And you love Grady, don't you?"

I laugh and nod. "Yeah. Like a lot."

He rolls his eyes, giving my hand a squeeze before letting go and slumping back into his chair. "Pretty sure he loves you too," he grumbles.

"Yeah." I grin.

"Like a lot." Wily gives me a pointed look. "He was gonna go down fighting for you last night. You should have seen him. You should have heard his voice when he knew you'd gone into that forest, in the dark, unprepared.

I thought he was gonna lose it." He looks at the wall, letting out a heavy sigh before softly admitting, "It made me realize this thing you two have going can't just be some mindless fling."

"It's not." My smile keeps growing. As much as I hate that I put Grady through those kinds of emotions, it's also kind of comforting to hear how worried he was. I mean something to him. Like a lot of somethings.

He loves me.

Wow.

He really loves me.

"Shit," Wily grumbles. "My teammate and my little sister. I'm hating it."

"Oh, come on. You'd hate whoever I dated. And he's a million times better than Nico and Simon, believe me." I bulge my eyes, kicking myself for bringing them back into this conversation.

Wily's expression darkens. "Seriously, butt face. What was up with that shit?"

"Don't even ask." I flick my hand through the air. "I was in a really messed-up place."

"But you don't feel that way with Grady?"

"No way. He's..." And there I go with the dopey smile. It grows over my lips, all silly and exaggerated. But I can't help it. "He's the one who makes me feel safe enough to be myself." I look at my brother, my gaze clear and steady. "I've never felt more free than when I'm with him."

CHAPTER 65
GRADY

Blake's been home for a few days now. Thankfully, she only had to spend one night in the hospital, and then we were able to bring her home and take over her care. She's sporting a walking boot, which she has to wear for one more week, then will start going to PT to strengthen her ankle back up again.

I'm carrying her around whenever I can and being the best nurse I know how. Everyone else is doing their best to hassle the crap out of the Wilson siblings as they limp around Football Frat. They're taking it like champs and dishing it right back out, finding flaws to tease.

The banter's been intense, but it's also lightened the mood around the place, and I'll take it.

Blake's parents showed up at the hospital on Wednesday, before she was released, and it was awkward as hell. They were full of sympathy and fuss, yet the quiet demand that she recover quickly so she can get her life back together was loud and clear.

It took everything in me not to shout them out of the

room. They were surprised she was dating me, but thankfully, they didn't make me feel as unwelcome as they'd first made Satch feel. Wily stepped in and stood up for me, which I was not expecting.

Needless to say, the visit wasn't exactly calming for anyone, and even though they tried to stick around, Wily convinced them to head back to Denver and come visit again when Blake was back on her feet.

"There are so many people to watch over her at Football Frat, she'll be feeling totally henpecked, so you don't have to worry."

And he's so freaking right. He's the worst of the lot, hovering around and making sure she's okay. Satch has had to force him to class, but she couldn't move my stubborn ass. I played watchdog for two days straight, because Blake needed her sleep, dammit, and I didn't want anyone disturbing her.

She slept like the dead for an entire day, and I finally headed back to class on Thursday morning, happy that she was looking like herself again.

Well, her new self. There's a peacefulness to her that wasn't there before, and I swear I want to spend my life memorizing every one of her smiles.

Despite Wily's assurances, his parents have been calling every day to make sure Blake hasn't bolted again or done anything stupid.

It's pissing me off, but I'm trying not to complain about it. I've got other things to worry about... like making Blake take her pain meds.

She's stubbornly refusing unless she has to. She's really taking the whole "turn my life around" thing seriously and hates the idea of needing any kind of substances to get through.

But she needs her meds, so I'm forcing her to pop pills when I can tell her ankle is throbbing so badly she can't even think straight. When I got back from practice on Friday and found her on my bed, white as a ghost and about ready to puke from discomfort, I coaxed a couple of stronger meds into her, then told her to stop being so damn brave.

She stared up at me, her eyes etched with agony. "I can't fuck up again."

"You won't," I promised her. "I won't let you... and neither will you."

I comforted her with soft kisses, and she eventually fell asleep. I spent the evening in bed with her. When she woke up, we whispered in the darkness, mapping out our next hiking trip. Despite what she went through, she's pumped to get back into the woods, and I've got a bunch of different spots I want to take her. She's promised me she'll never go out on her own again, and I'm confident she'll keep her word.

When the weekend rolls around, I get my studying out of the way first thing Saturday morning before heading off to a light training session. The team is shaping up nicely for next year, although Zander, Wily, and Tyrell are gonna be leaving a really big hole. I'll have my work cut out for me, but I'm pumped to do it.

When I started this year, I was dreading getting through to the summer, but I'm feeling pretty damn good about things now. I've really managed to let my pain over Teah go, and Blake has had a huge part in making that happen.

She laughed again for the first time on Sunday morning, and it made my heart freaking sing. Watching her face, I revel in her sweet expression. She's coming back, her cheeks getting that rosy tint again, her blue eyes dancing with amusement as she winks at me, then stares across the room at her brother.

We're hanging out in the living room downstairs. It's been converted back to its former glory now that Wily can handle the stairs. He still has to be careful and is down to using one crutch. He hates it, but he's not willing to do anything to jeopardize his chances with football. I've never seen the guy work so hard in my life.

But right now, he's taking a minute to relax. We all are, and I'm loving this chill vibe. His leg is propped in Satch's lap while Blake's is propped in mine.

We've all been sitting around teasing each other. Satch and I are accusing the siblings of being injury-prone, and they're saying they were totally fine until we came along.

I'm loving the banter flying between us, and the laughter popping out of Blake is all things beautiful. I smile at her, brushing my fingers up and down her leg, until there's a knock at the door.

I gently maneuver myself off the couch, setting Blake's ankle back down on a pillow before heading for the door. When I open it, my smile instantly fades, replaced with a frown that reflects this horrible twisting sensation in my gut.

Wily and Blake's parents are on our doorstep, and there is going to be nothing fun about this visit. They're both looking pale, their expressions grave.

I don't even have a chance to greet them before Mr. Wilson is gruffly saying, "We need to talk to Blake."

Part of me wants to stay put and say she's not available, but I can't get away with that, so I step aside and let them walk into the house.

They pause in the archway to the living room, and the second Blake sees them, that pink color drains from her cheeks and all that tension rushes back into her eyes. "What is it?"

"Your mother found an email in her spam folder today with some... photos attached."

Mrs. Wilson looks at her husband, and Blake looks about ready to throw up.

I dart around her parents and rush to her side, knowing exactly what this is about. She told me about her last text exchange with Cleo, lying against me, whispering into the darkness while I stroked her shoulder and tried not to show how badly I wanted to go to Chicago and pay Cleo a visit.

"Photos?" Wily face goes rock hard.

"You don't want to see them." Mr. Wilson shakes his head, giving his daughter a pained frown.

She watches him from across the room, her shoulders slumping. "I did warn you they might be coming. I told you not to look."

"Couldn't help myself." Mr. Wilson sniffs, rubbing a hand across his mouth.

Blake's expression buckles, her eyes glassing with tears. I reach for her hand, curling my fingers around hers as she sniffs and murmurs, "I'm sorry. I really lost my way there for a minute."

Her mother lets out a light scoff, bulging her eyes,

and I can only imagine what the images gave away. Blake told me about a few, and even I cringed as she described beer-covered nipples at a rock concert.

"But you're finding your way back." Satch's soft voice is so kind and sweet, her smile a perfect match. "And you're doing great."

Blake's lips curl with gratitude while Mr. Wilson darts a look at Wily's girlfriend. It's clear he doesn't want her having a say in this, but I'm fucking stoked.

Giving my girl's hand a squeeze, I add to Satch's assurances. "You are, Bee. Those photos are part of your past. It's done now. Cleo can't hurt you anymore."

"She'll still have more photos. What if she posts them online?"

"Then we'll take action. She can't go posting that kind of shit anywhere."

Blake sniffs and nods. "I guess she has access to the people I want to see it the least, so she's still winning."

"No, she's not," Wily growls. "We won't let her."

"And you're not letting her blackmail you anymore." I give her a proud smile. "She can send any photo she wants now, because—"

"They will be deleted every time they hit their inbox." Wily points at his parents. "Right?"

Mr. and Mrs. Wilson suck in their breaths, then nod.

"Of course." Mrs. Wilson gives her daughter a stiff smile.

"Can't believe you looked at them, Mom." Wily winces. "Seriously, what were you thinking?"

"They were right there, and I just..." She blinks and shakes her head.

"They have been deleted." Mr. Wilson slides his hand

down his wife's back and tucks her against him. "And I've sent a very strongly worded email to this Cleo person and told her to cease and desist or she'll be hearing from our lawyers."

"Good," Wily mutters, darting a quick glance at Blake before biting his lips together.

Oh yeah, there's plenty more to say, but I'm grateful he's not launching into some kind of rant about how this should have been dealt with weeks ago. Blake's already stressed enough and doesn't need more shit piled on top of her. She's working through it; they just need to let her do it at her own pace.

"We just... ah..." Mr. Wilson looks at his daughter. "We want to make sure you don't get 'lost' again, so we thought we'd come up and talk about what you want to do with your future." Walking into the dining room, he brings back two spare chairs and sets them down across from her. I hold my breath as her parents sit down and look at her expectantly.

Blake's fingers clench mine, and I can feel her body coiling with tension.

"Now that Chicago's out, we've been looking at other options for you," Mr. Wilson begins, glancing at his wife, who nods and smiles. "We were thinking—"

"Stop." Blake raises her hand. "You don't need to think for me anymore. I'm working this out on my own."

Their mouths drop open while my insides hitch with pride.

Yes! That's my girl.

"But, sweetheart," Mrs. Wilson sputters. "We're trying to support you."

"You can do that by trusting me."

Her mother blinks, her eyebrow arching. "You're asking us to do that after what we just saw on my computer?"

"That's her past," I softly growl. "Don't you dare hold that over her."

They look at me like I have no place in this conversation, but fuck that. I'm protecting my girl no matter what.

Blake squeezes my hand again, giving me a small smile before turning back to her parents. "As soon as my ankle's better, I'm going to get a job. The doctor said I'll be able to walk around normally within the next week. I'll still need to be careful, but I can at least start looking for work."

"Why do you need a job?" Mrs. Wilson looks mystified.

I turn away so she can't see my eye roll.

"To teach me some discipline, get me back into healthy habits. I want to work until the end of the summer, and then I'm hoping to enroll here at Nolan."

Her parents frown in unison, but her father does at least ask, "What are you planning on studying?"

Blake sucks in a breath, and I look at her with an encouraging smile. "I'm going to start over. Enroll as a freshman again. And I'm hoping to focus on photography and conservation."

Her mother's eyebrows rise. "And what do you plan on doing with that?"

Her smile tightens, her grip on my fingers increasing, as she can sense her mother's growing disapproval. "I'd quite like to become a wildlife photographer, Mom."

"A... what?"

She might as well have said "unemployed gypsy," and

I can't help a soft snicker. Seriously, her parents are too much.

"How will you ever make money doing that?" Her father shakes his head. "Blake, you're worth so much more. You're too smart to do... *photography*." He spits it out like it's some dirty word, and Wily huffs, tipping his head back with a cringing wince.

Blake clears her throat. "Actually, Dad, I'm smart enough to pursue something that makes me happy. It's not about the money. It's about taking classes that are interesting. Just because I'm good at something doesn't mean I love it. I want to love school. For the first time in my life, I want to enjoy going."

"But you do love school," Mrs. Wilson argues. "You've always loved school."

Blake shakes her head. "Not really. I just pretended to, because I knew you wanted me to be the study geek, and I was afraid if I wasn't that, then you..." Her expression flickers with doubt. "Then you wouldn't be proud of me anymore. All your love and attention would go to Wily, and there'd be none for me. If I wasn't performing up to your standards, I didn't think... you'd want me anymore." Her voice starts to wobble, the last few words coming out as a soft rasp that makes my chest hurt.

"Baby," I softly whisper, trying to catch her eye.

She's looking down at our hands, and I rub my thumb across her silky skin, desperate to assure her.

Mr. and Mrs. Wilson are gaping at their daughter but not saying anything. And the weight in the room is so freaking heavy it's almost hard to breathe. I'm two seconds away from asking them to leave. Unless they can say something reassuring, I don't want them here.

Her mother sucks in a breath, resting a hand over her chest, and then Mr. Wilson starts to blink like he's fighting tears. His expression crumples as he gets out of his chair and walks across the room.

"Aw, bean." Dropping to his knees beside the couch, he pulls Blake into a hug so tight that she lets out a little squeak. "Of course we love you. Always. You're our girl."

"You are," her mother blubbers, then looks at Wily and Satch. "She is."

Wily gives her a reassuring smile as she rises from her seat and walks over to join her husband. Running her hand down the back of Blake's hair, she smiles at her daughter with tears in her eyes, and I think this is the closest I will ever get to a Hallmark experience.

Darting my eyes across the room, I spot Satch's glassy smile, then share a look with Wily. He snickers, shaking his head as he plays with his football, giving it a squeeze, then catching his sister's eye.

"What do I do?" she mouths when her father still hasn't let her go.

Wily starts to silently laugh, then murmurs, "You wanted their love. You got it, sis."

She snorts and lets out a weepy laugh, which her parents seem oblivious to as they hug her and continue to reassure her of their unwavering devotion.

CHAPTER 66
BLAKE

My parents clung like limpets until I felt nearly suffocated. I guess it needed to happen. I'd never been so honest with them before, and I felt the toll like a heavy weight. But they do love me, and maybe deep down I've always known it.

I still can't help feeling like I'll be battling for their approval, though.

But do I really need it?

It'd be nice to have it, but I can't spend my life trying to please them.

It's time to look after myself, and they'll just have to love me through it.

"You good?" Grady glances at me.

I tuck a wayward curl behind my ear and smile at him. The sun is shining, we're driving out of town in his Jeep, music is pumping, I'm walking boot-free and feeling better than I ever have. I am so much better than good.

It's been a week since my parents' visit, and with each passing day, I've felt stronger and more determined to prove that I can make the biggest success of my life. I have a job interview lined up tomorrow at a place called Ponderosa Villa. It's for a cleaning position, which I'm a little nervous about since I grew up with housekeepers doing everything for me, but Grady ran me through how to clean a bathroom yesterday afternoon, and it's not that hard.

Wily lined up the interview for me, and I'll be meeting some woman named Rachel, who is apparently a sweetheart.

If I can get this gig, I'll be working five days a week, and although it's not a high-paying job, it's not about the money. I just need something to get me into healthy habits and keep me busy until the new school year begins. I'm worried if I sit around Football Frat twiddling my thumbs, I'll get antsy and want to do something stupid again.

Hopefully this job will work out just fine. Everyone's agreed to let me stay in Football Frat, and although I've still got that spare room, I've been spending every night by Grady's side.

I love how warm he is.

And his bed is so much more comfortable than mine.

He spoons me as we drift off to sleep, and it's seriously the best.

Turning off the road, Grady heads down a winding path that will take us to some peaceful spot he discovered in his first year at Nolan.

"Your ankle should be up for this," he's saying. "The ground is flat, and we'll take it slow and easy. It's just a short hike."

"I'm good."

"But you'll let me know if it gets too sore, right? You're not allowed to just grit your teeth through it because you think I'll be disappointed."

I wrinkle my nose at him, but he fires me a pointed look before facing the road again.

"Promise me, Bee."

"I promise," I assure him, then say it one more time for good measure. "I promise to be honest. Always."

His lips twitch, then curl into that grin I love so much.

This boy.

Raising the new camera Wily bought me the day I got my moon boot off (yes, he's the sweetest brother ever!), I snap a few pics of my man, then check the display screen with a grin.

My heart trills, my insides sizzling as I think about all the things I want to do with him. Now that my ankle's getting better and I can move around more freely...

"Okay, here we go." He pulls his Jeep to a stop, and we climb out.

Hitching the small bag onto my shoulders, I carefully settle the camera across myself before following Grady onto the track leading west. We weave through the trees, leaving the trail about five minutes later and heading into denser woods.

"You know where you're going, right?" I duck under a branch, watching my footing as I follow his line.

"Yeah, baby. Trust me." He slows his pace, and I catch up easily, tuning into the sounds of the forest and smiling at how full my soul feels every time I dive into nature.

I can't believe I'm only just discovering it all now.

Pausing on the trail, I lift my camera and line up a shot, then take a few more before framing a gorgeous one of my man hiking away from me. A shaft of light illuminates the leaves around him, and when I pull the camera back to study the shot I just got, I feel that sense of gleeful pride skipping through me.

"Damn, that's a good photo right there," I whisper with a grin.

"Come on, Bee," Grady calls to me, and I hurry after him, careful where I step.

He waits for me with a patient smile, and as soon as I reach him, I start gushing about the photo I just captured and how I'm going to frame it for his bedroom wall.

"Nice, baby." He reaches back for my hand and I take it, smiling as the sound of flowing water starts to register.

"Oooo." I grin, and he glances back with a smile.

"You're gonna love it."

And he's right.

As we clear the trees, a perfect little oasis opens up before us. Like a hidden treasure, this small waterfall dropping into a swimming hole is the most idyllic scene.

"I can't believe there's not a marked trail leading to this spot."

"I know, right?" Grady slips the bag off his shoulders. "But I don't want to tell anyone, because I kind of like how secret this place is."

"Yeah, for sure." I smile at him, this blooming sensation growing in my chest as I slip off my bag and camera, carefully setting them down before stepping up against him. "Thank you for bringing me here." I swing my arms around his neck, and he lifts me off my feet.

My legs wrap around him as he grins at me, then beckons me forward with a soft "C'mere."

I go without hesitation, crushing my lips to his, my

insides buzzing with anticipation. I instinctively know what's coming next, and I am so here for it.

As his hand splays across my back, sliding up to my neck, I slip my tongue into his mouth and sink into a mind-bending kiss. It's all I can do not to tear his clothes off. The energy between us is potent and addictive.

It's… cosmic.

Is that what he meant when he was trying to tell me he loved me?

I've been meaning to ask him, and why not throw it out there now?

"What…" I suck his tongue between my lips. "Did you mean…" I nibble down the edge of his jaw. "By the whole…" Pressing my lips to his neck, I inhale his luscious scent before finally finishing. "Cosmic thing?"

"Mmmm." He sighs before letting out a low chuckle. Squeezing me against him, I grin at the feel of his shaft growing harder by the second. "It's just something Teah said."

My insides coil.

"She was talking about her and Mac."

My insides relax.

"About how they had this cosmic connection. It was overpowering and unstoppable. And it made me think of you."

I grind against him, peppering kisses back up to his lips.

"We're…" He kisses me deep before murmuring against my lips, "We're like that, baby. From the second I saw you in that bathroom, I couldn't stop thinking about…" His tongue dips into my mouth again. "You. I wanted you so bad."

"I wanted you too," I pant against his neck, my body starting to catch fire.

"And it was like this powerful force I couldn't resist." He walks us around a rock, to a patch of grass bathed in sunlight.

Placing me on my feet, he keeps kissing and nipping my skin, working his way from my chin to my throat while his fingers wriggle beneath my shirt.

I moan in approval, the pads of his fingers gliding across my skin. Promising, promising, promising…

"Then we got to the forest and had that perfect time together, and I couldn't fight it anymore." His breath fans my neck. "I had to make you mine, Bee. Mine for good."

His hand cups my right breast and I tip my head back, the sun baking my skin as I smile up at the blue sky. "I'm yours. I was yours from the second you looked at me with those hungry eyes."

He laughs against my skin. "You make me so hungry, baby." With a playful growl, he hikes my shirt up even higher.

Lifting my arms, I help him out, loving the feel of the breeze kissing my skin as he drops my clothing to the ground.

He undresses me slowly, peppering my skin with nips and licks until my knees buckle. He catches me easily, lowering me to the grass and taking his sweet time with my body.

As he licks a path to my eager center, I tell him how hot he is and how I fell in love with him step by easy step. All the things he did for me, the ways he saved me, come tumbling out of my mouth until I can't breathe.

His tongue on my clit is knocking out my senses until the only one that's still functioning is pleasure.

It's pulsing a thick, strong beat as I scrape my fingers across his shoulders and let out a lusty cry. The air around me swallows the sound while the waterfall continues to tumble behind us.

When Grady parts my folds and licks a path back up to my clit, my entire body starts to vibrate, the promise of an orgasm building until my heart is knocked out of orbit.

"I'm coming," I gasp, digging my fingers into his short hair as shots of liquid fire dart through my body.

With a groan, I tip my head back as Grady's magic tongue destroys me. I stop breathing, my entire body going rigid before this orgasmic fire scorching my senses culminates into an explosive energy. It ripples through me, a cry punching out of my throat as my back arches and I'm lost to this mind-blowing sensation.

"That's it, baby. Enjoy the ride," Grady murmurs against my thigh, cupping my pussy as I writhe beneath him.

My heart is thundering as he crawls up my body.

The sound of his fly unzipping is the sweetest melody I've ever heard.

"Yes," I groan, frantically pushing his pants down. Wrapping my fingers around his cock, I stroke it while he kicks and slides his pants down to his ankles. He's still wearing his boots, too distracted by undressing me to bother with them at the time, and like hell I'm letting him bother with them now.

I need him inside me, and the second he's settled back over me, I line him up and let him plunge.

It feels fucking amazing, his long cock piercing me with a powerful thrust that makes us groan in unison.

"You're so hot, baby." He kisses my shoulder. "I love you wrapped around me."

"I love you inside me," I whisper, panting as I lightly scrape my teeth across his shoulder, then have to tip my head back as another cry punches out of me.

He feels so good, I can't even think.

I want to drown in this ecstasy.

I want time to stand still so that all that can ever exist is us and this coupling. Us in this beautiful oasis. Us connecting in the way only we can.

"Bee," Grady groans against my skin, thrusting deep and hard, his pace increasing as that rocket fires through him.

I can feel it build, expanding, gearing up to explode, and I encourage him with a kiss to his neck, scraping my nails lightly down his back before squeezing his ass.

Yes, yes, yes! my insides chant, my heart accelerating, and he fills me all the way to my soul.

He grunts, pressing his mouth against my cheek before brushing the tip of his nose across my skin.

"I love you," he mumbles. "I love you so fucking much."

I smile up at the sky, turning my head to meet his kiss. Our lips crush together, and he stills on top of me, his body vibrating as he drinks me in… then can't hold it anymore.

Ripping his mouth off mine, he rises on his hands, plowing into me over and over until I can't contain my cries.

The lusty sounds punching out of me probably scare the wildlife away, but I can't care right now.

There is only this.

Only us.

Yes!

He plunges deep, jerking back and then plunging again, the energy sizzling through his body reaching right inside me.

I feel that moment when he finally lets go. His release spurts into me, his body frenetic over mine until that high starts to fade and he sinks over me, lightly dropping kisses from my forehead down to my lips.

I giggle and he covers my smile with his mouth, his tongue gliding over mine with a tenderness that makes my chest swell all over again.

When he pulls back to gaze down at me, I show him everything. Every ounce of the love I have for him pours out of my eyes.

And he sees it.

He matches it.

With twitching lips, he leans down to brush his lips against mine, softly whispering, "Cosmic energy."

"The bee and the bear." I giggle before disappearing into his kiss.

CHAPTER 67
GRADY

Blake's at her job interview right now, and I can't stop thinking about her.

Wily hooked it up for her. He heard from his high school buddy Liam that his girlfriend was looking to hire a cleaner to help now that the villa is taking off.

He jumped all over it, arranging the interview, and man, I hope Blake's okay. She was raised in privilege, so she doesn't really know how to get her hands dirty. I've been cleaning my house since I was eight. And, for once, I'm actually grateful for that fact. I've been able to show Blake how to do the basics, and she's smart enough to pick anything else up along the way.

She was so nervous about going, but her father called just before she left. The second I saw his number, my stomach scrunched into a tight knot. Blake gave me an edgy smile before clearing her throat and answering the call.

"Hey, Daddy."

"Hey, bean." She put it on speaker so I could listen in,

and I moved around my room, getting changed in stealth mode so he couldn't hear me.

Blake smirked when I dropped my pajama bottoms and swapped them out for a pair of boxer briefs.

The heat in her blue gaze nearly took me out on the spot, so I had to turn away and focus on my bedroom wall, commanding my dick to calm the hell down. But that wasn't happening.

"I just wanted to wish you luck for your interview." Her father's voice was thick with emotion, and I stilled, wondering what'd be coming next.

"Really?" Blake's voice perked up in surprise. "Thanks."

"Honey, of course I want to wish you luck. We do support you, you know."

"Yeah... I... Thank you."

There was a pause as I slipped my boxers on, then spun to face her.

She gave me a cringing, helpless look, and all I could do was shrug.

"Well, um... thanks again." She scratched the side of her nose. When she lowered her arm, her pajama top strap slipped off her shoulder, and it was my turn to drink in that silky white skin of hers.

She noticed my gaze and started smirking all over again.

"Your mother and I have decided that..." He cleared his throat, interrupting the eye sex Blake and I couldn't help having. "If you get this job, we'll buy you a new car."

Blake gave a surprised blink. "But what about my Mini in Chicago?"

"I think it's best we sell that and get you something

else. We'll arrange to have the storage unit emptied and all your belongings shipped to Nolan. But a new car will be a fresh start, no bad memories attached to it, and you can get on with being the girl you want to be."

Blake kept blinking for a second, obviously not sure what to say.

"We don't like you driving around in that massive truck of Wily's. It's not a lady's car," her mother piped up.

Blake rolled her eyes, and I had to bite my knuckle to smother my laughter.

Blake?

A lady?

Yeah, her mother seriously does not know her at all.

"I was thinking a little VW Beetle or something peppy that you can get around Nolan in. What do you think?"

"I think..." Blake blinked some more, then let out a happy little laugh. "I think that would be amazing, thank you. That's really kind."

"Well, anything to get you back on your feet, sweetheart," Mrs. Wilson chimed in again, the underlying warning to stay on track loud and clear.

Blake doesn't need it. She's gonna do just great, with or without her parents' pressure. But I guess they're trying. Making sure she doesn't have to deal with any more shit in Chicago is a big gesture, and I'm glad Blake's not rejecting it.

She thanked them again, wrapping up the call before giving me an edgy smile. "Damn, I better nail this interview."

Striding across the room, I lifted her into my arms, kissing her soundly and assuring her, "You will."

And then Wily assured her over breakfast, and Zoey popped in with a picture she made.

"Oh, wow. Thank you, Zo-Zo." Blake grinned down at the scribble. "Can you explain it to me?" She pointed at the swirls of yellow. "Is that me?"

"Yup!" Zoey puffed her chest out proudly and tapped the picture. "Toiwet."

"And that's a..." Blake's expression buckled in confusion. "A toilet?"

Zoey nodded. "Keen toiwet!" She tapped the image again. "You keen toiwet."

"Right. Okay." Blake started to laugh, and Zoey tipped her head, confused by why that was so funny. Straightening out her expression, Blake gave the little girl a sincere smile. "I love it. And I'm gonna be the best toilet cleaner in this whole house."

"Yay!" Zoey punched her arms in the air, and Blake waited for the little girl to spin around and run out of the kitchen before wrinkling her nose at me.

"I'm gonna have to clean toilets. A whole lot of them."

"Yeah, baby." I gave her a pained smile and leaned across the table to kiss her.

"Would you two stop doing that in front of me," Wily groaned, tipping his head back in dramatic agony. "That's my sister. It's gross."

Blake narrowed her eyes at him before that cute little eyebrow of hers arched and she stood from her chair, then straddled my lap with a playful grin. "You don't like me kissing my boyfriend?" she teased him, holding my face and giving me a passionate kiss that was all tongue.

"Ugh! You guys are killing me!"

She grinned against my lips before diving in for

another, and I squeezed her ass until he was throwing pieces of toast at our heads.

Blake broke away with peals of laughter, and I caught the piece that was about to smack the side of her face. Giving her brother a look of warning, I popped it into my mouth and chewed.

We had a brief, silent standoff after that before he broke with a growl. But he was fighting a grin. At least I think he was.

So, yeah, he's okay with me dating his sister. I think he's starting to see how much I love her, and he can't fault that, right? I'll look after her. I promised him I would, and he's just gonna have to adjust to the fact that his sister is a grown-ass woman now.

A grown-ass woman with a very *fine* ass.

I squeezed it one more time for good measure, then had to let it go.

I skipped my workout so I could stick around and eat breakfast with her, then let her borrow my Jeep. I took Wily to his PT appointment, then headed off to class, and now I'm wandering beside Tyrell, anxiously waiting for a phone call.

Thank fuck she doesn't leave me hanging.

I've only been out of class a couple of minutes when my phone starts buzzing.

"How'd it go?" I answer after one ring.

"I got it!" she squeals.

"Really? Just like that?"

"Yes! She hired me on the spot, said Wily sang my praises, and she trusts any friend of Liam and Ethan's. It was so sweet! She knows it's only until the end of summer, but she's excited to work with me."

I grin, stoked by the excitement in Blake's voice.

"I met Tammy as well. You know the mom Sienna hangs out with sometimes? She was there with her boyfriend, Baxter. And her little son, Kai, is so cute! I played with the dog, Fezzik, and Rachel showed me all around the place. It's huge, and I'll be cleaning a lot of rooms, making beds, washing sheets, toilets, bathrooms, the floors, dusting. It's gonna be big, but I'm up for it."

"Is the pay okay?"

"Yeah, the guy who owns the place is awesome, apparently, and Rachel said I'll be getting more than minimum wage, which is amazing considering I've never worked a day in my life!" She laughs. "And she said I might get some tips, too, so that's pretty cool. Aw, Grady, I want to do, like, the best job for her, you know? I've never been more motivated in my life, and it's cleaning fucking toilets! What is wrong with me?"

I laugh, holding the phone to my ear and feeling this burst of pride rise through me. "It's your choice. That's what's so right about this. You're steering the ship this time, baby."

She lets out a sigh, and I can picture her pretty face. "I'm sure I'm not going to feel pumped like this every day, but you're right. It's nice to feel that sense of control."

"I'll motivate you on the days you don't wanna go. I promise."

"Ooo. Looking forward to that... I think. What does Grady motivation look like?"

My smile grows a little wider. "You'll just have to wait and see."

"Well, I look forward to it."

I nod, my brain already blooming with ideas.

"I better go. I was too nervous to eat this morning, so I'll grab a late breakfast, then call my parents, I guess. Time to pick out a new car."

I snicker and shake my head. "Don't let them talk you into anything you don't want."

"But it's their gift to me."

"If you want a big-ass pickup, then you ask for it, baby. Who gives a shit if it's not ladylike enough for your mother? You can drive whatever the fuck you want."

She giggles, and I picture her smile in my head.

"Love you, Bee."

"Love you, Bear."

We hang up, and I can't drop my smile. Tyrell snickers at me, shaking his head. "So loved-up. Damn, man. Now I'm flying solo. The only single in the house."

I wince. "Yeah. We really need to do something about that. Hey, why don't we go out tonight? We could celebrate Blake's new job and take her to Offside or something. We could get the whole crew together. It'll be fun."

"What? You gonna sit their snuggling with your women and pick out a girl for me?"

"Maybe." I grin.

He sticks out his tongue, obviously disgusted by that idea.

"Oh, come on. If you want to get yourself a girlfriend, you need to put yourself out there. You won't find anyone hanging out at home, and if you're not willing to do that online dating thing, then you need to go to places like Offside."

"I haven't been there in ages."

"Well, tonight's your night." I give him a soft slap on the shoulder, then point at him. "You're coming."

"Yes, sir," he mutters, obviously hating the idea.

I know what he's worried about. We'll make him go and talk to some random girl. She'll smile and flirt because she's not stupid. Tyrell's quality—it's easy to see that. And then after a few dates, he won't be feeling it, and then he'll have to do the whole "not sure I want to pursue this" speech. He's said it plenty of times before, but surely there's a girl out there who can get him past the two-to-three-date window.

"I believe in you, man," I say again as I open the door to Offside that night.

"Shut up," he softly mumbles, walking past me into the bar.

Carson snickers as he follows. Nylah's got his hand and is already waving at someone on the dance floor.

Sienna bounces in behind her, all bright and cheerful. She dropped Zoey off at Coach Jones's place about a half hour ago, and Mrs. Jones is in heaven having a little one in the house again. Nylah's sister has already set up a tea party apparently. I had to hear all about it on the car ride here.

Zander and I stayed quiet while the girls gushed about how cute Zoey is. I could see his lips twitching in the rearview mirror, though. Yep, that man adores his little girl.

Wily and Satch are already waiting for us inside. They scored us a great table between the dance floor and the dartboards. His arm's around her shoulders, his protective hand keeping her close as she darts her eyes around. She's so obviously out of her comfort zone, but I'm glad she's here. It means a lot to me that she wants to celebrate Blake's new beginning.

Zander and I head straight to the bar, ordering a round of drinks, and the first hour flies by. It's all laughter over french fries and pizza, teasing as we try to pick out a girl for Tyrell to flirt with.

He's squirming, shaking his head and telling us to "Stop, already. I don't need anyone's damn help to find me a girl. This is officially the worst idea you guys have ever had."

"We know you can find yourself a girl, man," Wily tells him. "It's about finding the *right* girl."

"And you guys are all experts?" He shoots a skeptical frown around the table.

"Hey, we've all scored."

He scoffs. "You lucked out. You didn't pursue shit. These girls found *you*." Pointing at each of them, he lists it off. "Baby mama appears back in your life. Coach's daughter throws a football at you. Tutor Girl is allocated to you. And you..." He gives me a little frown. "Actually, when did you and Blake get that spark? How did it happen?"

"Oh, um..." I squirm in my seat, flashing her an awkward look and wondering what the fuck I'm supposed to say here.

Blake grins. "The truth is, he walked in on me when I was butt-ass naked in the bathroom."

"What?" Wily sits up with a growl.

I shrink into my seat, pinching the bridge of my nose.

"Yep, that's right." My girlfriend continues to bury me. "I was shaving my legs, and he walked in on it, stood frozen, gaping at me for a second, and got himself an impressive hard-on. It was pretty beautiful, actually."

"Stop," I beg her, just waiting for Wily to jump out of his seat and thump me.

Satch giggles, slapping a hand over his mouth as Nylah starts howling with laughter.

Blake nudges me, her smile pure sunshine as she laughs out the rest. "I'm pretty sure he fell in love with me on the spot."

I groan, covering my eyes and getting a sharp kick under the table.

"Ow!" I wince and drop my hand to glare at Wily. "I didn't jump her in the bathroom, man."

"That's true," she backs me up. "He was a perfect gentleman."

"Yeah, right," Wily mutters darkly, and Blake starts giggling all over again.

"Love you, shithead," she sings.

"Shut up," he grumbles, his lips twitching as he gives his sister a side-eye, then mutters, "Love you, too, butt face."

Tyrell sits there shaking his head, still laughing while I rise in my chair and glide my arm around Blake's waist. Perching my chin on her shoulder, I kiss her cheek when she leans into me, then watch Tyrell jolt in his seat, knocking his beer glass over.

It's basically empty, so only a dribble spills out, but he doesn't even notice.

We all stare at him, but he's too busy looking over his shoulder.

"You good?" Zander asks him, but Tyrell doesn't seem to hear.

He's already rising from his chair and walking across to the bar.

"Where's he going?" Sienna asks, righting his beer glass before looking up to see where he is.

"No idea."

Nylah's eyebrows arch when she leans to the side to get a better view. "Looks like he's heading for that cutie behind the bar."

"Do you think he knows her?" Blake pops a fry into her mouth.

We all crane our necks as he calls something and the woman with the stunning smile turns, her face lighting with surprise.

Her springy curls bounce as she rushes down the bar, laughing and slapping the counter in front of him.

"They seem to know each other," Satch murmurs.

Wily runs his fingers down her arm. "Wonder what the connection is."

"He'll tell us when he's ready." Carson leans back in his chair. "Stop gawking at them, you guys."

We reluctantly turn away, and I shift my focus to the prettiest girl in the room.

She grins at me, her blue eyes dancing as I brush my finger down her cheek, then tuck one of her curls behind her ear. "Wanna dance or somethin'? Or we could play pool."

"I'm up for pool." Nylah slaps the table and rises from her chair. "Come on, Caveman. Let me kick your ass."

"Kick my ass? At pool? Kitten, you're dreaming."

She laughs. "Prove me wrong, then, hotshot."

"Oh, I have got to see this." Sienna jumps up from her

chair, following Nylah as she pulls Carson out of his seat and drags him to the tables.

I watch them go before turning back to Blake for an answer.

She tips her head, pursing her lips, and then that cute nose of hers wrinkles. "I'd rather go stargazing. You up for it?"

My smile grows in an instant. "Now we're talkin'." Turning to Wily, I'm about to ask if I can borrow his truck, but he's already holding out his keys for me. "Thanks, man. You want us to come back and collect you in an hour or so?"

"Nah, we can catch a ride with someone else."

I squeeze the keys in my palm, giving him a grateful smile. He nods, silently telling me to look after her, but he doesn't need to keep doing that. I'll always look after Blake.

We say goodbye, waving to the others, who are already setting up the pool balls.

"Catch you later!" Zander calls, and I cast one more look over my shoulder.

Tyrell's still caught up in an animated conversation, and my curiosity is piqued. Hopefully he'll tell all when he gets home... although I doubt it. The guy likes to keep to himself as much as he can.

Focusing back on the girl beside me, I drive her to the closest lookout, heading down the dark road until we pop out to a view that overlooks Nolan. The lights twinkle below us, but we climb into the back of Wily's truck and gaze up at the stars instead.

Blake snuggles against my chest, letting out a blissful sigh that's peaceful and sweet.

I think she's finally found it.

That peace I was hoping the forest would provide.

It's a humbling privilege to know that she's finding it with me.

Brushing my lips across her forehead, I squeeze her tight against me and silently promise to never let her go.

Because I've found my peace with her too. And I can't imagine it feeling any better than this.

CHAPTER 68
TYRELL

I can't believe it. The second I spotted Dani behind the bar, I thought I was hallucinating. She's a piece of my past that I never thought I'd encounter again.

When my family left Colorado Springs for Dallas, I planned on never going back.

And I haven't.

There's no way I want to set foot in that place again.

But I never expected a piece of it to show up in Nolan.

My heart started hurting the second I recognized her, but then before I could stop myself, I stood and wandered over to the bar.

It might hurt to look, but there's also a sense of nostalgia that I can't resist.

Dani Hill.

Damn.

Images from our days in high school flooded me, her smile and laughter filling my mind before I was taken out by thoughts of Atlas.

It nearly made me stumble. Nearly made me turn the hell back around, but my body had other ideas.

So I walked my ass to that bar, and I caught her attention.

And the second she figured out it was me, her face lit with that smile Atlas fell for the first time he met her.

Yeah, I walked through their entire romance.

Those two were made for each other, and my best friend was gone—hook, line, and sinker.

I helped arrange their first date, loaned him my car whenever he wanted to take her out. He even told me he was gonna marry her one day.

And then he died.

My throat swells as she says my name and lets out a delighted laugh.

"Tyrell Jackson? No way!" She rushes down the bar, slapping her hands on the wood. "What are you doing here?"

"What are *you* doing here?" I point at her.

She tips her head back, laughing some more. "I just moved here in January. New year, fresh start. You know how it is."

I nod, drinking her in. She's still pretty. It's a fucking crime that Atlas isn't here to enjoy it.

"So..." I lean against the bar, watching her carefully. "You doing okay?"

Her eyes crease at the corners as she shrugs, putting on a brave smile. "How about you?"

"Yeah." I nod, then lick my bottom lip and swallow. "Nolan's good. 'Bout to finish my senior year."

"Congratulations." Her voice is soft, her gaze dropping to the counter.

I nod, wondering if I should have kept in touch. But she wasn't my girlfriend. And all the shit surrounding Atlas's death? It was too much. I just had to get out of there.

"You ever gone back?" she murmurs.

I shake my head. "My family's in Texas now, so..."

"Okay." She nods, dipping her chin. "Yeah, I stayed for a while, but you know, he was just everywhere. It didn't matter how much time passed... I couldn't dodge the memories." Her eyes glass, and when she glances up at me, I can feel my heart breaking all over again.

I miss my friend.

I miss him so fucking much.

Sucking in a breath, she's obviously trying to steel herself as she crosses her arms. "It's been..."

"Two years, three months, and ten days," I finish for her, that night burned into my brain for all eternity.

I can still hear her screams as she held Atlas in her arms and begged him to wake up.

His eyes were blank, his face practically gray, and I will never get over that harrowing moment.

She gives me a sad smile and nods. "It's been really hard to move on, you know?"

"Yeah," I croak. "I get it."

"But I have to learn to live without him." She shrugs. "I'm hoping a change of scenery will help."

"It will," I assure her. "I wouldn't have survived if I hadn't had this place. I would have... drowned in Colorado Springs. He would have haunted me around every corner. Being up here has helped me... move on."

Her brown eyes shoot to mine. "Yet you still know exactly how long it's been since that night."

My forehead crinkles, and I've got no reply to that. I'll never forget. I can never forget.

"Hey, Dani! We've got people waiting," a tall guy down the other end of the bar calls. "Can I get a hand down here?"

"Sure thing." She holds up her finger. "One second." Her smile is warm as she looks back up at me. "It's nice to see you again, Ty."

"Yeah, you, too, Dani."

My throat is swelling again, and I can't explain it.

Part of me wants to ask her if she'd like to catch up for coffee sometime, but I don't know if I can.

Will we just sit there reliving the past? Wallowing in each other's pain?

It's taken a lot of work for me to get over losing the guy who was closer than a brother. We grew up together. Best friends since before we could walk.

Losing him gutted me.

And I've managed to keep him out of my life in Nolan. When Atlas first died, my teammates knew, but over time, they've quickly worked out that he's not a topic we talk about.

I somehow made it through the end of my sophomore year, and then I helped my family move to Texas. We spent the summer in Dallas, and for a second there, I wasn't sure I'd make it back to Nolan. But then Wily invited me to move into Football Frat, and my parents convinced me it was the right thing to do.

It was.

I came back here, and I let Atlas go.

But now I'm staring down at one of the closest connections I had to him.

She owned my boy's heart.

And I don't know if I'm strong enough to let her back into my life.

But I also don't know if I'm strong enough to ignore the fact that she's now living in Nolan.

Especially when Dani calls him in tears one night, asking for his help. There's no way Tyrell can turn his back on her, even when he's wrestling with buried grief and the fact that he's starting to catch feelings for his best friend's girl...

THE PERFECT PLAY is releasing December 2nd, 2025.

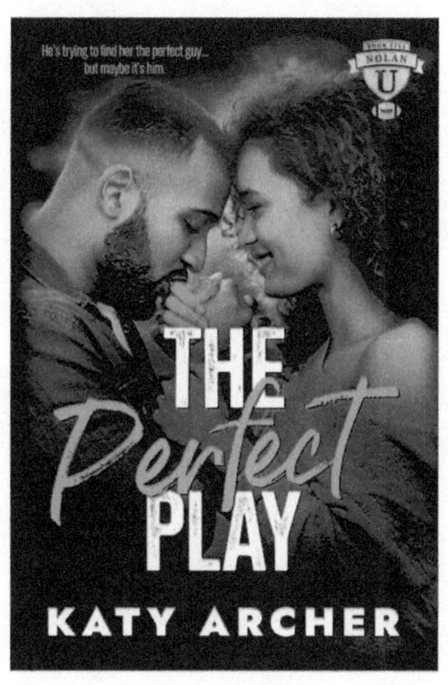

NOTE FROM KATY

Dear reader,

Thanks for reading Grady and Blake's love story. I had so much fun working on it. I love what a mess Blake is and the way Grady has to keep showing up to save her… and I love how she starts to find her courage. He's so patient with her and she's the electric shock he needs to get out of his breakup stupor. They're dynamite together and hanging out with them in the forest was the best! Those are some of my favorite scenes in the book.

I also love how many scenes there are with the Football Frat family and I'm very excited to let you know that there will be plenty more in the next book. Tyrell is going to need a lot of encouragement to find himself a girl… especially when the one he doesn't even know he wants is working at Offside. In fact, he's so oblivious to this fact, that he offers to help her find the perfect guy.

I'm sure you can imagine my glee at being able to write this one. Tyrell and Dani are gonna fall *hard* and they won't even see it coming 😏 Bring on December, right? I can't wait for you to read *The Perfect Play* 🩶

If you enjoyed *The Illicit Play*, I would so appreciate you leaving an honest review on Amazon and/or Goodreads. Even just a star rating is helpful. You don't have to write anything if you don't want to. But star ratings and even short reviews really help validate the book, letting readers know it's worth a shot. It also tells Amazon and Goodreads that this book is worth shining a spotlight on. I know there are a bunch of readers out there who love college sports romance just as much as we do. If you can help me reach them, then that would be freaking fantastic.
Thanks for the assist!

I'd also like to thank a few key people who have been instrumental in helping me get this book ready for you—Megan, Kristin, Beth and Rachael. Thank you for all of your advice, for catching those mistakes and helping me shape the story into something awesome. And thank you for the gorgeous cover and supporting me in releasing the book.

My IG peeps—I want to give a special thank you to all the people who helped me brainstorm character names: @bookingitwithsteph @angelataylorauthor @bookjunkie85 @g_i_026 @jw311 @bbthebookish @book-buddyinsights @roni3713 @shaelynrae11 @ac_storytime @tiarachevalley @makaylapaige2015 @airamjustairam

@slunita89 @cmbuelsing @cindy_lytal @stefanie.mulry. I love interacting with you and so appreciate your ideas and input.

Trudi and my writing lunch buddies—you are my favorite meal of the month. Thank you so much for making life amazing.

My review team—I love you all so much. Thank you for taking the time to read my books, share your thoughts and then promote them on social media. Seriously, you are the best!

My readers—thank you! I love the way you support me, fall for my characters and cheer them on. Your love is incredible and keeps me going 🩶

My amazing son, Jake—thank you so much for all your help and advice for all things first-aide and hiking related. I love how passionate you are about the outdoors and I can't wait to see all the cool things you're going to do with your life.

My first love—it doesn't matter if I'm a hot mess, you always have my back, you love me no matter what, and I am forever grateful for all you do for me. Thank you 🩶

xoxo
Katy

BOOKS BY KATY ARCHER

NOLAN U HOCKEY

Hockey House V-cards (prequel)
The Forbidden Freshman
The Heart Stealer
The Game Changer
The Love Penalty
The Only Goal
The Forever Game

NOLAN U FOOTBALL

Releasing in 2025
The First Play (prequel)
The Forever Play
The Off-Limits Play
The Surprise Play
The Illicit Play
The Perfect Play
The Christmas Play

NOLAN U BASKETBALL

Releasing in 2026 - 2027

NOLAN U - GEN 2

Starting in 2027

CONTACT KATY

I love to hear from my readers, so feel free to email me anytime. You can also find out more on my website.

EMAIL: katy@katyarcher.com

WEBSITE: www.katyarcher.com

And if you want to connect with me on social media, you can find me Addicted to College Sports Romance on...

INSTAGRAM:
www.instagram.com/addictedtocollegesportsromance/

FACEBOOK:
www.facebook.com/people/College-Sports-Romance-Books/61553919569131/

TIKTOK:
www.tiktok.com/@katyarcherbooks

www.ingramcontent.com/pod-product-compliance
Lightning Source LLC
Chambersburg PA
CBHW022234020726
47496CB00004B/891

* 9 7 8 1 9 9 1 4 0 3 0 1 8 *